"Ten vessels have landed on the hull," Uteln announced.

At that moment, a long, narrow metal shape emerged from the craft visible on the main viewscreen. As it neared the hull, several arms folded down at its base, like the fingers of a technological hand. It pushed flush against *Robinson*. Sisko expected a cutting beam to start carving up the ship, or even for the extended tool to begin rotating and physically cut through the outer plating.

But nothing like that happened. "What are they doing?" Rogeiro asked.

Suddenly, Sivadeki shot to her feet at the conn, her hands coming up to the sides of her head to cover her external auditory canals. She screamed and dropped to her knees. Sisko rushed forward to help her, but then a high-pitched screech pierced his ears. It felt as though long needles had been pounded into his brain. Black jots formed before his eyes. He staggered and tried to remain upright, reaching for the side of the conn with his uninjured hand. The main viewscreen winked off, and then the overhead lighting failed. Sisko held on for just long enough to glance behind him and see, in the reflected light of their consoles, the rest of the bridge crew crumbling. The emergency lighting came on with its ominous red tones.

Sisko fell forward and everything went black.

STAR TREK
DEEP SPACE NINE®
GAMMA

original sin

DAVID R. GEORGE III

Based upon *Star Trek*® and
Star Trek: The Next Generation®
created by Gene Roddenberry
and
Star Trek: Deep Space Nine
created by Rick Berman & Michael Piller

POCKET BOOKS
New York   London   Toronto   Sydney   New Delhi   Johcat

Pocket Books
An Imprint of Simon & Schuster, Inc.
1230 Avenue of the Americas
New York, NY 10020

This book is a work of fiction. Any references to historical events, real people, or real places are used fictitiously. Other names, characters, places, and events are products of the author's imagination, and any resemblance to actual events or places or persons, living or dead, is entirely coincidental.

™, ®, and © 2017 by CBS Studios Inc. STAR TREK and related marks and logos are trademarks of CBS Studios Inc. All Rights Reserved.

This book is published by Pocket Books, an imprint of Simon & Schuster, Inc., under exclusive license from CBS Studios Inc.

First Pocket Books paperback edition October 2017

POCKET and colophon are registered trademarks of Simon & Schuster, Inc.

For information about special discounts for bulk purchases, please contact Simon & Schuster Special Sales at 1-866-506-1949 or business@simonandschuster.com.

The Simon & Schuster Speakers Bureau can bring authors to your live event. For more information or to book an event, contact the Simon & Schuster Speakers Bureau at 1-866-248-3049 or visit our website at www.simonspeakers.com.

Manufactured in the United States of America

10 9 8 7 6 5 4 3 2 1

ISBN 978-1-5011-3322-0
ISBN 978-1-5011-3324-4 (ebook)

To Kirsten Beyer,
a woman of fierce talents and abilities,
a brilliant collaborator,
and, most important of all,
a wonderful friend

Historian's Note

The primary story of this novel commences in March 2386, not long after the events of the *Deep Space Nine* novels *Ascendance* and *The Long Mirage*. Finally freed from patrolling the sector around Deep Space 9 in the aftermath of the assassination of Federation President Nanietta Bacco, Captain Sisko and his *Robinson* crew finally set off on their mission of exploration into the Gamma Quadrant.

Original sin is that thing about man which makes him capable of conceiving of his own perfection and incapable of achieving it.

—Reinhold Niebuhr

Prologue

Catalyst

B rilliant light erupted from the improvised device, engulfing the man holding it as the explosion tore through his body. The detonation also felled the men and women standing beside Rejias Norvan, dropping them broken, burned, and bloodied to the ground. The blast triggered another device elsewhere in the crowd, and then another, and then still more. Explosions rent the perpetual night, great bursts of yellow-red fire that stood out dramatically beneath the cold black skies of Endalla.

From a safe distance, Radovan Tavus watched the chain of destruction unfold across the surface of Bajor's largest moon. Waves of flame rolled over those assembled like a fiery tsunami, its debris shrapnel, leaving death and devastation in its wake. When the conflagration had run its course, charred and battered bodies littered the ground. Beneath the slain Ohalavaru, the dull, uneven gray expanse of Endalla had been transformed by the intense heat into a smooth span of ebon glass.

A grim stillness settled over the landscape. The sudden quiet pinned Radovan where he stood. He stared at the gruesome tableau, unable to move in that moment any more than the hundreds of dead laid out before him.

But then Radovan saw motion. Near the flashpoint of the firestorm, an arm reached into the air. Attached to a body in a scorched environmental suit, it trembled for a moment before thrusting forward and down, as though seeking purchase.

Radovan hadn't even allowed for the possibility of survivors, but seeing one penetrated his shock. He rushed forward and into the grisly scene. He lost sight of the moving arm and the body to which it belonged, but he continued in that direction. He threaded his way through the field of singed and mangled corpses, stepping past inert bodies until he reached the blackened, twisted remains of Rejias Norvan. Radovan barely recognized the charismatic leader who had led an extremist Ohalavaru sect to Endalla in search of concrete evidence proving the veracity of the Ohalu texts.

Just past Rejias, the arm reached out again. Radovan looked over and saw the figure in the environmental suit, their helmet off. He recognized the man struggling to pull himself along, dragging his other arm behind him, useless. The man writhed fitfully across the ground, showing none of the dignity with which he typically carried himself, and yet the Emissary's grueling attempt to haul himself across the lunar surface possessed a certain desperate nobility.

Radovan looked ahead of Benjamin Sisko, searching for the dying man's intended goal. He saw only lifeless Bajorans, scorched heaps of inanimate flesh and bone rendered wholly equal by death. One carcass resembled the next. They all—

Wait, Radovan thought. *There*—

One of the fallen differed from the others—from all the other dead bodies strewn about the blast zone. Radovan headed in that direction, navigating through the killing field until he arrived at the apparent object of the Emissary's attention. So much smaller than any of the other cadavers, it obviously belonged to a child.

Not a child, Radovan corrected himself. *A toddler.*

He crouched beside the prone, unmoving husk and didn't wonder why Benjamin Sisko labored to reach it in what would surely be the final moments of his life. Still,

Radovan reached out and pushed at the toddler's side. The body rolled over easily, revealing a face somehow untouched by the explosions—a face known to all of Bajor. Nearly three and a half years earlier, the birth of Rebecca Jae Sisko had coincided with the return of the Emissary from the Celestial Temple after his mysterious sojourn there. Based upon ancient writings, the Ohalavaru deemed her the Avatar, and they looked upon her as a new hope for the people of Bajor, an augur of a growing collective awareness that would usher in clarity and a joyous future for their society.

The little girl stared up unseeing at Radovan. In death, she wore an expression not of repose, but of fear and surprise. Radovan saw the encumbrance of more years in her countenance than Rebecca had actually lived. It unnerved him in a way he could not articulate. He had never known what to make of the Ohalavaru claims about the Avatar, and her dying at such an early age confused him even more. He gazed at her frozen features and wondered about the capricious nature of existence.

And then Rebecca Sisko blinked.

Radovan shot to his feet so quickly, he almost overbalanced. He managed to catch himself, then watched as the toddler looked up at him and opened her mouth. In the instant before she spoke, Radovan expected that he would hear a deep, adult voice, like that of some cursèd entity—a Pah-wraith or a fire demon—that had seized control of the Avatar's dead body. Instead, he heard the small, plaintive voice of a little girl.

"What are you going to do?" she asked. Her eyes burned brightly.

Too brightly—too perceptively—*for someone so young,* Radovan thought. "I . . . I . . ." he stammered, unable to formulate a reply. Even in his everyday life, he had a difficult time determining how to live and what to do next;

he could not possibly expect to fathom what Rebecca Sisko wanted of him.

That's when Radovan felt a hand settle on his shoulder. He whirled around to see that Benjamin Sisko had reached his destination and climbed to his feet. Up close, the Emissary looked as dead as all the corpses cluttering the ground about them. Half of Benjamin Sisko's face had been burned away, the bone of his skull visible in places through his seared skin. His blackened tongue protruded past his teeth like a piece of charred meat. One of his eyes had turned to jelly.

"What are you going to do?" the Emissary demanded.

Radovan opened his mouth to scream—

—and bolted upright in bed. His heart thundered in his chest. A layer of sweat covered his body. His head pounded.

Radovan pulled his legs up to his chest and rested his arms atop his knees. He sat quietly that way in the darkness, attempting to calm himself. He reached up to his temples and slowly kneaded them, trying to overcome the feeling of his head being compressed in a vise. The memory of a shriek seemed to echo in his ears. Had he cried out in his sleep? He didn't know, but he thought—he *felt*—that he probably had. He idly dropped one hand to the top of his shoulder, to where, in his nightmare, the mortally wounded Benjamin Sisko had touched him. Radovan's hand found only his own bare skin.

Bare? That seemed wrong. Radovan always wore nightclothes to bed—typically underwear and a lightweight short-sleeve pullover. Why had he—

"You all right?" came a groggy voice out of the shadows beside him. Radovan threw the sheet back and hurled himself to his feet—even as some of the particulars of the evening percolated up in his mind. He remembered the woman in his bed, who had insisted on coming home with him after the Ohalavaru rally.

Radovan wanted nothing more than to fully rouse the woman—Winser Ellevet—and send her away, but he understood the bounds of propriety enough to know that he could not do that. Instead, he told her, "Go back to sleep," his own voice rough with slumber. He could not lie and claim that all was well—he'd never been particularly adept at conjuring falsehoods—but he knew how to avoid telling the truth. He held still, hoping that Winser would not completely waken. She said nothing more, and after a few seconds, Radovan heard her roll over. He continued to wait in the dark, motionless, until her breathing slowed and deepened, signaling her return to sleep. He then padded quietly across the unlighted room, feeling for the open door to the en-suite refresher. Once inside, he slowly swung the door closed, though he left the light off. After finding his robe by touch, he hurriedly pulled it on and cinched it closed. The utilitarian fabric covered his nakedness but did nothing to relieve him of his shame.

With his head still aching, Radovan opened the 'fresher cabinet and, out of habit, reached to the top shelf. His fingers found the various medications, palliatives, and painkillers used to treat his mother in her final year, which he'd taken with him when he'd cleared out her home. Realizing his mistake, he moved his hand down to the bottom shelf and felt around for the mild analgesic he kept there. He was not suffering from one of his migraines, but it had been a poor decision to accept Winser's invitation to a tavern after their post-rally dinner. Radovan rarely drank, and the throbbing in his head—coupled with his allowing Winser to come home with him—reminded him why. He opened the bottle of medicine, fumbled for two tablets, then let them dissolve under his tongue.

Finally feeling more like himself, he went back out into the bedroom and crossed to the other door, which he closed behind him. He moved down the short hall, past a closet to one side and the guest 'fresher on the other, to the living area of his flat. Light from the streetlamps outside seeped in through the gray curtains hanging along the front windows, sending a ghostly cast across the indistinct shapes of the furniture populating the room.

Radovan chose not to activate the overhead lighting panels. He skirted the small table and chairs by the replicator, then sidled behind the low wooden table in front of the sofa. He sat down heavily, exhausted—not just from his interrupted sleep, but from the emotions roiling within him. It seemed impossible that he had brought a stranger to his home in the first place, much less a woman who currently slept in his bed.

Radovan had first met Winser Ellevet almost a year earlier, at a local meeting of the Ohalavaru in the city of Johcat. Open to the public, the gathering had specifically invited people curious about the writings of Ohalu and the modern movement that had arisen around his ancient teachings. Radovan questioned many aspects of life on Bajor, and he had been drawn to learn about the relatively new sect because it diverged from the mainstream. He had never fit in anywhere, and although he hadn't expected to find a place among the Ohalavaru, he'd wanted to see if he could realize even the smallest comfort in their beliefs.

It was because of Mother, Radovan thought. Her death had been a source of both sorrow and relief, of both loss and liberation. After a lifetime spent playing the dutiful son, and several years ministering to his mother's ever-increasing healthcare needs, her passing had changed everything—freeing him from his arduous responsibilities while also robbing him of the most important person in his life.

"You weren't just set free," the counselor he'd briefly consulted had told him. "You were set *adrift*."

At the first Ohalavaru event Radovan had attended, he hadn't found succor, but he had found Winser. Or rather, she had found him. She had approached him at the refreshments table. She spoke to him easily, as though they already knew each other; more than that, she acted as though they had been in the middle of a conversation. She asked what he thought so far of the meeting, and also his general opinion of the Ohalavaru. Despite his impulse to excuse himself and withdraw, he carefully answered her—truthfully giving voice to some of the questions he still had, but also trying not to say too much. For all he knew, she could have been a believer in the tenets of Ohalu, sent to gauge his viability as a possible convert. Radovan did not care to be judged.

Winser listened to what he had to say, then offered some of her own opinions. Uncertain about the Ohalavaru, she echoed many of Radovan's own concerns. Despite his usual inclination to flee from public encounters, particularly those with strangers, he ended up talking with Winser for quite some time.

A month after that, at the next Ohalavaru meeting, Winser had arrived midway through the first speaker's address. She sat down next to Radovan, and later, she accompanied him to the refreshments table, where they once more conversed at length. At one point, she asked him if he might like to continue their discussion after the meeting, perhaps at a restaurant or a tavern. Radovan considered himself an average man—at least in appearance—but he realized that Winser was flirting with him. Although he did not find her a great beauty—she carried a few too many kilos on her small frame—her attention flattered him. At the same time, it made him uncomfortable, and so he politely declined her invitation.

Radovan had continued to attend various Ohalavaru gatherings, at which he'd often seen and spoken with Winser. From time to time, she invited him out. Eventually, during a particularly intriguing conversation about rumors of a possible Ohalavaru expedition to Endalla, Radovan acquiesced. He shared a meal with Winser at a local eatery, which went well enough that he subsequently had dinner with her after several other meetings.

And then we both went to Endalla, Radovan thought. The experience had been intense, though his bad dream that night did not accurately reflect what had actually taken place. Afterward, once they returned from the Bajoran moon, Winser asked him to join her for dinner apart from any Ohalavaru assemblies. Wanting to make sense of the events on Endalla, and feeling that he could talk to her about it, Radovan met her several times for meals.

He had done so that night. After they finished their dinner, Winser suggested they not end their conversation, but take it to a tavern. For the first time, Radovan said yes.

Why did I do that? he asked himself. And why had he chosen to order even one cocktail, let alone several? Drinking had clearly clouded his judgment, otherwise he would never have allowed Winser to come home with him. He could barely recall their trip back to his flat, and the memory of her coaxing him into bed ended with an awkward tangle of bare flesh. Radovan didn't think they had consummated their relationship, possibly because he'd been physically unable to do so—either as the result of the alcohol he'd imbibed, or because of his general disinterest in such encounters.

Except I wanted company, didn't I? Radovan's nightmare had not been the first he'd experienced; interrupted sleep had become the norm over the past months. Since returning from Endalla, his bad dreams had escalated in intensity, with that night's phantasm the most horrifying.

His heartbeat slowing to a normal pace, his headache receding, Radovan sat in the darkness and pondered the shock that had woken him. His bad dreams typically faded quickly, leaving him drained but with no recollection of what his sleeping mind had wrought. That night, though, the memory of his nightmare persisted.

The images that had risen in his mind had clearly been born out of the terrible events he had witnessed four weeks earlier on Endalla, but they did not match the reality of what had taken place. Radovan didn't understand why— why his subconscious would twist his awful experiences into something even worse. It made no sense to him.

I'm missing something, he thought. *Something about Endalla or the Ohalavaru.*

Radovan knew that sleep would not come just then, no matter how much he needed it. He shifted on the sofa and lay down, wanting to at least rest his tired body. Rather than attempting to relax his mind, he instead focused his thoughts, reflecting back on the incident that had spurred his nightmare.

Radovan peered through the port of the small civilian space vessel as it descended toward the barren surface of Bajor's largest moon. Two years prior, an isolytic subspace weapon had ripped away Endalla's thin atmosphere and obliterated its ecosystem. From his home on Bajor, Radovan could readily distinguish the transformation of the natural satellite; what had once been a brown-and-green sphere adorning the night had become an ashen pockmark in the sky. Viewing it from up close made the devastation even more apparent. Though Radovan had never before visited Endalla, he had throughout his life seen images of its surface, showing basic plant life and the various scientific settlements that had taken root there. From his seat aboard the spacecraft, he gazed out instead at a sterile, desolate landscape, an empty terrain shaded from a palette of grays and blacks.

"It's the color of gravestones," said Winser Ellevet. She leaned toward the port from where she sat beside Radovan. "It looks like parts of Bajor after—" Her voice caught, as though she might break down, but then she completed her thought. "After the Cardassians left."

Radovan nodded. He didn't trust himself to say anything for fear of what he might reveal. He could not quite define his relationship with Winser; though he wouldn't deem her a kindred spirit, he recognized her unease in social situations, and in that way found her a nonthreatening acquaintance. Whatever he called their association, Radovan wanted for the moment to preserve it. He could tell that seeing the destruction of Endalla up close affected her, but beyond a simple observational interest, Radovan felt nothing.

Once the ship set down on the lunar surface, Radovan and Winser disembarked with the other passengers. They did not require environmental suits; the first Ohalavaru teams to arrive on Endalla had assembled life-support equipment and set up a large hemispherical force field. The dome glowed a pale, translucent blue and maintained an artificially generated atmosphere.

As he and Winser walked down the ramp of their vessel, Radovan surveyed their surroundings. Other small ships had landed just inside the dome. Radovan recognized a large array of active transporter inhibitors ringing the center of the area, their operation filling the dome with a low-level drone. Several hundred people stood in clusters within that circle, working with large caches of gear, their voices adding to the clamor. The air smelled antiseptic, the hallmark of a recycled atmosphere.

At the base of the ramp, an Ohalavaru leader greeted Radovan and Winser and the other passengers. The tall, auburn-haired woman introduced herself as Vendoma Ani, and she led them to several unattended collections of equipment. Radovan saw more transporter inhibitors, along with a considerable number of portable excavators. A decade earlier, after the end of the Occupation, he had used such a device to carve out a new well for his mother when she had returned to her land. Those efforts largely went to waste, since her illness manifested soon after that, sending her to the hospital for the first of many long stays. She spent less time in the following years at her home than in medical facilities, and ultimately in a hospice.

Vendoma explained that everybody present would work together to mine the broad plain around the life-support dome. She revealed that an interpretation of the ancient texts—"controversial but compelling," she said—held that evidence confirming the Ohalu doctrine lay somewhere beneath that portion of Endalla's surface. Not yet wholly convinced of Ohalavaru beliefs, Radovan had come along in part because Winser had insisted, but mostly because he still sought answers that would help provide direction for his own life, which too often felt ungainly and purposeless.

Vendoma handed out personal access display devices to those assembled about her, then reviewed on the padds the operating instructions for all of the equipment they would be using. She emphasized the primary role of the excavators—large squarish metal boxes with control panels on their upper faces, standing atop curved feet that doubled as emitters. She picked up a transporter inhibitor—a long tube inlaid with lights—and deployed it on its tripodal base. She held up a thin rectangular device that resembled a padd with crosshatch metal mesh on one side and described it as a sensor mask. Vendoma also pointed out circular fist-size fasteners and attachable antigrav hafts.

Radovan found himself listening with only moderate interest. It seemed unlikely to him that the Ohalavaru would uncover anything of importance on Endalla, but he also knew that he wouldn't be able to leave until the end of the day, when the ships returned to Bajor. Vendoma walked everybody through the process of preparing to mine the lunar plain. She demonstrated how to initialize the transporter inhibitors and the sensor masks, and then how to affix them to the excavators using the fasteners. She showed how to utilize the antigravs to move the excavators to the ships that sat along the inner circumference of the dome. Other Ohalavaru stationed there would beam the configured equipment to a designated location out on the surface of Endalla. Once all of the excavators had been moved into position, their accompanying transporter inhibitors and sensor masks would be activated, and then the mining devices would work in concert to penetrate the lunar crust and exhume whatever lay beneath.

For most of the day, Radovan worked in silence. He had been assigned to set up and prime the transporter inhibitors—a task he could have carried out with his eyes closed—while Winser had been charged with helping convey the prepared excavators to the ship on which they'd traveled from Bajor. Their separation pleased Radovan, as it meant that he could perform his work without having to maintain the artifice of amiable conversation. Several Ohalavaru nearby did try to chat with him, but they found enough other willing participants for their discussions so that he didn't have to say much.

Mostly, Radovan thought about what the Ohalavaru leaders could possibly hope to find buried beneath Endalla. He also wondered about their elaborate plans. Given their use of sensor masks and transporter inhibitors, they clearly did not want anybody either to detect or to stop their efforts to strip-mine that section of the moon. The intended simultaneous operation of all the excavators also suggested that the Ohalavaru wanted to complete that phase of their mission in as short a timeframe as possible in order to avoid being discovered.

They never made it.

Just as Radovan finished working on a transporter inhibitor for one of his group's excavators, he heard somebody raise their voice in alarm. Several others also shouted. Radovan looked in that direction and saw another vessel descending through the faint blue of the force-field dome. As it alighted beside one of the Ohalavaru craft, the designation on the side of the new arrival's hull became visible: NCC-63719/3. Radovan read the shuttlecraft's name, written out in Federation Standard: *Prentares Ribbon*.

Almost as soon as the vessel had set down, a hatch slid open and a ramp folded out across the port nacelle. A man in a Starfleet uniform appeared and looked out across the interior of the dome. Almost all of the Ohalavaru turned at once in Radovan's approximate direction. The apparent attention chilled him even as he realized that everybody looked past him. Radovan turned to see the leader of the Endalla expedition, Rejias Norvan, stepping forward.

A uniformed Andorian woman—a *shen* or a *chen* or whatever they called their freakish four-way genders—joined the Starfleet officer and followed alongside him as he strode down the ramp of the shuttlecraft. Long, thick antennae, almost like misplaced albino fingers, extended from the top of the woman's head through a complicated jumble of white hair. The man, a human by the look of him, had a long face and a high forehead, and his close-cropped coif, beard, and mustache had all gone gray. He looked old, perhaps in his seventies or eighties, but as he marched forward, he carried himself with a confidence and dignity that suggested considerable experience and, perhaps, an even more advanced age. With the Andorian in tow, he cleaved through the crowd of Bajorans, having obviously concluded who served as their leader.

Radovan watched as, just a few meters away, the Starfleet officer approached Rejias. "I am Captain Elias Vaughn of the *U.S.S. James T. Kirk*," he said. "This is Ensign zh'Vennias."

"I am Rejias Norvan, Captain."

"Are you in charge here?" Vaughn asked.

Rejias shrugged—not as though he didn't want to answer, Radovan thought, but as though he believed the question unimportant. "I am one of the principal architects of this undertaking, yes, and therefore one of its nominal leaders."

Vaughn took a moment to regard Rejias, then peered past him and all around the dome. Radovan saw him examining both people and equipment. When he looked back at Rejias, the captain asked, "And what exactly is this 'undertaking'?"

The Ohalavaru leader raised his arms, palms up, and motioned to all those present. "As you can see, we are all native Bajorans," he said. "Endalla is a part of our sovereign territory, and so we have every right to be here." Rejias lowered his arms and stepped forward to stand facing Vaughn from just centimeters away. "You, on the other hand, are an outsider. On behalf of my people, I demand that you withdraw at once. Board your shuttle, fly it back to your ship, and leave the Bajoran system."

One side of Vaughn's mouth rose in what Radovan

judged an expression of genuine amusement. "Actually, Bajor joined the Federation more than three years ago," he said. "We're all fellow citizens, with an equal right to be here—or, in this case, with *no* right to be here. After the attack that wiped out all life on Endalla, the Bajoran government designated the entire moon off-limits to visitors. But I'm certain you already know all of that."

"I do," Rejias admitted. He spun and took a few paces away from Vaughn. When he came abreast of one of the excavators, he turned back toward the starship captain. "We have permission from the first minister to conduct a special operation here."

Vaughn smiled again, fully, but with no humor at all. "I'm afraid I know that's not true, Mister Rejias," he said. "My ship just arrived at Bajor, and on our approach to orbit, my crew noticed some anomalies on Endalla: a slight discoloration on the surface, some small and unexpected amounts of energy. Scans couldn't explain it, but a visual recon showed your dome, as well as other equipment distributed across the surface. We attempted to contact you, but in addition to blocking sensors and transporters, you're evidently also jamming communications." The information didn't shock Radovan, but he did wonder about the quality of the technological gear the Ohalavaru had acquired for their mission; at the very least, the network of sensor masks either had not been set up correctly, or it did not function with one hundred percent efficiency.

"We wanted to conduct our expedition in private," Rejias said.

Vaughn nodded. "I'm aware of that, since I contacted the authorities on Bajor to inform them of my crew's findings," he said. "I spoke directly with both Minister of Defense Aland and Overgeneral Manos of the Bajoran Militia.

Neither you nor anybody else have permission to be here, and I've been charged with ensuring that you leave."

"What if we decline?" Rejias asked.

"This isn't a request," Vaughn said. "If you and your people won't vacate Endalla voluntarily, I will have to forcibly remove you."

In one swift motion that startled Radovan, Rejias bent and swept a device from atop the excavator. He held it up in front of him and trained it on the captain. By the time he did, Vaughn's Andorian crew member had already drawn her phaser and leveled it at Rejias.

Radovan felt his body tense at the sudden threat of violence. He wanted to bolt, but he could not look away from the potentially explosive scene. He waited for the whine of the Andorian's weapon and the streak of its lethal—or at least suppressive—light. Instead, the starship captain reached out and placed his hand on the phaser. "That won't be necessary, Ensign," Vaughn said, and the Andorian lowered her arm. "I'm not even sure that Mister Rejias is holding a weapon."

The Ohalavaru leader glanced down at the tool in his hand, which had a tapering conic tip at the end of a handle, with what looked like power packs attached on either side. "It's a mining implement," Rejias said, "but I'm sure that if it can penetrate solid rock, it won't have any trouble cutting through your body."

"That sounds like a threat," Vaughn said. "You are already trespassing in violation of Bajoran laws. Don't compound a relatively minor infraction with something far more serious. Why don't you put that down and come with me." The starship captain offered the words not as a question or even as a suggestion, but as an order.

Rejias raised the mining tool higher, as though to emphasize his willingness to use it. "I'm not going with you," he said. "None of us are." He looked around at the other

Ohalavaru, including Radovan. At first, nobody moved, but then a number of those nearest to Rejias went to stand beside him. To Radovan's surprise, some of them raised their own handheld mining tools and pointed them at Vaughn and the Andorian. "Do you plan on arresting all of us?"

Radovan thought that the starship captain looked wholly unperturbed. "My orders are to find out who you are, what you're doing here, and to see that you leave Endalla," Vaughn said. "If necessary, yes, I will take all of you into custody and remand you to the Bajoran Militia."

"What we're doing here," Rejias said, his voice rising, "is exercising our right to religious freedom." Radovan thought the choice of words peculiar, given that the Ohalavaru actually disavowed the divinity of the Prophets.

Vaughn looked around—not at the people present, but at the excavator next to Rejias. "You're exercising your religious freedom with mining equipment?" he asked. "And by blocking communications and sensors and transporters? Help me understand that."

"I'm not interested in helping you understand anything," Rejias said. "I'm only interested in you leaving so that we can do what we came here to do."

"Which is?" Vaughn pressed.

"That's none of your concern," Rejias said, reacting sharply to the prying of the starship captain, but then the Ohalavaru leader appeared to think better of his response. He pointed the tool in his hand at the excavator beside him. "You've identified our mining equipment," he said. "What you don't know is that it's all networked together. You can try to remove us, but we're going to do what we came here to do—one way or another." He leaned down until the firing tip of his handheld tool touched the top of the excavator. The implication seemed clear: Rejias would see his followers mine the surface of Endalla using the machines as intended, or he would fire on the machine beside him, turning it into a bomb and triggering the detonation of all the others connected to it.

Radovan thought that it might be a bluff, but he saw some of the Ohalavaru recoil at the threat. Vaughn did not, but neither did he push Rejias. "There's no need to escalate the situation," the captain said. "Can we find a middle ground here? Perhaps you can explain to the proper Bajoran authorities why you want to be here and what you hope to accomplish."

Radovan saw a smile blossom on Rejias's face, plainly signifying not goodwill, but cynicism. "The 'proper' Bajoran authorities would not hesitate to deem all of us—" He waved the handheld mining tool around to include the other Ohalavaru. "—as *im*proper Bajorans." Rejias shook his head. "No," he said emphatically. "No, we will not negotiate our right to seek the truth." He raised his empty hand to the mining tool and twisted a collar at the wide base of its conic end. Still pointed at the excavator, the forward tip of the instrument began to glow.

Vaughn didn't move. Around the dome, Radovan saw, people didn't quite know how to react. Some moved back, while others froze. The half-dozen Ohalavaru standing near Rejias watched the Ohalavaru leader and Vaughn intently.

For Radovan, the moment seemed to elongate. He stared at the mining tool in Rejias's hand, wondering when it would discharge and how long it would take for the first excavator to explode. Some part of Radovan wanted it to happen.

Captain Vaughn slowly raised his hands in a placatory gesture. "Ensign zh'Vennias." The Andorian immediately started back toward the Starfleet shuttlecraft, and Vaughn followed. Radovan marveled at the terse but effective communication between them.

Along with everybody else, Rejias watched the two Starfleet officers go, but he did not move. He pointedly kept the emitter end of the mining tool pressed against the excavator. Once Vaughn and the Andorian had boarded the shuttlecraft, all of the Ohalavaru turned to Rejias, clearly looking for direction. He said nothing, but after a few moments, when *Prentares Ribbon* remained where it had landed, Rejias lifted the mining tool and fired over the heads of the Ohalavaru. An amorphous yellow ring of energy shot from the emitter, growing from just centimeters across to several meters by the time it struck the side of the shuttle. A loud boom filled the air. When the energy ring dissipated, it left behind a black circle seared into the vessel's hull.

At once, the craft lifted off. Radovan expected its bow to swing around so that it could open fire on the Ohalavaru, but it continued upward. The shuttlecraft left the azure dome, causing the force field to spark a deeper blue as it passed through it. The vessel grew smaller as it rose, until Radovan could no longer see it.

Vendoma hastened over to Rejias. "They'll be back," she told him.

The Ohalavaru leader nodded his agreement. "We probably don't have much time," he said. He surveyed the scene within the dome. "How close are we to completing our preparations?" Multiple voices responded, but the consensus suggested that the Ohalavaru would need another hour or so to complete seeding the excavators across the lunar plain. Several people spoke up to suggest that they should abandon their efforts, at least for the time being, but Rejias would have none of it. He implored everybody to work as quickly as they could to accomplish their goals. Some people returned at once to the tasks they'd been assigned, but others moved more slowly, at least at first. As more Ohalavaru picked up their tools and got to work, though, the pace of their efforts increased.

Radovan returned to the cache of transporter inhibitors. He selected the nearest one and activated it. He toggled the device on, initialized it, and ran a diagnostic to confirm its setup. He then handed it off to Vernay Falor, the man working next to him, so that he could attach it to an excavator.

As Radovan made his way through the remaining inhibitors, he thought about Rejias's decision to continue on with their operation despite their discovery by Starfleet. Vaughn had been forced to depart, but it seemed unlikely that he or other authorities wouldn't return. But if the Ohalavaru left Endalla with the intention of completing their mission at a later time, they would either have to recover all of the excavators and other equipment spread across the surface around the dome—which would be difficult to do in the face of Starfleet interference—or they would have to procure replacements for all that gear. It made sense to stay. *Plus we're not that far off from slicing a huge swath into the ground.*

As he toiled over the transporter inhibitors, Radovan repeatedly gazed around, checking for any sign of the Starfleet shuttlecraft coming back. He saw nothing in the dark skies beyond the dome. As the Ohalavaru neared finishing sowing the excavators across the lunar plain, he began to believe that Rejias and his followers might be able to achieve the goals they had set themselves on the Bajoran moon—at least to the point of strip-mining the surface, even if they didn't actually uncover anything of importance.

But then a flurry of yells went up, and Radovan knew that Starfleet had returned. He looked in the direction of the raised voices and saw people pointing—not skyward, but straight ahead of them. Radovan stared at the dome until at last he spotted the objects of their attention: figures out on the unprotected surface of Endalla, clad in environmental suits, approaching the force field.

Rejias wheeled around, peering in all directions. Radovan did the same, understanding that the Ohalavaru leader believed they would be attacked from all sides. But all around the dome, the sterile landscape stretched away, empty of anything except the excavators.

Just as Radovan looked back toward the oncoming figures, the first of them passed through the dome. Six more individuals followed, arranged in a *V*-shaped formation, three to the left and three to the right. All of them had their hands raised and opened—demonstrating, Radovan supposed, that none of them held any weapons. The faceplates of their helmets reflected the pale blue of the dome, obscuring their identities, but Radovan assumed that Captain Vaughn led the group.

Once more, everybody looked to Rejias. When he raised the mining implement and pointed it at the seven interlopers, the Ohalavaru all moved out of the way, allowing him an unobstructed line of fire. The figure in the center of the intruders slowly reached to the sides of their helmet, twisted it a quarter turn, then lifted it off.

It was not Vaughn, Radovan saw. It was Benjamin Sisko.

Radovan felt his jaw drop open at the unexpected sight of the Emissary, who had been a prominent presence in Bajoran life for more than a decade. Instantly recognizable, the charismatic Sisko gazed across the inside of the dome with a penetrating stare. Radovan had always found Sisko enigmatic, having seen the religious icon numerous times on the comnet over the years, and twice in person. Not long after the end of the Occupation, when Radovan had been in Ashalla as part of a work crew repairing the capital's infrastructure, he'd seen the Emissary speak at a reconstruction rally. Years later, after his return from the wormhole, Sisko had visited Radovan's hometown of Johcat, presiding over the opening of the restored Nirvat Sanctuary, a historic temple that had been left in ruins by the Cardassians.

Radovan's views about the Emissary had varied over time, ranging from suspicion and distrust to confidence and regard. Radovan's mother had been more consistent in her estimation of Sisko, believing that it made no sense for such an esteemed position to be occupied by an alien. Then again, she'd never had much faith in the Prophets either. "Where were they during the Occupation?" she used to ask. "If they're Bajor's gods, we'd be better off without them."

The Emissary leaned toward the figure on his right, who raised a hand and motioned at Rejias. His helmet dangling from the fingertips of one hand, Sisko strode toward the Ohalavaru leader with assurance. Rejias lowered the mining tool to his side as the Emissary reached him.

"Are you Rejias Norvan?" Sisko's voice sounded rich in timbre, and his dark brown skin appeared lustrous, almost as though glowing from within. Radovan thought that the Emissary's bald head and goatee lent him a formidable countenance.

"Yes, I'm Rejias Norvan."

"I'm Benjamin Sisko."

"I . . . know who you are, Emissary," Rejias said. He spoke with a reverence that Radovan found odd. After all, Sisko occupied an important and venerable place in the mainstream Bajoran religion—a religion to which the Ohalavaru did not subscribe. Still, Radovan supposed, the Emissary had discovered the wormhole, had communicated with the Prophets and spent time with them in the Celestial Temple. Whether you considered the Prophets gods or simply powerful aliens, Sisko's relationship with them counted for something. "We *all* know who you are."

"Good," Sisko said. "Then I hope you'll accede to my request that you and your people vacate Endalla at once."

"I'm afraid we do not accept Starfleet's authority in this matter," Rejias said.

"I'm no longer in Starfleet," Sisko said. "I haven't been for years."

"With respect, Emissary, you are wearing one of their environmental suits," Rejias said. "And so are they." He pointed toward the six people who had accompanied Sisko across the surface of Endalla and into the dome. Radovan saw that they no longer stood in a *V* formation, but had spread out in a wide arc. As he watched, they slowly moved farther apart and forward, as though attempting to render their presence as nonthreatening as possible.

Sisko glanced back over his shoulder. "Yes, they're Starfleet officers," he said. "One of them is Captain Vaughn. After he spoke with you, he reached out to me on Bajor."

"Why would he contact you?" Rejias wanted to know. "Because we're Ohalavaru?"

The Emissary blinked. "Until this moment, I didn't know who you were," he said. "Does that have anything to do with why you're here?"

Rejias hesitated, and for a moment, Radovan thought that he didn't know how to respond. He obviously didn't want to reveal the plans of the Ohalavaru, but he probably didn't want to lie to the Emissary. Finally, Rejias said, "It doesn't matter why we've come to Endalla. We're Bajorans, which gives us the right to be here."

"Mister Rejias, I'm not a peace officer or a court official," Sisko said. "I'm not here to arrest you or to judge what you do and don't have the right to do. I'm here because Captain

Vaughn contacted me at my home in Kendra Province and asked me to come."

"Starfleet has no authority to force us to leave Endalla," Rejias maintained.

Sisko breathed in deeply, then exhaled slowly. "As I said, I'm not in Starfleet. Yes, Captain Vaughn was charged with removing you, but you met his request with a threat of violence. He asked me to come here in my role as the Emissary of the Prophets in an attempt to resolve this situation peacefully."

Rejias waved the handheld mining tool in the direction of Vaughn and the other Starfleet officers. "And yet you brought armed officers with you."

Sisko nodded slowly. "Yes, they're armed, but only for self-defense. You can see that none of them have drawn their weapons." Radovan looked over at Captain Vaughn and the members of his crew and confirmed what the Emissary had said: all phasers remained holstered. "As for me, I'm not even carrying a weapon." Sisko held his arms out, palms up, in a gesture of openness. "I agreed to come here as a mediating influence. I wanted to come alone, but Captain Vaughn couldn't allow that. I didn't want to exacerbate the situation, and so I convinced him to beam down to the surface and then walk here, rather than coming in an armed shuttlecraft." Radovan believed that the Emissary had genuinely wanted to avoid provoking Rejias and his followers, especially after the Ohalavaru leader's threat to Vaughn that he would detonate the network of mining devices, but he also thought that approaching the dome on foot had allowed them to investigate the equipment sown across the lunar plain. "We don't have to be adversaries. This doesn't have to be hard."

"No, it doesn't," Rejias agreed. "If you leave now with Captain Vaughn and his crew, we can complete our mission here and depart as quickly as possible."

"Your mission," Sisko said, seizing, Radovan thought, on the implied scope of the word. "What would that be?"

"It . . . it doesn't matter," Rejias said. He clearly didn't want to reveal the reason he'd led hundreds of Ohalavaru to Endalla.

"It seems to me that it does matter," Sisko said. The Emissary pointed to the device beside Rejias. "You and your people have planted mining equipment all over this part of the lunar surface. You plainly intend to excavate here, but the Chamber of Ministers and the Vedek Assembly have deemed Endalla hallowed ground. In addition to intruding on land that the Bajoran government has declared off-limits, and to preparing to conduct unsanctioned mining operations, you're desecrating the place where thousands of people lost their lives. This is their tomb."

"More than that died during the Occupation," Rejias said. His words sounded angry, but he had actually softened his voice. "In that way, Emissary, all of Bajor is a tomb. We have not abandoned our planet."

"No, of course not, but there are numerous sites on Bajor that are closed to the people," Sisko said. "The locations where the Cardassians committed their worst acts of butchery have not been turned into museums or memorials open to the public; some of them have been razed, while those that remain have been walled off as grim reminders of a period in history that should never be forgotten."

Rejias looked down, as though resigned to the verity of Sisko's words. Radovan wondered what the Emissary would think of their plans to uncover a potentially greater truth. Would he be at all intrigued by their efforts to put the lie to the divinity of the Prophets? Or would he work even harder to thwart them in their quest to vindicate Ohalu? Radovan didn't know for sure—Sisko had for some time, at least initially, sought to distance himself from his

place in Bajor's religion—but the latter possibility seemed
far more likely.

With his head still down, Rejias said, "You and others
may consider Endalla a tomb, and rightly so, but what we
do will not tarnish the memories of the scientists who perished here." Rejias finally looked back up at Sisko. "Quite
the opposite, Emissary. Our work will honor their lives by
following in their footsteps."

"What does that mean?" Sisko asked. "You can't be
claiming to have come to Endalla to study its ecosystem."

"No, not to examine the environment of a barren moon,"
Rejias said. "But we are looking for evidence of something
far more important."

"Evidence of what?" Sisko asked. Rejias declined to answer. The Emissary peered around at the people nearest to
him. When Sisko looked in his direction, Radovan felt a
physical sensation, as though a surge of electricity had raced
through his body. A formless whirr rose in his ears. He
stared back at the Emissary and felt a connection to him—a
connection not well defined or easily comprehended, but
nevertheless palpable.

"It doesn't matter what we're looking for," Rejias said.
"What matters is that we're not leaving until we find it." He
sounded resolute. Radovan envied him his certainty and
clarity of purpose.

The Emissary regarded Rejias silently for a moment, evidently taking his measure. Then he looked past the Ohalavaru leader. "I am Benjamin Sisko," he said again, raising
his voice to be heard throughout the dome, above the background purr of the transporter inhibitors. "You know who
I am, and I now know who you are. What matters is that
we are all of Bajor."

Radovan felt his brow crease at the description. *Of Bajor?
What does that mean?* Despite his status in their religion and

his relationship with the Prophets, Sisko could no more be considered a Bajoran than any other human—or any other alien from any other world.

"And because we are all *of* Bajor," the Emissary continued, "we all want the same things *for* Bajor: a vibrant society filled with good works and opportunity, built on the principles of amity and inclusiveness and peace." Sisko turned in place as he spoke, addressing everybody present. "You are Ohalavaru. I am not. But that is of no consequence. I am not here because of our differences. The Bajoran government is not asking you to leave because of who you are or what you believe; right now, they don't even know who you are. They only know that you are defying the current prohibition against visiting Endalla."

"I didn't agree to that," a man called out. Radovan tried to look through the group of Ohalavaru to see him, but couldn't tell who had spoken.

"Maybe not," Sisko said. "Maybe you have a legitimate grievance with the Bajoran government. But there is a right way and a wrong way to pursue your goals. If you want permission to be here, to find the proof you seek, go through the proper channels."

Everybody stared silently at Sisko. Everybody stood their ground. Radovan thought about Vaughn and the other Starfleet officers. When he looked for them, he saw that they had ranged out farther, though they still stood on the periphery of the crowd.

"As you can see, Emissary, we refuse the order to leave," Rejias said. "We wish only to be left alone. We do not seek confrontation, but we will not back down." Rejias raised the handheld mining tool and once more aimed it at the excavator beside him.

Sisko's gaze darted toward the potentially explosive device. When he spoke again, it was not to Rejias, but to all of the Ohalavaru. "The decision to seal off Endalla was not just a matter of protecting the sanctity of the memories of those who died here," he said. "An isolytic subspace weapon tore away this world's atmosphere and obliterated all life. That was just two years ago. Subspace might still be fragile here."

Radovan had never fully understood the nature of the weapon the Ascendants had unleashed in an attempt to destroy Bajor, other than that it attacked the underlying fabric of existence. And nobody seemed to know exactly how a Jem'Hadar soldier had foiled that effort, except that the cost of saving Bajor had been the loss of life—and the ability to sustain life—on Endalla. But Radovan had never heard that the surviving moon remained in any danger.

"What are you saying, Emissary?" Rejias asked.

"If you carry out your labors to mine Endalla, you run the risk of damaging subspace more," Sisko said, responding to the question but still speaking to all the Ohalavaru. "You run the risk of completing the destruction of Endalla that the Ascendants started, and losing your own lives in the process."

A murmur of voices went up in the dome, coinciding with a wave of movement as many of the Ohalavaru, seemingly out of instinct, stepped back from where the Emissary stood with Rejias. Radovan didn't move. He studied the two men facing off against each other, wondering who would prevail in their battle of wills.

But then the quality of sound within the dome changed. At first, Radovan thought that people had simply stopped talking, but then he realized that the hum of the transporter inhibitors had decreased. He frantically looked around for Vaughn and the other Starfleet officers, seeing first one and then another with their gloved hands on inhibitors. The lights on those devices had gone dark, signaling that they had been deactivated. Radovan knew what would happen next even before he heard the high-pitched whine of a transporter beam.

Around the dome, bright white motes and vertical streaks of light formed over people. Rejias immediately lunged forward and grabbed up an inhibitor from the pile of those being attached to excavators. As he switched it on, Vendoma and several others did so too. In his mind's eye, Radovan envisioned himself doing the same, but he found himself frozen in place, unable to move. The whine continued as people began to dematerialize, while the transporter effect around Rejias and Vendoma and the others who had picked up and activated inhibitors faded.

The Ohalavaru leader pointed his handheld mining tool at the excavator. As Radovan's vision started to fade, he knew that Rejias wouldn't depress the triggering pad. Though Radovan judged him steadfast and determined in wanting to prove Ohalu's doctrine, he didn't think the Ohalavaru leader possessed the strength of will to take extreme action.

Then Rejias fired.

In the final instant before his vision went dark, Radovan saw the bright yellow beam shoot into the excavator. The mining device exploded in a fiery light that consumed Rejias and the others who had stayed with him. Everything glowed red, and then everything turned black. In a subjective moment that could have been a second or a year, Radovan wondered whether he'd been safely beamed away from the inferno, or he'd been caught in the blast and brought to the precipice of death.

Both possibilities excited him.

Lying on the sofa in the living area of his flat, Radovan thought about when he had materialized aboard Vaughn's

Starfleet vessel, *U.S.S. James T. Kirk*. Several scores of Ohalavaru stood beside him on the rectangular platform of what he recognized as a large-scale cargo transporter. Everybody looked around in confusion—everybody but Benjamin Sisko, who had also been beamed up from the surface of Endalla.

From everything that had taken place, Radovan had gleaned Vaughn's plan. The Starfleet captain employed the Emissary as a distraction. Sisko's interaction with Rejias gave Vaughn and his crew time to shut down enough inhibitors to allow them to beam everybody up in the dome using multiple transporters. Perhaps the initial strategy had been for Sisko to convince Rejias and his followers to leave Endalla of their own accord, but it didn't matter. In the end, Vaughn succeeded in moving the Ohalavaru off the Bajoran moon.

Afterward, Radovan and the others had been taken back to Bajor, where they'd faced questioning at Militia headquarters. Only then did they learn the fate of Rejias Norvan, who had indeed fired his handheld mining tool at the portable excavator beside him. Six other Ohalavaru managed to activate transporter inhibitors so that they would not be beamed away by Vaughn's crew, but Radovan doubted that any of them had expected Rejias to trigger the detonation of all the excavators they'd networked across that plain on Endalla. All seven of them perished in the resulting firestorm, the heat of which turned that section of the lunar surface into a frozen lake of black glass.

All of the Ohalavaru had been released on probation. The subsequent investigation found Rejias responsible for what had taken place, and the powers that be found little reason to charge his followers with anything beyond trespassing. The Bajoran government did request assistance from Starfleet in establishing a security presence on Endalla in order to prevent other Ohalavaru from returning to the moon to seek the alleged proof of their beliefs.

In the darkness of his flat, Radovan stared up toward the ceiling. He did not feel like himself. Even disregarding the naked woman lying in his bed at that very moment—an incident completely out of character for his life—his ongoing bad dreams left him feeling hollowed out almost every night. Lately, he walked through most days in a state of mental grayness, his interrupted sleep weighing down his waking hours with constant fatigue.

The dreams about the events on Endalla hadn't started immediately after Radovan's return to Bajor, at least not that he could remember upon waking. But soon enough, they filled his nights. Initially, the images that played across his slumbering mind echoed the actual events on the moon, but as the days passed, they morphed into something different—something darker. He imagined ghastly scenes with more violence and death than he had witnessed on Endalla. His nightmares showed him more: charred, bleeding bodies in the form of Ohalavaru corpses and a dying Benjamin Sisko.

Why? Radovan asked himself, not for the first time. It didn't make sense to him. He had come back to Bajor feeling no worse than when he had gone to Endalla. In fact, he hadn't found his time on the moon very satisfying, and so leaving early had been a boon. He didn't care about Rejias or the others who'd died, and Radovan held no particular animus for the Emissary, even considering his mother's opinion of Benjamin Sisko.

But my dreams didn't just include hundreds of Ohalavaru dead, Radovan thought. *And not just a dying Emissary.* There had been another presence in his recent nightmares: Rebecca Sisko.

The Avatar.

Radovan swung his legs from the sofa and pushed himself up to a sitting position. The toddler occupied a special place in the prophecies of Ohalu. In the meetings he had attended, Radovan had heard many discussions about Rebecca Sisko's significance to the Ohalavaru. Most believed that the mere fact of her birth proved Ohalu's foresight and demonstrated his understanding of the Prophets. A small minority also thought that a day would come when Rebecca Sisko would play a larger role in Bajoran life.

Radovan didn't know how to interpret her death in his dreams—as a sign of loss, or as a necessary step on the road ahead. He had never fully understood the Prophecies, either from the Bajoran canon or from the Ohalu texts. At times, they seemed to make sense of the universe, to offer up context for the mysteries of existence and a clear way forward into the future. At others, they sounded like so much propaganda, bald invention intended to calm and control a perpetually troubled people. Radovan read the Prophecies with a vague sense of confusion and disappointment. He had been asking questions all his life, and yet he had never received any satisfactory answers—not from the mainstream religion and not from the Ohalavaru.

Except—

Something clicked inside Radovan. He stood up in the murky shadows, his hand moving to his temple as his thoughts swirled. He realized that his frenzied reimagining of events marked a metamorphosis from simple nightmare into something far heavier: a mystical vision—an Orb shadow, or perhaps even a *pagh'tem'far*.

Or a prophecy, Radovan dared to think. All at once, he realized that the Prophets, whether gods or aliens, had gifted him with future sight—and a mission. He suddenly interpreted his dreams as the prospect of Bajor facing destruction. The idea didn't entirely distress him, but his frenzied psyche provided him with a view forward. Though blurry at the edges, he saw the start of a path that he could walk—that he was *destined* to walk.

At long last, Radovan perceived a purpose to his life. Answers seemed tantalizingly close, just over the horizon. He only had to get there. He knew that he would need to take action, that it would be difficult for him, even to the point of having to break the law. He might even have to risk his own life, but he made the decision to do whatever he had to do.

Even, he thought, *if it means that he would have to hurt the Emissary.*

Or worse.

Chapters

Reaction

Gamma Quadrant, 2386

The *Galaxy*-class starship jolted hard, as though it had slammed into something while soaring through the Gamma Quadrant. A tremendous roar filled the *Robinson* bridge as the impact hurled Captain Benjamin Sisko from the command chair. The deck canted beneath him and he flew over the operations console. Pain flared in his knee as it struck the back of Commander Gwendolyn Plante's head. He landed in front of the main viewscreen, trying to cushion his fall with his outstretched hands. Agony sliced through Sisko's right wrist as it gave way. He heard the snap of a bone not through his ears, but inside his body. Instantly nauseated, Sisko ignored both the feeling and his injury.

"Status report," he called out. The captain had to raise his voice to be heard above the shrill quaver of the automated shipwide alert that blared on and off in time with visual signals flashing red. The ruddy tint of emergency lighting suffused the bridge.

"We've dropped out of warp," said a voice from right beside Sisko. The captain saw that Anxo Rogeiro had been hurled from the first officer's chair to the front of the bridge. The commander made his declaration from where he sprawled on the deck, without the benefit of consulting a control panel or a padd. Sisko immediately realized how his exec made such a determination: despite the call of the red alert, the resonant background hum of the faster-than-light drive would have been audible, and the low-level vibrations it produced would have translated through the structure of the ship, if it had still been operating. The captain could neither hear nor feel the effects of the warp engines.

"Confirmed," called Lieutenant Commander Sivadeki from her position at the conn. During whatever had happened to the ship, she had somehow kept herself anchored to her station. "The warp engines are off-line. We're tumbling."

"Impulse power," Sisko ordered, raising his voice to be heard above the din. "Bring the ship under control." He pushed himself up from the deck, sending a thunderbolt of pain slicing through his broken wrist. He saw that the area around his injury had already begun to swell. "Plante," he yelled, intending to direct her to quiet the red-alert klaxon, but she must have anticipated him because the sound ceased. He saw her working the ops console even as she climbed back into her chair. Sisko must have knocked her from her position when his knee hit her head.

"Power levels are fluctuating," Plante said. "The main generators are down. The backups are active but unstable."

"What happened?" As Sisko raced through the gap between the conn and ops panels, back toward the command chair, Lieutenant Commander Uteln reported from the tactical station on the raised aft section of the bridge.

"We struck a . . . a pocket of energy," he said. "It did not breach the hull, but it collapsed our warp field and overwhelmed the shields."

"A 'pocket of energy'?" asked Rogeiro, who had followed the captain back to the center of the bridge. "A natural phenomenon? Or a weapon?"

Uteln's hands danced expertly across his panel. "Impossible to tell," he said. "But navigational deflectors didn't stop it and sensors didn't detect it until too late."

"Maybe a mine," Rogeiro suggested.

"Tune the sensors to scan for other pockets," Sisko told Uteln. The captain bent his arm and held his broken wrist against his chest to steady it. The pain had eased to a dull throb. "Conduct a full sweep of local space."

"Aye, sir."

"Captain, the impulse engines are not responding," said Sivadeki from the conn. "The *Robinson* is continuing to tumble."

"Thrusters," Sisko said. "Bring us to a full stop." The captain turned and looked at the main viewer, across which the span of stars reeled, reflecting the ship's uncontrolled pitch through space.

"Engaging thrusters," Sivadeki said. The stars immediately began to slow and stabilize.

But then the viewscreen went blank. The emergency lighting failed, as did the visual red-alert signals, leaving the bridge illuminated only by the glow of control panels. A moment later, they too failed, plunging Sisko and his command crew into absolute darkness. An eerie silence descended.

Sisko remained where he stood, confident that the *Robinson* officers at their stations knew their duties. He tapped his combadge, which warbled in response. "Sisko to engineering."

"Relkdahz here, Captain," came the disembodied voice of the ship's chief engineer. His words, interpreted from the alternately slurping and squealing sounds of his native language by a portable translator, sounded reedy and robotic. *"We experienced an energy surge all over the ship. It knocked us out of warp, overloaded relays, and damaged the main engines. It also caused feedback in our systems and shut down*

the primary generators. The backups engaged, but a residual charge from the surge sent them into quiescent mode."

"What can we do?" Ahead of Sisko, a beam of light winked on at ops, where Plante had retrieved a handheld beacon from its storage location at her console. The rest of the bridge became faintly visible in flat shades of black and gray and white.

"We've initiated a full restart of the main generators," Relkdahz said. His voice sounded unusually loud in the otherwise silent bridge. Another beacon flared on behind Sisko, at the tactical station, and then Sivadeki activated a third at the conn. *"It'll take thirteen minutes to restore main power, but we're cycling the emergency generators; they'll be back in less than two minutes. The state of the impulse engines is unclear."*

"Acknowledged," Sisko said. "Warp drive?"

"We won't know with certainty until we can get in there and fully assess the damage," Relkdahz said.

"What's your best estimate?" the captain asked.

For a moment, the chief engineer did not answer. Sisko thought that the combadge signal might have failed. The captain waited for a moment, the leaden ache in his wrist pulsating in time with the beat of his heart.

Then Relkdahz said, *"I'd guess at least a day . . . maybe two."*

"Keep me informed. Sisko out."

In the dim light thrown by the handheld beacons, the captain returned to the command chair. Rogeiro sat down beside him, shaking his head. "Days, not hours," the first officer said. "If we did hit a mine, we could be in for some company." His words carried the gentle accent of his Portuguese heritage.

"You think it could be a trap," Sisko said.

"Probably not meant for us," Rogeiro said.

"No," Sisko agreed. The *Robinson* crew had departed Deep Space 9 and entered the Bajoran wormhole three months earlier. They set course away from the Dominion and into space unexplored during any of Starfleet's previous forays into the Gamma Quadrant—the three-month journey of *Defiant* a decade prior, *Robinson*'s six-month mission three years ago, and the aborted joint effort of *Enterprise* and the Romulan vessel *Eletrix*. "We have neither friends nor foes this far from the Federation."

"Until the warp drive is repaired, I should lead a team of shuttlecraft to patrol the area," Rogeiro suggested.

In general, the idea appealed to the captain. Where *Robinson* had been rendered blind and unable to protect itself, the auxiliary vessels possessed fully functioning systems. In addition to providing reconnaissance of nearby space, the shuttles could also defend the starship if needed. But the plan lacked one essential.

"Our sensors couldn't detect the energy pocket until too late," Sisko told Rogeiro. "Whether it was a mine or something that occurred naturally, there could be more of them. Until we can tune the shuttlecraft sensors accordingly, I don't want to send anyone out there."

"Sir, the ship isn't under control, and we're not sure when we're going to get the impulse engines back," Rogeiro said. "If there are more pockets of energy, the *Robinson* could hit another one. I think it's worth the risk to send at least one shuttlecraft out to seize the ship with a tractor beam and bring it to a stop."

"You're right," Sisko said at once, understanding the danger to *Robinson*. "Get down to the shuttlebay—"

In front of Sisko, the conn and ops stations glimmered back to life. Sivadeki and Plante wasted no time in working their controls. All around the bridge, other panels flashed on, and the rest of the bridge crew returned to their tasks.

Finally, the emergency lighting came back on, imbuing the scene with its crimson tones.

At the front of the bridge, the main viewscreen remained blank. Sisko ordered Plante to activate it, and a moment later, a moving starfield reappeared there. "Do we have impulse drive?" Rogeiro asked.

"It's just come back online," Sivadeki said.

"Bring us to a full stop," Sisko said.

"Yes, sir."

The soft drone of the impulse engines rose to permeate the bridge, the almost imperceptible tremors of their operation like the ship's heartbeat. It felt to Sisko as though the wounded *Robinson* had been revived. The array of stars began to slow their slantwise march across the viewscreen, until at last they settled into a motionless image.

"Engines answering all stop," said Sivadeki.

Sisko stood back up. "Sensors, full sweep," he said. "Find out if that pocket of energy is still intact after we collided with it. I also want to know if there are any others out there."

"Aye, sir," said Uteln.

"Lieutenant sh'Vrane," Sisko said, addressing the ship's lead science officer, "study the sensor readings we already have from just before the collision. See if you can determine whether the energy pocket was of natural or artificial origin, and if it was manufactured, try to figure out its purpose." From the sciences station on the aft perimeter of the bridge, the Andorian acknowledged her orders.

Rogeiro stepped up beside Sisko. "Commander Sivadeki," the first officer said, "are there any solar systems in the area?" Sisko thought he asked the question as though he already knew the answer—which he undoubtedly did, since *Robinson* had been cruising through a relatively barren region of space.

"Negative, Commander," Sivadeki said. "The nearest are between five and ten light-years away and unlikely to contain life-sustaining planets. The system we were headed for has a main-sequence star, spectral class K, absolute magnitude of plus five. It's eleven-point-two light-years distant."

"What are you thinking?" Sisko asked his exec. "If there are civilizations orbiting any of those stars, we're too far out for the energy pocket to be some kind of defense or early-warning system."

"Right," Rogeiro said. "That wouldn't make any sense. It's—"

"Captain," Uteln interrupted, "we have multiple sensor contacts dropping out of warp. I read six incoming vessels—no, eight—twelve." He operated his controls, clearly trying to identify the scope of the approaching threat. "There are two dozen ships. No known configuration. They're about four times the size of a runabout." Uteln continued to work the tactical station, coaxing information from the sensors. "Scans show they have defensive shields and . . . they also have emitters on their bows and concentrated energy behind them."

"Weapons," Rogeiro concluded.

"Shields up," Sisko said. "Ready main phasers and arm quantum torpedoes."

"Aye, sir," said Uteln.

"Bring us about, full impulse," Sisko said. With the warp drive out, *Robinson* could not outrun the incoming ships, but it could at least make itself into a moving target. "Prepare for evasive maneuvers."

"Setting course, full impulse," said Sivadeki.

As *Robinson* settled onto a new path, Rogeiro spoke to Commander Plante, who served the ship not only as its operations manager, but also as its second officer. "Put the ships on-screen."

The image on the main viewer shifted and a swarm of vessels appeared. Other than by virtue of their proximity to one another, the ships did not look like a coordinated squadron. They traveled along differing nonlinear trajectories and in no discernible formation. Sisko saw no two vessels that matched in color. He focused on one with a greenish gray hull that had no axial symmetry, looking more like a fusion of differing, many-angled shapes. When he studied a second ship, he saw that, even apart from its orange exterior, it in no way resembled the first; it comprised three spheres joined by cylindrical projections.

"Those ships look different from one another," Rogeiro said, giving voice to Sisko's thoughts. "There's no uniformity of design."

"Hailing frequencies," Sisko said. With Uteln preparing the ship's weapons and defenses, Plante took over communications. She tapped at the ops panel.

"Channels open, Captain," she said.

"This is Captain Benjamin Sisko of the *U.S.S. Robinson*," he intoned. "We are representatives of the United Federation of Planets on a peaceful mission of exploration." He waited for a response, and when he got none, he tried again. "This is Captain Sisko from the United Federation of Planets. We come in peace."

"Nothing, sir," Plante said. "I can't tell if they're receiving us."

On the viewer, a jumbled batch of vessels peeled off from the others and dove toward *Robinson*. "Here they come," announced Uteln.

"Target the lead ships," Sisko said without hesitation. He loathed the idea of first contact with an unknown species coming at the potentially lethal end of a phaser, but he would do what he needed to in order to protect his crew. "Phasers only. Prepare to fire on my order."

Sisko and Rogeiro retreated to their chairs as tense seconds passed. As the phalanx of alien vessels approached *Robinson*, the captain dreaded the onset of battle. From a philosophical standpoint, they had embarked on their mission to encounter unknown civilizations, to learn about them and from them, and to establish friendly, mutually beneficial relationships; they had not set out into the Gamma Quadrant with the aim of making new adversaries. On the practical side of the ledger, Sisko had no way of knowing the strength of the alien weaponry. He hoped that the advancing vessels, all far smaller than *Robinson*, would pose no real threat to his crew, though he feared that the aggregate power of so many ships could prove overwhelming.

"Captain, two more sets of ships are breaking off from the main group," Uteln said. "They're moving to outflank us . . . but . . ." Sisko heard the chirps and twitters emitted by the tactical console as Uteln worked his controls. "Sir, none of the vessels are aiming their weapons at the *Robinson*."

Before the captain could question the conclusion, jagged bolts of energy leaped from the bow of one ship. The blistering white streaks looked more than anything like bolts of lightning. Sisko did not understand how that could possibly be the case, given that such planet-based phenomena followed low-resistance paths through the atmosphere; there should have been essentially no resistance in space, and so discharges of electrical energy should have traveled along straight lines.

The bolt terminated well short of *Robinson*. Where it ended, a lattice of brilliant, interconnecting filaments blazed into existence. The mesh-like formation burned brightly for several seconds, then vanished. The captain stood up and stepped to the center of the bridge, his gaze locked on the main viewer.

"Analysis," Rogeiro said, rising from the first officer's

chair and moving to stand beside Sisko. "What kind of weapon is that?"

"Scans read it as plasma based," Uteln said.

"Is it some sort of barrier?" Rogeiro asked. "Could they be seeding pockets of energy out in space like the one we hit?"

"Negative," Uteln said. "The energy dissipated, leaving nothing behind . . . but . . . I'm also detecting some unusual subspace variances."

A second vessel fired, sending another dazzling bolt jinking through the void. Two more ships followed suit, and then two more. Networks of radiant strands illuminated different volumes of space, though none of them came close to landing on *Robinson*.

"Sensors are showing more ships dropping out of warp ahead of us," Uteln said.

"On-screen," Rogeiro said.

The image on the main viewer jumped, from displaying the patchwork of weapons fire to another farrago of small vessels. "There are twenty-five ships in the new group," Uteln said. "They're approximately the same size as the others." The arriving vessels moved similarly to the first, along nonstandard, nonconforming flight paths. As best Sisko could tell, no two ships shared either a hull color or a design.

As the captain watched, many of the vessels dispersed, some moving off to port, some to starboard, some upward, some down. The half-dozen ships in the center blocked *Robinson*'s course ahead. "Target the vessels in front of us," Sisko said. "If they don't get out of our way when we get close, open fire. We'll punch our way through if we have to." The captain moved forward to stand beside Sivadeki at the conn. "Use evasive maneuvers," he told her. "Keep us away from their weapons." Sisko did not know how effective the plasma bolts would be against *Robinson*, but he didn't want to find out—particularly considering the subspace anomalies sensors had revealed.

On the viewscreen, one of the vessels fired, casting a luminous, angular bolt out into the night, culminating in an irregular web of glowing fibers that, like its predecessors, quickly faded. In succession, the other ships unleashed their weapons. One energy framework appeared and evaporated, only for another to develop nearby. They all eventually disappeared.

"Phasers locked on multiple targets," Uteln said. "Firing range in ten seconds."

"Evasion course plotted," Sivadeki said. "Ready to implement as soon as we attack."

"Five seconds," Uteln said.

The vessels ahead of *Robinson* all fired simultaneously. Ragged, gleaming tendrils tore through the darkness, each ending in an uneven grid of light beams. For a moment, a growing patchwork appeared, like a great chain-link barrier of energy, but then it too vanished.

"Firing phasers," Uteln said. *Robinson*'s weapons seared through space, six red-tinged yellow rays of powerful coherent light shooting toward the alien ships blocking the Starfleet vessel's course. Sisko hoped that the phasers would significantly reduce the effectiveness of their unknown adversaries' shields, or even eliminate them entirely; he wanted to end the conflict as quickly, and with as few casualties, as possible.

On the viewscreen, the beams raced on-target toward the six alien vessels—and then vanished. Sisko blinked, unsure of what he had just seen. Each of the phaser strikes had closed on their objectives, suddenly dimmed at a particular point, and then stopped, as though they had struck an invisible wall. As the alien ships fired again, Sisko said, "What just happened?"

"Scanning," Uteln said.

Another piecemeal wall of crisscrossing energy strings flashed up across *Robinson*'s bow. At the conn, Sivadeki rapidly worked her controls. The view of the firing alien vessels slipped off to port as she altered course.

"Do those ships have superior shields?" Rogeiro asked. "With extended range?"

Sisko glanced back toward the tactical station and saw Uteln poring over the data on his console. "Negative," the lieutenant commander said. "Sensors read shields similar to ours, though less powerful, but . . . the phasers dispersed at the point where we detected abnormal subspace variances."

On the viewer, another group of mismatched ships appeared in front of *Robinson*. Sisko watched as they fired, generating additional matrices of energy. The strange formations flared and then faded.

"Fire phasers and quantum torpedoes, full spread," he ordered. Uteln worked his control panel. The reddish-yellow beams of the phasers flew once more from *Robinson*, joined by the blue-white bolts of the quantum torpedoes. Sisko waited for the weapons to land, hoping that they would provide an escape route for his ship.

But the alien vessels sent up another assemblage of misshapen energy grids. The phasers passed through them, dimmed, and then died. The quantum torpedoes struck them and exploded, well short of their marks.

"Evasive," Sisko said, even as Sivadeki operated the conn to take *Robinson* in another direction. The viewscreen revealed only more alien vessels, their unusual weapons continuing to create the strange energy patterns. Sivadeki altered course again—up, down, to port, to starboard—but she could not find a way out for *Robinson*.

"We're surrounded," Uteln said.

"But why?" Rogeiro said.

Sisko shook his head. Possibilities occurred to him: that *Robinson* had crossed into the territory of a violently xenophobic race, or that the pocket of energy the ship had inadvertently struck had been useful or meaningful in some way to the aliens, perhaps sacred. Whatever the reason, it didn't matter at that moment, unless it helped Sisko determine how to extract his crew from the danger they faced.

Sivadeki struggled at the conn, but no matter the direction *Robinson* moved, alien vessels appeared on the viewscreen, still discharging their energy bursts. With each moment, the weapons fire drew closer, though the ships remained at a distance.

"Captain, if we keep moving, their energy blasts are going to hit the ship," Sivadeki said.

"Full stop," Sisko said. "Open hailing frequencies." At the conn and ops, Sivadeki and Plante followed their orders.

"Engines at full stop."

"Channels open."

"This is Captain Sisko of the *Robinson*," he said. "You have threatened our ship and surrounded us, but we don't know why. We are explorers, seeking only to expand our knowledge of the universe and to meet and befriend other civilizations. Our aims are peaceful. We fired on your ships only after you fired on us." Sisko waited for a response he knew would not come.

"But . . . they haven't fired *on* us," Rogeiro noted. "They've fired all around us, but no weapons have touched the ship." He looked toward the main viewscreen, and Sisko followed his gaze. The energy webs drew nearer, even though the alien vessels had yet to specifically target *Robinson*. "Why?"

Plante glanced up from the ops station. "They're not trying to destroy the ship," she said. "They're trying to capture us."

For Sisko, the question remained: *Why?*

"Captain," Uteln said, "the energy discharges are getting very close to the ship."

"Shield status?" Sisko asked.

"Shields are up full," Uteln said, "but until the main generators are back online, we can't fortify them."

Sisko exchanged a glance with Rogeiro, then said, "Shut down the weapons systems. Take additional power from there."

"Sir?" Uteln asked.

"Do it," Sisko snapped.

"Aye, sir."

To Rogeiro, Sisko quietly said, "Our weapons are ineffectual; there's no point in keeping them online." The first officer nodded in agreement.

The captain looked back at the main viewer to see a writhing web of energy approaching *Robinson*. He expected it to dwindle into nothingness, as the others had, but it didn't. The ship trembled.

"One of the energy nets has struck us," Uteln said.

"Damage report," Rogeiro said.

Uteln frantically worked his console. He looked to Sisko as though he didn't believe what his readouts told him. A sheen of perspiration showed on his hairless scalp. "There's no drain on the shields," he said. "There's virtually no effect at all . . . except . . . a subspace variance."

"What kind of variance?" Rogeiro asked.

"It's nothing I can identify, sir," Uteln said. "The energy has dissipated . . . it doesn't seem to have done anything but produce those subspace irregularities."

"What kind of irregularities?" Sisko wanted to know.

"It's just . . . the readings show discontinuities," Uteln said. "It's almost as though subspace has been torn apart."

Suddenly, the normal bridge lighting came on. Sisko

appreciated the banishment of the claustrophobic red glow in favor of the brighter white tones. *"Relkdahz to bridge."*

"Sisko here. Go ahead, Commander."

"Primary power is back online," the chief engineer said. *"The ship is in good shape except for the warp drive. We're still examining the main engines, but we've got twenty burned-out power relays, plus damage to several transfer junctions and the theta-matrix compositor."*

"Can you make repairs?" Sisko asked.

"We can," Relkdahz said, *"but we'll need to replicate new relays, as well as new parts for the junctions and the compositor. We'll have to install and calibrate all of it. It will take at least twenty-four hours."*

"Get on it," Sisko said. "I want a status report every four hours."

"Yes, sir."

"Sisko out." He stepped over to the ops station. "Anything at all?" he asked.

"Still no response, Captain," Plante said.

"Continue transmitting my message," Sisko said. "Keep trying to get through." He regarded the main viewer. The alien vessels had stopped firing their weapons and remained motionless in space, neither approaching nor retreating from *Robinson*. "Full magnification on the nearest ship."

"Full mag," Plante said. The image on the viewer blinked, and one of the alien vessels filled the display. It comprised a series of four disk-shaped structures connected unevenly along their flat edges, with a conic aft section. Sisko had never seen anything like it. It looked neither functional nor artistic, though both measures doubtless depended on the nature of its builders.

Suddenly, the unusual ship turned, and from the lateral side of the second disk, another shape hurtled out into space.

A sphere etched with an asymmetric pattern of curling lines, it had four protuberances arranged in a square on the near side. "Is that an auxiliary craft?" Sisko asked.

"It appears so," Uteln said, consulting his panel. "Ten of them have been launched from the alien vessels. They're all headed toward *Robinson*."

"Boarding craft," Rogeiro said.

"Standard view. Bring our weapons back online," Sisko said. He waited for the tactical officer to make that happen. When Uteln confirmed that he had done so, the captain said, "Lock phasers and quantum torpedoes on the approaching vessels." Despite the ineffectiveness to that point of the weapons, the captain would not allow his ship to be boarded without a fight. Before that, though, he would once again try diplomacy. "Hailing frequencies."

"You're on, sir," said Plante.

"This is Captain Sisko," he said. "We are tracking your boarding vessels. We do not wish to fight, but we will not allow you access to our ship. If we have trespassed in your territory, or committed some other transgression against your people, it was unintentional. We apologize. We seek peaceful coexistence, but we will gladly withdraw and never return if that is what you wish. But if you attempt to board this ship, we will defend ourselves."

Sisko waited as the auxiliary craft grew to fill the main viewscreen on its approach to *Robinson*. "Standard view," he said, and the image on the viewscreen pulled back to show the collection of alien vessels ahead. Boarding craft approached from two of those. As with their parent ships, neither of the boarding vessels resembled each other. Sisko didn't expect a reply, and he received none.

Plante confirmed it: "No response, sir."

"Fire all weapons." Sisko heard the feedback tones that signaled the discharge of phaser banks and the launch of quantum torpedoes. But as he watched the main view-screen, he saw no bright beams of destructive power.

"Phasers fired," Uteln said, "but they produced no discernible output." The blue-white glow of quantum torpedoes did shoot out into space toward the boarding craft. The captain waited for them to strike their targets, but when they did, the torpedoes simply flew apart with no resultant explosions.

Sisko didn't wait for an explanation. "Evasive maneuvers, full impulse," he said. "Look for an opening to get past them. In the meantime, let's not make it easy for them."

"Full impulse," Sivadeki said, and she worked the conn. Sisko heard her controls respond to her touch with the appropriate sounds. The pulse of the impulse drive rose on the bridge.

But the ship didn't move.

"Captain, I've engaged the impulse engines," Sivadeki said, confusion and anxiety in her tone. "They read active and operational, but we're not moving."

Sisko peered down at the conn and read the details spelled out across the panel. Everything appeared normal, but when he glanced up at the main viewscreen, he could see that *Robinson* remained motionless in space. "Bridge to engineering."

"Engineering. This is Relkdahz."

"Are the impulse engines functioning?" Sisko asked.

"Yes," Relkdahz said, *"the impulse drive is online and operating at peak efficiency."*

"The ship's not moving," Sisko said.

"I don't know how that can be," Relkdahz said. *"Stand by."*

"Let me know. Sisko out."

"Captain," Uteln said. In just the single word, Sisko heard apprehension in the voice of the usually unflappable tactical officer. "Sensors are returning readings I've never seen before. All around the ship, space-time appears to have . . . broken down. We're adrift in . . . nothingness."

"Broken down?" Rogeiro repeated.

Uteln studied his console. "Everywhere the aliens fired their energy nets, the fabric of existence has been destroyed . . . down to subspace."

"That was the reason for the variances you detected," Sisko said.

"Apparently," Uteln agreed.

"That's why we're not moving," Sivadeki said. "There's nothing for the impulse engines to drive against."

"What about thrusters?" Rogeiro asked. "Can we at least move?"

"I can try," Sivadeki said, and she married her actions to her words, working over her controls at the conn. "I've activated the thrusters, but we're still stationary."

"At their current velocity, the auxiliary vessels are three minutes out," Uteln said.

"Route all available power from the primary and secondary generators to the shields," Sisko said. "Intruder alert. All crew to arm themselves, all civilian personnel on lockdown."

As Plante prepared the ship to be boarded, Sisko watched the viewer as the alien craft descended on *Robinson*. As he did so, all of the doors on the bridge parted in short order. Armed two-person security contingents entered and took protective positions.

"Tractor beam," Sisko said, searching for some means of preventing his ship from being boarded. "Target the craft directly ahead of us. I want to hold it in place." If they could use a tractor beam to secure one of the approaching vessels, perhaps they could route enough power to freeze all of them.

"Engaging tractor beam," Uteln said. Not surprisingly,

the blue-white beam that should have emanated from *Robinson* did not appear. "The tractor will not operate in the zone of dead space."

"Of course not," Rogeiro said, clearly resigned to the failure of another of the ship's systems.

Sisko retreated to the command chair and sat down. As he did so, he noticed the flesh around his swollen wrist had grown discolored, sporting patches of mottled purple and yellow. His first officer resumed his position beside him.

"What are our options?" Rogeiro asked.

"If they can board us," Sisko said, "we'll have to fight them hand to hand."

Rogeiro lowered his voice. "And if they're able to commandeer this vessel?"

Sisko fixed his exec with a long, cold stare. He knew what Rogeiro asked of him: to what lengths would the captain go to prevent *Robinson* from falling into the hands of an adversary—even a new and unknown adversary? "I cannot allow that to happen." The first officer nodded soberly. Sisko had confirmed that, if necessary, he would initiate the ship's self-destruct protocols.

The bridge quieted as all eyes fixed on the main viewscreen. As the ships neared *Robinson*, they began to pass out of sight on the bottom of the display. "Lock viewer on the lead vessel," Sisko said. Plante complied. The captain and the rest of the bridge crew watched as the auxiliary craft rotated, bringing the four segments protruding from the sphere toward *Robinson*'s hull, making their function as landing pads obvious.

Seconds later, the vessel touched down on *Robinson*'s primary hull, landing in the middle of the ship's Starfleet designation: NCC-71842. Sisko heard the dull thump that coincided with touchdown. The shields flashed blue below it.

"Can we increase the power of the shields momentarily?" Sisko asked. "Effectively send a surge through them that might incapacitate those ships."

"I can try," Uteln said. "I'm increasing the power to the defensive grid, but keeping the amount of power to the shields capped at the transmission nodes." He worked his controls. "Power levels are building up at the nodes. I'll need to release it before they overload."

"Do it," Sisko said.

Uteln waited, then tapped a control. On the viewscreen, the shields hugging the hull of *Robinson* flashed a darker blue as the increased power distributed across the grid. The auxiliary craft remained unaffected.

A hatch on the bottom portion of the spherical vessel withdrew and moved out of sight, revealing a dark opening. Sisko stood back up as he waited to see who or what would emerge. At first, nothing did.

"Ten vessels have landed on the hull," Uteln announced.

At that moment, a long, narrow metal shape emerged from the craft visible on the main viewscreen. As it neared the hull, several arms folded down at its base, like the fingers of a technological hand. It pushed flush against *Robinson*. Sisko expected a cutting beam to start carving up the ship, or for the extended tool to begin rotating and physically cut through the outer plating.

But nothing like that happened. "What are they doing?" Rogeiro asked.

Suddenly, Sivadeki shot to her feet at the conn, her hands coming up to the sides of her head to cover her external auditory canals. She screamed and dropped to her knees. Sisko rushed forward to help her, but then a high-pitched screech pierced his ears. It felt as though long needles had been pounded into his brain. Black jots formed before his eyes. He staggered and tried to remain upright, reaching for the side of the conn with his uninjured hand. The main viewscreen winked off, and then the overhead lighting failed. Sisko held on for just long enough to glance behind him and see, in the reflected light of their consoles, the rest of the bridge crew crumbling. The emergency lighting came on with its ominous red tones.

Sisko fell forward and everything went black.

The rocking movement had a rhythm to it, almost like sound. It seemed a long way off, like a wave that starts in the middle of the ocean and becomes the barest swell by the time it reaches shore. It lapped beneath Sisko, swaying him gently one way, then the other. In some subjectively immeasurable amount of time, the sensation expanded, took on a fullness that became audible.

Aaa nnn . . . aaa nnn . . . caaa tnnn . . . caaa tnnn . . .
Over and over, making no sense, until all of a sudden, it did.

"Captain."

Sisko opened his eyes to see the blond-haired visage of Lieutenant Commander Diana Althouse, the ship's counselor. The petite woman kneeled over him, her hands on his upper arms, apparently trying to shake him into consciousness. She wore a haggard expression that the captain thought spoke less to her sense of concern for him and more to whatever ordeal she had just endured.

Sisko's thoughts swam. He blinked, searching for focus. He looked at Althouse, wondering just why she had come to his cabin. But then Sisko gazed past the counselor to the overhead, to the recognizable transparent dome. *I'm on the bridge,* he thought with surprise. He pushed himself up and saw other members of his crew blearily pulling themselves off the deck. "What . . . what happened?" he asked.

"The ship struck a pocket of energy and fell out of warp—" Althouse said, and all of it came back to the captain.

"We were attacked." Sisko pushed himself up. A stab of pain flared in his wrist, which he saw had expanded to twice its normal size. As he climbed back to his feet, Sisko tottered and Althouse steadied him. "That sound . . ."

"It knocked the entire bridge crew out," the counselor said.

Behind Althouse, Commander Plante tried to hoist herself up on the operations console, but then she lost her grip and staggered backward. Sisko stepped past the counselor, caught his second officer, and lowered her into her chair. Plante shook her head quickly from side to side, her long golden hair loosed from its knot and whipping around as she tried to clear the cobwebs from her mind. "I'm . . . I'm okay," she said, and she began checking her control panel.

"Siva!" the captain heard Althouse say. When he turned, he saw that the counselor had moved to the side of the conn, where Lieutenant Commander Sivadeki lay motionless on the deck. A rust-colored stripe of blood had leaked from the Tyrellian's earhole and pooled beneath her head. "She's not coming to," Althouse said. The counselor felt along the inside of Sivadeki's elbow. "Her pulse is weak." Without waiting for the captain's order, Althouse followed ship protocol by reaching over and tapping the conn officer's combadge. "Computer, emergency medical transport." As the counselor rose and stepped back, the whine of the transporter filled the bridge and Sivadeki disappeared in a haze of coruscating white light, beamed directly to *Robinson*'s sickbay.

Sisko looked for his first officer and found him settling shakily back into his chair. The captain paced over to him. "Are you all right?"

"Yes," Rogeiro said. He rubbed at his temple. "I've got a headache, but I'm all right."

Sisko waited a moment to confirm his exec's condition, then told him, "Sivadeki's been injured. Get Lieutenant Stannis up here to take over. Meanwhile, fill in at the conn."

"Aye, sir," Rogeiro said. He stood and made his way over to Sivadeki's station.

Sisko looked to Uteln, who had recovered enough to return to his console. "Tactical, report," the captain said. "How long were we out?"

"Seven hours, thirty-one minutes," Uteln said. He continued to study his instruments, then raised his head and looked over the captain, toward the main viewscreen. "The aliens are gone." Sisko turned and followed the tactical officer's gaze. The viewer showed the section of *Robinson*'s primary hull where an alien vessel had alit. The unusual craft no longer sat there, but in its stead, a clean, circular hole had been cut into the ship's external plating, eliminating parts of the numerals *8* and *4* in its registry. As Sisko watched, a force field flickered blue across the cavity. "There are no more vessels on the hull, and internal sensors reveal no intruders aboard." He tapped furiously at his controls. "External scans show no sign of any ships at all within range."

"And the *Robinson*?" Sisko asked.

"The hull has been breached in all ten locations where the alien craft landed," Uteln said. "Automatic force fields are in place."

"Dispatch repair teams to those locations," Sisko said.

"Aye, sir."

"Commander Plante," the captain said, "ship's status."

"The warp drive remains down," Plante said. "Otherwise, all systems have been restored and are functioning within normal parameters. Casualty reports are coming in from all over the ship, mostly minor injuries. Sickbay lists four emergency transports . . . all for Tyrellian members of the crew. There are no indications of any fatalities, but . . . I'm receiving word of several people missing from their last known location."

"Missing?" Sisko said. He strode over to stand beside Plante. "How many?" he asked as the operations officer worked her panel.

"Of the ship's complement of one thousand, three hundred, forty-seven crew and civilian personnel," Plante read from her display, "eighty-seven are unaccounted for."

Sisko's eyes widened as anger welled up within him. It did not require a sophisticated line of reasoning to identify what had happened: the alien boarding party had abducted almost ninety people from *Robinson*. The captain could only hope that they had been taken alive and were unharmed.

The faces of Kasidy and Rebecca flew across Sisko's mind, but he pushed them away. He couldn't think about the personal risk to his family. No matter who had been removed from the ship, the captain and his crew would do whatever they had to do to recover them.

"Where were they taken from?" Sisko asked.

"From several different areas," Plante said, consulting her displays. "But all on the residential decks." Sisko watched as she scrolled through a list of names. She touched a heading, and an indicator appeared on each row. "Captain, only civilians are missing."

Sisko could not prevent himself from feeling a pang of fear for his wife and daughter. He fought the urge to ask if they numbered among the missing. He could not show favoritism for his family; he had a responsibility to every individual aboard his ship.

Plante continued to parse through the data, searching

for additional information. Eventually, her hands stopped moving across her console and she looked up at Sisko. "Captain," she said, "all eighty-seven of the missing are children."

Sisko stood in the center of the cabin he shared with his wife and daughter, his back to the open door that led to Rebecca's room. She wasn't in there. She wasn't anywhere aboard *Robinson*.

"What are we going to do?" Kasidy asked. Sisko could see her obvious concern and seriousness of purpose, but also noted that she showed no signs of panic, for which he felt grateful. He had to make a conscious effort to tamp down his own fears, which otherwise would have threatened to overwhelm him.

When Kasidy had regained consciousness after the alien attack, she had raced to their daughter's classroom to make sure that Rebecca had not been injured by the sound-based weapon that had incapacitated everybody aboard ship. To her horror, she discovered Rebecca missing, along with a number of other children. Kasidy allowed the appropriate ship's personnel to contact the bridge to notify the command crew of the situation, and then she withdrew to their quarters to wait for word from her husband.

For his part, Sisko had learned on the bridge that Rebecca was among the missing children. He remained there for as long as it required him to discharge his immediate duties, which included determining the extent of what had happened aboard *Robinson*, ordering repairs to the warp drive, and setting his engineering, piloting, and scientific teams the task of finding a means of moving the ship beyond the region of destroyed space-time it currently occupied. Sisko also told Uteln to lead the tactical staff in finding a method of protecting the crew against another sonic attack—for the captain had every intention of tracking and engaging the aliens who had stolen most of the children aboard *Robinson*.

When Sisko had finally returned to his family's quarters, he'd found his wife anxiously pacing in the living area. Her gaze settled on his swollen, discolored wrist, but only briefly, and she said nothing about it. Sisko noticed the door to Rebecca's room standing open, but he resisted the impulse to go there, to peer in and explicitly confirm his daughter's absence. Instead, he went to his wife, meaning to take her in his arms, to console her, to promise that he would not rest until they got Rebecca back. But once they embraced, Kasidy pushed away from him and continued her march across the cabin. She told him what she had experienced.

Kasidy had been thrown into a bulkhead when *Robinson* had suddenly lurched and its inertial dampers had faltered, though she had come away with just a bruise on her shoulder. She watched through a port as the strange energy webs had blossomed around the ship, felt the crew's attempts to evade them, and witnessed the small vessels approaching. As best she could recall, she heard the high-pitched siren for only a moment before it had driven her to her knees and then into unconsciousness.

Sisko had explained all the details of those events from his perspective, from the pocket of energy the ship had struck to the alien force that had boarded the ship. Kasidy cared about none of it. She didn't want to know what had already transpired; she only wanted to know what would come next.

"The first thing we've got to do is get the ship repaired and back into normal space," Sisko told her.

Kasidy stopped a few steps from him. "I mean, what are *we*—" She pointed to Sisko and then to herself. "—going to do."

The half statement, half question hit him like the blunt shock of a phaser set to heavy stun. Sisko had heard his wife utter the same words before, in the same tones, combining her hopes and fears, her determination and dread, stitched together with a thread of accusation. As Kasidy's husband and Rebecca's father, Sisko had brought them aboard *Robinson*, and as the commanding officer of the ship, he had allowed their daughter to be taken from them. Replace the Starfleet vessel with the planet Bajor, and his position as captain with that of Emissary, and they had been there before. Sisko knew that his wife, in that moment, did not blame him for what had transpired, any more than she had meant to do so six years earlier, but no matter how she thought about it—either then or now—he understood that she felt it.

"What we're going to do is find our daughter," Sisko said, "and bring her home safely." He didn't know the precise language he had used back when Rebecca had been taken as a toddler, but he realized it must have been close to what he'd just said. He didn't really want that to be the case—he had no desire to mirror those baleful days back on Bajor on any level—but he could not deny the parallels of the two situations.

"It's happening again," Kasidy said quietly, as though reading his thoughts.

"No," Sisko told her out of reflex, understanding what his wife needed to hear—what they *both* needed to hear. "The circumstances are similar, but no."

Kasidy appeared to consider his claim. Sisko, remembering, saw the rest of their conversation play out in his head. She would say it out loud, ascribe their bad fortune to the choices he had made, the responsibilities he had accepted.

But that didn't happen. Kasidy crossed the cabin to him, reached up, and put her hands on his upper arms. She looked deep into his eyes, searching for strength or truth or maybe something else. He didn't know, but he stood tall and met her gaze, trying to bolster her, but also to find his own fortitude.

"Tell me it's not the same," Kasidy said. "Tell me that the Prophets haven't spoken to you, that somebody seeking the Emissary or the Avatar hasn't done this."

"The Prophets haven't spoken to me," Sisko said honestly and earnestly. "And I don't see how this could be about the Bajoran faith. We're traveling deeper and deeper into the Gamma Quadrant, and Rebecca wasn't the only child taken." He decided not to say the other half of what he thought— namely, that he wished the abduction of the children from the ship *did* have to do with the Bajoran religion. Despite that the Prophets had essentially abandoned him after his return from the Celestial Temple, and later had sent a vision of Kira Nerys to release him from his service to Them, They had ultimately helped him to keep his family safe. It hadn't always been easy, but he genuinely felt that the Prophets had guided him along the path that had allowed Kasidy and Rebecca to remain alive and healthy, and to bring them fully back into his life.

Kasidy dropped her hands from Sisko's arms and wrapped her arms around his waist. She pulled in close to him, folding herself into his body. Sisko held her as best he could without setting his broken wrist tightly against her back. He wanted to protect her and make her feel safe. "What are we going to do?" she asked him again.

"I'm going to command this ship," Sisko said, trying to project as much confidence to his wife as he could. "The crew is going to repair the warp drive, find a way out of here, and pursue those who took our children. We're going to get all of them back, including Rebecca."

"And what am I going to do?"

"You and the rest of the diplomatic corps and first-contact specialists are going to study our encounter with the aliens," Sisko said. "You're going to search for clues in how to deal with them once we locate them."

Kasidy pulled away from Sisko and regarded him carefully. He suspected that she might think he sought only to keep her busy during this difficult time. "Do you think that will help?" she asked.

"I think it may be critical," he told her. "I couldn't even get them to respond to us—not when I tried to greet them, not when I told them who we were and what we wanted, not even when I threatened them and then fired on their ships. We need to find out what will work."

Kasidy nodded. "Right," she said, as though attempting to convince herself of the need for her efforts. "I'll get right on it."

"Good," Sisko said. "I have to get back to the bridge."

"Get down to sickbay first," Kasidy said, holding a hand out to indicate his injured wrist.

"I will," Sisko said. He leaned in and pressed his lips to his wife's. "I love you, Kasidy."

"I love you, Ben."

"We'll get her back," he said, and then he headed for the door. On the way to sickbay, he vowed again to himself that he would not stop until he brought all of the missing children back to *Robinson*. *Rebecca was taken from us once before,* Sisko told himself, *and we rescued her and brought her back home.* He swore they would do so again.

But he couldn't prevent himself from remembering how horrible it had been the first time their daughter had been abducted. Nor could he forget how, even after she had been recovered, the incident had almost destroyed their family. Most of all, he couldn't stop thinking about how close they had come to losing Rebecca.

Bajor, 2380

Kasidy stopped in midstride after starting down the center aisle. On the display table to her right stood a large sculpture, perhaps a meter long and half as tall. It depicted a nude male figure diving into a river, the body captured in bronze, the water in some green-tinged crystalline material. Only the fingertips of the man touched the crest of one wave, the point of connection so minimal that Kasidy wondered if the artist had integrated a small antigrav into the work.

"Is this piece by Flanner Posh?" she asked, calling over to the owner of the gallery, who sat at a desk along a side wall of the shop. Rozahn Kather—whom everybody called Kit—looked up from the ledger she'd been perusing.

"That it is, dearie," she said, her voice loud and friendly. She rose and made her way over to the sculpture and peered at it from the other side of the table. Since Kasidy had first come into Kit's establishment almost four years prior, time had added a few more kilograms onto the older woman's stout frame, and had etched deeper and longer lines into her face. "It's a real departure for him."

"I know," Kasidy said. "I wasn't sure initially because of the subject matter, but that coarse metalwork and its kinetic feel . . . it just had to be Flanner."

"It surprised me when he brought it in last month," Kit said. "I might not have believed it if he hadn't told me."

Kasidy studied the piece. The style screamed Flanner Posh, but the theme in no way resembled any other sculpture of his that she had ever seen—and she had seen quite a lot of his work over the years. As far as Kasidy knew, he had previously concentrated exclusively on Bajoran individuals during the Occupation—enduring a hardscrabble existence under the oppression of the Cardassians: seeking moments of the slightest reprieve, praying to the Prophets for liberation, living hand-to-mouth in the ghettos, performing hard labor in the camps.

"I don't really know how to feel about it," Kasidy said. "It has all the striking elements of his artistic style, but it somehow seems . . . I don't know . . . wrong."

"He told me he woke up one day and decided the time had come for him to move on from the Occupation," Kit said. "He thought to try sport because he figured he could find nobility in the physical and mental effort of it."

"Well, I can certainly see that in this piece," Kasidy said, "but I guess because I know so much of his work, this puts me in mind of a young man on the run and trying to escape from Sharhite or Gallitep or one of the other labor camps."

"Now that you mention it—"

"Hi, Kit!" The woman's bushy eyebrows went up when she heard Rebecca speak. She craned her neck to look over the sculpture and down past the table.

"Is that the wee one with you?" Kit asked. She started to come around the table.

"Yes, we just decided to go out for a walk this afternoon," Kasidy said. She leaned down and unstrapped her daughter from the antigrav stroller, knowing that Kit would want to hold her and that Rebecca would want to be held; the toddler often behaved shyly around other children, but she seldom had trouble interacting with adults.

As Kit came down the aisle, Rebecca reached her little arms out to her. Despite her thickset form, the older woman had no difficulty bending down and scooping up Kasidy's daughter. She plopped Rebecca into the crook of her elbow. "How are you, my sweet girl?"

"Goo-ood," Rebecca said, stretching the word out into a second syllable. "Thank you."

"Oh, my," Kit said. "Ain't you polite?"

"Yes," Rebecca said.

Kasidy smiled. "She's just started doing that," she said. "Thanking people like that, I mean. It's amazing to me how she just picks up things."

"And don't you know that's gonna be a blessing and a curse," Kit said with a chuckle. "So I'd say *thank you* is a good place to start."

"I'd say you're right," Kasidy agreed.

"You know," Kit said, chucking Rebecca on the chin, "I just might have a little something sweet in my desk. Would you like that?"

"Yes, yes," Rebecca said excitedly.

"Should we ask your mother if that's okay?"

"Mommy, Kit wants to give me sweets," Rebecca said. "I think you should let her."

"Oh, you do?" Kasidy said. She glanced outside and saw that the afternoon had dimmed as sunset approached. "All right, but just one. It's getting late, and we'll be eating dinner soon."

"Yes," Rebecca told Kit in a whisper, as though uttering the word any louder could have induced a change of heart by her mother.

As Kit carried Rebecca over to her desk, Kasidy moved the stroller off to the side, out of the way, and continued browsing. She visited the gallery often enough that she had seen much of the work before, including paintings by Bajoran artists such as Acto Viri, Denik Alash, and her favorite, pointillist Galoren Sen. But Kasidy saw some new pieces, and one in particular caught her notice: projected from a base that looked like a spherical segment of a star, a holographic kinetic sculpture took the viewer on a moving tour through a wheeling solar system filled with planets, moons, asteroids, comets, and other astronomical objects, all rendered in differing malleable materials. She noted the name of the programmer-sculptor, Waska Veneeda, so that she could ask Kit about her. By the time she finished her circuit through the gallery, though, Kasidy saw that dusk impended, and she wanted to get home before darkness fell.

She headed to the desk, where Rebecca sat on Kit's lap, the end of a red *jumja* roll sticking out of the toddler's mouth. Amid all of the artwork in the shop, Kasidy's daughter worked on her own masterpiece. Crayons of various hues lay strewn across the desktop as Rebecca used a green one on a canvas to color in the tops of a dense cluster of trees.

Kasidy circled around so that she could view the drawing in its proper orientation. She saw that the trees Rebecca had sketched circled around a clearing. A large dark shape sat inside the ring of trees, with a smaller form beside it. "That's very pretty, honey," Kasidy said. "What's that?" She pointed to the dark object.

"I don't know," Rebecca said. She didn't look up, but continued to add leaves to the tops of the trees.

Kasidy chuckled. "Okay," she said. "Then what's that?" She gestured to the smaller figure.

"That's me."

"That's you?" Kasidy asked, surprised. "And just what are you doing out in the middle of the woods." Rebecca responded by offering an exaggerated shrug, a fairly new means of communicating for her.

"Quite the imagination," Kit said.

"There's no doubt about that," Kasidy said. "Honey, the sun's going down, so we need to get going. Daddy will be home soon."

"Where is the mister today?" Kit asked. "He didn't come into town with you?"

"No, he's out at B'hala today, helping on the dig." Kasidy tried to keep any note of disapprobation out of her tone, though she didn't know how successful she was. Ben had started working at the archaeological excavation about six months earlier—not long after the tragic deaths of their friends Prylar Eivos Calan and his wife, Audj. Kasidy hadn't been in favor of her husband returning to B'hala. The city had been lost for twenty millennia, until Ben had rediscovered it, back when he'd been commanding Deep Space 9. His search for the ancient site led to him suffering a serious plasma shock, which resulted in an unstable neurological condition. Ben subsequently claimed to have visions—pagh'tem'far, according to the Bajoran religion—but the injury to his brain threatened his life. Despite that, he had wanted to forgo curative surgery in favor of continuing to experience what he considered to be mystical, prescient dreams. Ben had eventually collapsed, suffering a seizure and falling into unconsciousness. Kasidy had nearly lost him, and would have, had Jake not overridden his father's medical directive.

When Ben had returned to her from his time with the aliens inside the Bajoran wormhole, just in time for the birth of their daughter, Kasidy had been elated. He didn't return to Starfleet, but instead settled into the house he had planned to build before he'd vanished after the end of the Dominion War, and that she had completed. They finally became the family Kasidy had dreamed of during Sisko's absence.

Those first couple of years together on Bajor, in the house they shared in Kendra Province, had been close to idyllic. While Kasidy continued to oversee the operation of her freighter, *Xhosa*, and intermittently to command the ship during some of its short-range cargo runs, Ben faced few demands on his time. Various Bajoran spiritual leaders, including Kai Pralon once she'd been elected, initially encouraged him to speak publicly about his experiences in the Celestial Temple, but he almost always declined. Later, they sought his participation in various religious events, but he seldom chose to do so. Far more often than not, he simply stayed at home to help raise their newborn daughter. They did socialize, frequently welcoming family and friends to their house. Jake met Azeni Korena, and the two married and lived on Bajor; they visited a lot. Friends and colleagues also made their way to the house: Wayne Sheppard, Brathaw, Luis García Márquez, and others from *Xhosa*, Kira Nerys, Nog, Ezri Dax, Elias Vaughn, and others from Deep Space 9. Kasidy and Ben also grew close to people they met on Bajor, most especially Calan and Audj.

Kasidy had to admit that life had not been perfect. Ben occasionally seemed distracted and troubled, though he refused to admit it, let alone talk about whatever weighed on him. She sometimes found him staring out the picture windows in the front room, or sitting out on the porch, in the dead of night. He always claimed simple insomnia, but Kasidy knew him better than that. She could tell that something bothered him, but she knew that he would discuss it with her if and when he saw fit. She contented herself in the understanding that whatever gnawed at him had nothing to do with their life together; Ben could not have been a more loving or devoted husband and father.

But then Calan and Audj had died in a fire. Kasidy and Ben both felt the loss deeply, and they helped each other through it. Almost seven months after the accident, sadness remained, but time had eased the pain brought on by the tragedy.

Except that, since the fire, Ben's sleeplessness had grown more frequent and his melancholy deeper. Kasidy at first attributed it to the deaths of their friends, but Ben's sorrow somehow seemed broader than that, perhaps aggravated by a sense of discontent. He decided, even over her objections, to contribute his time and efforts to the work going on at B'hala. He claimed that he did it to honor the memory of Eivos Calan, who had toiled relentlessly at the ancient city, but Kasidy felt that more drove her husband. Lately, she began to wonder if Ben had developed doubts about their marriage.

Kasidy said none of that to Rozahn Kather, but her voice must have conveyed some of her concerns, because Kit raised an eyebrow. The gallery owner offered no other response, though, but instead turned her attention back to Rebecca. "All right, then, little miss," she said, "I guess it's time you and your mama were on your way."

Rebecca plunked the green crayon down on the desk and looked up at Kit. "Okay." The older woman lifted Rebecca into her arms again and stood up.

"You can take her canvas home so she can finish it," Kit said, "or you can leave it here for next time."

"What do you think, Rebecca?" Kasidy asked.

"Next time," Rebecca said without hesitation.

"Well, I guess that's that," Kit said. She followed Kasidy back over to the antigrav stroller and set Rebecca down into the seat. "I'll see you next time, my sweet girl."

Unexpectedly, Rebecca raised her hands up toward Kit, who bent back down. Rebecca wrapped her arms around the woman's neck. "I miss you," the little girl said.

Kit laughed, a round, hearty sound. She stood back up and said, "You need to leave before you can start missing me. But when you do, I'll miss you too."

"Thanks for the jumja roll and the picture," Kasidy said. She headed the stroller for the door. "I'm sure we'll see you again soon."

"Take care, dearie," Kit said with a wave. "You too, my sweet girl."

"Bye!" Rebecca said, fluttering her hand about in a gesture that looked less like a wave and more like somebody flopping around the arm of a ragdoll.

Back out on Adarak's cobblestoned main thoroughfare— which had once been called Central Avenue, but, after Ben's return from the wormhole, had been renamed Avenue of the Emissary—Kasidy headed west, along a line of leafy trees that ran down the median. In the distance, the striated fall clouds shined pink and orange in the dying light of B'hava'el. As she pushed Rebecca along in her stroller, the traditional oil lamps hanging from the poles on both sides of the avenue came on, their yellow flames dancing in the twilight.

The number of pedestrians had increased since Kasidy and her daughter had arrived in town earlier that afternoon. Many of them, she saw, headed for one or another of the restaurants nestled in among Adarak's many shops. Morova's Kitchen, which specialized in modern interpretations of traditional Bajoran fare, appeared particularly busy. Kasidy also saw few empty tables inside The Federation; the much newer eatery featured menu items culled from a score of worlds across the UFP, including Earth. She and Ben had yet to try it, but they'd talked about doing so sometime soon.

By the time Kasidy and Rebecca reached Nerak Lane, dusk had deepened to the threshold of night. The temperature had dropped a degree or two as well, but not so much that she felt the need to put a jacket on Rebecca or herself. She knew that winter was fast approaching, and so she felt grateful for the fall mildness.

"Here we are," she told Rebecca when they reached the public transporter. Kasidy pushed the stroller through the wide, open doorway to the passenger terminal. Several people exiting the facility nodded and smiled to her as they passed—none, thankfully, showing any signs of wanting to approach her. It had been different when she had first relocated to Bajor, and again when Ben had come home from the wormhole. In those days, people had often recognized her as the wife of the Emissary and felt compelled to pass along their best wishes to her, or take a holophoto with her, or ask her advice on personal matters. Fortunately, the locals had grown respectful, and even protective, of Kasidy and Ben's privacy.

"Pleasant day," she said as the people passed her. The interior of the circular terminal had been designed in blacks and grays on the horizontal surfaces, and garnet on the walls. Inside, Kasidy saw all four transporter platforms empty. Two of the round stages stood side by side to her left, and two to her right. Between them, at the far end of the depot, Kasidy saw a young man sitting behind a freestanding control console. He had been on duty earlier, when she and Rebecca had beamed in from home. Kasidy had first met him several months before, when the Bajoran Militia had originally assigned him to Adarak. "Hi, Pol."

"Hello, Ms. Yates," he said, looking up. Kasidy had invited him to call her by her given name, but he had never done so. She guessed that his youth—Nendi Pol couldn't have been much more than twenty—prevented him from being so familiar with a mere acquaintance more than twice his age. The towheaded transporter operator had soft features and a slight build that actually made him look even younger. "I hope you and Rebecca had a pleasant afternoon in town."

"Hi, Pol!" Rebecca said.

"Hello, Rebecca."

"We did have a nice time today, thank you," Kasidy said. "I hope things haven't been too hectic for you here."

"Oh, you know, we just had a bit of a rush," Pol said. "It'll get even busier as we get deeper into the dinner hour, but that's okay; the shift goes faster the more that people come through."

"Then I hope everybody in Kendra Province south of the Yolja River is hungry and doesn't feel like eating a replicated meal tonight," Kasidy said, for which Pol rewarded her with a big smile.

"Are you headed home, Ms. Yates?"

"We are," Kasidy said, moving to one of the scanners in front of the platform currently designated for outbound traffic. She waved her wrist before the sensor, and the device read her combracelet, which stored both her identification and her home transporter coordinates. The scanner chirped its affirmative response when it registered her data. She inclined the stroller so that the antigravs would adjust to the steps, then pushed Rebecca up onto the platform.

"You're all set," Pol said.

Kasidy set Rebecca's stroller in place, then stepped onto the adjacent pad. "Thank you, Pol. Have a pleasant evening."

"Thank you. Pleasant evening to you too." The young man worked his console. The squeal of the transporter sounded, and then the white specks that accompanied dematerialization clouded Kasidy's vision. The terminal faded from sight, replaced by the familiar view outside the front of the house: the Kendra Mountains off in the distance, with the dark form of the Yolja River snaking before them. She turned toward the stroller to take her daughter inside.

Rebecca wasn't there. Neither was the stroller.

Panic gripped Kasidy, but she realized that Pol must have made a mistake in beaming her home. *Or maybe the transporter malfunctioned,* she thought, but then she pushed that idea away; even in the late twenty-fourth century, transporter accidents still accounted for a number of injuries—and worse—every year.

She tapped her combracelet and raised it to her lips. "Kasidy Yates to Adarak Transporter Terminal," she said. She dreaded any delay in receiving a response, or in hearing any note of concern, but the operator replied right away in a normal voice.

"Pol here," he said. *"Did you forget something, Ms. Yates?"*

"Just my daughter," Kasidy said, thinking that she had somehow erred in her placement of the stroller on the platform, and that Rebecca still sat there in front of Pol.

A moment passed before the operator responded, and Kasidy's fears rose up again. *"What?"* Pol said, sounding confused. *"She's not with you?"*

"No," Kasidy said as she broke into a run.

Sisko had just pulled a saucepan from one of the kitchen cabinets when he heard the front door open. Footsteps followed. He opened his mouth to welcome his wife home, but before he could say anything, Kasidy called out to him.

"Ben! Are you here? Ben!" He heard an inflection he didn't know if he'd ever perceived in his wife's voice: terror.

Sisko sped out of the kitchen into the dining room and peered to his left, toward the front door. Kasidy stood between the sitting area around the fireplace on one side and the living room proper on the other. With her body tensed and her eyes wide, she looked prepared to spring into physical action. "Kas, what is it?" he asked her. "What's wrong?"

"I just transported home from Adarak with Rebecca," she said, "but when I arrived here, she wasn't with me."

Sisko reacted immediately. His gut tightened into a knot because of the depth of love he felt for his daughter, but owing to his training as a Starfleet officer and his years in command of Deep Space 9, he still moved. He dropped the saucepan—it clattered on the hardwood floor—and rushed to Kasidy. He took her hands in his and looked into her eyes. "Did you contact the transporter operator?" he asked. "Maybe Rebecca just didn't get beamed out with you."

"I did," Kasidy said. "Rebecca's not there."

Holding on to one of his wife's hands, Sisko raced outside with her. He realized that he didn't have a communications device with him, and so he told Kasidy, "Have them beam us back to Adarak."

She activated her combracelet, which twittered in response. "Kasidy Yates to Adarak Transporter Terminal."

"This is Nendi Pol, Ms. Yates," the Militia officer replied with an edge of concern. *"Did you find—"*

"No," Kasidy interrupted. "I want you to beam my husband and me to Adarak right away."

"Yes, ma'am."

Sisko squeezed his wife's hand just as the transporter effect took hold of them. They materialized on one of the platforms in the Adarak passenger terminal. He saw nobody inside the facility except Nendi, who jumped up from his chair and came out from behind his control console.

"Is Rebecca here?" Sisko asked, though he already knew the answer. He whirled around in the middle of the terminal, searching for his daughter. All four transporter platforms stood empty.

"No," Nendi said. "The two of you—" He pointed at Kasidy. "—beamed out together."

Sisko heard voices, and he turned toward the terminal entrance to see two men walking in from outside. He didn't have to think about what to do. He knew that he had to secure the—

The accident scene. The phrase skittered through his mind like unwanted vermin across a basement floor.

Sisko threw his arms wide and strode toward the two men. "I'm afraid the terminal is temporarily closed," he told them. "It shouldn't be long." One of the men started to protest, but the other appeared to recognize Sisko and grabbed his companion's arm.

"It's okay, Danol," the second man said. "We'll wait." He redirected Danol and the two stepped back outside.

Sisko quickly paced back toward the control console and its operator. Kasidy went with him. "Close the entrance," he told Nendi, hiking a thumb back over his shoulders in the direction of the front of the terminal.

The young man froze, awash in uncertainty. "I'm . . . I'm not in Starfleet," he said, obviously trying to explain why he couldn't simply follow Sisko's orders.

"Neither am I," Sisko said. "But I *am* the Emissary." *And the father of a little girl who went missing on your watch,* he thought. He would also say it aloud if he needed to, but he didn't want to spook the young man into inaction.

Nendi almost thought about it for a second too long, but then he returned to his console and worked the controls. The front doors glided closed, coming together with a latching sound. "I beamed Ms. Yates and Rebecca together," he said. "To the same coordinates." He regarded Kasidy. "When you contacted me afterward, I checked the real-time log and confirmed the transport." He motioned toward his panel.

Sisko went around the console. Early in his Starfleet career, he had logged many hours crewing the *Livingston*'s transporters, and during his time as an engineer aboard *Okinawa*, he'd been charged with maintaining those systems. He reviewed the log to which Nendi referred. Just as the young man had said, the records verified the successful transport of both Kasidy and Rebecca.

Sisko reached up and tapped at the control surfaces. They buzzed in response, denying him access to the information he sought. He tried again, without success.

"Can I help, Emissary?" Nendi asked. "What are you looking for?"

"I want to see the point-to-point settings," Sisko said. "Maybe Rebecca's destination got established incorrectly." He actually hoped that hadn't been the case. Theoretically, if the end-point coordinates had somehow been set incorrectly or had been changed in error, Rebecca could have materialized a kilometer underground, inside solid rock, or a kilometer in the air, with nothing to stop her from plummeting to her death. Engineers designed transporter systems to prevent that from occurring, but Rebecca hadn't beamed to her destination, so anything could have happened.

"Here, sir," Nendi said, pointing to a display on the other side of the console. "I checked that too." Sisko crossed behind him and studied the readout. It listed both the origin and destination coordinates for Kasidy and for Rebecca. The pairs of numbers matched precisely.

"Ben?" Kasidy asked. "What's going on? Where's Rebecca?" The questions came like pleas, revealing Kasidy's fears. She asked where their daughter was in order to cling to the hope, ever more desperate, that Rebecca was actually anywhere instead of having been transported to her death, either by beaming to the wrong place or by never rematerializing at all, the pattern of her atoms lost to dissolution.

Sisko brought the side of his fist down on the panel. "This doesn't make sense," he said, trying to puzzle out what had happened. "The coordinates are right." He gazed across the console at his wife, who seemed on the verge of breaking down. "You beamed out together. Why didn't the two of you both . . ."

Sisko's voice trailed off as a thought occurred to him. "Ben, what is it?" Kasidy asked, but he barely heard her. He touched the display currently showing the transporter coordinates and brought up a control menu. He began navigating through a series of selections and submenus, but he couldn't find the right one.

"Pol," Sisko said, "I need the carrier-wave transmission logs."

"The transmission . . . ?" Nendi echoed. "But we have the origin and destination verified."

"Get them!" Sisko ordered, ignoring the fact that he did not actually command the young man.

Nendi quickly raised his hands to the display in front of Sisko, triple-tapped to call up the topmost menu, then traversed down into the data. Twice, he chose incorrect paths and had to backtrack. Finally, he reached a list of frequencies, the digits marching to well right of the decimal place.

"That's it," Sisko said. Nendi withdrew his hands, and Sisko accessed a pop-up menu to sort the data in descending order by time. "Did you transport anybody in or out after Kasidy and Rebecca?"

"No," Nendi said.

"That means that these are the entries for their transporter signals," Sisko said, pointing to the top two lines. He touched the first and it expanded to a graphical representation of the symmetrical carrier wave. It looked normal.

"What is it you're looking for?" Nendi asked, but Sisko paid no attention. Instead, he touched the second entry.

When the graph of that carrier signal appeared, he immediately saw a problem. "What . . . what is that?" Nendi pointed to the place where the wave deviated from one frequency to another.

"It's Rebecca's carrier signal," Sisko said. He looked up at his wife. "It was intercepted."

"Intentionally?" Kasidy asked.

"I don't know," Sisko admitted. "It could have been a glitch in the system. Or maybe the effect of a solar flare or some other natural condition."

"But what does that mean?" Kasidy asked.

"It means that Rebecca materialized somewhere else," Sisko said.

"Somewhere else *where*?" Kasidy said, her voice rising. "Inside a tree? In the middle of a lake? Out in space?" She sounded frantic.

"No, no," Sisko reassured her. "The system has safeguards to prevent that." He didn't know if he could be certain those technical protections had actually worked, but he needed to keep his wife calm. "Can you track this signal?" he asked Nendi.

"Yes, yes," the young man said. He quickly worked the panel, and the display in front of him rapidly changed. Sisko watched as Nendi isolated the second part of Rebecca's carrier wave and initiated a trace. A map of the Kendra Valley appeared, on which a green dot blinked at the point marked *Adarak*. A red line emerged from that point and drew a shallow arc across the screen. The image pulled back to a view of the Bajoran globe. The red line curved south from Kendra Province, past the equator, until it ended and another flashing green dot appeared. The display zoomed into a map of Tozhat Province, near the city of Johcat. A new set of destination coordinates appeared.

"That's it," Sisko said. He mapped the new materialization point for his daughter and confirmed that she had successfully transported to a location on the ground. "Rebecca just ended up beaming to another location, but she arrived there safely." He moved out from behind the console and headed for an outbound transporter platform. "Beam me to her location," he told Nendi. "I'm going to bring her back."

Kasidy started after him. "We'll both go."

"No," Sisko said, turning to stop his wife. "The Bajoran Militia needs to know about this. Contact Colonel Jalas." Jalas Dren served as the top Militia officer in Kendra Province. "Tell him everything that's happened." He addressed Nendi. "Other than for me, keep this transporter shut down until it's been checked out." Sisko spoke as if he blamed what had occurred on a technological problem, but he did that only in an attempt to ease Kasidy's concerns. He didn't know if she fully believed that explanation, but she surely *wanted* to believe it. So did he, but he worried that something else had happened—something bad.

Sisko remembered that he had no comm device with him. He asked Kasidy for hers, then stepped up onto one of the outbound platforms. "Energize," he told Nendi. As the transporter terminal receded around Sisko, he glanced at his wife, who looked as worried as he felt. Then his vision grew dark.

When his sight cleared, he saw that twilight in Kendra had been replaced by midday in Tozhat. Further, the blacks and grays and deep reds of the transporter terminal had been exchanged for the greens and browns of an undeveloped wilderness. It pleased Sisko that he had beamed onto solid ground, which meant that his daughter had as well, but any hope he had of finding her there quickly faded. He looked all around him, but did not see her.

"Rebecca!" Sisko called out. "Rebecca!" He waited, straining to hear any sound that could have been made by his daughter. He heard nothing like that. He wished he had a tricorder, but he knew that the Bajoran Militia would be out there soon enough with the proper equipment to scour the area.

In the direction Sisko faced, a veldt stretched far and wide into the distance. The grassy flatland featured only a few scattered trees and bushes between his location and the mountains that rose up along the horizon. He saw movement and faraway shapes out on the plain, but too distant for Rebecca to have walked there from the transport point in so short a time.

Sisko cupped his hands to his mouth and screamed out his daughter's name, once, twice, a third time. Eventually, he pivoted to look in the opposite direction. Twenty or thirty meters away, a dense wood began. He could see little beyond the first few lines of trees. Again, he called out Rebecca's name but received no response.

Sisko raised Kasidy's combracelet to his mouth, ready to transport back to Adarak to ensure the Militia's aid in the search, when a glint of sunlight caught his eye. He peered back at the woods, but whatever had shined had done so only briefly. Sisko moved around, trying to see it again, and at last he did: at the edge of the forest, a flash of light like a reflection on a mirror or a metal surface.

He lost sight of it as he ran through low-lying brush toward it, but he didn't stop until he reached the tree line. He stepped past the first trunk and hunted around it, to no avail. He moved on to the next tree along the edge of the wood, and that's when he spotted it: an antigrav stroller. It sat on the ground, tipped over and not functioning.

"Rebecca," he said—not so that she could hear him if she was nearby, but involuntarily, under his breath. Sisko's heart beat so hard it felt as though it might burst out of his chest. His pulse thundered in his ears. For a moment, he thought he might pass out, but he fought his way past the sensation.

Sisko hurried over to the stroller. He picked it up and examined it, then thumbed on the power button at the top of the *U*-shaped handle. It hummed into operation. The stroller hadn't been broken; it had been deactivated.

Sisko closed his eyes and did something he hadn't in a long time: he offered a personal prayer to the Prophets. Rebecca was too little to have reached the switch on the stroller. Somebody else must have done so.

Which meant that Rebecca had been abducted.

Gamma Quadrant, 2386

S isko sat in the command chair on the bridge, resisting the impulse to rise and pace the deck. The ship's chief medical officer had repaired his broken wrist—a distal radius fracture, Doctor Kosciuszko had called it—knitting his bone back together with one of his surgical instruments. The CMO had also prescribed an anti-inflammatory, and in the almost twenty-four hours since Sisko had been injured, the swelling had gone down.

The captain's anxiety about his missing daughter and the rest of the abducted *Robinson* children, and his eagerness to find them and bring them back home, translated into extreme nervous energy. He wished he had a baseball with him so that he could hold it, focus his mind on the tactile sensation of it: the weight and shape of it that allowed it to fit confidently in his hand; the firmness that had just enough give in it to make batting a fair proposition; the elevated roughness of the 108 double stitches; the feel of setting his index and middle fingers across the seams to hurl a rising fastball, or hooking them in the horseshoe formation to drop a curve. If Sisko had a ball with him, he would toss it in the air above him and catch it when it came down, indulging in the satisfaction of both ritual and physical accomplishment.

No, Sisko thought. *What I would do is wind up and heave*

the ball as far as I could. He knew well the energy he would expend making such a throw, how it would center him and calm his nerves, but he also appreciated the metaphorical aspect of such an act. In the midst of calamity, he would relish the ability to capture that distress, compress it, and send it hurtling away.

In the nearly full day that had passed since the ship had struck the pocket of energy, scans had revealed that *Robinson* presently perched on a small island of the normal space-time continuum, with the hull extending out into the inert region around it. The ship remained essentially stranded. Attempts to utilize the impulse engines at various speeds and in various configurations to move *Robinson* had all met with no success. Likewise, even employing the thrusters to push the ship, however slowly, out beyond that region of dead space had also failed. Relkdahz and his engineering staff believed that the warp drive, still undergoing repairs along with the hull, would provide the crew with their best chance to escape the area of destroyed space-time.

Meanwhile, Uteln and his tactical team had scanned nearby space and beyond for any sign of the alien attackers. *Robinson*'s sensors successfully reached across the inert zone surrounding the ship, but they showed vessels neither in the area nor at longer range. Uteln also reported no trace of any ion trails by which the crew might eventually track the alien craft, but theorized that such telltale signs of faster-than-light travel could be detectable once *Robinson* cleared the dead space.

Sisko rubbed at his eyes, though that did not help the ache behind them. He had barely slept, and when he had, the experience had hardly been restful. The same had been true for Kasidy. *And probably for all the other parents on board,* he thought. Sisko had always championed the idea of including crew family members on starships, particularly on those vessels conducting long-term missions of exploration. It always made sense to him to mitigate the hardships that service in Starfleet could impose on officers by allowing them to bring along those closest to them. He still believed that, despite what had happened—and despite that, once before, he had experienced the worst consequences of that policy.

Prior to Kasidy and Rebecca taking up residence on *Robinson*, Sisko had discussed with his wife the positives and negatives, the benefits and dangers of such a choice. It had been a long road for them to travel from the idea to the reality, but they had come to the decision together. It had been a settled issue between them for some time—even when, after the assassination of the Federation president more than half a year earlier, *Robinson* had been ordered to the Helaspont Sector for a possible confrontation with Tzenkethi forces.

But this . . . this is different, Sisko thought. *For almost all of the children—and* only *children—to be taken from the ship without warning or explanation . . .* He could not find words to describe the enormity of the situation.

How would we go on? Sisko asked himself, thinking of his crew and their mission. He did not want to admit the possibility that they might not be able to recover or even find the children, but as the commanding officer of *Robinson*, he had no choice but to consider such an eventuality. With so many lost, and with so many grieving families left behind, Sisko would have little recourse but to turn the ship around and head back to the Federation. *And what would that mean for Kasidy and me? Could our relationship survive so great a strain?* Once, he would have thought so, and all that they had already withstood during their relationship of nearly a decade and a half demonstrated the strength of their bond. *But this—*

At the forward portion of the bridge, the turbolift doors beside his ready room opened with a whisper. Lieutenant Commander Althouse stepped out and crossed to her position, in the chair to Sisko's left. "Captain," she said. Dark circles beneath her eyes and drooping lids suggested not that she had slept badly, but that she had not gone to bed at all. "The counseling staff are overburdened right now." The statement surprised Sisko, not for its content, but because Althouse typically came at a subject obliquely; she did not employ directness very often, so doing so at that moment doubtless spoke to the severity of the situation, as well as to her evident fatigue. "With so many parents of missing children distraught and seeking some form of counseling, the three of us cannot adequately address their needs." Lieutenant Haroun al-Jarjani, from Alpha Centauri, and Ensign Aldora Vint, from Betazed, rounded out Althouse's staff.

"I understand," Sisko said, "but I would think that the parents would be consumed by their duties at this critical time, intent on doing what they could to find the children and bring them home."

"They are," Althouse said, "but not all of the parents are in Starfleet. And while it's all hands on deck, some people are better equipped to deal with it than others. There are also a handful of young people aboard who have lost siblings."

"Do you have a recommendation?"

"I do," Althouse said. "I want to suggest employing a group dynamic."

"I'm not sure what that means."

"I want to bring the parents of the abducted children together in a support setting," Althouse explained. "I want to be able to address their concerns, answer their questions, and help them figure out for themselves the best way forward."

"That sounds reasonable," Sisko said. "Do you think it needs to be mandatory?"

"No," Althouse said. "Not yet. But allowing people access to a group setting is a better solution than having to turn them away because we don't have the psychological support resources."

"Agreed."

"But there's something more that I want to do," Althouse said. "I don't have a child on this ship, and neither do Lieutenant al-Jarjani or Ensign Vint. I'm thinking about asking one of the parents to help with the groups—preferably one with experience in diplomacy."

Sisko took a beat before stating the obvious: "You're talking about Kasidy."

"With your permission and her willingness, of course," Althouse said.

Sisko trusted the professional acumen of the ship's lead counselor, but he took a moment to envisage Kasidy's reaction to such a request, and to estimate her ability to do the job. He thought his wife would accept the appeal for her assistance because it would provide a more concrete means of dealing with the situation than his nebulous orders to the diplomats and first-contact specialists about preparing to deal with a completely unknown alien race. But the captain thought that she would also genuinely want to render whatever aid she could to other parents—particularly the civilians—simply because of her natural empathy. He thought Kasidy capable of handling the responsibility, and her insights into having a child kidnapped would make her all the more valuable.

From a personal standpoint, Sisko reckoned that occupying herself in that way might prevent Kasidy from fixating on blaming him for another major threat to Rebecca in her short life. It seemed inconceivable that, just six months

shy of her tenth birthday, she had been abducted for a second time. Sisko could not argue that his decisions—first
to accept his role as Bajor's Emissary of the Prophets, and
then to take command of *Robinson*—had not directly led
to both incidents.

"All right," Sisko told Althouse. "I'll have Kasidy come
up to my ready room and we can discuss—"

"Engineering to bridge."

Sisko glanced at the control panel set in the arm of his
chair and checked the chronometer. He had charged his
chief engineer with providing a status report every four
hours, but his current call to the bridge had come forty-five
minutes early. Sisko hoped that boded well for the repairs
to the ship. He pointed out the time to his first officer, who
sat to his right.

Before Sisko responded to Relkdahz, he addressed Althouse. "Go talk to Kasidy," he said. "Tell her I approved
your request." The counselor nodded and headed at once
for the turbolift. Responding to the contact from engineering, Sisko said, "Bridge here. Go ahead, Commander."

"Captain, we've restored the warp drive," Relkdahz said.

"You're ahead of schedule," Rogeiro noted.

*"Because we replaced only twelve of the twenty failed power
relays,"* Relkdahz said. *"To compensate, we replicated more
advanced relays that have higher capacities. We reconfigured
the transfer junctions, both the damaged ones we repaired and
those left intact."*

"Is there a trade-off, Commander?" Sisko asked. "Are we
sacrificing safety?"

"Not safety, sir, no, at least not in the short term," Relkdahz said. *"Over time, the new relays could cause the transfer junctions to fail, but simulations tell us that won't happen
for at least a month's flight at normal cruising speed, or half
that at emergency velocities. By that time, we'll have repli-*

cated more relays, and we can install them in less than a day. I thought that, in the current situation, you'd want the flexibility of traveling at warp sooner rather than later."

"That's good work, Commander," Sisko said. "How long before we have a full engine restart?"

"We have it now," Relkdahz said. *"Warp speed is available on your order."*

"Well done," the captain said. "Sisko out." Unable to contain his fervor to finally begin the search to find Rebecca and the other missing children, he stood up and paced to the center of the bridge, just behind Plante to his left and Stannis to his right. Though Sivadeki would recover, she remained in sickbay after undergoing surgery to repair a torn aural membrane caused by the sonic attack on the *Robinson* crew. "Lieutenant, set course along the path of the alien vessels when they first appeared."

"Aye, Captain," Stannis said.

"Commander Uteln," Sisko said, "you've calibrated the sensors to detect any pockets of energy like the one the ship struck yesterday."

"Aye, sir," the tactical officer said. "Alerts will automatically be routed to the conn."

"Good," Sisko said. "Lieutenant Stannis, ahead warp one."

"Warp one," Stannis said.

Sisko tensed as he waited for the lieutenant to carry out his order, irrationally concerned that the repaired drive would not function. But then the captain felt the vibrations of the warp engines as Stannis worked his console. The bass thrum of the faster-than-light drive provided a second tangible confirmation of its operation. But as Sisko watched the main viewscreen, he saw no indication of movement.

"Stannis?" Rogeiro asked as he joined the captain at the center of the bridge.

The pilot consulted his console. "The warp engines are operational," he said. "But we're not moving."

"Bridge to engineering," Sisko said.

"Engineering, Relkdahz here."

"What's happening with the warp drive?" Sisko asked. "It's engaged, but we're not going anywhere. Is this because of fewer relays and replaced junctions?"

"Negative, Captain," Relkdahz said confidently. *"All instrumentation shows the drive is functioning to specifications and well within all tolerances."* There was a pause, during which Sisko imagined the chief engineer seeking an explanation for *Robinson's* remaining in place. *"We should be traveling at the speed of light."*

"Sir, I've found the problem," Stannis suddenly said. He wiped his fingers across a display on his panel with an expanding gesture, and a top-down depiction of *Robinson* appeared. "Here is what is supposed to happen when we accelerate to warp factor one." He pressed a control on the display and several lines roughly tracing the contours of the ship expanded out into space around it. Sisko recognized the traditional representation of a warp field. "But here is what's actually happening." The lieutenant toggled a switch, resetting the diagram to its initial state. As Sisko watched, he saw a warp bubble begin to expand around *Robinson*, but then it collapsed back into the ship. It occurred several times before Rogeiro spoke up.

"But why is that happening?" the first officer asked.

"Because space-time has been destroyed all around the ship," Stannis said, "down to and including its foundation. There is no subspace here to support the expansion of the warp field."

"How do we fix it?" Rogeiro asked, but Sisko already knew the answer. Stannis confirmed the captain's worst fears.

"We can't," the lieutenant said. "None of our drive systems will work here."

The exec looked over at Sisko with a grave expression on his face. The captain could tell that Rogeiro wanted his commanding officer to put the lie to the pilot's conclusions, or to offer up another option the crew could pursue to get the ship moving again. But Sisko couldn't. He could only voice the truth.

"We're stranded."

Bajor, 2380

Kasidy sat at the table in the dining room, staring off into the middle distance, her body numb to sensation. Her mind did not wander, though; she listened to every word spoken in her presence, whether directed to her or not. She heard a great deal. That morning, a troop of Bajoran Militia officers had descended on the home where she and Ben had raised Rebecca. But for all the people moving around inside and out, for all the equipment that had been delivered and set up, for all the voices and all the noise, the house felt empty.

The previous evening, after Ben had followed the rogue transporter signal that had stolen their daughter away, Kasidy had done as her husband had asked: she'd contacted Colonel Jalas Dren—or she'd contacted his office. With the colonel unavailable, she spoke to one of his aides, who listened to her description of events and promised to dispatch the appropriate personnel to Adarak. Although Kasidy heard her urgency reflected in the man's tone and in his pledge of immediate action, it didn't satisfy her. For the first time, she explicitly traded on Ben's distinction among the Bajorans, demanding the direct involvement of the colonel as soon as possible.

Five minutes later, Jalas and three of his officers had materialized in the Adarak terminal, beaming there by way of the Militia transporter in the provincial capital of Renassa. The colonel set his subordinates to work while he personally ministered to Kasidy. At first glance, his appearance resembled that of a kindly grandfather, tall but slightly stooped, with thinning gray hair above a well-lined face, and a waistline that had gone a bit soft. But when he spoke, he did so with confidence and authority, a man accustomed to having his orders followed to the letter.

Jalas had started his conversation with Kasidy by vowing that, whether Rebecca had gone missing because of a transporter mishap or because she'd been kidnapped, the Bajoran Militia would find her and bring her home. His assurance, though blatant mollification, still brought a degree of comfort. The colonel could not possibly have made such a guarantee based on any real information—he knew no more at that moment than Kasidy did—but she would hold him to his word until she once more held her baby in her arms.

The three officers who'd accompanied Jalas had swiftly sprung into action. A woman with the rank of sergeant began studying the transporter logs, while a second woman, wearing a lieutenant's insignia, followed after Ben, again utilizing the Militia's transporter in Renassa. The third, a man the colonel introduced as Sergeant Elvem Rota, interviewed Kasidy about what had taken place. Together, the trio in short order confirmed the sequence of events, including the intentional commandeering of Rebecca's carrier signal and her abduction from the location out in the wilderness to which she had been beamed. Kasidy and Ben subsequently spent several hours in the Militia's provincial headquarters in Renassa, speaking with members of their investigative unit. Jalas assigned a man he called his best agent, Major Orisin Dever, to lead the case.

Afterward, Kasidy and Ben had returned to their house

in Kendra Valley, accompanied by an armed detail that would keep watch over them until the situation had been resolved. They arrived back at their home to find a forensic team wrapping up its work. While Kasidy and Ben had been answering questions and telling Orisin everything they could, the major, with the couple's permission, had sent investigators to search their house for anything that might be relevant to Rebecca's abduction.

They found nothing.

Kasidy and Ben had never gone to bed that night, knowing that circumstances would not allow them even a moment's slumber. They sat together on the sofa in front of the unlit fireplace, where the mantel featured a bevy of family photographs. They held each other in the darkness, the only light that of the two moons peeking in the windows on the other side of the front room, behind them. They spoke quietly about their daughter, focused primarily on all of the people presently searching for her. Before long, they lapsed into silence, and soon after that, exhaustion took hold of them and they both mercifully drifted off.

They had awoken shortly after dawn, when Major Orisin had appeared at their front door. He did not come alone or empty-handed. He brought with him quite a bit of equipment, along with the personnel to operate it. Although like most buildings on Bajor—and throughout the Federation—Kasidy and Ben's home had been built with materials that impeded beaming into and out of the structure, the major extended the transport-free zone well beyond the house with a sizable ring of inhibitors. A security team comprised armed guards outfitted with individual tricorders and a central sensor unit. Orisin's staff also brought with them several dedicated computer interfaces that linked directly to various law-enforcement databases and the Bajoran comnet. A portable companel connected to the archives of both the Vedek Assembly and the Chamber of Ministers, while another maintained open communications with the Militia's provincial command center, as well as to the offices of both Asarem Wadeen and Pralon Onala. Both the first minister and the kai had been informed of the situation, though Major Orisin had decided for the time being to withhold the news of Rebecca's abduction from the public.

Kasidy sat in the dining room amid all the turmoil. Across the table from her, a Militia officer worked over one of the computer interfaces. In the front room, the furniture stood pushed up against one wall, which had allowed others to set up their equipment and operate it. Voices abounded. The technological sounds of myriad panels joined the tumult, added to it, filled the house.

And still it feels hollow, Kasidy thought. She knew that it would until Rebecca was there again. Until then, everything would be different, and nothing else would matter.

"Ms. Yates?" Kasidy looked up to see Orisin standing before her. A couple of centimeters shorter than Ben, who stood beside him, the major possessed a solid but unimposing physique. His youthful features suggested a man who had moved rapidly up the ranks to his present position, but the numerous strands of silver running through his blond hair bespoke considerable experience—or perhaps hard-fought experience. Either way, his presentation and manner instilled confidence.

Sometime during their interaction the previous night, Kasidy had told Orisin to call her by her given name, but he had so far declined to do so. She reasoned that he wanted to preserve a professional relationship for her sake—as a sign of respect, and to foster her trust in his efforts. She suspected that it helped the major as well, as a means of preventing himself from becoming too personally involved.

"Yes?" Kasidy said. She had heard Orisin out in the front room ask Ben to join him just a minute or so prior.

The major glanced at Ben and gestured to the chair next to Kasidy. "Please," he said. Ben sat down, while Orisin stayed on his feet. "We know that somebody abducted your daughter, and our primary goal is to effect her return to you, unharmed and as soon as possible. That's not just for your sake, but for hers."

"Of course," Ben said. Although his voice remained level and his face a mask of stone, Kasidy could see his frustration at having to listen to such an obvious statement. She didn't know if Orisin perceived Ben's irritation, though she suspected that, in his role as an investigator, he had developed considerable skill in reading people.

"The question for us is: how do we find your daughter?" the major said. "We know how she was taken: by hijacking her carrier signal out of the Adarak terminal, altering her destination and materializing her there—but the kidnappers still utilized the Adarak transporter to do that. Why? We believe it's because they don't have the use of their own transporter, and we found evidence to support that conclusion. A forensic team traveled to the location where your daughter's stroller was left. They found, on two bare patches of ground, patterns in the soil that could have been caused by a travel pod. We checked with the Ministry of Transportation, who coordinated with the Consolidated Space Center in Musilla. Satellite guidance for surface vehicles tracked a travel pod's transponder to that location from Johcat and back again in the relevant timeframe."

"Johcat?" Ben asked as Kasidy's heart started to race. When Ben had attempted to find Rebecca by following her modified transporter signal, he'd ended up in the southern hemisphere, in the Deserak Wilderness, a massive undeveloped expanse in Tozhat Province. The city nearest to that location was Johcat. To Kasidy, the information about the travel pod sounded more than positive; it sounded like a solid lead on their daughter's whereabouts.

"I sent Sergeant Elvem and several other officers to the city in search of the travel pod," Orisin said. "I also sent an alert to transporter stations worldwide. Without identifying your daughter, I transmitted her DNA signature as part of a missing-persons protocol. If anybody tries to beam her anywhere on the plant, or to a ship in orbit, her pattern will be flagged and the transport interrupted. She and anybody with her will be beamed into separate holding cells at the nearest Militia facility." Kasidy appreciated the preemptive action. "In the meantime," Orisin said, "there's another question we need to ask."

"Why?" Kasidy blurted out, even before she knew she would speak. "You want to know why the kidnappers abducted Rebecca."

"Yes," Orisin said. "During our conversation last night, I asked each of you about your personal history—since you came to Deep Space Nine and Bajor, but even before that."

"You were looking for enemies," Ben said. The word evoked images in Kasidy's mind of the Dominion and the Typhon Pact, of massing armies and starship battles.

"Essentially, yes," Orisin said. "But more to rule out that possibility than to give it credence. In general, average people do not have enemies. There are always going to be individuals who don't get along with you, sometimes from a simple clash of personalities, sometimes for cause, but it's truly unusual for anybody to develop strong enough and violent enough emotions to seek revenge by committing a heinous crime."

"Are you saying that Rebecca's abduction has nothing to do with us?" Kasidy asked. "That it's . . . random?" She didn't know which prospect scared her more—that somebody took their daughter out of vengeance, or that they did so for no reason at all.

"No, I don't think that what happened is random, because you two are not 'average people,'" Orisin said. "As the Emissary of the Prophets, Captain Sisko holds an eminent place in Bajoran society. As his wife, Ms. Yates, so do you. But it was still important to check on your histories. Through the night, I had a team of investigators comb through your lives. Before and after you became the Emissary, Captain, you had a long career in Starfleet, and you, Ms. Yates, spent years on freighters, eventually to the point where you commanded your own ship." The major's eyebrows dipped momentarily, as though in sudden realization. "In fact, I should be addressing you as *Captain* Yates."

Kasidy waved her hand before her in a dismissive gesture. "*Ms.* is fine," she said. She thought to tell him again to call her by her given name, but chose not to bother.

"At any rate," Orisin continued, "it can't be said that people in such positions don't ever end up with adversaries, but those are typically professional—meaning political or martial in nature for you, Captain Sisko, and commercial for you, Ms. Yates. But such relationships rarely lead to an incident like this. It seems improbable to me that what's happened came as the result of a promotion Captain Sisko failed to give a deserving candidate in Starfleet, or of a victory in a military confrontation, just as it's unlikely to be because Ms. Yates won a delivery contract over a competitor. Still, I wanted to check possibilities like those. To that end, Overgeneral Manos enlisted the aid of Starfleet Command, and Minister Wintik that of the Federation Department of Commerce." Manos Treo occupied the highest position in the Bajoran Militia, Kasidy knew, and Wintik Barr led Bajor's Commerce Ministry. "We did identify several professional incidents where somebody professed their hatred for Captain Sisko, as well as a number of other instances that could have—whether reasonably or not—earned him somebody's enmity. We found fewer such occurrences for Ms. Yates, but there were still a couple. For both of you, though, we saw nothing that caused us particular alarm."

"So if you don't think this is professional," Ben said, "then you think it's personal."

"It could be," Orisin said, "but I don't think so. If somebody sought revenge on either one of you, why would they do this?" He shrugged, as though to underscore his point. "To hurt you for some real or imagined slight? All right, but then why wouldn't they do more than this?"

"More?" Kasidy asked. She could conceive of only one action worse than taking Rebecca away from her temporarily, and that would be to take her away permanently.

"If somebody sought revenge against you, why wouldn't they physically injure you, or even kill you?" the major asked. Kasidy noticed that he studiously avoided proposing that they could have harmed Rebecca. "And if motivated by a thirst for vengeance, why do so anonymously? If this act was specifically intended to hurt you, then it succeeded, but if it was meant to avenge a particular wrong that one of you perpetrated—or that somebody thought that you perpetrated—it's failed."

"Because we don't know who did this," Kasidy said. "Because we don't know why they did it."

"Precisely," Orisin said.

"Somebody could still contact us," Ben said.

"And I think somebody will," Orisin told them. "But not to inform you of the reason they wanted to hurt you. That just doesn't make a lot of sense to me. They'll contact you in an attempt to extort a ransom."

"A ransom?" Kasidy said. "That makes even less sense. We have nothing of value that anybody would want—at least, nothing that any other Federation citizen couldn't get for themselves."

"For the most part, I'd agree," Orisin said. "But there is one thing you possess that nobody else on Bajor has."

Kasidy understood what the major meant, and Ben said it. "The title of Emissary."

Orisin nodded. "Yes, you're the Emissary," he said. "And according to the Ohalavaru, your daughter is the Avatar."

"You think Ohalu worshippers did this?" Kasidy asked. She knew the place they afforded Rebecca in their faith, but she also understood that their convictions painted them more as believers in science than in the divinity of the Prophets. In many ways, Kasidy's views lined up more with the Ohalavaru than with those of the traditional Bajoran faithful.

"I don't know," Orisin said. "It's unclear whether an Ohalavaru or a mainstream believer would have more of a motive to do this. It's conceivable that a traditional adherent wanted to make a statement, or to somehow undermine the tenets of Ohalu."

"In either case, the question of why remains," Sisko said. "What is it they could possibly want?"

"I am of the strong opinion that whatever demand they make will be of a religious nature," Orisin said.

"Like . . . what?" Kasidy asked.

"Maybe . . ." Ben began, and then he stood up. "Maybe they'll want me to renounce my title as the Emissary or . . . repudiate Rebecca's status as the Avatar." He peered down at Kasidy, and though he didn't smile, she could see—

What? she wondered. *Satisfaction? Excitement?*

"I can do that," he told her, and then he repeated it to Orisin.

"We'll have to hear their demands," the major said. "It could be the reverse; they could want you to proclaim yourself kai, or insist that you demand Rebecca be worshipped by all Bajorans."

"I don't care," Sisko insisted. "If they want me to make some sort of public pronouncement—even if it's contrary to my own beliefs—I'll happily do it. It means nothing compared to getting Rebecca back." He sat back down.

It did not entirely surprise Kasidy to hear Ben make such a declaration, but she felt relieved to actually hear him say it. In her heart, she believed that, like her, he would make virtually any sacrifice to preserve the well-being of their daughter. But Kasidy also had to admit, at least to herself, that another aspect of Ben's avowal merited her approval: the potential of him formally abdicating his role in the Bajoran religion. She wanted to chastise herself for the sentiment as soon as she felt it, but she discovered that she couldn't. Although she had grown more accustomed over time to her husband's place in the beliefs of Bajorans, she had never completely accepted it—or trusted it. As the Emissary, Ben had faced death—had on one occasion even chosen to risk his life for the possibility of experiencing a sacred vision.

And the wormhole aliens took him away from me for eight months, Kasidy thought. She had been so thankful that Ben had returned in time for Rebecca's birth, but she still feared that, someday, the Prophets might remove him from her life again. *And from the life of our daughter.*

To Ben, Orisin said, "It's good to know what you're willing to do," but his demeanor seemed tempered. "What you do, and what we do, will depend on—" The major cut himself short as another officer stepped up beside him, a Bajoran padd in her hand. "You have a report, Lieutenant?"

"Yes, sir," the woman said. The day before, she had been the officer to follow Ben out into the Deserak Wilderness. She had short red hair and only three shallow ridges on the bridge of her nose. Kasidy wondered if she had a fully

Bajoran heritage, but then noticed that the lieutenant's ear tapered up almost to a point. From just casual observation, she looked as though she could have a Vulcan forebear among her Bajoran ancestors. Kasidy had never heard of such a coupling, but she didn't doubt that they took place. "Sergeant Elvem just transmitted his findings from Johcat. They found the travel pod." She held up the padd. Orisin quickly took it from her and perused its contents.

"What about Rebecca?" Kasidy asked, though she realized the foolishness of the question the moment it left her mouth. If their daughter had been recovered, the lieutenant surely would have led with that information.

"There's no sign of her yet," the lieutenant said.

"Where is the travel pod?" Ben asked. "Has it been scanned for DNA?"

"The pod was found in a municipal square in Johcat," Orisin said, still consulting the padd. "It's a public vehicle, meaning that it's available to any citizen who needs to use it. It could therefore be difficult to isolate individual, untainted DNA samples."

"There's more on that, sir," the lieutenant said, and she pointed to the bottom of the padd's screen. Orisin read from the device before continuing.

"The record of the digital IDs used to activate the pod was wiped," he said. "Scans of both the interior and exterior of the pod show that it was recently irradiated. That destroyed any biological evidence that might have been left behind." He handed the padd back to the lieutenant. "Tapren, instruct Sergeant Elvem to have his team canvass Johcat, visually and with sensors. Send whatever resources he needs. I want you to review the transporter logs into and out of the city since the abduction, and to check boarding manifests for any space vessels launched from the surface. Check with the Musilla CSC if necessary."

"Right away, sir," the lieutenant said, and she quickly headed back into the front room.

"You think that Rebecca was taken out of Johcat?" Kasidy asked. She could barely think about the fact of her daughter's kidnapping without breaking down, but the idea of Rebecca being carted around from place to place by strangers horrified her. It also made her angry.

"We have to consider the possibility that she's been moved since being brought to the city," Orisin said. "I think it may be time to make your daughter's kidnapping public."

"What?" Ben said, clearly uncomfortable with the idea. "Why would we do that? Wouldn't that just threaten the kidnappers? Push them toward acting in desperation?"

"They've abducted your child. They're already desperate," Orisin said. "Announcing their crime to the public could draw them out, force them to make their demands of you sooner rather than later. Everything we know tells us that the kidnappers want your daughter alive. If they wanted to harm her, they would have done so already. But they transported her out into the Deserak Wilderness rather than beaming her into a tree. They took her to Johcat in a travel pod instead of leaving her somewhere out in the wild." He paused to grab another chair from the table. He set it before Kasidy and Ben and sat down to face them at eye level. "By making the abduction public, we effectively deputize the four hundred thousand people of Johcat—the entire population of Bajor, really. People will take note, and if they see your daughter, they'll report it. If they observe an everyday detail that seems out of the ordinary—a neighbor who stops coming out of their home, a colleague who becomes furtive and distrustful, a flat or a building that's been empty but suddenly appears occupied—they'll report that. It will generate plenty of false leads, but we'll follow every tip until we find the one that's true. We only need one of them to point us to your daughter."

"But the kidnappers will know that," Kasidy said. "If we announce what's happened, they could get scared . . . decide to abandon their plans and . . . and . . ." Kasidy couldn't say aloud the worst possible outcome.

"I understand your concerns," Orisin said. "I can't tell you that your fears aren't justified. I think making a public statement now could help us, but it's not yet critical. We just found the travel pod. It's possible that we'll find more clues in Johcat."

Kasidy turned to Ben. The flesh beneath his eyes had a purplish tint. He looked drawn and worried and scared and angry, all at the same time. She felt the same things and knew that he would be able to see that. They didn't say anything to each other, but they didn't have to; he knew what she thought.

"For right now," Ben said, "let's wait to announce the abduction."

Orisin hesitated. Kasidy suspected that he weighed whether or not to push them on the issue. He didn't. "All right," he said. "We won't say anything publically yet, but I want the two of you to think about it more. I'd like you to consider it as an option for us at some point . . . a tool we can use. Even if you believe it's not appropriate to use that tool now, there may come a time when it becomes not just potentially helpful, but necessary."

Ben nodded. "We'll think about it."

"Good." Orisin stood up and placed the chair back at the dining room table. "If there's anything you need, please let me or Lieutenant Tapren know." The major headed back into the front room.

Ben took Kasidy's hand in his. "It'll be all right," he told her. She nodded, though she didn't know if either one of them believed that.

As they sat quietly together, Kasidy wondered why Orisin had suggested going public, especially since the major believed that the kidnappers would soon issue their demands. She wanted to hear those demands, and then to accede to them as quickly as they could—anything to bring Rebecca back to them without putting her in any further danger.

Kasidy thought about the next steps that the Militia's investigators would take. Orisin had ordered them to surreptitiously search the city, visually and with sensors, and to double-check transporter logs. They needed to find the next link in the chain that would take them from the transporter terminal in Adarak to wherever Rebecca had been taken.

With a jolt, Kasidy realized why Orisin wanted to announce the abduction to the public. Ben had followed Rebecca's transporter signal to the Deserak Wilderness, and the major and his team had tracked her from there to the city of Johcat. But in the square where the public travel pod had been flashed clean and then abandoned, the trail had gone cold.

Gamma Quadrant, 2386

Commander Anxo Rogeiro followed the captain and the rest of the senior bridge crew into the observation lounge in silence. The first officer knew that Sisko did not favor calling his officers together in so formal a manner. The captain preferred to discuss issues either on the bridge or with smaller groups in his ready room. Even though the gravity of the situation demanded a meeting of the entire senior staff, that needn't have taken place in the observation lounge. Rogeiro suspected that the dispiriting mood on the bridge—brought about by the abduction of the children and the marooning of the ship—had motivated the captain to put himself and his officers in motion, to get them on their feet and moving, to provide them with a change of scenery, if only briefly.

Sisko positioned himself at the head of the long, arc-shaped table, and Rogeiro took the chair to his right. Sivadeki, recovered from her aural surgery, sat down with Plante, Uteln, and Althouse, all of them across from the first officer, their backs to the large ports that spanned the length of the compartment. Corallavellis sh'Vrane moved to the far end of the table, while Ambrozy Kosciuszko, the ship's chief medical officer, arrived from sickbay and took the seat beside Rogeiro. The exec noted the absence of *Robinson*'s chief engineer.

"Where's Relkdahz?" he asked. He activated his com-badge with a touch, but before he said anything, the second set of doors to the conference room parted with a whisper. The chief engineer entered in a rush, appearing to glide across the deck. An Otevrel, Relkdahz possessed an upright, generally cylindrical physique that narrowed slightly at his midsection. A row of small tentacles circled his green body about a third of the way up, with a second set of larger tenta-cles a third of the way down. Most of Relkdahz's appendages functioned exclusively as muscular hydrostats—extremely dexterous structures capable of contracting and elongating, of bending, twisting, and hardening—but two of his upper stalks ended in optical receptors, while two others ended in auditory nodes. He wore a black tubular garment around the lower portion of his body and a gray, gold-collared uni-form around the upper half.

"I'm sorry I'm late," Relkdahz said as he made his way to his species-specific "chair" at the end of the inner side of the table. Otevrel could not bend their bodies in a manner that allowed them to sit. Rather, they leaned against a shallowly inclined flat, which had two pair of stubby arms, one upper and one lower, about which they could wrap their tenta-cles. Relkdahz settled his almost two-meter length into his chair. "We were exploring a means of reinforcing the warp field when we engage the main engines," he said to explain his tardiness. "We're trying to find a means of keeping the warp field up even without a foundation of subspace to support it." His words sounded tinny and a bit mechanical after being filtered through the portable translator he wore around the base of one of his upper limbs. Like all members of his species, he spoke by way of a vibrating flap atop his body. His unprocessed speech always reminded Rogeiro of somebody humming a song with an unfamiliar melody.

"The meeting's just starting," the first officer told Relkdahz. Rogeiro considered asking the chief engineer to expand on his staff's labors with respect to enabling the ship to travel again at warp speed, but he instead turned toward Sisko so that the captain could officially begin the meeting. The exec's professional dynamic with his commanding officer worked exceedingly well. In the five years they'd served together, they had developed a conversant functional relationship that helped the two of them—and consequently the crew—to perform at the highest levels of efficiency.

That hadn't always been the case. Starfleet Command transferred Rogeiro to *Robinson* not long after the Borg Invasion, at the same time that Sisko took command. Unexpectedly, the new captain came aboard with a despondence and a reticence that did not track with either his service record or his reputation. In particular, his unwillingness to communicate complicated the first officer's ability to meet the needs of his commanding officer, and therefore of the ship and crew. Rogeiro initially attempted to work around the situation, hoping that the captain would ultimately emerge from his melancholy and self-imposed isolation. When that showed no sign of happening, the first officer confronted Sisko. Months passed after that with little alteration in the captain's behavior, to the point where Rogeiro considered reporting the issue to Starfleet Command. But it turned out that the exec had planted seeds of change because, at last, Sisko softened and grew more expressive. The atmosphere aboard *Robinson* improved virtually overnight. Only later, after the two men became friends, would the first officer learn of the incredibly difficult circumstances that had brought the captain so low and driven him so far down.

Off Rogeiro's glance, Sisko looked to Relkdahz. "What about those efforts with the warp drive, Commander?" the captain asked. "Are we any closer to being able to move the ship?"

"We theorized about deploying a tractor beam to strengthen and stabilize the warp field, but we haven't been able to propagate the beam in the inert region around the *Robinson*," Relkdahz said. "We're now trying to adjust the tractor's power and frequency. Lieutenant Gsellman is leading those tests, but the mathematics of it are not encouraging."

"Why not?" Rogeiro asked.

"Because engineering theory comes from our understanding of physics, and its practice relies on the natural laws of the universe," Relkdahz said. "Without the fabric of space-time in which to operate our equipment, without subspace beneath it, reality breaks down."

"But not *all* reality," Plante said. The second officer wore her long golden hair pulled back into a chignon. A human, she had been raised on Alpha V, though she spoke with no trace of an accent. "The ship is still here. *We're* still here."

"The space-time we occupy, and the subspace underpinning that, still exist, for the most part," Uteln said. Unlike Plante, the Deltan did speak Federation Standard with a distinct enunciation, overpronouncing his words in a stilted manner. "But the continuum has been destroyed all around us, and even beneath the outer edges of the *Robinson*. We are effectively surrounded by a moat of nonexistence, with the ship extending out into that moat, but we have no ready means of crossing from where we are back to normal space."

"I understand the warp field being unable to expand and sustain itself in the region of null space," Rogeiro said, "but why can't we use the impulse drive or the thrusters?"

"For one thing, the impulse engines employ subspace field coils," said Sisko, who started his Starfleet career as an engineer.

"That's accurate, Captain, but there's more to it than

that," sh'Vrane said. "Theoretically, both the impulse drive and the thrusters should work since they function based on Newton's Third Law of Motion."

"For every action," Sisko said, "there is an equal and opposite reaction."

"More specifically, the mutual actions of two bodies on each other are equal and opposite," the science officer said. "That makes the failure of the impulse drive and the thrusters puzzling. When either system creates force, movement is generated by pushing not against space, but against the physical structure of the motors themselves."

"But then why aren't they working?" Rogeiro asked.

"In the case of the impulse drive, a part of the problem could be what the captain noted, which is that it uses subspace field coils, although we are still working to confirm that," Relkdahz said. "But the thrusters . . ." The chief engineer's upper limbs—those without visual or aural purposes—fluttered up and down in a gesture that Rogeiro had come to recognize as the equivalent of a human headshake. "It is difficult to explain their inability to operate as designed."

"Could it be the null space around the ship . . . beneath it?" Sivadeki asked.

"Yes," sh'Vrane said. "It demonstrates that the physical laws of our universe do not apply where the space-time continuum and the subspace that serves as its foundation no longer exist."

"But . . . wouldn't that have a greater effect on the *Robinson* than simply preventing the thrusters from operating properly?" Plante asked. "Wouldn't the ship, or parts of it . . . I don't know . . . come unmoored? Crumble to dust? Cease to exist?"

"The edges of the ship are, in a sense, unmoored, extending out into the area of nothingness," Uteln said. "For the moment, the ship remains intact."

The tactical officer's qualifying phrase sounded a red alert for Rogeiro. "'For the moment'?" the exec asked.

"It is difficult to know with certainty," Uteln said, "but the extension of the ship into null space seems at best precarious."

"What does that mean?" Sisko wanted to know. "Is the ship in immediate danger?"

"We don't know for sure," sh'Vrane said. "We are continuously scanning the impacted sections of the ship and analyzing the results. The *Robinson* is so far unaffected, but there is evidence that the region of undamaged spacetime that we occupy could break down. The null space around the ship appears to be exerting stress on the intact continuum."

Rogeiro noticed the Andorian's antennae crook slightly, an indication that the situation concerned her. The first officer found the idea that a section of the universe essentially no longer existed around *Robinson* troubling enough, but he categorized the possibility that the disappearance of reality beneath the edges of the ship could spread as a clear and present threat. Pursuing the aliens in order to find and rescue the kidnapped children provided reason enough to restore *Robinson*'s propulsion systems as quickly as possible, but it also seemed plain that if the ship remained in place, it could imperil the crew.

"Why didn't they just destroy us?" Rogeiro wondered aloud.

Nobody said anything for a moment. The silence extended and grew uncomfortable, until Doctor Kosciuszko finally responded. "The aliens didn't destroy us because they wanted to board the ship," he said. "Because they wanted to take the children."

Rogeiro bowed his head and closed his eyes, frustrated with himself for asking a question that could be interpreted in such an insensitive way. Among the officers on Sisko's senior staff, none had brought children aboard other than the captain, but his daughter had been among those abducted. "I meant afterward," Rogeiro clarified in a quiet voice. "Why didn't they destroy the ship after they departed?"

"Maybe once they completely surrounded the *Robinson* with null space," Uteln hypothesized, "their weapons no longer worked across that void."

"Maybe," Rogeiro said, but then something else occurred to him. "Wait. The aliens boarded the *Robinson* after destroying space-time around it. But their ships traveled *through* null space, so we know it must be possible to do that."

"But the ships that obliterated space-time were in normal space when they attacked, and afterward," sh'Vrane said. "The auxiliary craft they sent to board the *Robinson* could have utilized any functional drive system to propel them toward us in normal space, and then simple momentum could have carried them across the void."

"I'm not talking about when they sent their ships to board the *Robinson*," Rogeiro said. "I'm talking about after that . . . when they left."

"It's possible that they have a different type of drive system," Uteln suggested. "One that can operate in null space."

"Maybe," Relkdahz said. He stood up from his leaning chair and reached down with a tentacle to a control panel on the conference table. The skewed chevron of the Starfleet emblem flashed onto the large display in the bulkhead behind Lieutenant sh'Vrane. Everybody looked up at the screen as a still image replaced the insignia. It showed the exterior of the underside of *Robinson*'s primary hull, where one of the alien craft had alit. Unlike the spherical vessel that the bridge crew had watched land atop *Robinson*'s Starfleet registry, the one on the display had an angular, rhombohedral configuration. "There are no warp nacelles," the chief engineer said, "but we already know that warp fields cannot be sustained. That also rules out these craft using any sort of impulse drive."

"They could be fitted with some form of propulsion with which we're not familiar," Uteln suggested.

Relkdahz tapped at the control panel on the conference table again. The image on the display shifted, zooming in on the bottom of the alien craft's hull. A trio of red circles appeared around three conical structures. "These appear to be chemical thrusters."

"But I thought we just concluded that thrusters don't work in null space," Sivadeki said.

"They don't," Relkdahz said. "Which means that these vessels must be driven by some other form of motive force—a form that *does* work in null space." As the chief engineer studied the image of the alien craft, he wrapped his upper limbs clockwise around his body—a contemplative posture, like a human folding their arms across their chest. "The ship is relatively small," Relkdahz said, "so the drive could be rudimentary."

"Wait a minute," Rogeiro said, thinking about what the bridge crew had witnessed during the boarding. He quickly reached to the control panel in front of him on the table and toggled on the computer audio interface. "Computer, display the vessel that landed on the ship's registration number." An image of the spherical craft appeared. It stood on four landing pads. Rogeiro pushed back from the conference table, stood up, and walked over to the screen. He pointed to the area below the vessel, between its landing pads, where a metal shaft extended downward to press with multiple prongs against *Robinson*'s hull. "What about this?" Rogeiro asked.

"That came into contact with the ship right before the

sonic attack," Sisko said. "I assumed that was how they transmitted the weaponized sound."

"Maybe it was," Rogeiro said. "But afterward, what if the aliens used this to physically push their vessel away from the *Robinson*?"

"Just . . . push away?" Sivadeki asked.

"Lieutenant sh'Vrane just talked about momentum being able to carry the alien craft across null space," Rogeiro said. "If that's true, then all they had to do was find a means of imparting velocity to their vessels vectored away from the *Robinson*. Once they began moving, they just needed time to cross the void and back into normal space, where they could use traditional propulsion." He regarded all of the senior staff, but then specifically looked to the chief engineer. "Can we do that?" Rogeiro asked. It seemed like a very basic idea, but because of that, he thought it all the more likely to work.

"You want to *push* the ship back into normal space?" Relkdahz replied. "That would require that the *Robinson* push *against* something, or that something push against it."

Rogeiro pictured himself out in space, in an environmental suit, his gloved hands against the ship's hull, trying to force it to move. But then he thought about sh'Vrane's description of how the thrusters worked, and a different image rose in his mind. He saw a shuttlecraft in the main bay, beams streaking from it inside the *Robinson*.

Rogeiro looked at the captain and said, "I know how to get the ship moving."

Beside Sisko, the first officer's chair sat empty. After Commander Rogeiro had contrived a possible solution to the marooning of *Robinson* in null space, Relkdahz and his engineers worked with sh'Vrane and her scientists to ascertain the feasibility of the plan. They had no problems proving the theory, but the effects of the destroyed space-time continuum around the ship had already produced unforeseen consequences. Relkdahz and sh'Vrane both thought that the first officer's proposal *should* work, but neither committed to saying that it *would*—or even that it would be safe to try. As a result, Rogeiro volunteered to pilot the shuttlecraft he believed could free *Robinson*.

Except that calculations had demonstrated that a more viable solution replaced a single shuttlecraft with the two runabouts Sisko had requested for the crew's exploration of the Gamma Quadrant. Lieutenant Commander Sivadeki stepped up to pilot the second vessel, but the captain wanted his most experienced conn officer at *Robinson*'s helm for the crew's escape attempt. Sisko assigned Lieutenant Stannis to the task.

To the captain's right, past the empty exec's chair, sh'Vrane walked down the curved ramp from the aft section of the bridge. Sisko saw that the science officer carried a padd. "Status, Lieutenant?"

"We've conducted multiple simulations," sh'Vrane said. "Lacking the ability to sustain their drive systems, the two runabouts can generate the greatest force not by solely using their tractor beams, but by reversing them and adding a tightly focused deflector." Rogeiro's plan had been to utilize a shuttlecraft to impart a force against *Robinson* from inside the main bay, and thereby push it into motion, but Uteln and sh'Vrane had suggested using the tractor beams of the auxiliary vessels to the tow the ship in order to get it moving.

"Commander Rogeiro's proposal turns out to be the best choice after all," Sisko said. "It'll be better to push than to pull." The captain glanced over at the bridge's main viewscreen, which showed the two *Danube*-class vessels sitting next to each other in *Robinson*'s shuttlebay. They did not face aft, as though preparing to launch into space, but forward, toward the interior bulkhead, as though they had just landed. During preparations, the shuttlebay crew had opened the massive compartment's wide hatch in the hope that the rapid decompression might move the ship. It hadn't, and so Rogeiro's plan had proceeded. The crew closed the hatch and repressurized the shuttlebay, then worked to reinforce the inner bulkhead.

"We've also scanned the shuttlebay and mapped the areas within it where space-time has broken down," sh'Vrane said. She held out the padd to Sisko. "At the deepest point, the null space surrounding the *Robinson* extends twenty meters into the hangar."

"Twenty meters," Sisko repeated as he took the padd and examined its display. "That should leave enough room for the runabouts to maneuver." The screen showed an overhead representation of the main shuttlebay. An undulous red line cut across the deck in front of the broad, closed hatch. He also saw several misshapen splashes of color. Sisko pointed to them. "These are the areas where space-time has broken down within the ship?" For the most part, *Robinson* sat atop the normal continuum, but null space encroached along the periphery of the ship and in small amounts throughout it.

"Yes, sir," sh'Vrane said. "Commander Rogeiro and Lieutenant Stannis have programmed the areas of nonexistence into their helm systems. When the *Robinson* begins to move, they'll navigate around them."

"Very good," Sisko said, and he handed the padd back to the science officer. As sh'Vrane returned to her station, the captain said, "Commander Uteln, are the pilots ready?" Normally, Rogeiro and Stannis's efforts would have fallen under the aegis of Sivadeki, the ship's primary flight controller, but because of the nature of the operation, Sisko had handed it over to the tactical officer.

"Aye, sir," Uteln said.

"Then let's begin," Sisko said.

"Channel open to the *Acheron* and the *Styx*," Uteln said. "Commander Rogeiro, Lieutenant Stannis, commence operation." Sisko heard both officers acknowledge their orders, then watched the main viewer as both runabouts lifted from the deck. "Thrusters and antigravs are engaged on both vessels," Uteln said. The antigravs, Sisko knew, would help to counter the force of the reverse tractor beams, allowing the runabouts to impart momentum to *Robinson* rather than being driven backward by the far more massive starship.

The captain waited as the vessels hovered in the shuttlebay. When nothing more happened, he feared that their reasoning had been invalid, or their measurements, and that the null space around and within *Robinson* would prevent the runabouts' tractor beams and deflectors from functioning, and that the crew's attempt to get the ship moving had failed even before it began. But then a tight collection of gray-white shafts of light shot from the bottom of each vessel, striking the reinforced bulkhead at the front of the shuttlebay. Though tractor beams—or, in the current instance, reverse tractor beams—did not technically qualify as offensive weapons, it still disquieted Sisko to see them discharged inside his ship. He expected to feel *Robinson* shudder, as though under attack, but he didn't.

"Reverse tractor beams at half power," Uteln said.

"I'm reading stresses on the reinforced hull, but it's holding," sh'Vrane said. Seconds passed. Sisko waited for something to happen, waited for Uteln or sh'Vrane to announce progress in pursuit of their goal. Instead, the science officer said, "The ship isn't moving."

"Increase reverse tractor beams to full," Uteln said. On

the viewscreen, the gray-white streaks brightened. The nearer of the two runabouts suddenly flew backward several meters before stabilizing. "*Acheron*, what's your status?" Uteln asked at once.

"*I had to boost power to the antigravs,*" replied Stannis. "*The increased force of the reverse tractor beam overwhelmed them. Recalibrating.*"

"Acknowledged," Uteln said. "Do you copy, *Styx*?"

"*I copy, Lieutenant Stannis,*" Rogeiro said. "*Recalibrating my antigravs as well.*"

"The reinforced bulkhead is still holding," sh'Vrane said, "but I'm detecting vibrational stresses in the *Robinson*'s hull." Sisko heard the electronic feedback tones of the sciences station as sh'Vrane worked her console. "There's a shearing force acting on the ship. It's . . . it's as though the *Robinson* is trying to move forward, but some part of it is frozen in place . . . as though the reverse tractor beams are working to drive the ship ahead into null space, but there's too much resistance from the normal continuum."

Sisko imagined attempting to push a heavy crate across the sand on a beach. The solution would be to find a means of decreasing the friction between the two, either by lifting the crate or by introducing a slick intermediary surface at the point of interaction. The captain could not determine how such an analogy could be put into practice in the present circumstances.

"Deploy concentrated deflectors," Uteln said. "Half power." On the viewscreen, red beams sprang from the bows of the runabouts to join the reverse tractor beams. They slammed into the reinforced bulkhead.

"Captain, the region of null space is seeping farther into the shuttlebay," sh'Vrane said.

"What?" Sisko asked. "Why?"

"I don't know," sh'Vrane said. "It appears that the normal continuum the ship inhabits is fragile where it borders null space. It may be that the thrusters and antigravs of the runabouts, or the focused power of the tractor beams and the deflectors, are having an impact on it, or it could be the vibrations of the *Robinson*." Sisko hadn't initially noticed anything, but all at once he could feel the deck trembling beneath his feet.

"Suggestions?" Sisko asked, rising and moving to the middle of the bridge, but he already knew the answer. If null space expanded far enough into the shuttlebay to reach the runabouts, their thrusters and reverse tractor beams would fail, and possibly their antigravs and deflectors as well. The crew's attempt to cross null space and escape back into the normal continuum would fall short, with no other practicable solutions even on the drawing board. Before sh'Vrane could respond, Sisko said, "Increase the runabouts' deflectors to full power."

Uteln echoed the captain's order. The red beams on the main viewer did not noticeably change, but both Rogeiro and Stannis acknowledged the tactical officer. The ship began to shake even more.

"Vibrations are increasing throughout the ship," sh'Vrane said. "The stresses on the hull are approaching maximum tolerance."

Sisko felt *Robinson* struggling around him, trying to fling itself off the island of normal space it occupied and across the gulf of null space that separated it from the rest of the familiar, intact universe. "Divert power to the structural integrity systems. Increase power to the tractor beams and deflectors," he ordered. He knew he risked damaging the various sets of systems and emitters on the two runabouts, or destroying the interior bulkhead of the shuttlebay, but none of that would matter if they couldn't overcome being stranded.

"Increase reverse tractor beams and deflectors to one

hundred ten percent," Uteln said. The gray-white rays from both runabouts grew brighter still. Both vessels immediately jerked backward before steadying.

"*Acheron* is dangerously close to the edge of null space inside the shuttlebay," sh'Vrane said. "Stresses are at maximum tolerance on the reinforced hull, which is showing signs of buckling. The ship . . ." Sisko waited for sh'Vrane to finish her statement, sure that the science officer would signal the end of their efforts to get to the normal continuum. Instead, with a note of wonder in her voice, she said, "The ship is moving."

Sisko almost could not credit what he heard. He glanced over his shoulder at *Robinson*'s science officer. As the deck quaked beneath the captain's feet, a rumble rose to accompany it. "How long can the bulkhead hold up?"

"It could collapse at any time," sh'Vrane said. "But the ship is accelerating." On the viewscreen, *Styx* banked to starboard and moved laterally in the shuttlebay, then jinked back to its previous position. Sisko understood that his first officer had just avoided a patch of null space as *Robinson* moved forward.

"Increase power to tractor beams and deflectors," the captain said again, raising his voice to be heard over the growing roar. In truth, he wanted Rogeiro and Stannis to shut down their runabouts. The crew had cleared the area on the other side of the reinforced bulkhead, but it remained an open question how much damage the ship would sustain if the front of the shuttlebay collapsed. Sisko knew, though, that the crew might not devise a better means of freeing themselves. He also understood painfully well that each moment that passed with *Robinson* unable to pursue its missing children made the task of finding and rescuing them that much more difficult.

After Uteln conveyed the orders to the runabout

pilots—boosting the reverse tractor beams and deflectors another ten percent—Sisko watched on the main viewscreen as the different beams intensified. This time, neither vessel fell back, but *Acheron* jogged to port, then quickly to starboard, and once more to port. *Styx* shifted rapidly as well, Rogeiro and Stannis clearly trying to avoid instances of null space as *Robinson* moved forward.

The ship bucked hard. Sisko bent his knees and threw his arms out wide, barely keeping his balance. He retreated to the command chair, where he could take hold of its arms to steady himself, but he did not sit.

"I'm reading a fracture in the reinforced bulkhead," sh'Vrane said. "A complete failure is imminent."

Sisko continued to watch the tractor beams and deflectors pound into the shuttlebay bulkhead. While *Robinson* thundered and shuddered around him, the captain resisted his strong desire to order the two runabouts shut down. Both vessels veered again, multiple times. *Acheron*'s reverse tractor beam faltered, blinking off and then on again before failing completely. The red rays of the runabout's deflector vanished as well, and the vessel dropped heavily onto the deck of the shuttlebay.

The bridge lurched violently to port. The inertial dampers failed momentarily. Sisko grabbed for the arm of the command chair and missed, but he managed to catch the control console beside the first officer's position. On the viewscreen, the reverse tractor beam and deflector of *Styx* quit, and the runabout fell back to the shuttlebay deck.

No, Sisko thought, but then the massive tremors pervading the bridge ceased, the accompanying reverberations quieted.

"We're free," sh'Vrane announced. "The *Robinson* is moving through null space."

"The ship is rolling and pitching," Sivadeki said. She operated her console. "I'm unable to engage any of our drive or maneuvering systems."

As expected, Sisko thought, but then his mind turned to the immediate danger to the ship. "Lieutenant sh'Vrane, status of the shuttlebay bulkhead?"

"There is a fracture, but it stopped growing once the runabouts ceased operation," sh'Vrane said.

Sisko moved back to the center of the bridge, directly behind and between the operations station and the conn. "Commander Plante," he said, "dispatch repair teams to the main shuttlebay at once."

"On their way, Captain," Plante said.

"Very good," Sisko said. He peered up at the main screen, where he saw the hatch of *Styx* open. As the captain watched, Rogeiro disembarked the vessel. "Let's see where we're headed," Sisko told Plante, who toggled the display from a view of the shuttlebay to the panorama directly ahead of *Robinson*. Stars traced long arcs up and down across the screen as the ship rotated on its lateral and longitudinal axes. "How fast are we moving?" Sisko asked. "Will we be able to reach normal space?"

Sivadeki, already working the conn, read off the ship's velocity—a velocity not only far slower than warp travel, but even well below the slowest impulse speed. "We are decelerating, but at an infinitesimal rate," she said. "Accounting for that, on our current trajectory, we will negotiate null space and reach the normal continuum in seven hours, forty-three minutes."

Seven hours, Sisko thought. While he had hoped for a swifter escape, he also knew that the situation could have been worse—that it could have taken days or weeks or even months, or that they might never have been able to secure their freedom. Under the circumstances, he counted seven-plus hours as a victory.

Sisko strode back to the command chair and stood before it, addressing Uteln at the tactical station. "I want all available resources working to find where the alien ships went," Sisko said. During the crew's time ensnared in the region of null space, the bulk of their efforts had been directed at extracting *Robinson* from its ad hoc prison, but the captain had also assigned personnel to scan surrounding space and beyond for any trace of the vessels that had attacked them. With the ship free, Sisko wanted as many of the crew as possible working on the problem.

But even if we find the aliens' trail, the captain thought, *it'll be seven-plus hours before we can begin to chase after them.* As *Robinson* limped across the inert region and back toward normal space, Sisko felt the weight of time elapsing. He feared that, with each passing moment, the aliens carried the missing children—including his own daughter—farther and farther away.

The doors at the rear of the auditorium slid open quietly, and from her vantage leaning back against the front of the stage, Kasidy saw her husband enter. The scores of people scattered about the seats turned to follow her gaze. Like her, they had suffered—continued to suffer—the abduction of a child during the alien attack. On the recommendation of Counselor Althouse and with Ben's official endorsement, Kasidy had set up group sessions to help those aboard—and in particular civilians—cope with the situation. She didn't know whether or not it actually helped—although she couldn't deny that talking and visiting with people similarly afflicted did provide her a measure of comfort. She hoped the same held true for the other parents.

Whispers rose in the group at the captain's arrival. Kasidy heard her husband's name and rank mentioned by more than one person. If Ben had come simply to observe, she didn't think he'd be able to do so. She could tell already that his presence would change the dynamic among those present. For the better part of ninety minutes, they had been sharing their feelings about what had happened. Kasidy revealed her own past experience with her daughter's abduction as a toddler, which quickly became a focal point of the discussion, and for some, a touchstone. The story of Rebecca's kidnapping on Bajor and her safe return provided hope for their own children's homecoming.

"Captain," Kasidy said as he approached the stage down the left-hand aisle. Though everybody knew of their marriage, Kasidy endeavored to address him professionally whenever Ben was in uniform outside their cabin. They had never actually discussed the issue when she and Rebecca had first relocated to *Robinson*, but it had seemed to her the proper choice; although not in Starfleet, she did serve in her diplomatic and first-contact roles as a member of the crew.

Ben nodded to her when he reached the front of the auditorium. "Counselor Althouse told me that you were meeting," he said. "I wanted to address the group."

"Of course, Captain," Kasidy said. She stepped away and took a seat in the front row, beside Ensign Jozell Dorson. An unjoined Trill, she served in sickbay as a nurse. Her ten-year-old daughter, Elent, had been among those taken from the ship. Kasidy would never have wished any child to be stolen from their home, but both she and Jozell had spoken of the one positive aspect of Rebecca and Elent *both* being abducted: over the past year and a half, the two girls had become best friends. Wherever they had been taken, they would be frightened, but at least they would have each other.

Taking Kasidy's place in front of the stage, Ben said, "Obviously, not all the parents of missing children are here, though it looks like most of the civilians are." Only a few of those present served in uniform. Kasidy knew that many of the Starfleet officers who'd had a son or a daughter taken were currently on duty, while others were on their sleep shift—though she doubted that the latter group were getting much rest. "I wanted to update you on our efforts."

"Thank you, Captain," said Harry Danvers, who sat in the front row. A human, he served the crew in the ship's salon. Several others quietly added their appreciation for Ben's visit.

"As you know, five hours ago, we managed to force the *Robinson* into motion," Ben said. "We're still more than two hours from reaching normal space and being able to use the warp drive again. Currently, the crew is utilizing the ship's sensors in an attempt to track down the aliens who attacked us."

Kasidy saw some people nodding in response to Ben, but they did so absently, as though they really didn't hear what he said. *Or maybe they heard it,* Kasidy thought, *but they don't believe it—don't believe that we're going to be able to bring our children home.* She understood such skepticism; she felt it too.

"Who did this, Captain?" asked a male voice from several rows in back of Kasidy. She peeked around several people and saw Anatoly Seitzer. He taught secondary education aboard ship. Kasidy had spoken with the man on a couple of occasions and had found him erudite and perceptive, though his question impressed her as foolish—doubtless born out of frustration.

"We don't know," Ben said gently. "We're in unexplored territory, far from the Federation and the known space of the Alpha and Beta Quadrants. We tried repeatedly to make contact with the aliens, but we received no reply."

"Did we learn anything about them?" Crewman Indray Karza asked. The Klaestron transporter operator sat beside Seitzer. "Do we have any idea why they did this?"

"We know almost nothing about our attackers beyond what we observed of their ships and their behavior during the attack," Ben said. "Their motives are a mystery, but it seems noteworthy that they left us alive and the ship intact."

Kasidy thought her husband's interpretation of events optimistic, but not terribly compelling. Yes, the aliens hadn't murdered anyone, but they had trapped the ship in the middle of a destroyed region of space and then abandoned them. It could be that the attackers refrained from killing everybody aboard not as an act of beneficence, but because they believed that death would necessarily follow.

"Are you . . . are you confident that you'll be able to rescue the children?" Jozell asked. She sounded timid, as though fearful of the answer she would receive.

"I am confident," Ben said. "We're working nonstop toward the goal of finding the children and bringing them back to the *Robinson*."

"'Finding the children'?" Seitzer said. "I thought you told us you were tracking the alien ships."

"We're using sensors to search for them," Ben said.

"You mean the alien vessels are gone," Seitzer said, his tone flat, not asking a question, but clearly stating his fears, "without leaving any trail?"

Regardless of the truth, Kasidy hoped that Ben would not confirm the statement. The parents of the missing children had suffered a trauma when they'd regained consciousness after the attack to find their sons and daughters gone, and they continued to bear the stress of uncertainty.

At the moment, they needed hope more than anything else, a reason to look forward. Later, there would be time enough for reality.

"Yes, the alien ships are gone," Ben said. Kasidy closed her eyes. She hadn't needed to hear that; neither, she felt sure, had anybody else. Still, she willed her eyes open. For the sake of the others, she wanted to show the conviction that all would end well, to demonstrate that she possessed the strength to withstand the ordeal. "It's also true that we have been unable to detect an ion trail or a warp signature," Ben went on. "But within the last hour, our scans discovered another region of null space. It stands to reason that it was created by the same weapons the aliens used to trap the *Robinson*."

"So then . . . what?" Seitzer asked. "You have a possible bearing on which to search? What if the aliens didn't travel in a straight line? Or what if they didn't head in that direction, but came from there? Of what if the aliens weren't even the ones to cause it?" As he spoke, Seitzer's voice increased in volume—not to the point of yelling, but there could be no mistaking his agitation. Kasidy understood the man's anger. She felt the same way, but she also recognized that her fury—and likely his—stemmed from multiple sources: fear for the life of her child, rage at the abductors, frustration for her inability either to prevent the kidnapping from taking place, or to take action to end the nightmare.

"Mister Seitzer, we are certain that the second region of null space identified by the sensors was caused by the aliens who attacked us," Ben said, his manner firm but not combative. He walked over to stand directly in front of Seitzer. "My crew are very good." Ben moved back to stand before the center of the stage and looked out at all the worried faces turned toward him. He gazed from one side of the auditorium to the other, from the front to the back, as though making eye contact with everybody—including Kasidy.

Finally, Ben said, "When we departed Deep Space Nine three months ago, we crossed seventy thousand light-years and then traveled still farther, to places wholly unknown to us, to seek out new knowledge, new life, and new civilizations. We did so to better our understanding of the universe and our place in it. That is a noble purpose." Kasidy didn't quite understand why Ben had chosen to speak about their lofty goals. He had to know—had to feel—that nothing he said about their mission, no matter how well intentioned or true, could mitigate the horror of the situation.

"That *was* our purpose, and I hope we soon return to it," Ben continued. "But our mission has changed. Our primary goal—our *only* goal—is to find our children and bring them home. I will do whatever it takes, this crew will do what it takes, to make that happen. We will not stop until all of our children are back on the *Robinson*."

Kasidy had already known everything that Ben had said—she understood his resolve better than anyone except, perhaps, for his son—but clearly not all of the parents had. As she looked around the auditorium, she saw expressions of determination on many faces. As the captain of the ship, Ben had said the right things.

Kasidy stood up and joined her husband. "Maybe that's a good place for us to end today," she told the assembled parents. "I'll hold another gathering here tomorrow at the same time. If any of you need to talk between now and then, Counselor Althouse and her staff are available, or you can ask to speak with any of the other parents, including me." She paused and glanced up at her husband before adding, "We're all in this together."

Ben nodded in agreement. Kasidy stood with him at the front of the auditorium as the other parents rose and filed out quietly. Several of the people peered in her direction and offered a moment of connection—a voiceless, mouthed

Thank you; a close-lipped smile; a nod. Kasidy returned each gesture, trying to convey strength to these parents whose fears she shared.

She only hoped that they would not have to mourn together.

Kasidy came out of the refresher and walked down the short hall to find the living area of her family's quarters empty. She quickly doubled back, between the 'fresher and the closet, and ducked into the bedroom she shared with Ben. She expected to see him there; if he'd been called to the bridge, he would have let her know before he left.

Their bedroom was empty.

Kasidy looked around—almost as though she might have somehow missed seeing her husband. Her gaze came to rest on the two rounded rectangular ports that ran vertically up the outer bulkhead. Earlier, she had blacked them out. When the crew had gotten *Robinson* moving again, sending it somersaulting sidelong through space, the wheeling view of the stars had disturbed her equilibrium. *Not that I wouldn't have felt off-balance anyway.*

Kasidy walked over and touched the control pads on the bulkhead. The opaque tint of the ports faded, becoming first translucent and then transparent. Out in space, the stars continued to roll past in tall arcs, up and around, down and around, again and again. It passed muster as a fair metaphor for Kasidy's thoughts. Her efforts to meet with the other parents aboard the ship had been difficult. She hoped that it helped the others. It had actually done her some good, giving her purpose at a time when her role as a mother had been stolen from her. It also provided a distraction from her own dread.

No, it was more than just purpose, more than just a distrac-

tion, she thought. In order to express her assurance to the others, she'd had to find that strength in herself. It didn't hurt that she knew what to expect since she'd been through the experience before.

Except that it does *hurt,* she had to admit to herself. Kasidy thought she'd long found her way past what had happened six years prior, but in the time since her daughter and the other children had been taken, those terrible days on Bajor had come back to her. Because of the events on *Robinson,* Kasidy felt fear and desperation for Rebecca, echoes of what had come before, and her memories revived those original emotions, and more: anger and resentment surged within her and threatened to erupt.

Pressure swelled behind Kasidy's eyes and her jaw set. She quickly restored the ports to their opaque setting, then closed her eyes. She focused on her breathing, calming it down, then unclenched her teeth. She slowly counted to ten.

Finally, Kasidy went back into the living area of their quarters. She did not see her husband, but she hadn't expected him suddenly to be there. She knew him well enough to know where he'd gone.

Kasidy crossed by the blacked-out ports and the sitting area on one side of the living space, and the dining table and desk on the other. She walked up to the open door that led to Rebecca's bedroom. Darkness greeted her. The lighting panels within had been extinguished, and the ports—which Kasidy had earlier rendered opaque—admitted no starlight. Only a thin band of illumination from the living area reached into the compartment; it ran across the deck, onto the bed, and over her husband's legs. As Kasidy's eyes adjusted to the dim light, she saw that he sat on the edge of the mattress, his head bowed.

"Ben?"

"I'm here," he said without looking up.

The question *Are you all right?* rose in her mind, but she had no need to ask it. Ben wasn't all right, and neither was she. They wouldn't be until . . .

"What have I done?" Ben asked. The pain in his voice tore through Kasidy. She went to him in the shadowy room, dropped to her knees, and took his hands in hers.

"This wasn't your fault," she told him. "You can't blame yourself for the actions of beings you didn't even know existed."

"Can't I?" Ben said. His voice sounded heavy, emblematic of the tremendous burdens of his position.

"I know you're the commanding officer of this ship, and that Starfleet holds you responsible for everybody on board . . . that *you* hold yourself responsible," Kasidy said. "But you didn't incapacitate the *Robinson*, you didn't fire on it, you didn't . . ." She had been about to say that Ben hadn't abducted the children, but she couldn't force the words from her mouth. "You didn't do anything wrong."

Still looking down, Ben shook his head. "It's not about being the captain," he said. "I know I didn't make any errors in judgment on the bridge, but . . ."

She allowed him time to finish his thought. When he didn't, she asked, "But what, Ben?" She wanted to help him, and he clearly needed to talk.

"I brought you and Rebecca aboard," he said. "I rejoined Starfleet, and when we reconciled, I asked you to join me on the *Robinson*." He finally looked up and met her gaze. "I *wanted* you to join me."

Kasidy understood her husband's point. He knew—better than most—the dangers of life aboard a Starfleet vessel. Still, she could not allow him to hold himself solely accountable for a decision they'd made together. More than that, she wanted to absolve him of his guilt, or at least to diminish it.

"You wanted us to join you because we're a family," Kasidy said. "We belong together. I wanted that too."

"You wanted us to be together and you wanted to leave Bajor," Ben said. "We could have done that by going back to Earth or any other planet in the Federation. I didn't have to stay in Starfleet, or I could've taken a desk job. I was selfish and stupid."

Kasidy rose from her knees and sat down on Rebecca's bed next to her husband. She put her arms around him. "We made the decision together."

"You didn't want to raise our daughter in space."

"No, I didn't," Kasidy said. "At least, not out patrolling the edge of Tzenkethi space or facing down Breen starships. But Starfleet was sending the *Robinson* out on an extended mission of exploration. I saw what that meant to you when you first ventured into the Gamma Quadrant for your six-month assignment . . . how thrilling it was for you . . . how much you got out of the experience. Yes, the universe can be a dangerous place, but it can also deliver marvels. I realized how much Rebecca could learn in that kind of environment, how beneficial it could be for her. It's helped make you the person you are. I love you, and part of your identity is being a Starfleet officer. I never wanted you to change."

Ben unexpectedly pulled away and stood up. He stepped over to Rebecca's dresser and picked something up, though his body hid it from Kasidy's view. "Didn't you?" he asked her, still facing away. "Didn't you want me to change?"

"Ben . . ." Even though they had rarely discussed it at any length, Kasidy knew he referred to the first time Rebecca had been kidnapped. They had been so happy to bring her home unharmed, and cautiously optimistic—and eventually thrilled—that she'd manifested no emotional wounds from her abduction. Kasidy and Ben engaged Doctor Lennis Delah, a professional specializing in early-age trauma, who initially met with their daughter three times each week, and then just twice, and finally only once. After a couple of months, the doctor declared additional sessions of no particular value to Rebecca and suggested that they continue on an as-needed basis. They never had cause to send their daughter back; they simply concentrated on providing a safe and loving environment for her. They occasionally attempted to draw Rebecca out on what she'd been through, but she never spoke of it outside her counseling sessions, and so neither did they, even to each other—almost as though avoiding the subject would somehow rob the incident of its grim reality.

Ben turned around from the dresser. With her eyes accustomed to the darkness, Kasidy saw that he held a model of a Starfleet vessel, *Wellington*, which Jake and Rena had brought back from Earth a couple of years prior for Rebecca. "You never liked my being the Emissary."

Kasidy immediately reproved herself for bringing up the Prophets the day before. She thought that she and her husband had gotten past that part of their lives, and Ben had confirmed that after the attack on *Robinson*, when she'd asked if he thought it had anything to do with the Bajoran religion. "I never said I didn't like you being the Emissary," she told him. "I know I mentioned the Prophets yesterday, but that was the first time in a long time."

"I know that it's always bothered you, that you've never really accepted it."

Just as it had a few minutes earlier, anger ignited within Kasidy—anger and resentment. She stood up quickly, the strong emotions driving her to her feet. "I don't think that's fair," she said. She strode out of Rebecca's room and back into the living area. She made it almost all the way to their bedroom door when Ben called after her.

"Kas, I'm not blaming you," he said. She stopped and

turned to face him. He stood in the doorway to Rebecca's room. "I think, more than anything right now, I'm blaming myself. I wasn't sensitive to how hard it must have been for you."

"That's not fair either, to you or to me," she said. Kasidy paced back to the center of the living area. "Look, I'll admit that I haven't always been comfortable with your role in the Bajoran religion." She shrugged as she decided to admit the truth. "Maybe I've never been comfortable with it. But you were already the Emissary when we met, and that didn't prevent me from falling in love with you or from marrying you. It didn't stop me from giving birth to our daughter or from wanting to spend the rest of my life with you."

"I shouldn't have moved us to Bajor."

"You didn't, Ben; *I* did," Kasidy said. "You were off in the Celestial Temple when Jake and I built our house. You acquired the land for it and designed it, but I made a home on Bajor before you ever did."

"But you did that for me," Ben said.

Kasidy crossed the other half of the living area to stand directly before her husband. "I did it for *us*," she said. "You know . . . it *was* a strange experience to have you occupy a significant place in the Bajoran religion. And it wasn't always easy. I watched you almost die because it was so important for you to experience mystical visions imparted to you by the Prophets. You risked your own son's life in order to enable the defeat of a Pah-wraith. And when I was carrying our child, the Prophets took you away from me—for eight months, but I didn't know that at the time; it could have been for a year or a decade or the rest of my life. But *I* moved to Bajor and made a home there—a home for *us*, but without *you*. So, yes, you can say that you being the Emissary bothered me, or that it was difficult for me, but don't tell me I didn't accept it. I have always stood by you."

Ben nodded. "You're right," he said. "I'm sorry." He reached out and pulled her toward him, wrapping his arms around her shoulders. Kasidy hugged him back, her hands circling around his waist. They stood quietly that way for a few moments, until Ben pulled back. He held her at arm's length and looked into her eyes. "I'm blaming myself for what's happened, but I'm more concerned that you are too . . . because I think you blamed me for Rebecca being taken from us the first time."

Kasidy wanted to refute her husband's claim in order to spare his feelings, but also because she didn't want it to be true—she had never wanted it to be true. She strived to be a better person than that, but how could she deny it when, just a short while earlier, that old anger and resentment had resurfaced in her? "I didn't blame you for Rebecca's abduction on Bajor," Kasidy said. "But I did feel bitterness toward the Bajoran religion. How could I do otherwise, when our daughter was taken and almost killed by a zealot?"

"He wasn't a mainstream adherent," Ben said. "He was an Ohalavaru."

The response felt like a slap. "Does that matter?" Kasidy asked. She loosed herself from her husband's grasp and marched away from him, but she didn't go very far before rounding on him. "When you found B'hala and Istani rediscovered Ohalu's writings, it essentially brought the Ohalavaru out of the shadows. It all centers around the Prophets and what the Bajorans believe about them." Kasidy hesitated before going on, but if she truly hoped to put her resentment behind her, she knew she had to say more. "It also has to do with what you think about the Prophets."

"Because I left you?" Ben asked. "I did that only because I had to . . . because I had to protect you and Rebecca."

"But don't you see?" Kasidy asked. "You believed that because the Prophets told you to believe it."

"But They also brought us back together," Ben said. "Through Kira, They reunited our family."

"I know," Kasidy said. "But don't you understand how difficult all of that was for me? For major events in my life to be dictated by mystical impressions given to you by the hidden members of an alien race? Even if you believe that they're omnipotent beings—even if they *are* omnipotent beings—I don't care. I don't want them meddling in my life—in our lives—especially when it ends up, directly or indirectly, putting the well-being of our daughter at risk."

"I'm sorry," Ben said again, his voice full of regret.

"No," Kasidy said, shaking her head. She took herself to task for bringing up their past struggles. She needed to deal with the resuscitated anger and bitterness she felt, but she didn't have to wound Ben in the process. "I'm sorry. Just because I thought those things for a time doesn't mean I was right, and it doesn't mean that I still believe them." She once more crossed the living area to stand in front of him. She placed her hands flat against his chest. "Ben, it wasn't your fault six years ago when a mentally unstable man kidnapped Rebecca, and what's happened now isn't your fault either." Thinking about their daughter brought fresh tears to Kasidy's eyes. "I feel helpless," she said. "How could we have allowed Rebecca to be taken from us again? It's not our fault, it's nobody's fault but those who took her, but it still feels like we keep failing our little girl."

As a tear spilled from Kasidy's eye, Ben seemed to steel himself. He reached to her face and wiped away the tear on her cheek. "We're going to get her back."

"I want to believe that," Kasidy said, "but you don't know for sure."

"I know that we got Rebecca back once before," Ben said, projecting a confidence she wished she also felt. "I know that Rebecca came home safely, and that she suffered no ill effects from the incident."

"We don't really know that either, do we?" Kasidy asked, facing yet another uncomfortable reality. "We don't know how much or in what ways Rebecca has been impacted by what she endured. We don't even truly know everything that happened to her."

"We know she wasn't physically harmed," Ben said. "We know that she wasn't molested. And Counselor Lennis told us that, even after months of regular appointments, she could find nothing emotionally wrong with Rebecca."

On a day of confronting unspoken truths, Kasidy decided to challenge one more. "Didn't that seem strange to you, that Rebecca could come home after being kidnapped and be perfectly fine?" she asked. "It seems strange to me even now."

"Maybe, but not in an unhealthy way," Ben said. "She's always been strong and steady."

"The counselor alerted us to watch Rebecca for any behavior that strayed from the norm," Kasidy said. "Our daughter is strong and steady, and she's smart, and she's happy. Maybe that's why we don't talk about it—why I can't usually admit it to myself—but Rebecca is not normal."

Ben regarded Kasidy without saying anything, then pulled her into an embrace. He held her quietly for so long that she didn't think he would respond to what she'd said, but then he did. "No, our daughter is not normal," he allowed. "But that's always been the case, even before she was kidnapped. She was always different from other children her age—more like an adult than a child."

With her head still pressed against the front of her husband's shoulder, Kasidy agreed with him. "She's so calm, so accepting of whatever's going on around her."

"Maybe that's what helped her survive when she was

taken six years ago," Ben said. "Maybe that will help her now."

"Maybe," Kasidy said, hoping that her husband spoke from more than mere wishful thinking.

"We're going to find her," Ben said. "We're going to find all the children, and we're going to bring them back to the *Robinson*."

Kasidy cinched her arms tightly around him. She wanted to believe. She just didn't know if she could.

Robinson felt whole again. On the main viewscreen, the stars shined in a stable pattern, the ship no longer unfixed and spinning uncontrolled through null space, but soaring on course through the normal continuum. The bridge deck plates pulsed with the deep tones of the warp drive.

Except that the ship isn't whole, Sisko thought. He sat in the command chair, eager for *Robinson* to reach its destination, but anxious about what the crew would discover there. To that point, they had found virtually nothing.

Once *Robinson* had cleared null space, Sisko had ordered a marker buoy anchored nearby to transmit warnings to approaching ships. Scans continued to detect no trace of the alien vessels. The only notable sensor contact came from the distant region of dead space they'd already identified. With no other reasonable options, the captain ordered the ship on that heading.

Almost another entire day had passed as *Robinson* raced through the Gamma Quadrant at high warp. Time elapsed, for Sisko, like a form of slow torture. Everybody aboard recognized that the longer it took to locate the abducting aliens, the less likely that they would succeed in rescuing the missing children.

The crew had continued scanning for any hint of the

alien vessels, but they'd met with no success. Scans did pick out a third and fourth zone of inert space, both much smaller than the one in which *Robinson* had been stranded and the one to which the ship presently sped. The alien ships had vanished.

"We are approaching the second expanse of null space," Sivadeki reported from the conn.

"Captain, sensors are picking up a single vessel," said Uteln. Sisko shared a look with Rogeiro, who sat beside him. The first officer didn't hesitate.

"Shields up. Yellow alert," Rogeiro said as he rose and made his way up the starboard ramp. "Is it one of the ships that attacked us?"

"Running comparative analysis now," Uteln said. Sisko heard the tactical officer operating his console. "Negative," he finally said. "The vessel we're seeing is much larger— about half again the size of the *Robinson*. Scans show two cylindrical projections mounted in parallel."

"Warp engines," Rogeiro said after arriving beside Uteln.

"It appears so," the tactical officer said. "I'm reading dilithium and antimatter, but I'm also seeing significant amounts of illium six twenty-nine."

"Meaning that the dilithium has decrystallized," Sisko said.

"Aye, sir," Uteln said. "And the antimatter exists only in trace quantities . . . more like a residue than an amount being contained as fuel."

"We're in visual range," Rogeiro said. "Commander Plante, put it on-screen, maximum magnification."

The viewer wavered and a dark shape appeared at its center. Barely more than a shadowy smudge against the backdrop of stars, it gave off no light of its own. Sisko could not even identify it as a ship.

"Enhance for low light levels," Rogeiro said.

"Enhancing," said Plante, working the ops console.

On the viewer, the image popped, revealing a large vessel motionless in space. It had a single main hull, long from bow to stern, not very wide, and quite shallow. A pair of pylons extended laterally from it on each side and supported a thick, squat nacelle, plainly recognizable as a warp-drive configuration. Illustrations in various colors covered the flat surfaces of the ship, some of which appeared to depict cyclopean faces.

"There are no matches for this ship design in any of our databases," Uteln said.

"Life signs?" Sisko asked.

"None, sir," Uteln said. "I'm also reading no movement and no heat signatures. There's an atmosphere aboard: seventy-two percent nitrogen, eighteen percent oxygen, seven percent hydrogen, as well as water vapor, carbon dioxide, and trace amounts of noble gases."

Sisko stood up and walked to the center of the bridge, where he perched his hands on his hips and studied the viewscreen. "Commander Rogeiro, what's your impression of that vessel?"

The first officer circled down from the aft section of the bridge to stand beside Sisko. "Even with its narrow hull, it's big."

Sisko acknowledged Rogeiro's reply with a noncommittal grunt. Then he asked, "What about you, Commander Plante? What comes to mind for you?"

The operations officer shrugged. "Art," she said. "I've seen ships with creative architecture, but the markings on them, if they have any, are usually prosaic, employed for the utilitarian purpose of identification."

Sisko nodded. He couldn't argue with either Rogeiro or Plante, but neither officer saw what he saw, so he tried again. "What about you, Commander Sivadeki?"

"To me, it looks old, Captain."

"Yes," Sisko said. "It gives me the sense of age as well, though I can't really say why. Is there any way to date that ship?"

"No, sir, not without more information," Uteln said. "But it's in the middle of a region of null space, so it's possible that it could have been there for months, years, decades, even centuries."

"I may have something, Captain," sh'Vrane said from the sciences station. "I'm measuring the interface between the normal continuum and null space here. I would describe it as considerably less dense than what we traversed." When *Robinson* had finally cleared null space, the transition back to the normal continuum had sent tremors through the ship, like a shuttlecraft moving through turbulence.

"What are the implications of that?" Sisko asked.

"From the readings we collected while we were stranded, it appeared that the interface between null space and the normal continuum grew more integrated over time . . . smoother, for want of a better word."

"Meaning that you think that this region of null space is older," Rogeiro said. "Can you estimate how much older?"

"It's difficult to know for sure without more data," sh'Vrane said. "I can calculate the rate of smoothing we observed, but we don't know if that process is constant; it could slow down or accelerate over time."

"What's your best guess?" Rogeiro asked.

"Based on our readings, I'd say that this region of null space was created at least decades ago . . . and perhaps more than a century."

"Meaning that if that vessel was marooned in null space with its crew," Rogeiro said, "then they died there."

Sisko regarded his first officer. "It looks like we're not the first ship to be attacked out here."

"Attacked and left to die," Rogeiro agreed. "Do we drop another marker buoy?"

"Affirmative," Sisko said.

"Drop us out of warp," Rogeiro ordered. "Bring us to a full stop and prepare to dispatch marker buoy."

"Yes, sir," Sivadeki said. As the deep background beat of the warp drive slowed, Sisko returned to the command chair. The first officer followed and sat beside him. The hum of the impulse engines rose to fill the bridge, until it too dwindled. "Engines answering all stop."

"The relevant data has been uploaded to the marker buoy," Uteln said. "Ready for launch on your order."

Sisko nodded to Rogeiro, who said, "Dispatch buoy." A sound similar to the firing of the ship's phasers followed.

"Buoy away," Uteln said.

"Still no trace of the alien ships?" Rogeiro asked.

"Negative," Uteln said, "but in addition to the third and fourth regions of null space, sensors are now detecting three more such areas."

"We have to assume they were all caused by the aliens who attacked the *Robinson*," Sisko said, at last seeing a way forward. "Commander Uteln, I want full and continuous sensor sweeps for more occurrences of null space. Lieutenant sh'Vrane, can you use the existing data points to determine the most likely origin point for the aliens?"

"Yes, sir," sh'Vrane said. "I can use various methods of interpolation to construct a set of new data points. We'll have to make some assumptions, including that the aliens are operating from a particular base—a planet or a star system. The more regions of null space we can detect, the better our mathematical model will be, and the likelier we are to find our attackers."

And the children, Sisko thought. "Commander Uteln, send the coordinates of all the known areas of null space to the conn. Commander Sivadeki, set course for the nearest region until Lieutenant sh'Vrane can provide better places to search."

"Transferring coordinates, aye," Uteln said.

After a moment, Sivadeki said, "Coordinates received." She studied her console for a moment. "The nearest zone of null space is point seven-three light-years away." She tapped at her controls. "Course laid in, Captain."

"Ahead warp nine," Sisko said.

As Sivadeki worked the conn, *Robinson* hummed to life once more.

Bajor, 2380

When Radovan Tavus looked up from his hardbound copy of *The Book of Ohalu*, it surprised him to see that shadows had climbed halfway up the curtains on the front windows. He glanced to his right, into the corner of the living area where his flat's companel sat. The clock verified what the setting sun had just told him: hours had passed while he'd read the prophecies that anchored the convictions of the Ohalavaru.

Except that Radovan hadn't simply read Ohalu's writings. He studied them, analyzed them, tried to dissect them in a way that would more fully reveal his own purpose. The incident on Endalla had started Radovan on his path, and his dreams had ushered him through the first part of his journey: choosing the instigating action, planning it, preparing for it, and finally setting it all in motion. Everything had come to pass precisely as he'd envisioned it, but he did not know what came next. He had devised and executed his blueprint almost perfectly, but only for the foundation of the structure he wanted to build.

It will come, he told himself, although it hadn't that afternoon.

Radovan collected the yellow ribbon marker, pulled it down the inside of the page he'd been reading, and closed the book. He'd acquired the volume at the very first Ohalavaru meeting he'd ever attended. Though not a particularly handsome edition—it had a plain, featureless cover, with the title printed in block letters on the spine—it did have a pleasing heft to it, and its vellum pages a satisfying coarseness to the touch.

Radovan set the book down on the sofa and stood up. He crossed to his left, past the small table and chairs where he typically took his meals, and down the short hall. As he approached his bedroom, he dug his hand into his right pants pocket, but his fingers found nothing there.

Anxiety clutched at Radovan. His heart raced as he tried to shove his hand farther down, as though his pocket possessed some distant reach inaccessible with normal effort. When he only confirmed the emptiness of his pocket, he froze. Had his noble efforts failed already, undone by the mere misplacement of a key?

As a part of his preparations, Radovan had installed a strong lock on the door to his bedroom. He specifically chose a device that could not be opened with a code or by manipulation of a magnetic field, but only by way of a physical key, and only from outside the room.

If I can't open the door—

A number of possibilities occurred to Radovan, none of them good. The door must not stay closed, but he could not very well contact emergency services to help him. He could probably cut through the door, or even break it down, but that would leave it breached and defeat the purpose of putting a lock on it in the first place. To overcome that lock in its current configuration, he knew, would require nothing short of explosives—hardly a solution since one or more of his neighbors would doubtless inform local law enforcement.

Desperate, Radovan plunged his other hand into his left pants pocket, though he knew he would not find the key there. But he touched a hard metal object, which he wrapped his fingers around and pulled out. He held his hand up before his face and opened it, like a magician completing an illusion. On his palm sat the key. Colored a matte black, it had an elliptical bow and two cylindrical shafts, both of which featured crisscrossing, meandering indentures cut into their lengths.

Radovan smiled. He remembered pocketing his key earlier that afternoon with his left hand because his right had been occupied carrying a lunch tray. He could have gone into the kitchen first and deposited the tray and its contents there before coming back to relock the door, but he wanted to take no chances. His success would rely not just on careful planning, but on attention to detail.

And I will *succeed,* he told himself. Wherever his path led him, he would follow. Whatever as-yet-unknown goal lay before him, he would achieve it.

Radovan clasped the two-shafted key and inserted it into the dual plugs of the lock. It didn't get very far before jamming in place. He withdrew the key, reversed the placement of the twin shafts, and pressed it back into the lock. It shot home with a reassuring click, and when Radovan turned it, he heard the scrape of metal against metal as the thick bolt retracted from its secured position. Unwilling to risk being confined to his bedroom—as ridiculous a turn of events as that would require—he removed the key and put it back in his pocket—his *right* pocket. Then he slowly twisted the knob and pushed open the door.

The Avatar sat on the edge of the bed, her arms at her sides, hands tucked under her thighs, legs dangling from the mattress. She sat in the fading light of dusk seeping in through the windows on either side of the bed—windows Radovan had been sure to render effectively reflective on the outside and to seal closed. The girl did not move when he entered the room, yet her dark eyes focused on his face, as though she had been watching him through the door. Her attention unnerved him, as did her stillness.

In his adult life, Radovan had spent little time with children, but he didn't need much experience to know that they seldom stayed tranquil for long. Already the girl had demonstrated that. He could only surmise that the combined effects of the drugs he had administered to her had not yet fully abated. The previous day, when he had commandeered her transporter signal and rematerialized her in the Deserak Wilderness, he'd been armed with a hypospray and one of the two ampoules of soporific that he'd taken from his mother's home after her death. Radovan administered the injection to the girl as soon as she beamed in, and it took immediate effect. He loaded her small body into a large travel bag, which he then bundled into the public travel pod he'd procured for his trip.

Back in the city, Radovan had surreptitiously returned the vehicle to a service bay that saw virtually no traffic at that time of day. He took pains to wipe the travel pod's log clean, and to eliminate any physical evidence of his or the girl's presence in it. Then he carried the large bag to his home, sticking to heavily trafficked pedestrian thoroughfares, reasoning that people would be less likely to notice him in a crowd.

In his flat, Radovan had settled the girl on his bed. He knew she had only recently turned three and a half, but her diminutive size still surprised him. He had no familiarity with growth charts for children—let alone for *human* children—but he thought her small for her age. When he changed her into pajamas—he'd gotten a week's worth of clothing for her based on her age—the large fit confirmed her below-average stature.

The girl had slept through the afternoon and into the evening. Radovan installed a night-light and checked on her regularly, ensuring that she did not suffer any physical distress. At midnight, when she had still not woken, it occurred to him that he had erred in injecting her with a full dosage of the sleep-inducing drug. He searched for the medical directions that had come with the ampoules, but he'd obviously not brought them from his mother's home. He considered perusing the comnet for information, but dismissed the idea, concerned about leaving any digital footprints that could be considered suspicious by law enforcement. Such caution had driven him, during his planning, to visit various libraries to find the information he needed.

That morning, the girl had finally woken, after twenty hours asleep. Though groggy, she asked questions: *Where's Mommy? Who are you? Where is this?* Radovan did his best to answer her in a way that would prevent her from being scared and that would keep her quiet. He told her that her mother had needed to visit her freighter, *Xhosa*, and also that her father had gone to Deep Space 9, figuring that she would recognize the names of the ship and space station. He claimed to be a family friend who had been asked to look after her during the days her parents would be away. He introduced himself as Hayl, a relatively common given name among Bajoran men his age.

The girl had whined and cried, but fortunately, she'd remained bleary from the soporific, limiting the energy she had to make a nuisance of herself. She also complained about needing to "go potty" and about being hungry. It delighted Radovan to learn that the girl required only a small amount of assistance to use the 'fresher, and he congratulated himself on having the foresight to obtain a child's toilet seat and step stool. He helped change her from pajamas into a jumper and pullover shirt.

Radovan had served her—and himself—a simple breakfast of cold cereal, sliced fruit, and juice. They ate together in his bedroom, off trays. Afterward, he gave her a child's padd, on which he'd loaded a number of games, stories, drawing programs, and contemporary entertainments appropriate for her age. He started to operate the device for her, but the girl showed him that she already knew how to use it. She navigated through the menus and selected an animated feature called *Princess Bonna and the Rainbow Waterfall*, which she evidently had watched several times before. Nestled in a clutch of pillows, she gave all of her attention over to the cartoon.

When Radovan had checked on her later, he saw that the girl had either finished or simply stopped watching the animated feature, and she had begun playing a game that asked her to identify animals. When she saw him, though, she quickly abandoned the padd and demanded his attention. She wanted her mother, she wanted her father, she wanted to go home. She needed to use the 'fresher again. She wanted to go outside and play.

Radovan had distracted her as best he could. He picked up the padd and helped the girl identify various animals, though she had an easier time recognizing several creatures from Earth than he did. Many, such as elephants and chameleons, could easily be compared to Bajoran fauna, such as *kulloth*s and *verrior*s, but others, such as jellyfish and platypuses, confounded him because of their bizarrely alien natures.

When the girl had grown bored with the animal game, she talked again about going home. Radovan attempted to engage her with a counting program, and when that failed to work, he ventured back to the entertainment menu. Nothing succeeded, and the girl began to fidget and whine. Radovan found her more difficult to deal with than adults, which he hadn't thought possible. It astonished him that such a little creature could irritate him so quickly and so thoroughly.

Radovan had forced himself to maintain his composure—a skill he had cultivated over time in order to avoid standing out. When the girl yelled and cried and carried on, he wanted to scream at her to shut her mouth. When she flopped around the bed, ran all over the room, and pounded on the door, he felt the compulsion to grab her and throw her into a wall.

But he hadn't. Instead, he either talked to her or ignored her, whichever tactic proved more useful. He refused to respond to her tears, but when she said she was hungry again, he told her that he would make lunch for her. He left the room—locking the girl in—and returned shortly with a *jevi* nut paste and *moba* jam sandwich on *mapa* bread, along with a glass of cold *kava* milk. She wolfed it down, along with the half tablet of sedative he'd crushed and put in her food.

It had concerned Radovan to give the girl two such drugs in the span of twenty-six hours, but he needed some peace, as well as time to probe *The Book of Ohalu*. He did have the directions for the sedatives, and they contained contraindications for the soporific, but only if taken together. Radovan also reasoned that if the girl died from ingesting the two drugs in such close proximity, he would finally know his destiny. In general, he had no desire to harm her, but he also recognized that it could fall to him to be the instrument of the Avatar's death.

After that, Radovan had checked on her several times to find her still alive and, fortunately, sleeping. Now, stopping just inside the door, he saw that the drug had worn off. "You're awake," Radovan said to the girl.

She continued to stare at him from the edge of the bed, motionless, without saying a word. She remained so still that he wondered if she might somehow be asleep, though he had no idea how she could stay sitting while dozing. He took a step forward, and at last the girl moved. She pulled her hands from beneath her legs, spun around, and threw her little body onto the bed, then slid down the mattress to the floor. She then raced over to him and started slapping her hands against his leg.

"I want Mommy!" she yelled. "I want Mommy!"

Radovan looked down at the caterwauling child. Thankfully, he didn't *have* to silence her, since his flat sat on the third and highest floor, at the end of the building, so that his bedroom shared no common walls with another unit. Additionally, the flat below his had gone unoccupied for the past couple of months. In a way, the girl's behavior fascinated him, but he discovered that his patience quickly grew thin. He felt himself grit his teeth, but he once more made an effort to restrain his temper.

Radovan crouched down and caught the girl's hands in his own. She struggled to free herself from his grip, but quickly abandoned the effort. She stopped yelling and looked into his eyes. "Your mommy is on board her ship," Radovan said. "She'll be back in a few days to get you."

"No!" the girl shouted into Radovan's face. He shook her hands once, firmly.

"Yes," he told her.

The girl puffed out her cheeks. "No," she said again, though at a much lower volume. "I want Mommy." She dropped her head and looked down. Tears pooled in her eyes. Radovan felt sorry for her, though he knew he could not afford to indulge such sympathies.

Somebody knocked at the front door.

Both Radovan and the girl whipped their heads in the direction of the unexpected sound. "Mommy!"

"No, it's not your mommy," Radovan snapped at the girl.

"Mommy! Mommy!"

Radovan reached out and slammed the bedroom door, then grabbed the girl. She squirmed in his hands, trying to get away, as he picked her up and carried her over to the bed. Radovan thrust her into the pillows and pinned her to the mattress. He leaned in, bringing his face close to the girl's. Her eyes went wide, and Radovan felt satisfaction in seeing her fear; he needed her to mind him.

"That's not your mommy," Radovan said again, and he realized that he wanted to convince himself as much as he did the girl. He had planned so meticulously, but then he'd forgotten to take the girl's stroller from the Deserak Wilderness. If law enforcement had tracked him down, though, would they knock on his door?

Maybe, if they're not sure I'm who they're looking for, Radovan thought. *Maybe they want to interrogate me . . . or search the flat.*

The knocking came again. Though muffled by the closed bedroom door, it still sounded louder, as though the visitor had decided to pound rather than merely knock.

Radovan reached up and pointed in the girl's face. "Be quiet," he said sternly. The girl didn't say another word, but she also didn't look away.

Radovan pushed away from the bed and quickly exited the bedroom. As he pulled the door closed behind him, he saw that the girl hadn't moved from where she lay against the pillows, but had turned her head to glower at him. Despite the knocking, he almost felt relieved when he pulled the key out of his pocket and secured the lock.

The pounding stopped. Radovan waited, hoping that whoever had chosen to pay a call on him had thought better of it and left. He couldn't imagine who would have come to his door other than law enforcement. He had no living family—most had perished during the Occupation, while his brother had died later, in an off-world accident. He also had no real friends, only colleagues and acquaintances, and he—

"Tavus?"

Radovan knew the voice on the other side of the front door at once. It belonged to Winser Ellevet, the woman who'd come home with him after an Ohalavaru rally two weeks earlier. Radovan hadn't attended any events since then, nor had he seen or even spoken with her. She'd attempted to contact him several times, leaving both written and verbal messages for him, but he hadn't responded.

"Tavus, can you hear me?" Winser said. "I went by E.T.T. Three today, so I know you're sick."

The declaration enraged Radovan. How dare this woman visit his occupational site—this woman who didn't really know him, who had for months pursued a friendship with him, only to eventually entrap him to sate her carnal desires. How dare she.

Radovan marched to the front door, intending to throw it open and confront Winser. He wanted her to know that she had violated his boundaries, and that he would have nothing more to do with her. And he wanted to tell her *loudly.*

At the door, Radovan reached for the knob . . . and then froze. *Is this smart?* he asked himself. If he faced her, if he yelled at her, she would discover that he had lied about being sick. Did she know that he had been away from E.T.T. 3 all week? Radovan feared doing anything that could prove suspicious to law enforcement, or that could cause Winser to begin asking questions, especially if the abduction of the Avatar became public.

Radovan leaned in close to the door. "Ellevet, is that you?" He spoke just loudly enough for her to hear him, but softly and roughly enough to suggest he actually suffered from an illness.

"Yes, Tavus, it's me," Winser said in an animated tone. "Let me in so I can help you."

"Thank you, Ellevet, but I shouldn't. I'm still contagious."

"What's the matter with you?"

"Just a bad coryza," Radovan said. "It's nothing serious, but I just need time and rest to get better."

"Do you need me to bring you a doctor?" Ellevet asked. She sounded genuinely concerned.

"No, no," Radovan said, adding a couple of hoarse coughs. "I'm already under a doctor's care. I've got medication for my congestion and inflammation."

"It doesn't sound like it's working very well."

"Believe me, I'm much better than I was."

Winser was quiet for a few seconds, and Radovan anticipated what would come next. "I've been worried about you," she said. "I've tried to contact you a few times since you brought me back here."

Since I *brought* you *back here?* Radovan thought, furious at the characterization. Winser had manipulated him, plied him with alcohol, and forced herself on him. He barely remembered that night or their encounter, and he felt grateful for the hazy memory. Once more, he tamped down his anger in the service of his greater destiny.

"I received your messages," Radovan said. "I'm sorry I haven't been in touch, but this coryza has really knocked me out. I've mostly been in bed." He immediately regretted mentioning his bed, worried that Winser would draw some inference from it, or perhaps make some licentious reference to their one night in his flat. Mercifully, she stuck to talking about his illness.

"I feel bad that you've been so sick for so long," she said. "Since you need to rest, I'd be happy to come in and help take care of you . . . serve you meals, keep you hydrated, bring you your medication."

"That's very generous," Radovan said, though he actually believed Winser's offer less selfless and more an attempt to ingratiate herself to him. "But I'm managing well enough, and I'd feel terrible if you were to become ill because of me."

Again, Winser got quiet. Radovan waited for her footsteps, but when he didn't hear them, he wondered what he would have to do or say to make her leave. Finally, in a low voice he could barely make out, she said, "I hope you'll let me know when you're better. I'd really like to see you again."

"Of course," Radovan said, though he had no intention of ever seeing Winser again.

"Okay," she said, though she sounded less than convinced. "Promise me you'll get in touch if you need my help with anything."

"I certainly will," Radovan said. "Thank you for coming by. That was very thoughtful of you." The words tasted mealy in his mouth.

"I'll see you soon," Winser said. Radovan thought the hope in her voice pathetic. He knew he should answer her in kind, telling her that, yes, he would see her soon, but he couldn't.

"Bye," he said, and he at least tried to inject a note of optimism into his tone. Once more, he waited for Winser to walk away, and at last she did. Radovan closed his eyes and breathed in deeply, pleased that she had finally gone.

He headed for the replicator in the wall beside his small dining table and chairs. He needed to order dinner for the girl. He decided that he would include a jumja stick for dessert, hoping that the sweet confection would placate her.

But Radovan's thoughts remained on Winser Ellevet. He knew that she would return. Maybe not the next day or the day after, but he did not doubt that she would come back to his flat. He could again refuse to allow her inside, but would she accept that? Or would she instead make a scene? Radovan could not risk any unwanted attention.

And that means I can't simply wait for inspiration to strike me, he realized. *At least not here in my flat.*

Radovan decided he would have to make a new plan. He would have to determine how best to get the girl out of the city without being detected. He would also have to figure out where to take her.

The sudden change to his plans should have flustered Radovan, but it didn't. He chose to interpret it not as a setback, but as an acceleration of his timetable. Sooner than he'd thought, he would fulfill the purpose for which he had been born.

Perhaps very soon indeed.

Gamma Quadrant, 2386

Nearly two full days after the abduction of the children, *Robinson*'s tactical officer and chief of security, Lieutenant Commander Uteln, stood at his console on the bridge and monitored the ship's progress through the Gamma Quadrant. To that point, the crew had identified twenty-seven regions of null space spread across multiple sectors. Based on the dispersion of those dead zones, Lieutenant sh'Vrane's science staff—in particular Ensign Dalisay Dari Aquino, who specialized in numerical analysis—had utilized the data to pinpoint half a dozen possibilities for the most likely place from which the attack on the ship had been launched. The crew had already investigated two of those locations, finding nothing. The third had likewise proven empty, but a main-sequence star in the vicinity suggested another possibility. The captain had ordered Sivadeki to set course for the solar system.

Uteln studied his display as the ship's long-range sensors gathered information from what lay ahead. "Scans show a seven-planet system," he announced. "It's populated mostly with gas giants, with two inner, terrestrial worlds. The rocky planets both have daytime surface temperatures in excess of four hundred degrees, far too hot to host any known kind of humanoid life."

"Let's conduct a survey of the system," Captain Sisko said from where he sat in the command chair.

"Sir?" asked Commander Rogeiro, seated beside the captain.

"I know," Sisko said, "but this is the best lead we've had."

The captain spoke evenly, without betraying the deep levels of concern and anxiety that had to be churning within him. As a Deltan, Uteln possessed innate empathic abilities, but he didn't need to use them to understand what Sisko must feel. A Starfleet captain, by definition, assumed responsibility for the lives and well-being of every individual under his or her command, and aboard starships that carried families of crew members, that extended to the civilians. That those abducted from *Robinson* were children exacerbated the situation, and that Sisko's own daughter had been taken could have driven the captain to despair. Uteln had two children himself, and though both had reached adulthood more than a decade earlier, he couldn't imagine the devastation he would have felt if they had been taken from him in their youth, or if either one of them preceded him in death. Captain Sisko's composure impressed the tactical officer.

"Is it really a lead, Captain?" Rogeiro asked. "A star system with no habitable planets?"

"Either the beings who attacked us have a home somewhere or they're nomads," Sisko said. "If they continuously roam, we may never locate them, or if we somehow pick up their trail, we may not be able to overtake them. But if there's a world that they call their own, we need to find it."

For his part, Uteln concurred with the captain's assessment. Though the tactical officer could cite examples of species with no fixed home, who traversed the universe as a way of life, he also knew that the vast majority of spacefaring races founded and maintained planetbound civilizations, across one or more worlds. "Initiating solar-system survey protocols," Uteln said. "What about probes, sir?"

"No, let's not launch any probes yet," Sisko said. "If there's any chance of the children's abductors being in this system, I want to retain the element of surprise." From a tactical standpoint, Uteln agreed that the *Robinson* crew should attempt to remain concealed from their adversaries as long as practicable.

"Commander Sivadeki, set course for the system," Rogeiro said. "Tangential approach, rapid deceleration, and hide us in the Kuiper belt. Commander Plante, prepare the ship for its lowest functional profile." The conn and operations officers acknowledged their orders and worked their consoles. On the main viewscreen, the field of stars streaked off to starboard and up as Sivadeki set *Robinson* onto its new heading.

While the ship sped toward the outer reaches of the planetary system, Uteln programmed *Robinson*'s sensors to methodically scan the planets and their moons, the star, and the space in which they all dwelled. As the ship eventually dropped out of warp and took up a position beside a large asteroid in the Kuiper belt, Uteln studied the results, as did Lieutenant sh'Vrane. Three hours after arriving in the system, the science officer spoke up.

"Commander, I'm detecting an orbital anomaly in the second planet's moon," she said, addressing Uteln from her sciences station along the aft section of the bridge. "Can you confirm?"

"Checking," Uteln said. He accessed the gravitational data collected for the second planet, which showed that only one natural satellite revolved around it. He also called up the information gathered for the moon. Using the mass of the two astronomical bodies and the distance between their center points, he calculated the barycenter of their paired system, then plotted the planet's wobble and the moon's orbit. He then matched his results against the corresponding sensor data.

They didn't match.

"I see a discrepancy too," Uteln told sh'Vrane. He locked down the tactical console and stepped over to the sciences station behind him. He examined sh'Vrane's display and confirmed that they had both discovered the same divergence. Uteln pointed to the number on the screen that measured the difference between the moon's expected orbit and its actual orbit. "That's not much of a variance," he said. "Could the gravitational pull of one of the gas giants account for it? Or several of them?"

"No, the orbits of the gaseous worlds are too far away to account for it," sh'Vrane said. "And the two planets in the next higher orbits are both on the other side of the star right now." Her antennae curled slightly downward, in a movement that Uteln had learned to read in the Andorian as puzzlement. "It may not be a large disparity, but it is significant."

Uteln grasped for another explanation. "Could the system contain a microsingularity?"

"I considered that possibility as well, but our scans are negative," sh'Vrane said. She stared at the display on her console. "Orbital perturbations don't just happen. There has to be another mass out there."

"Another mass?" Uteln asked.

"Probably another planet, but in a much closer orbit than any of the gas giants," sh'Vrane said.

"Are you suggesting a *cloaked* planet?" Uteln asked, unable to prevent skepticism from entering his voice.

"Not necessarily," sh'Vrane said. "I know we only detected seven planets, but is it possible that we missed one?"

Uteln beat back his inclination to reject the science officer's suggestion out of hand and instead considered the situation. "We conducted preliminary scans to determine the gross characteristics of the system, such as the number of planets, via long-range sensors," he said, thinking through the problem. "That means that we identified worlds visually, by way of their reflected light against the blackness of space, or by their darkness created by their transit in front of their star."

"In theory, our scans could have failed to find a planet if it absorbed most of the light that shined on it," sh'Vrane reasoned, "or if it somehow shined brilliantly on its dark side while passing in front of its sun."

"It's possible," Uteln said.

The science officer stared at the display on her console, and Uteln watched as her antennae slowly straightened. "There *has* to be another mass out there," she said again.

"Can you tell what it might be, and where?" Uteln asked.

"I think it must be a terrestrial world, between one and two astronomical units from the star, and on this side of its orbit," sh'Vrane said. "I'll create a search grid."

"Transfer it to the tactical station," Uteln said. "I'll adjust the sensors."

As the science officer deftly operated her controls, Uteln returned to his station. Once sh'Vrane had plotted out a search pattern and sent it to the tactical console, Uteln programmed it in and started a sensor sweep. Then he reported to the captain and first officer the discrepant readings and the corresponding actions he and sh'Vrane had taken.

Two hours later, the scans registered a contact.

"Sensors are detecting an object fifty-seven million kilometers from the second planet," Uteln read from his console. "Mass: six point two-one times ten to the twenty-first kilograms. It reads like a rocky world—" The tactical officer abruptly stopped talking. He had based his characterization of the object as a planet based on its mass, but other data suggested something else—something he had never before seen and that he did not understand.

"Commander?" Rogeiro asked.

"The object is not a planet," Uteln said. "But I'm not sure what it is. Its dimensions don't make any sense."

"Put it on-screen," Sisko said. "Maximum magnification."

"Aye, sir," Uteln said. The tactical officer worked his console, and the starfield on the main viewer vanished. In its place appeared a massive, curved geometric shape floating in space.

"What . . . what is that?" Rogeiro asked.

Uteln studied its dimensions before raising his head to see the object. It looked like a great, thick square, the corners of which had been pushed in the same direction to form a saucer-like shape. The area visible on the outside of the object shined brightly, while on the inside, it resembled the surface of an inhabited world, painted in browns and greens, blues and whites.

"It looks almost like an expanse has been removed from the crust of a planet and transplanted by itself out into space," Plante offered from the ops station. "Except that the civilization lives on the inside, like a section of a Dyson sphere." The second officer's comparison struck Uteln as an apt descriptor.

"The Dyson section has a dense metal core," the tactical officer said, attempting to make sense of the readings on his console. "Gravity on either side measures one point zero-seven-seven *g*. It is in regular orbit about the star. It is in synchronous rotation, with its inner, concave side always facing the sun, and its outer, convex side facing away. Frozen water blankets the entire surface on the far side; the edges are catching the sunlight, which is the source of the illumination. On the near side, I'm detecting an atmosphere; based on pressure and elemental composition, it's breathable for us."

"Life signs?" Sisko asked.

Uteln called up a display of biological and related measurements. "I'm getting confusing readings. There is a general sprawl of structures and thoroughfares, but nothing aggregated into what we would call cities. There is a tremendous amount of heat and movement, but life signs are sporadic and difficult to interpret."

"Why?" Rogeiro asked.

"It could be the result of something interfering with our scans—particular metals in the structure, or noise from their communication systems, or even just our distance from the object," Uteln said. "It also could have to do with the nature of the life-forms."

"Can you isolate human or other specific readings?" Sisko asked. Most of the children taken from *Robinson* had been humans, although the group also included Bajorans, Andorians, and several others.

"Negative, not at this distance," Uteln said.

"Do you read any defenses?" Rogeiro asked.

Uteln worked the sensors to check for emitters anywhere on the object, but found none. He then scanned the skies above the inner surface of the Dyson section. He saw movement at once. "There are vessels maneuvering through the atmosphere and—" For the second time, the tactical officer stopped speaking midsentence—not because he saw something he had never seen before, but because he saw something he recognized. "Captain, some of the ships are identical to the ones that attacked us."

Sisko stood up and moved to the center of the bridge as though propelled from the command chair. "We found them."

Uteln felt a moment of elation that the *Robinson* crew had

at last located the beings that had taken the children—and therefore, hopefully, that they'd located the children as well. But then the sensors revealed another detail. "Captain," Uteln said, "the entire object is surrounded by null space."

Sisko toggled off the intraship comm system. Seated in the command chair on the bridge, he had just finished informing the entire crew that they had tracked down the beings who'd attacked *Robinson*. The captain wanted the parents of the missing children to know that, after two days of dread, they had made major progress in their rescue efforts. Sisko felt a sense of hope that had been missing since the abduction, and he aimed to provide that to everybody aboard— including his wife.

"Captain, we're receiving telemetry from the probe," Uteln reported. After finding the odd, obviously artificial world and confirming the presence there of *Robinson*'s attackers, Sisko had ordered the launch of a reconnaissance probe. Using the gas giants as cover, the sensor-laden device navigated into the system. "It has arrived and deployed the full range of its sensors."

"Can you locate the children?" Sisko asked.

"A bank of sensors is dedicated to the task," Uteln said.

"Visual," Rogeiro said.

On the main viewscreen, an overhead view of the Dyson section appeared. It looked like the unremarkable surface of many class-M planets that Sisko had seen: brushstrokes of brown and green marked landmasses, patches of deep blue revealed oceans and lakes, and streaks and swirls of white showed clouds scudding above the geography. But where every planet the captain had ever seen formed a circular aspect out in space, the one below the probe showed as a rounded square. It put him in mind of human history, when conventional wisdom held to a flat Earth, and old maps warned mariners of the dangers of sailing off the edge of the world.

"High magnification," Sisko said.

The main screen jumped to a closer view of the surface. Buildings spread widely across the land with no discernible order, while thoroughfares cut through them in tortuous routes. The disarray suggested organic rather than planned civic growth.

"Captain, sensors confirm a great deal of movement on the surface," Uteln said, "but life signs are still confused. There are biological markers, but they're inconsistent."

"Inconsistent?" Rogeiro asked. "In what way?"

"Both internally and externally," Uteln said. "There don't appear to be enough biological processes to define a single being, but taking each set of readings, it's as though there are thousands of different species."

"What is the level of their technology?" Rogeiro asked.

"Scans show several fusion reactors scattered across the surface, but most of their power is generated by high-efficiency solar-collection units," Uteln said. "Their ground vehicles contain fuel cells. It's unclear how those are charged, but they probably utilize solar power."

"What about radiation lev—" Rogeiro started to ask, but Uteln cut him off.

"Captain, sensors have detected human life signs," the tactical officer said.

The news sent energy flooding through Sisko's body. "How many?" he asked.

"Collating, Captain," Uteln said. "Scans show seventeen humans . . . five Bajorans . . . one Trill . . . one Orion . . . one Vulcan . . . and two Andorians."

"That's all?" Rogeiro asked, echoing the words that had arisen in Sisko's mind.

"Yes, sir," Uteln said. "A total of twenty-seven individuals. They are all in relatively close proximity to one another inside a—*wait!*" Sisko's heart seemed to lurch in his chest at the tactical officer's single excited word. "Sensors are picking up more human life signs . . . and Andorian . . . Betazoid . . . Lorillian . . ." Uteln tapped at his controls before continuing. Sisko realized he was holding his breath, and he forced himself not to do so. "Captain, I have eighty-seven life signs corresponding to all of the missing *Robinson* children."

"Where are they?" Sisko wanted to know.

"They are in three clusters, of twenty-seven, thirty-one, and twenty-nine," Uteln said. "They're in separate, neighboring buildings. I should be able to pinpoint them visually." As the tactical officer worked his console, the view on the main screen tracked across the surface of the Dyson section in a blur of motion. When it stopped, Sisko saw a complex of connected buildings, all of different shapes and sizes. "They're here," Uteln said, and three red circles appeared on three adjacent structures.

"Can we beam them out?" Sisko asked.

"Scanning for transporter inhibitors," Uteln said. Sisko waited for the answer, certain that the solution would not prove quite so simple or easy. At last, the tactical officer said, "Sensors detect no active inhibitors, but they're also not showing any transporter beams anywhere on the surface. This society may not possess the technology."

Sisko could not have asked for better circumstances. If this civilization had not developed the transporter, then it seemed unlikely that they would know how to shield themselves against it. But another potential problem occurred to Sisko. "What about the effects of null space on the transporter?" he asked. "Will we be able to beam the children through to the ship?"

For a moment, nobody responded, which suggested the uncertainty involved in attempting such a rescue. Finally, sh'Vrane said, "It's difficult to know, Captain. Our drive systems failed in null space, as did phasers and tractor beams, but sensors do function."

In the first officer's chair, Rogeiro turned toward Sisko. "If we want to be certain of the efficacy of the transporters, we could travel to the nearest region of null space outside the system and execute a test."

The captain acknowledged the suggestion with a nod, though he immediately disregarded the option. Since they had finally found the children, Sisko and his crew needed to act at once. The abductors had clearly not intended to obtain some form of ransom, because they had neither made any demands nor left a trail to follow. That told Sisko that they had other aims for the children, and without knowing the nature of those aims, he could not risk taking any longer than necessary to stage a rescue.

The captain knew that Federation values, Starfleet guidelines, and his own ethics dictated that he resolve situations using diplomacy whenever possible, but he saw an opportunity to retrieve the children with no loss of life simply by rushing into the system and transporting them back to *Robinson*. By issuing such orders, he risked provoking another battle, but the beings who had gone to considerable lengths to incapacitate his ship and crew in order to carry out their abduction had also refused to respond to all communications. That led Sisko to believe a diplomatic solution unlikely. More than that, if he embarked on such a course and failed, they would lose the element of surprise. The time for negotiation had passed.

"Red alert," Sisko said. "We're going in."

Bajor, 2380

The door signal tolled, an up-and-down chiming of bells. Asarem Wadeen looked up from the jumble of padds and books crowded between the computer interface and the dedicated companel on either side of her desk. Her office door glided open and Enkar Sirsy, one of her assistants, stepped inside.

"Minister, you asked me to inform you when your first appointment arrived." Enkar wore dark-blue slacks and a pink floral blouse, topped by a black jacket that complemented her long red hair. She had formerly assisted the previous first minister, Shakaar Edon, but had withdrawn from public service after his assassination. Asarem had stayed in touch with her, and six months after the memorial, she'd coaxed Enkar to join her staff, where she had served for more than three years.

"Yes, thank you, Sirsy," Asarem said. "Please show them in."

Enkar peered back through the doorway into the outer office and gestured inside. "Please come this way," she said. "The minister will see you." Asarem stood up and came around to the front of her desk as Benjamin Sisko and Kasidy Yates entered.

At first glance, the couple looked every bit as striking as they usually did. Sisko—tall and broad-shouldered, with dark eyes and dark flesh, a smooth, bald pate, and a goatee—carried himself with an air of authority, doubtless a vestige of his long tenure commanding Deep Space 9. Yates, a head shorter than her husband, had an almost regal appearance: her straight, black hair cascaded down to her shoulders and framed a lovely face notable for its warm, silky complexion and high cheekbones. But as Asarem approached to greet them, she saw signs of the toll that the last day and a half had taken on the pair. They both moved with a leadenness that suggested fatigue and the burden of a heavy weight—understandable, considering the terrible circumstances. Discolored crescents beneath Sisko's eyes betrayed a lack of sleep, and a deep, vertical worry line creased Yates's brow.

Asarem reached out and took the Emissary's hand in both of hers, then repeated the gesture with his wife. The first minister met Yates's gaze and held it an extra beat. The first minister could not pretend to know precisely how difficult the past thirty-nine hours had been for her, but she understood firsthand the nature of a mother's loss. Asarem's only child, a daughter she'd named Eloija, after her own mother, had died in infancy, during the Occupation, a victim of a bitter winter and a dearth of healthcare and medicine in the Karnoth resettlement camp. Eloija had lived only three weeks, but a quarter of a century later, even amid the demanding schedule and responsibilities of her office, the first minister thought about her virtually every day.

"Thank you so much for coming," Asarem told her visitors. "I would have traveled to Adarak to meet with you, but given the requirements of my security team, I thought it would be too disruptive, especially at this time." Both Sisko and Yates murmured their understanding. "Please, why don't we have a seat." The first minister motioned toward a sitting area on the other side of the room, where two sofas and a number of comfortable chairs surrounded a low ceramic table. The early-morning sun shined in through the tall, narrow windows in the wall beyond, sending striated bars of light across the marble floor. Just past the casements, the columns that flanked the Great Assembly stood guard. Beyond them stretched Ashalla, Bajor's capital, a vibrant city comprising elegant structures, broad pedestrian thoroughfares, lush greenswards, and meandering waterways.

As Sisko and Yates sat down together on the near sofa, Asarem asked if they would like something to drink or to eat. They both demurred. The first minister dismissed her assistant, who quickly withdrew, the door sliding closed behind her. Asarem took a seat across from her visitors.

"I'm so sorry about what's happened," the first minister said. "I can only imagine how difficult it must be."

"Thank you," Yates said. Her response seemed more pro forma than anything else; she moved and spoke stiffly, as though struggling to connect with the world around her. She sat hunched slightly forward, with her knees and elbows together, almost as though reacting to being punched in the gut. Asarem thought Yates would say more, but she didn't. Beside her, Sisko seemed aware of his wife's discomfort, but he neither said anything nor reached out to her. Strangely, as much as Sisko and Yates surely needed each other, they appeared isolated—not just from each other, but even from their surroundings.

"I've been in touch with Major Orisin," Asarem said before the silence could grow awkward. "I want to assure the two of you that the Bajoran Militia is doing everything it can to find your daughter and bring her home safely."

"We haven't seen the major yet this morning," Sisko said, "but he's been helping us . . . working with us . . . keeping us informed."

"If you haven't spoken with Major Orisin today, then you may not know what's been accomplished overnight," Asarem said. "Per the Militia's request, my office has expedited processing with the Ministries of Defense, Justice, and Transportation. The records you provided of your daughter's DNA have been disseminated, without attribution, throughout Bajor's transporter network. If an attempt is made to beam Rebecca anywhere on the planet or into orbit, her signal will be detected and immediately isolated, and she will automatically be transported to safety. The Militia has also begun to inspect all ships leaving the surface, and they've begun scanning public spaces, all under the guise of trying to locate stolen goods." It occurred to Asarem that such a justification actually made for a true, if unflattering, description. "In addition to that, because of the apparent expertise involved in the abduction, the Militia are checking on the backgrounds and movements of all transporter technicians on Bajor."

Sisko looked at his wife, as though he expected her to react to the information Asarem had provided, but she remained quiet. "Thank you, First Minister," Sisko said. "We appreciate the Militia's efforts, and yours. We're also grateful for your concern and support, as well as everything you've told us."

Sisko's words, however genuine, made the first minister uncomfortable. She hadn't chosen to pull the Emissary and his wife away from their home, at such an impossible time, just to offer up her sympathy, or to provide information Major Orisin could have given them. "Mister Sisko, Ms. Yates, there's another reason I wanted to speak with you in person."

At last, Yates appeared to engage. She looked over at Asarem, and then to her husband. "Minister, if you need Ben for some reason . . . if you need the Emissary to—"

Appalled at the idea that she had called Sisko and Yates to her office for her own purposes, Asarem interrupted. "No, no, no," she said quickly. "I'm sorry if I gave you the impression that this is about anything other than your daughter."

"It's all right, Kas," Sisko said. He reached over and took his wife's hands, which she held clasped tightly together on her knees. "What is it, Minister?"

"I wanted to speak to you about a woman named Jasmine Tey," Asarem said. "Do you know her?"

Sisko and Yates both shook their heads. "The name doesn't sound familiar," the Emissary said. "Should we know her?"

"No, there's no reason that you should," Asarem said. "I just thought that you might have met her at some point. Until recently, she was a member of my security detail."

"I suppose I might have seen her," Sisko said with a shrug.

"It doesn't really matter whether you have or not," Asarem said. "I'm bringing her up because I think she could be of use to you."

"Of use?" Sisko asked. "Do you think that Kasidy and I need personal security protection?"

"No, that's not what I'm suggesting," Asarem said. "Agent Tey is relatively young, particularly for the positions she's held, but she has been highly trained and has a distinguished record. Her skills and experience include criminal profiling."

Yates seemed to take particular note of the last detail. "Do you think she can figure out who did this?"

The first minister knew that she needed to step lightly. She did not want the Emissary and his wife to doubt the efforts already being made to find their daughter. "I've been told that Major Orisin is excellent at his job, so I have no reason to doubt his capabilities," Asarem said, choosing her words judiciously. She did not wish to say anything untrue, but at the same time, she genuinely believed that Jasmine Tey could prove a vital asset in locating Rebecca Sisko. But the first minister had built a solid relationship with Overgeneral Manos and the Bajoran Militia, and she had no interest in jeopardizing that by forcing them to add a civilian to their investigation. If Sisko and Yates requested Tey's assistance, though, Manos would likely allow it; such an appeal would also likely insulate Asarem from any political consequences.

"If you don't doubt Major Orisin's abilities," Yates asked, "then why are you recommending someone else?"

"I don't think that's what the first minister is saying," Sisko told his wife.

"No, it's not," Asarem agreed. "I'm not advocating replacing Major Orisin, or anybody else, for that matter." The first minister leaned forward, wanting to emphasize what she would say next. "But I've known Agent Tey for five years. She has an exceptional record: degrees in criminal justice and forensic psychology, training in law enforcement, not to mention a skill set that includes hand-to-hand combat and the use of numerous small arms."

"You make her sound like a one-woman security force," Sisko noted. Asarem appreciated the observation since, if they could rescue Rebecca, the Emissary and his wife would probably seek some form of everyday protection for their family. The first minister believed that, if offered the opportunity and if she accepted it, Tey could provide that and more for Sisko, Yates, and their daughter.

"I have tremendous regard for Jasmine Tey, both as a security officer and as a person," Asarem said. "She has training and experience, but perhaps just as important, she possesses a dogged determination and an acute insight into criminal behavior." She paused, again wanting to underscore the words that would follow. "She would be a tremendous resource in the efforts to find your daughter."

"I don't understand," Yates said. "If this Agent Tey would be so helpful, why don't you just assign her to the search?"

"When Agent Tey resigned from my security detail, she also stepped away from her professional life," Asarem explained. "She's now a civilian. I have no authority over her. But she hasn't yet taken another position, though I believe that she is looking for an opportunity offworld. For the moment, she's still on Bajor."

Sisko looked at his wife. "What do you think?" he asked.

"I . . . I'm not sure." Yates gazed over at Asarem and then back to her husband. The first minister understood the body language.

"Why don't I give the two of you privacy so you can discuss it?" Asarem said, standing up. "Take your time. I need to check on another issue with my assistant." Without waiting for either Sisko or Yates to reply, she strode across the room and through the door, into the outer office. Enkar looked up from her own desk.

"Is there something you need, Minister?"

"No, thank you, Sirsy," Asarem said, then thought better of it. "Actually, have we received the Agriculture Ministry's report on the soil reclamation project in Zhentu Province?"

"It came in late last night, ma'am," Enkar said. She leaned to her right and nimbly tapped in an access code on one of the drawers in her desk. It responded by popping open, and Enkar pulled out a padd, which she held out to the first minister. "I've already uploaded and indexed it for you."

"Thank you, Sirsy." Asarem took the proffered padd and spent a few moments reviewing its contents. She saw that the soil reclamators recently sent to the northernmost climes of Zhentu had so far had little success in decontaminating the lands there. It discouraged Asarem that, more than a decade past the end of the Occupation, some of the physical damage the Cardassians had done to Bajor remained. Of course, the scars covering the deepest wounds from those times would endure for generations.

When Asarem looked up from the padd, Enkar said, "I should also tell you that Minister Belwan has already arrived for your meeting."

Asarem checked the clock on the wall across from Enkar's desk. "He's early," she said. "Again."

"Yes, ma'am, and this time, he brought Prylar Novor with him," Enkar said. "Theno has shown them to your conference room, and he's . . . keeping them entertained."

Asarem smiled. Another of her aides, Altrine Theno relished such assignments. With an arch sense of humor, he delighted in laying bare the foibles of those in high places. It amazed the first minister that one official or another hadn't demanded that she dismiss him; frankly, for as long as he'd been a member of her staff, it surprised her that *she* hadn't chosen to fire him. "If time in a conference room with Theno, and an audience in Prylar Novor, doesn't teach Minister Belwan not to show up early for our meetings, nothing will."

"I believe you're right, ma'am," Enkar said, matching the first minister's smile with her own.

Just then, the door to Asarem's office skimmed open. The Emissary and his wife stood there. Yates appeared sharper than she had earlier, more *present*. "First Minister," she said, "based on your recommendation, we'd like to enlist the aid of Agent Tey."

"Excellent," Asarem said. "I'll set up a meeting at once." The first minister truly believed that Jasmine Tey would help find Rebecca Sisko. Asarem could only hope that her former protector would agree to join the investigation—and that it wasn't already too late to save the life of the young girl.

And to prevent lasting psychological and emotional damage.

Hyperspanner in hand, Radovan stepped back from the wall and examined his handiwork. It looked like a disaster. The back panel of the replicator and two of the access plates above the materialization shelf had all been removed and set aside, revealing a bewildering welter of technological elements. The control panel for the device had been loosened from its mounts and hung aslant, providing access to an array of isolinear chips and pressure-sensitive pads. Twists of fiber-optic cables spilled down like convoluted waterfalls, descending from the replicator and then climbing back up to connect, reroute, and bypass various components.

Radovan had begun the work the previous evening, after he'd sent Winser away and served the girl dinner. When he initially brought her the meal, she refused to eat, but he professed not to care. He left the tray on his night table, locked the bedroom door again, and went back out into the living area, where he started modifying the replicator.

Later that night, when he checked on the girl, he saw that she'd eaten most of the dinner he'd prepared for her. She'd also fallen asleep on the floor. Beside her lay the child's padd he'd given her, and when he activated it, he saw that she'd drawn several pictures. One clearly depicted the girl with her parents in front of their house, while another showed the three of them with a second man and woman—probably her half brother and his wife.

The third picture drew Radovan's particular interest. It featured a background of trees, with the girl on one side and a much larger figure on the other. Radovan recognized himself. All of the other people in the drawings had brown skin and all but the brother's wife had flat-bridged noses, while his image had been colored with pink flesh and rhinal ridges. In the picture, the girl and Radovan faced each other, but she had sketched a pale yellow circle around herself.

What was she trying to depict? he asked himself. *A force field?* That didn't seem quite right. Did she intend to set herself apart, to assume a special status because of her identity as the Avatar? Even with the girl's place in the beliefs of the Ohalavaru, he didn't think such ideas occupied the mind of a three-and-a-half-year-old.

Radovan set the padd aside and picked the girl up from the floor. She stirred but did not waken. He tucked her into bed without bothering to change her out of her clothes. Then he locked her in and returned to the living area, where he resumed his modifications to the replicator. She called out once, around midnight, and he carried her to the 'fresher. He helped her there, then changed her into her pajamas and put her back to bed. Afterward, Radovan worked on the replicator late into the night, and then continued early that morning. His determination that he needed to take the Avatar out of the city sooner rather than later pushed him to complete the alterations as quickly as possible.

As he stood examining the results of his efforts, Radovan realized that he couldn't be sure of the reliability of illicit blueprints. He'd acquired the plans on the black market, from an Yridian information merchant. They'd looked reasonable to him when he'd first inspected them, but his technological education had come in a related but different area. If he'd been deceived about the modifications, he would be hard-pressed to make his way safely out of the city anytime soon—at least in the way he'd envisioned.

There's no way to find out but to try, Radovan told himself. Hearing his mother's oft-used saying ramble through his mind surprised him. She had reiterated those words again and again throughout his life, haranguing him into doing what she thought best. She'd been wrong so many times, but he had to admit that she'd also often enough been right.

Radovan went to the closet in the short hall just outside his bedroom. He got down on his knees, grabbed up the several pair of shoes he owned, and tossed them into the hall. He then reached into the far corner, to where he kept a heavy, fireproof safe. He kept important documents there: the registration of his birth, his school transcripts, his training documents. *The official report on the accident that killed Jendo,* he thought, recalling how traumatizing it had been to learn of his older brother's death at an ore-processing plant on Dytallix B. He kept his mother's will in there as well—not that she had left him much of anything, and not that he had any reason to hold on to it any longer.

Radovan wrapped his arms around the safe and tried to haul it out of the corner. Already heavy and unwieldy, it did not slide easily across the carpeting on the floor of the closet. Radovan opened the hinged top of the safe, propped it in place, then gripped the top of the near side and jerked the safe toward him. By degrees, he moved it out of his way.

Beneath where the safe had been, Radovan pinched the corner of the carpeting between his thumb and forefinger. He peeled it back to reveal a wood floor below. He pulled a gravity knife from his back pocket, flipped it to its open position, and slid the blade between the floorboards, which he levered upward. After setting the short lengths of wood aside, he closed his knife and slipped it back into his pocket, then reached in and rummaged around the concealed compartment. His hand came back carrying a transparent bag filled with a scanner and a slew of isolinear chips.

Back in the living area of his flat, Radovan spilled the contents of the bag out onto the dining table. He read the coded tags he'd attached to the isolinear chips and selected the one he wanted. Peeking past the control panel, he singled out the slot he had earlier emptied. He pressed the isolinear chip into the opening until it locked in place. Then he studied the control panel, tapped in the appropriate command sequence, and took a step backward to watch the replicator.

Radovan held his breath, concerned that nothing would happen, but almost immediately, he heard a familiar hum. On the replicator shelf, a haze of glittering white light appeared in a long, narrow shape. When the glow faded, Radovan reached for the object left behind.

A roll of thick gray material about half a meter wide, it looked right. Radovan unfurled it on the table, then activated the scanner and analyzed what he had just replicated. Still half expecting to be disappointed, he satisfied himself that the readings actually confirmed the nature of the material—a commodity not typically reproducible by a home replicator.

Radovan fabricated several more rolls of the gray material, then switched out that isolinear chip for another, and then another, and then still more. He replicated various pieces of equipment—technological and otherwise—a collection of chemicals, a small, basic medkit, and multiple sets of ampoules. As each object materialized, he scanned it to ensure its authenticity.

Once he finished replicating what he needed, Radovan moved the equipment and chemicals into the recess beneath the floor, along with the scanner and the proscribed isolinear chips. He then replaced the floorboards, put the carpeting back down, and shoved the safe back into the corner. He felt energized by his efforts, eager to carry on with his plan. He still hadn't deciphered the relevant prophecies in *The Book of Ohalu*—he hadn't even determined which passages referred to him—but he had confidence that he would know what to do when the time came. Based on what had happened with the Ohalavaru and the Emissary on Endalla, and on Radovan's dreams based on those events, he had some vague notion of the shape his deeds would take. Despite lacking certainty, he felt good about his decision to take further action. He had initially planned to keep the girl in his flat until he figured out the next step in his path, but because of Winser's attention, he didn't dare wait.

To continue with his preparations, Radovan would need to retrieve his large antigrav trunk—one of the few items he'd inherited from his mother. He kept it in his storage locker in the basement of his building. He didn't really want to leave the girl alone in his flat, but he would keep the bedroom door locked and he wouldn't be long.

Before leaving his flat and heading downstairs, Radovan pulled out his dual-shafted key. He quietly unlocked the bedroom door and pushed it open so that he could check on the girl. He saw that she remained asleep in a jumble of sheets and blankets.

As Radovan closed the door and relocked it, his mind wandered again to his mother's antigrav trunk. He wondered what she would have thought about one of her own possessions being so intimately involved with the fate of the Avatar. And what would she have made of his participation? Would she have been proud of his contribution to Bajor?

Radovan didn't know, and he told himself that he didn't care. It only mattered that he traverse his path and do what he was meant to do. He turned from the bedroom door and walked back into the living area. He would go downstairs, bring up his antigrav trunk, and prepare it for the journey ahead. He paced to the front door and opened it—

Winser Ellevet stood just outside, one hand raised, about to knock. When she saw him, her face brightened. "You're better," she said. She stood half a dozen or more centimeters shorter than he, though she probably weighed almost as much. Though she had short hair, two clumps of her drab, brown locks tumbled across her forehead and over her eyes.

As Radovan stammered that he still hadn't fully recovered from his illness, Winser bustled inside and past him. He visualized physically stopping her: grabbing her by her upper arms and casting her out of his flat, but he understood that he could not do that. Committing a violent act against Winser risked raising her suspicions, and worse, having her contact law enforcement.

Radovan closed the front door and turned to see Winser standing by his dining table, staring at the modified replicator. "What is this?" she said. He looked at the kludge of mismatched circuitry and components, but then his gaze fell to the surface of the table. There, the medkit he'd replicated lay open, its contents—a hypospray and a medical scanner—sitting beside it. The ampoules, which he intended to load into the kit's empty storage compartment, also sat scattered about the table. He'd left all of it out in case he needed to use the drugs on the girl.

Winser followed the direction of his eyes. She took one of the ampoules and held it up, though she did not look at it closely. "Are you making your own medicine?" she asked. She glanced back at the modified replicator. "Is that what all this is? Bypassing the safeties so you can render your own medication?"

Radovan suddenly imagined throwing Winser not out the front door, but into a wall. He quickly beat that thought back and forced a sheepish smile onto his face. He looked down, as though abashed. "You . . . you won't tell anybody, will you?" He crossed to the table, took the ampoule from her fingers, and placed it in the medkit. "It's just that I was very sick, and I hate doctors." As he spoke, he gathered up the other ampoules and packed them into the kit, along with the hypo and scanner.

"Of course you hate doctors, Tavus," Winser said. She reached out and put her hand on his arm. Radovan forced himself not to flinch away from the intimate gesture. "After everything you went through with your mother, I can understand wanting to keep your distance from the medical profession, just to avoid the emotional associations."

My mother? Radovan thought, startled. *Emotional associations?* He'd never told her anything about his mother's illness . . . unless— *The night she came here.* He'd drunk with her. He knew that the alcohol had taken its toll on him, but he hadn't realized how much. He barely remembered anything from that encounter, other than his massive headache and deep embarrassment.

"You know I won't tell anybody, Tavus," Winser said. She squeezed his arm. "But you have to be careful with something like this." She pointed to the medkit, which he held in one hand. "The laws prohibiting anyone other than medical professionals from replicating drugs exist for good reason. Self-medicating can be dangerous."

"I know, you're right," Radovan said, agreeing with Winser just so that he could get her to leave as quickly as possible. He set the medkit back down on the table, as if by doing so he could distance himself from her criticism. "But I haven't harmed myself, and I am on the mend . . . although I'm really still recovering—"

"Which is why I brought these," she said, holding up three isolinear chips. "I wanted to make you some meals from healthy, restorative recipes my great-grandmother passed down to me." She peered back over her shoulder at the replicator. "If that thing still works."

"Actually, I already ate this morning," Radovan said. "Right now, I just really need to rest." He did his best to hint that she should leave.

"You go right ahead, Tavus." She cocked her head to one side and ran her finger up along his upper arm. "If you want, I can lie down with you."

The indecent suggestion brought Radovan's one night with Winser back in full force. He suddenly felt sick to his stomach. He decided to try to use that to his advantage. "That sounds nice, Ellevet, but I don't want to make you ill," he told her. "I just want to crawl back in bed by myself and get some sleep." Radovan realized that the pillow and bedclothes he'd used the last two nights were still on the sofa. Fortunately, Winser apparently hadn't noticed.

"Oh, you poor dear," she said, and she placed her hand against the side of his face—an expression of affection that further sickened him. "I'll go, but I'll leave these here." Winser set the three isolinear chips she'd brought with her on the table.

"Thank you," Radovan managed to say with no trace of the acrimony he felt. "It was very thoughtful of you to bring those over."

"It's my pleasure," Winser said. "I'm just glad I got to see you, if only for a few minutes." Radovan stepped aside to let her leave, but instead, she glanced down the hall. "Can I just use the 'fresher before I go?"

No, no, no! Just get out! Radovan thought. But he said, "Yes, of course."

Winser headed down the short hall and into the re-fresher. When its door had closed, he quickly moved to the sofa and gathered up the bedclothes and pillow. He carried them to the far end of the living area and shoved them behind a long, low cabinet, where Winser couldn't see them when she came back out.

Radovan shook his head. To that point, he had planned his actions so carefully, but he obviously hadn't taken into account that woman showing up at his flat multiple times. He would have to make it clear to her that he would contact her when he felt better, and that she shouldn't return until he did. She'd already demonstrated that she wouldn't listen, but he hoped it would at least keep her away for the rest of the day—enough time for him to complete his preparations and get out of the city.

Radovan leaned heavily on the cabinet. He hadn't gotten that much sleep, and so he really did feel tired. Maybe once Winser left, he actually should lie down again—

A scraping noise rose behind Radovan . . . like the sound of metal sliding against metal. In the instant before he turned, he knew that, in his eagerness to make his way down to the basement to get his antigrav trunk, he had left the key in his bedroom door. When he pushed off the cabinet and spun around, it felt as though he did so in slow motion. Winser had come out of the 'fresher and unlocked his bedroom door. Had curiosity overcome her? Had she decided to get into his bed despite his stated preference for her to leave? Had she jealously—and errantly—suspected he had another woman in there? Or had the new and powerful lock made her suspicious in another way?

All of those questions flooded through Radovan's mind as he ran across his living area—past the sofa and low table, past the amended replicator and the dining table and chairs, down the short hall between the guest refresher and the closet. Did he call out to Winser, yell at her to stop, to leave his flat at once? He didn't know, and he wouldn't be able to remember later. But he would recall seeing her push the bedroom door open and look inside.

"Who's that?" she asked loudly, and Radovan didn't know if Winser thought an adult woman might be in his bed. She took two steps inside, and by the time he reached her, he saw that the girl was sitting up in bed and peering toward the doorway. "That's—" Winser said, pointing as she turned toward him, but he seized her and threw her to the floor.

Winser shrieked, a sound like the wail of a wounded animal. On the bed, the girl began to scream. "Quiet!" Radovan roared, though it had no effect. He saw Winser trying to scramble up, and he threw himself on top of her, his knee coming down hard in the small of her back. She grunted and collapsed back to the floor as he realized he had the medkit in his hand. He must have snatched it from the table as he ran past.

Beneath Radovan, Winser struggled to throw him off and get back up. He opened the medkit, grabbed the hypospray, then fumbled his way through the ampoules to find the right one. He finally snapped one into place and pressed the hypo to the side of Winser's neck. Radovan heard its sibilant hiss, and in just seconds, her body went limp. She fell face-first back to the floor.

Behind him, the girl's screams had stopped, reduced to heaving sobs. Radovan clambered to his feet and walked over to the bed. "Be quiet," he said in a tone that sounded surprisingly calm, even to himself. The girl looked up at him, but she continued to cry. "I just put her to sleep," Radovan tried to reassure her. "She'll be all right when she wakes up."

The girl just stared at him.

Radovan went back over to where Winser lay facedown on the floor. He regarded her for a few silent moments, attempting to figure out exactly what to do with her. He found the slight movements of her body as she breathed hypnotic.

Finally, Radovan positioned himself at her head, where he reached down and took hold of her under her arms. He lifted the upper portion of her body off the floor and scampered awkwardly backward. He dragged her out into the hall and set her down. Stepping over her unconscious form, he returned to the bedroom and looked in at the girl. "I'll be back in a few minutes with some breakfast for you." He pulled the door closed, locked it, and pocketed the key.

Then Radovan did what he had to do.

Gamma Quadrant, 2386

S eated in the command chair, bathed in the blood-red tint of alert lighting, Rogeiro felt the sheer power of *Robinson* as the ship soared deeper into the star system. A cocoon of plangent sound and vibration sheathed the bridge, accompanying the transformation of the crew from stranded survivors to unshackled liberators. *Robinson* sprinted ahead at warp speed, despite traveling *into* a planetary system and not out of it, but the first officer had confidence in Sivadeki's ability to safely navigate the inherent dangers.

In just minutes, the ship descended from the Kuiper belt to the inner system and decelerated to sublight velocity. The softer, steadier rhythms of the impulse engines replaced those of the warp drive as *Robinson* hied toward the strange world the crew had discovered. Uteln confirmed the shields active and the weapons at full power, while Plante verified all of the ship's transporters on standby.

"Approaching target," Sivadeki said from the conn. "Sixty seconds out."

"Let's see it," Rogeiro said. On the main viewer, the distant smudge in its center suddenly filled the screen. The object more or less described a spherical square in space, with its inhabitants occupying the perpetually sunlit bowl of its inner side.

"Sensors have detected all the children," Plante said. "They are still assembled in three separate groups." Her fingers marched rapidly across the ops panel, which issued a corresponding series of cheeps and tweets that sounded almost like a song. "Targeting the transporters. I'm prepared to lock on and beam them up as soon as we're in range." Plante had rerouted the control systems of every transporter aboard *Robinson* to the operations console, where she could manage them collectively. She would beam up all of the children at once.

"Commander, we're being scanned," Uteln reported. "A squadron of ships already airborne within the atmosphere is altering course to intercept." Without the first officer having to issue an order, Plante adjusted the main screen again. A magnified view showed a dozen or more vessels streaking up from the Dyson section. Many of the ships looked familiar to Rogeiro from the first attack on *Robinson*, with no two of them identical.

"Thirty seconds to transporter range," Sivadeki said.

"Lay down covering fire above the null space," the first officer said. Nobody on the bridge had expected their gambit to go unnoticed or the unusual world to go undefended. "Phasers and quantum torpedoes, continuous discharge in random patterns." Rogeiro stood up as the feedback tones of the tactical console confirmed the sustained launch of *Robinson*'s weapons.

Plante again adjusted the image on the main screen, which pulled back to show a wider view. Multiple filaments of destructive yellow-red energy shot from the bow the ship. Glistering blue-white shells joined the fusillade. Rogeiro stepped forward to stand beside Sivadeki at the helm. "Evasive maneuvers," he told her. "You need to find us ten point one seconds."

"No return fire yet," Uteln said. "Their ships are still crossing the null space surrounding their world."

"Be ready when they reenter the normal continuum," Rogeiro said. The *Robinson* crew had already seen that phasers and quantum torpedoes failed in null space, but if the advancing vessels possessed similar energy weapons, the aliens would doubtless employ those armaments once they reached normal space.

Rogeiro studied the main viewscreen and watched the enemy ships approaching. Ahead of them, *Robinson*'s phaser beams swept irregularly through the void, dying as they reached null space. The quantum torpedoes—programmed to detonate at random, but prior to leaving the normal continuum—exploded in brilliant flashes of light.

"We're in range," Sivadeki said.

"The first ships are entering normal space," Uteln said. As though to punctuate the development, a blue beam shot from the lead vessel and slammed into *Robinson*. The ship trembled in response.

"Commencing evasive maneuvers," Sivadeki said. The view of the vessels and the Dyson section behind them slipped away on the main screen as *Robinson* changed course.

"Minimal damage to the shields," Uteln said. "Their weapons are laser based—about a third as powerful as our phasers." They apparently didn't want to use their space-time weapon so close to their world, which the captain had anticipated. The ship shook again as another shot landed.

"How many hits can we take with the shields down?" Rogeiro wanted to know.

"Before the ship sustains serious damage?" Uteln said. "That depends on the placement of the strikes and how many we take at once. It could be as many as ten or twelve, maybe as few as six or eight."

Rogeiro made the decision in less time than it took to give the order. "Do it now."

Uteln responded at once. "Shields are down."

"Energizing transporters," Plante said.

Just ten seconds, Rogeiro thought, and he counted out, *One.* In that instant, two blasts struck *Robinson* in rapid succession, and then a moment later, a third.

"More of the vessels have exited null space and opened fire," Uteln explained.

Two.

At the conn, Sivadeki's hands moved with impressive speed, but with so many enemy ships, *Robinson* had only so many routes open to it. In his head, the first officer continued counting: *Three . . . Four.* Another blast landed, and then another hit especially hard, throwing Rogeiro forward. He fell to the deck in front of the main viewscreen.

"Simultaneous hits on the port nacelle," Uteln called out.

Five.

Rogeiro climbed back to his feet and peered over the conn at Sivadeki. "Protect the port nacelle."

"Aye, sir," Sivadeki said, even as she operated her controls, directing the ship on a winding path through space.

Six.

Robinson quaked again, and then multiple blasts hammered the ship one after another.

Rogeiro stumbled again and slipped down to his knees. A tremendous din filled the bridge. It sounded as though the ship would fly apart at any moment.

Seven.

"Another hit on the port nacelle and two on the starboard," Uteln said, shouting to be heard. "Three strikes on the impulse cowling."

They're targeting our drive systems, Rogeiro thought, and then: *Eight.*

But then somebody else yelled, "Raise the shields!" It took Rogeiro a second to realize that it had been Plante. He could not recall ever hearing her countermand an order.

"Shields up," Uteln called out, following the second officer's command. *Robinson* immediately took more weapons fire, but the defensive screens easily withstood the assault.

"Commander," Plante said to Rogeiro as he staggered back up, "the transporters can't function across null space. I tried twice to beam up the children, but the dematerialization sequence failed both times."

"Understood," Rogeiro said. He then addressed Sivadeki. "Get us out of here," he said. "Best possible speed." The first officer quickly strode between the conn and ops, making his way back to the command chair. "Uteln," he said, "get me the captain."

Sisko acknowledged the coded message with one of his own, which he and his first officer had decided upon before embarking on their two-pronged rescue mission. The captain had anticipated the failure of the transporter across null space, and so he and his crew had formulated a backup plan. While *Robinson* dove into the planetary system to attempt to beam the children to safety, the ship's two runabouts, *Acheron* and *Styx*, followed at a distance and headed for the far side of the Dyson section.

Sisko closed the channel, then looked to the woman seated beside him at the main console of *Styx*. "Go," he told her. Ensign Anissa Weil reached forward and tapped a series of control surfaces in rapid sequence.

"Engaging thermal conduits," Weil said. "Signaling the *Acheron* to do the same." Olive skinned, with short black hair, dark brown eyes, and a hawk nose, the ensign served aboard *Robinson* as an engineer, though she also had considerable experience as a pilot. She had helped install heating elements along the undersides of the two runabouts' warp nacelles.

Robinson's run past the inhabited surface of the Dyson section had served not only as an attempt to rescue the children, but as a distraction should that attempt prove unsuccessful. With Lieutenant Stannis at the conn of *Acheron* and Sisko piloting *Styx*, the two officers took the runabouts to the artificial world's convex, dark side. They each maneuvered their vessel to exit the normal continuum with the landing pads facing down. Momentum carried *Acheron* and *Styx* through null space until they settled with a thud beside each other on the far surface of the Dyson section.

In addition to adding improvised heating elements, the crew had installed emergency evacuation modules in the runabouts. The preconfigured compartments included high-capacity transporters and accommodation for scores of passengers. If the *Robinson* crew couldn't beam the children across the gulf of null space, Sisko had figured, he would solve that problem by using the runabouts to cross the inert region and land directly on the odd world.

Once the two vessels had alit, the transporter officers—Crewman Stokar aboard *Acheron*, and Crewwoman Jentzen Spingeld on *Styx*—had scanned for the children, but sensors had been unable to penetrate through the dense metal core of the Dyson section to the populated side. That meant that the away teams would have to bring the runabouts closer. Knowing that might be necessary, Uteln had already devised a covert means of doing so.

With word from Rogeiro that the *Robinson* crew's attempt had failed, Sisko took the next step in their secondary plan. An ice sheet kilometers deep covered the dark side of the Dyson section. Lieutenant sh'Vrane theorized that the frozen expanse functioned as part of the artificial world's hydrologic cycle, acting essentially as a fresh-water ocean, to which water was added and frozen, and from which it was melted and retrieved. Uteln's scans revealed a series of large tubes running between the inner and outer surfaces, a majority of them utilized to deliver water through filtration systems to the frozen side for purification and storage, and the rest used to return water to the inhabited side for use.

"The ice is melting beneath both runabouts," Weil said as she monitored the sensors. "It shouldn't take long before—" *Styx* suddenly shifted, not as though it had dropped in the thaw below it, but as though something had struck the hull. "It's the interface at the edge of null space. The runabout is reentering the normal continuum." Like *Robinson* when it had been stranded, the Dyson section existed on an island of ordinary space, surrounded by nothingness. Once *Acheron* and *Styx* fully left the inert region, their crews could once again make use of their weapons.

Sisko turned in his chair to face the other five members of his away team. Along with Spingeld on the transporter, that included *Robinson*'s chief medical officer and three security officers: Lieutenant Harris Rogers, who crewed the weapons panel, along with Ensigns Rita Bevelaqua and Grandal. "When the runabout fully exits null space, I'll reorient the *Styx* to travel into the ice, toward the opening of the tube," the captain said. "The *Acheron* will be right behind us. Use low-yield phasers on a wide-dispersion to liquefy the ice ahead of us, until we reach the tube and liquid water. If we encounter any structures inside the tube that we can't navigate past, use the sensors to determine if we can cut or blast our way through, although our preference is to remain hidden. Our goal is to reach a point where we can lock on to the children on scans and beam them all back to the runabouts."

Styx shuddered again.

"The runabouts are back in normal space," Weil said.

Sisko spun back to the main console and gazed through the forward ports, which sloped inward from the bow of the vessel. Directly ahead, filling three-quarters of the view, stood a wall of ice. Above it stretched a star-speckled span of the Gamma Quadrant night. The captain brought the impulse engines back online, then used the thrusters to alter the direction of *Styx*. The runabout rose and then pitched forward. The stars vanished, leaving the ship facing a wall of ice. "Fire phasers," Sisko said.

"Firing phasers," replied Lieutenant Rogers.

Twin cones of reddish-yellow light fanned out from the runabout's bow and merged in a broad circle on the ice, which immediately began to melt. Sisko pushed *Styx* forward. The runabout entered the water, phasers still ablaze.

"The *Acheron* is directly behind us," Weil said.

As the two runabouts burrowed deeper into the ice sheet, the melting point of the frozen water marginally decreased with the rising pressure—approximately three four-hundredths of a degree per atmosphere of pressure, a distinction without a practical difference. Leading the way, *Styx* made slow but steady progress through the enormous glaciated mass. Piloting the runabout, Sisko ensured that he remained on course for the outer opening of the tube they had chosen to traverse, which emerged on the inner side of the Dyson section at the bottom of a massive lake, closer than any of the other tubes to the three locations of the children.

Eventually, they reached the outer surface of the artificial world and entered the tube, the runabout's phasers still firing. The ice continued to melt beneath the assault, until it eventually gave way to liquid water inside the tube. Beyond that point, sensors picked out a series of sieve-like structures, each increasingly finer. They had clearly been designed to prevent rogue chunks of ice or other solid material from advancing through the tube. Lieutenant Rogers used the *Styx*'s phasers to carve out holes in the filters large enough to allow the runabouts passage.

Much of the center length of the tube contained no obstructions, and *Acheron* and *Styx* made swift progress. At the other end, Rogers once again had to use phasers to slice through a series of filters. Finally, the two runabouts emerged on the inner surface of the Dyson section. The captain set *Styx* down on the bottom of the lake, and *Acheron* landed beside it. Outside the ports, a blackness deeper than space prevailed.

"Report," Sisko said. Sensors had failed to penetrate to the inner side of the Dyson section during the entire journey through the tube.

"Scans show all eighty-seven of the children," Spingeld replied. "They are still separated into three groups."

Sisko worked the controls on the main console to open a tightly focused, short-range, scrambled channel to the second runabout. "*Styx* to *Acheron*."

"*This is Stannis,*" came the immediate response. "*Go ahead, Captain.*"

"We've got all of the children on sensors, at three different sites," Sisko said. "Do you?"

"*Crewman Stokar reports that we do, Captain,*" Stannis said. The lieutenant spoke with the deep, ragged voice common to many Corvallen men.

"Crewwoman Spingeld will transmit the coordinates of one of the sites," Sisko said. "On my order, Crewman Stokar will beam up the children from that location, while we beam up the others."

"*Understood.*"

The captain glanced over his shoulder at Spingeld, a petite human with dark, wavy hair. She set to operating her panel, and after a moment, she nodded. "Coordinates sent," Sisko said.

"We've got them," Stannis confirmed. *"Crewman Stokar is targeting the* Acheron's *transporter."* The lieutenant paused, then said, *"We're ready, Captain."*

"Energize," Sisko said.

The captain had graduated the Academy and begun active duty with Starfleet more than three decades earlier; he had served aboard half a dozen starships and as the commander of the most important space station in the Alpha Quadrant; he'd conducted espionage on Romulus, and fought in the Tzenkethi and Dominion Wars, as well as during the Borg Invasion. His first wife had died aboard a starship where he held the position of first officer. Yet with all of that time in uniform, the experience that stood out at that moment took Sisko back to Deep Space 9, to when a Pah-wraith had taken over the body of his son to do battle against a Prophet. He had allowed the confrontation to take place when he could have stopped it—worse, in the service of Bajor's future, he had *wanted* it. Jake had survived the ordeal and immediately professed his understanding for what his father had done, but Sisko had never forgiven himself. His son had told him he had done the right thing, but in the years since, that had seemed irrelevant. Sisko's first duty lay neither with Starfleet nor with the Bajoran people; he had come to belief that, as a father who had brought two children into the universe, he owned no greater obligation than to the well-being of his son and daughter. Rebecca had been taken from him and Kasidy once before, and they had been fortunate to get her back. Losing Jennifer had almost killed him; losing his daughter would. He needed for the transporter to pluck Rebecca and the other children from the bizarre world to which they had been taken and deposit them aboard *Acheron* and *Styx.*

But then Spingeld looked over at him with an expression that told him that wasn't going to happen. "Captain, the children are visible on sensors, but it's impossible to establish a transporter lock on them," she said. "There is equipment at each location that I can't identify, and it's interfering with the carrier wave."

"Crewman Stokar confirms the same results, Captain," Stannis said.

Sisko thought of his daughter and all the other children, frightened after being ripped from their home by unknown beings and taken to an unfamiliar place. He thought of his wife and the other parents, and he knew how they felt. He would not let them down.

"Break out the weapons," Sisko told the two away teams. "If we can't beam the children out, then we'll have to go and get them."

Bajor, 2380

With Ben next to her, Kasidy marched alongside the top-floor railing of the three-story residential building. The staccato beat of their shoes clacking along the hard-surfaced walkway trailed them like a dog nipping at their heels—except that she would have preferred an animal chasing them to the heartache actually in pursuit. It had not quite been two full days since Rebecca had gone missing, but it might as well have been two weeks or two months or two years; Kasidy felt her daughter's absence as a physical sensation, as though her body had somehow been drained of that which formed her identity, as though she had been emptied out and the inside of her leftover shell scraped clean.

Although the sun had risen high in a mostly clear sky, the afternoon carried an autumnal chill. Kasidy fastened her light jacket against the cool air. She wished that she had worn something heavier when they'd left the house.

I'm lucky it occurred to me to put on any sort of a coat at all, she told herself.

Since Rebecca's disappearance, Kasidy had spared few thoughts for anything but her daughter's safe return. It troubled her to be away from home for the second time that day, after she and Ben had earlier met with Asarem Wadeen. Kasidy had confidence that if the Bajoran Militia found Rebecca, or if they learned anything, or if they required additional information, Major Orisin would let her and Ben know at once. Still, it felt wrong to be out of the house, as though it made their daughter's return less likely—as though being at home provided a beacon for Rebecca to follow, to find her way out of the wasteland. Kasidy understood that such a notion made no sense: their daughter had yet to reach the age of four; Rebecca would not return on her own—somebody would have to find her and bring her back.

After meeting with the first minister that morning, Kasidy and Ben had gone back home to discover a message waiting for them. Prior to that, they had wrestled with whether or not to contact Jake and his wife to let them know about what had happened. The young couple had recently traveled across the quadrant to Milvonia III so that Rena could study for a season under the tutelage of Deniskar Treyna, a painter she admired. Kasidy and Ben hadn't wanted to disrupt that experience, but they believed that Jake and Rena would want to know about Rebecca's abduction. Ben had tried to reach his son, but had ended up having to leave a message of his own.

After their visit to Ashalla to see Asarem, Kasidy and Ben found that Jake had attempted to contact them in their absence. He told them that Rena was busily making arrangements for their immediate journey back to Bajor. It would take them days to make their way home—arriving after Rebecca had been safely recovered, Jake was sure—but he and Rena wanted to be there. They sent their love and would reach out again during their trip.

Ben stopped three-quarters of the way along the building and pointed to the door there, set back from the walk inside a gated patio. Kasidy saw from the unit ID on the door—*A13*—that they had reached their destination. She glanced to one side, over the railing and down, at the large, hexagonal park on which fronted the six buildings of the Delisa Gardens housing complex. The waters of a fountain danced in elaborate patterns at the center of the greensward, while a playground occupied one corner, and a set of picnic tables another. Several tall trees, their remaining leaves a blend of fall colors, bordered the park, while numerous low bushes, their flowers gone, dotted the landscape. Kasidy saw only a few people about, doubtless a consequence of summer's recent departure.

Ben pushed open the gate and held it ajar for his wife, who preceded him onto the patio. An outdoor table and chairs stood to one side in front of a window, but Kasidy saw nothing else: no plants or jardinières, no adornments on the walls, no signs at all of recent use. It made her suspicious and reinforced her feeling that they shouldn't have bothered making the trip to the purlieus of Ashalla.

As her husband touched the welcome panel next to the hunter-green door, Kasidy rubbed her hands up and down along her upper arms, trying to warm herself. She regarded Ben and realized that she expected him to offer her his coat, or to put his arms around her, but he didn't appear to notice her discomfort. He simply stared at the door.

His mind is elsewhere, Kasidy thought. Her husband's inattention might have bothered her if she hadn't understood it. *He's thinking about Rebecca too.*

Kasidy wondered if Ben had considered her role in their daughter's disappearance—if he *resented* her for it. *Does he blame me?* She knew that he wouldn't, that she had not been negligent in her care of Rebecca, but the victim of a horrible crime. And yet the truth of that hadn't prevented Kasidy from condemning herself for what had happened.

The door opened, revealing a slim young woman, about Kasidy's height. She had light-brown skin and Asian features, which included a wide, flat nose. Her straight dark hair spilled down past her shoulders and curled inward, and the commas of her well-defined eyebrows perfectly crowned her deep-brown eyes. She wore tan slacks, with a black belt and a loose white blouse. A simple gold bracelet circled one wrist. Kasidy thought her lovely.

"Captain Yates, Captain Sisko," the woman greeted them. "I'm Jasmine Tey. Won't you please come in?" She moved aside, allowing Kasidy and Ben to enter.

Inside, they stepped into a small parlor, decorated sparingly. Covered in white patterned fabrics, a love seat and a pair of undersize easy chairs filled the area. A couple of nondescript little tables sat scattered about, while a few mundane paintings hung on the walls. Plain white curtains covered the front window, which looked out on the patio.

It hasn't been decorated sparingly, Kasidy realized. *It's been furnished to make it* appear *that somebody unexceptional lives here.*

Tey followed them into the room and gestured through a wide archway to the adjoining space, where four tall chairs sat around a rattan-topped pedestal table. A tea set had been laid out on a tray atop it. "I just made a pot of *deka* tea," Tey said. "May I pour you a cup?"

"Yes, thank you," Ben said.

They followed as Tey walked into the dining area and reached for the teapot. "Captain Yates?" the young woman asked.

"Kasidy and Ben will do," Kasidy said. It always felt odd to her to be called by her position when not aboard ship, and Ben hadn't been active in Starfleet in more than four years. "Nothing for me, thank you."

Kasidy knew better than to judge an individual solely by their appearance, but under the circumstances, she couldn't help comparing Tey to what she and Ben had been told about her. A human, she had a modest frame and a demure bearing, and she looked even younger than her twenty-eight years. Kasidy had trouble imagining her working in security or law enforcement, much less as the formidable, highly experienced figure about whom the first minister had spoken.

They all climbed onto the tall chairs at the table. Tey placed a cup of tea before Ben and another in front of herself. Kasidy watched her husband take a jumja cube from an open bowl and stir it into his tea. She thought only that she wanted to end their visit as quickly as possible and get back to their house.

"I don't know what the first minister's told you," Ben said, "but she thought you might be able to help us."

"Minister Asarem contacted me after she spoke with you this morning," Tey said quickly and without inflection. "She asked me if I would be willing, as a personal favor to her, to assist in an investigation. When I agreed that I would, she reinstated my security clearance, and I was invited to the provincial Militia headquarters in Renassa. There, I was informed about the situation and received a full briefing on your daughter's abduction."

Kasidy stared at Tey—not because of what she had just said, but because of how she had said it. Until that moment, the young woman had behaved with a mannerly deference and an unaffected politeness. With just a few statements and a shift in her comportment, Tey commanded the room.

"We're grateful for your willingness to help," Ben said, "though I'm not sure what more you can do than Major Orisin and his people."

"I understand that Major Orisin has suggested you consider going public about the abduction," Tey said. "I would counsel against that." She seemed very sure of herself. Even though Kasidy agreed with her conclusion, she wanted to hear her justification.

"Why?" Kasidy asked.

"The kidnapper employed great care in taking Rebecca. His efforts involved considerable planning and split-second timing," Tey explained. "That indicates that he is unlikely to risk being caught by taking her to a public place. Announcing the abduction would therefore offer no reward, but it could potentially anger or pressure the kidnapper."

"You're saying 'kidnapper,'" Ben noted. "Singular."

"And using masculine pronouns," Kasidy added.

"A lone male likely perpetrated this crime," Tey said. "Most likely middle-aged, probably single and poorly socialized, with emotional problems." She offered no explanation for her conclusions, but Kasidy understood that Tey based her reasoning on her training and experience. Despite her youthful and unimposing appearance, she suddenly seemed older than her actual age.

"So if we shouldn't make the abduction public, then what do you think we should do?" Ben asked. "Wait for the kidnapper's demands?"

"There isn't going to be a ransom," Tey said. Again, she sounded sure of herself. Her opinion worried Kasidy, who glanced over at her husband. She saw her concern mirrored on Ben's face.

"If the kidnapper didn't abduct Rebecca so that he could make demands, then what is his motive?" Kasidy asked. "And how does that affect the chances of getting our daughter back?"

"The question of why Rebecca has been taken is of critical importance," Tey said. "Because of your daughter's significance to the followers of Ohalu, I agree with the consensus that there is likely a religious motive behind the abduction—either on the part of an Ohalavaru hoping to validate or fulfill those beliefs, or by a traditional adherent wanting to refute or obstruct them. But I also think that's only one part of the explanation."

"What other reason could somebody have?" Kasidy asked.

"It's not necessarily about reason," Tey said. "The kidnapper is probably deeply troubled. So much so that it's even possible that he selected Rebecca at random, although I think it more likely that she was taken specifically and deliberately, in the service of some unknown end."

Kasidy physically recoiled in her chair. "'Some unknown end,'" she echoed. The phrase evoked terrible possibilities. "What does that mean?"

"It only means that we don't know for what purpose your daughter was taken," Tey said. "If not at random and not for ransom, then it probably has to do, at least in part, with Rebecca's alleged place in the belief system of the Ohalavaru as the Avatar. I began rereading the Ohalu texts this afternoon, in search of any potential goal somebody might have that would be aided by kidnapping your daughter."

"*Re*reading?" Ben said. "Are *you* an Ohalavaru?"

"I do not subscribe to any religious system—Bajoran, human, or otherwise," Tey said. "I intend no offense, Mister Sisko."

"I take no offense," Ben said. "So then you're an atheist."

"I am," Tey said. "I believe that there are powerful and remarkable beings in the universe, but I don't think that any of them are gods, or that there is some existential 'creator.'"

It pleased Kasidy to hear that. If Rebecca had been abducted for religious reasons, somebody invested in those belief systems could allow their personal biases to cloud their view of the investigation. Of course, a majority of Bajorans hewed to the divinity of the Prophets—including, more than likely, most of those working to locate Rebecca.

"I first studied *The Book of Ohalu* not long after it was rediscovered during the archaeological excavation of B'hala," Tey continued. "At the time, I was a member of the security detail assigned to protect the first minister. It was therefore incumbent upon me to research the Ohalavaru in order to assess any potential threat they could pose to Minister Asarem."

"Did you find anything?" Kasidy asked. "I mean, when you reread the texts today?"

"It buttressed my opinion that the kidnapper does not intend to make any demands—of the two of you as parents, of Mister Sisko as the Emissary, or of the kai," Tey said. "I also concluded that he does not intend to return Rebecca."

"What?!" Kasidy said. The idea horrified her. From the moment Rebecca had disappeared from her side, Kasidy had been consumed by concern for her daughter's safety. But the prospect of Rebecca surviving her ordeal but never coming home spoke to another fear—namely, that Kasidy would never see her daughter again.

"Actually, such a motivation could work to our benefit," Tey said. "I believe that the kidnapper is an Ohalavaru, and that he wants Rebecca to satisfy her prophesied destiny as the Avatar, perhaps hoping to raise her to take on that role when she reaches adulthood. If that's the case, it would mean that he intends her no physical harm." Kasidy understood Tey's reasoning, but it didn't address the psychological and emotional damage Rebecca could suffer while in the clutches of the kidnapper. "With the security measures that the Militia has put in place, it will be very difficult for him to take your daughter off Bajor," Tey went on. "That means the only thing we need to do is find her."

"You make it sound easy," Ben said, more than a wisp of disapproval in his tone.

"It will not be easy," Tey replied. "But I will not give up in the search for your daughter."

Kasidy appreciated the former security agent's avowal, not least of all because it fell short of those others had made. Colonel Jalas, Major Orisin, the first minister, even Ben, had all proclaimed that they *would* find Rebecca and bring her home. Tey made no such promise, pledging only to continue working toward that goal. The honesty of that oath, though it failed to guarantee what Kasidy most wanted, somehow encouraged her. It made Tey seem as though she understood the situation better than the others—better, even, than Ben—and so her declaration never to abandon her efforts to find Rebecca provided hope.

Still, Kasidy wanted something more concrete. "What makes you think the kidnapper won't harm our daughter?" she asked.

"There is a passage in *The Book of Ohalu* that I believe supports that view," Tey said. She raised her hands from her lap, revealing that she held a Bajoran padd. Kasidy had not seen her carrying it when Tey had greeted them at the door, nor had she seen it on the table. The young woman also wore civilian clothing that did not appear to contain any pockets or pouches capable of carrying the device, which made its appearance feel like a magic trick.

"It occurs eighty percent of the way through the text, in a chapter titled 'Progress,'" Tey continued. She tapped at the device, then turned it around so that Kasidy and Ben could see its display. Words marched down the screen in Old Bajoran. Kasidy could not read the ancient tongue, though she had seen it enough to recognize it from its similarity to the current form of the language. Indeed, the characters of the chapter heading bore enough resemblance to modern Bajoran that she read it as the word *Progres*.

Tey turned the padd back to herself and operated it.

"The passage reads, 'She shall know departure as arrival, and through her journey, the future shall unfold as an era of grace and love. The many paths must diverge again and again, yet there is but one way ahead: through her *shebbe toth*.'" She showed the display to Kasidy and Ben again. The words had all been translated into Federation Standard, but for the final phrase that Tey had read.

"'*Shebbe toth*,'" Ben repeated. "That roughly translates as 'agony of maturity.'"

"Agony?" Kasidy said. The word sent a jolt through her.

"That is one way to read it," Tey agreed. "It's how I read it. It carries a connotation different from what you might think."

"If I remember my idiomatic Old Bajoran, it refers to puberty," Ben said. "To the often awkward and difficult process of moving from childhood to adulthood."

"Yes," Tey said.

"And that makes you think that an Ohalavaru took Rebecca so that he could ensure she grows up," Kasidy asked.

"So that she can then achieve her prophesied destiny as the Avatar of Peace," Tey said.

"Why hasn't anybody on the Militia's investigative team told us this?" Kasidy wanted to know.

"Probably because, although I'm sure they've studied the Ohalu texts in the last two days, none of them arrived at the same conclusion."

"Why not?" Ben asked.

"For two reasons," Tey said. "First, because there is no explicit mention of the Avatar in this chapter. It is therefore a matter of some debate as to whom these passages refer. The prevailing belief is that it is an allusion to the spiritual leader of the people. Militia officers studying *The Book of Ohalu* would know that and probably agree."

"Then why should we accept your version?" Kasidy

asked. She discovered that, because Tey had been so impressive, she wanted to trust her.

"Because of my training and experience in criminal profiling," Tey said. Kasidy didn't see the connection between a set of ancient writings and attempting to get inside the mind-set of a kidnapper, but then Tey explained it. "It's actually unimportant how I read the passage. What matters is how the man who took Rebecca reads it."

Kasidy and Ben looked at each other. She could see her husband trying to gauge the value of Tey's opinions. Finally, he asked, "What's the other reason the Militia haven't reached the same conclusions as you?"

"Because of the final phrase," Tey said. "In the original text, it is written as one word—*shebbetoth*—but there is no such word in Old Bajoran. Almost all current translations render it as *sheb betoth*, rather than as *shebbe toth*."

"Of course," Ben said. He appeared to understand Tey's argument, though he did not seem particularly pleased by it. "But I have to ask why we should trust your interpretation over the consensus of scholars."

"As I mentioned, what I think doesn't matter," Tey said. "It's what the kidnapper thinks." Ben nodded, evidently accepting that answer.

"But wait," Kasidy said. "What is the usual translation? What does *sheb betoth* mean?"

"It means *sacrifice*," Tey said.

Once more, Kasidy felt as though an electric shock passed through her body. "You're telling us that the kidnapper has interpreted the Ohalu texts as meaning that he has to make sure Rebecca reaches adulthood, but also that he might think he needs to—?" Kasidy forced herself to say, "Sacrifice her."

"Yes, that's possible," Tey said. "But if the kidnapper is Ohalavaru and has taken your daughter in order to validate his beliefs, and if he has emotional issues—all of which I believe is the case—he will seek to draw out his experience with the Avatar as long as he can. He will want to inflate his importance to the cause. Even if he reads the passage as 'sacrifice' instead of as 'agony of maturity,' he will delay the outcome of his efforts so that he can inhabit the role of hero as long as possible. That will give us time to find him before any permanent harm comes to Rebecca."

Kasidy wanted Tey's assertions to be true, and for that reason, she didn't trust herself to judge the security specialist's conclusions. "I want to believe what you're saying, but I don't know if I can."

"Fortunately, there's no need for you to do so," Tey said. If Kasidy's doubt insulted her, she gave no sign. "If I was the only person searching for your daughter, it would matter. But I'm not. Major Orisin and his teams—scores of people—are also trying to locate Rebecca, taking multiple tacks. Frankly, I'd be content to discover that my conclusions are completely wrong and for Major Orisin to find your daughter in the next five minutes. But until she is found, I'm going to use my instincts and experience to follow wherever the evidence leads me."

"How are you going to proceed?" Ben asked. "You said that your security clearance has been reinstated, but we know that you resigned your position in the Bajoran government, so what authority do you have to actually conduct an investigation?"

Kasidy expected Tey to balk at being asked to detail her renewed credentials, especially just after having her conclusions questioned. Instead, she said, "Per the first minister's request, Minister Menvel this afternoon appointed me as an at-large investigator." Menvel Swee, Kasidy knew, served as the head of Bajor's Ministry of Justice. "Overgeneral Manos then officially requested my attachment to the

Militia and assigned me to assist in the search for Rebecca. I report directly to the commandant, so I have a great deal of autonomy, along with full access to the resources of the Militia. I have already been in touch with Major Orisin to coordinate my efforts with those of his teams, in order to ensure that there will be no duplications of effort."

"What will your first step be?" Ben asked.

Tey blinked, hesitating for just a second. "I have already taken quite a few steps, Mister Sisko," she said. "By learning the details of Rebecca's abduction, by being briefed on the actions of the Militia, by examining the Ohalu texts." She did not sound angry or even annoyed to have her methods scrutinized, but she did appear eager to get on with those methods. "My *next* step will be to ask you and Ms. Yates some questions."

Ben gazed at Kasidy, as though to appraise her willingness to revisit everything that had happened. Kasidy looked to Tey. "Please," she told the young woman, "tell us what you need to know."

For the next hour, Kasidy and Ben sat with Tey and gave her answers. Some of the woman's questions trod the same ground as those posed by Major Orisin and his investigative teams, but then she would focus on issues and details different from what the Militia personnel had. Where Orisin had asked about any other patrons Kasidy might have seen in Rozahn Kather's gallery the afternoon of the abduction, Tey wanted to know about her experience in the art shop— what she'd looked at, what she'd said to the owner, and the like. Where the major had questioned her about whether or not she'd followed a routine during her visits with Rebecca to Adarak, Tey wanted to know about the experience of that particular visit—how comfortable the temperature had been, whether she and Rebecca had enjoyed anything in particular, those sorts of things. Kasidy initially thought the interrogation inexpert, even clumsy, to the point where she considered calling it to a halt. Eventually, though, she came to understand that by asking such personal and subjective queries, Tey managed to construct a different but still accurate picture of what had transpired on that terrible day.

Kasidy and Ben also responded to questions about how the people in and around Adarak had treated them over the prior year. They spoke about the house fire that had taken the lives of their friends Calan and Audj. Tey also asked about Ben's standing as the Emissary, and about the nature of his recent experiences in that context. He explained that, while the people of Bajor still regarded him as holding that role, he had begun to feel otherwise. Only once in recent times had Ben explicitly acted in that capacity: during the Ohalavaru occupation of Endalla.

The information appeared to pique Tey's interest. She explained that, while she'd heard about the incident, she didn't know much about it. At the time, she'd recently resigned her position in the Bajoran government and had taken a trip back to Kuala Lumpur in her native Malaysia on Earth. "So you traveled to Endalla to speak with the Ohalavaru there specifically as the Emissary of the Prophets?" Tey asked.

"Yes, based on the request of Captain Vaughn, whose starship crew first discovered the Ohalavaru presence on the moon," Ben said. "He had already confronted them on the surface of Endalla, but he'd failed to remove them. He believed that my presence there, both as the Emissary and as the father of the Avatar, might help influence the Ohalavaru to leave peaceably."

"Did you identify yourself in those ways?" Tey asked.

"No, but I didn't have to," Ben said. "Rejias Norvan, the leader of the Ohalavaru group on Endalla, addressed me as 'Emissary.'"

"But not as the father of the Avatar?" Tey asked.

"No, but they all certainly knew my identity," Ben said.

"Did that help de-escalate the situation?"

"It's difficult to know," Ben said. "Everything on Endalla happened rapidly. I think my presence could have had an impact on some of those present, but not on Rejias Norvan, the Ohalavaru leader there. He did not seem stable."

Tey regarded Ben quietly for a moment, obviously considering what he'd said. "Major Orisin has ordered his people to search for any possible links between Rejias and the abduction," she said. "He's sent investigators to question the families, friends, and colleagues of those who died in the explosion, but maybe that's not the right place to look . . . maybe what took place on Endalla functioned as an instigation for your daughter being taken."

Kasidy leaned forward over the table and placed her hand atop her husband's. "Do you mean that you think Rebecca's kidnapping is retribution?" she asked.

"It's possible," Tey said, "but that's not what I meant." She pushed back from the table and stood up. "I need to review a report of the incident on Endalla."

Tey clearly intended to end the meeting. Kasidy and Ben stood up. They thanked Tey again for her willing participation in the search for their daughter, and she assured them that she would be in touch soon. Though Kasidy had told her to use their given names, she called them "Ms. Yates" and "Mister Sisko"—a middle ground between familiarity and the more formal use of their titles.

As she and Ben headed for the front door, Kasidy noticed the tea that Tey had poured had gone untouched.

Radovan closed the closet in the hall, then dug around in his pants pocket for the two-pronged key. He unlocked his bedroom and pushed the door open. The girl sat on the bed, a partially eaten meal on a tray beside her. She did not look up as he entered the room.

"I'm glad to see you're eating," Radovan said, though in truth, he didn't really care one way or the other. After his explosive encounter that morning with Winser Ellevet, the girl had screamed herself hoarse before breaking down into tears. When finally she quieted, her racked sobs at last run dry, Radovan brought her breakfast, but when he returned for the tray, he saw that she had overturned it and sent her meal spattering to the floor. The girl shrank away from him as he yelled at her to clean up her mess, but then he ended up doing so himself. When he later took lunch into the bedroom, he warned her not to repeat her bad behavior. The girl hadn't dumped that food, but neither had she eaten it.

Radovan crossed to the bed and picked up the tray. He saw that, while the girl had moved the food around on the plates, she really hadn't eaten anything. It didn't matter to him whether or not she kept herself sated, but he did want her to consume enough for the sedative he'd put in her food to take effect. If not, he'd have to resort to the hypospray.

Radovan hovered beside the bed, glaring down at the girl. She refused to look up at him. He closed his eyes and imagined grabbing hold of her, shaking her violently, and forcing her to pay attention to him. Radovan knew it would feel good to do that, to demonstrate the power he had over the Avatar, but he also believed that the time had not yet come to end their journey together. He needed to proceed cautiously in order for them to reach their destination— their shared destiny.

As Radovan carried the tray toward the door, the girl surprised him by speaking. "What happened to that lady?"

Radovan stopped in midstride and turned back to the

bed. Several possible responses spun through his head, but he settled on the one he hoped would ultimately provide the path of least resistance. "What lady?" he said.

"That lady," the girl repeated. "That lady." She pointed to the floor in front of the door, to the location of Radovan's physical altercation with Winser.

"I don't know what you're talking about," he said. "There was no lady here." It occurred to Radovan that his last statement had the virtue of being true: Winser, with her incessant talking, her alcohol intake, and her sexual aggressiveness, could hardly be considered a lady. "You must've been dreaming."

The girl stared at Radovan. He could tell from the look in her eyes that his assertion had set gears turning in her little mind. Even though he had taken her from her mother and imprisoned her, she wanted to believe him. As an adult, he held a natural sway over her, a de facto authority formed by his age, size, and behavior.

But the girl didn't believe him. He knew that. Instead of telling him that, though, she said, "I want to go home."

Radovan saw an opportunity. "If you want me to take you back, you have to be a good girl," he said. "That means that you can't scream and you can't cry and you have to eat the meals I prepare for you." He crossed back to the bed and set the tray back down beside the girl. She looked down at the food for a long moment before finally picking up a carrot stick. She bit into it with a loud crunch.

"That's a good girl," Radovan said. He reached to pat her on the head, but she shied away from his touch. He chose to ignore the insult and started back toward the door. As he pulled it closed behind him, the girl spoke again.

"I know you're lying," she said. "You're never gonna take me back home." She stared across the room at him with her dark eyes. He met her gaze and stepped back inside, wanting to intimidate her—to show her that she should not talk back to him, that she should not disrespect him. But the girl continued to stare. "You're never gonna take me home," she said again, "but I'm going home anyway."

Radovan saw red. He raced back across the room and cocked his fist, his desire to strike the girl palpable. He knew that he could kill her—that if a single blow didn't end her life, he could rain down violence upon her tiny body until he had broken it beyond repair. *But it's not time yet,* Radovan told himself. That hour might come round, but it would be one he designed, one he curated, not some random moment into which the girl or anybody else goaded him.

The girl simply looked up at him. She did not cower or in any way show fear. That made no sense, and it only enraged Radovan more. He felt his fingernails digging into the palm of his closed hand, still pulled back and ready to strike. He wanted very badly to hit the girl, to confirm his strength, to show his control of the Avatar, to take the next step in doing what Rejias Norvan could not: prove the truth of *The Book of Ohalu* and the Ohalavaru beliefs.

Radovan spun away from the bed and rushed back across the room. He sped through the hall to the dining table. He grabbed the medkit, opened it, pulled out the hypospray, then selected the appropriate ampoule for his purposes. He ran back into the bedroom and—

The girl was gone.

Radovan felt his eyes widen in surprise—and in fear. If she somehow got free—

Radovan's arm shot out, his hand clutching at the door-jamb. He wrenched himself back into motion, reversing course and dashing back into the living area of his flat. The front door remained closed and locked.

Of course it is, Radovan thought. The girl could not have

gotten past him. And even if she had, she could not possibly reach the locks on her own, nor could she have manipulated them in order to free herself. Radovan's decision to confine her to his bedroom had come from an abundance of caution.

He headed back down the hall, taking a moment to peek into the guest 'fresher. When he didn't see the girl, Radovan continued on into the bedroom. He slid open one side of the closet doors there, then the other. He glanced on the other side of the bed, then checked in the en-suite refresher. Finally, he dropped to his stomach and pulled up the comforter that hung down from the bed all the way to the floor.

The girl gazed back at him. For a moment, neither of them moved, but then Radovan scrambled forward. The girl shrieked and tried to crawl away, but his hand found her forearm and clamped on. He yanked her from under the bed. As she attempted to prize his fingers from around her wrist, Radovan swung his other arm around and brought the hypospray up to the side of her neck. The girl froze when she heard the medical device's hiss, then frantically tried to free herself, flailing her arms and legs. Her efforts lasted only a few seconds before her body went limp.

Radovan stood up with the girl in his arms. He hadn't wanted to leave his flat, nor had he intended to vacate the city. He always recognized that he might have to do so, but never had he envisioned the time coming so quickly. But then he also hadn't counted upon Winser Ellevet to inadvertently interfere with his plans.

It's time to go, Radovan thought. After his confrontation with Winser, he'd spent the rest of the day preparing for his departure. For *their* departure.

Radovan carried the Avatar out of his bedroom, more certain than ever that he was on his way to fulfill his fate.

Gamma Quadrant, 2386

The bright white sparks of materialization dissolved from before Sisko's eyes, leaving him standing amid a kaleidoscope of shapes and colors. Because of the veritable rainbow of multiform hues shining on him from every direction, it took the captain a moment to discern the overall profile of the wide, rectangular corridor into which he had beamed. The variegated surfaces—walls, ceiling, floor—lent the surroundings a carnival-like atmosphere, but paradoxically, the cool, dry air smelled of antiseptic.

Sisko glanced to either side to ensure that both security officers Rogers and Grandal had successfully transported with him from *Styx*. Like the captain, they had their phasers drawn, set to heavy stun. Also like Sisko, they wore in their ears special comm units, designed by Lieutenant sh'Vrane to block the effects of the sound-based weapons used against the *Robinson* crew during the boarding of the ship.

Seeing no beings in the corridor in either direction, the captain looked to Rogers, who, in addition to his phaser, also carried a tricorder. "Life signs in the building are erratic and uncertain, but . . . I am detecting the group of twenty-nine children," the lieutenant said. "Down another corridor to the left, about fifty meters ahead, and then inside a large chamber."

Sisko had ordered separate three-member away teams to

the trio of locations housing the *Robinson* children. He'd left a pilot, transporter operator, and physician aboard each of the runabouts, with orders to vacate the Dyson section—and to return later—if the vessels came under attack. Lieutenant Stannis aboard *Acheron* and Ensign Weil aboard *Styx* would await signals as the away teams sought to free the children and bring them to points where they could be beamed to the runabouts and then taken back to *Robinson*. The captain hoped to rescue all of the children at once, but short of that, the away teams needed to conduct reconnaissance efforts to determine how best to accomplish their goal.

Gesturing with his phaser, Sisko motioned ahead. He started forward down the corridor with Rogers and Grandal flanking him. They had proceeded ten or so meters before the lieutenant spoke up again.

"Sensors show movement ahead," Rogers said. "Still indeterminate life signs, but they're coming in this direction, toward the second juncture." The lieutenant pointed along the left-hand wall. Sisko could make out a series of intersecting corridors. The captain flattened himself against the near wall and leveled his phaser at the second junction, as did Grandal beside him. Rogers took up a similar position against the opposite wall.

From a distance, a confused racket emerged, a disordered agglomeration of noises that grew louder even as the din failed to cohere. Sisko tried to imagine troops advancing to intercept the away team, but he did not hear the cadence of soldiers marching in unison, nor even the intentional breaking of stride to avoid mechanical resonance. It sounded like chaos.

Suddenly, a frenetic throng spilled from the mouth of the second passage up ahead. Sisko could not immediately absorb what he saw. Ten or twelve figures rushed toward the away team, but the captain had trouble registering them as living beings. The captain saw flesh, but also metal casings, and though some appendages looked like arms and legs, and some projections like heads, he also spied wheels and drums, lights and readouts.

But then Sisko spotted one of the approaching horde aiming a device at the away team, a pistol-like armament with a parabolic emitter. The captain heard a high-pitched whine for just an instant before the specialized comm units in his ears canceled out the potentially debilitating sound. Another squall rang out, but originating with the away team and accompanied by first one and then another reddish-yellow beam as Rogers and Grandal discharged their weapons. Sisko squeezed the firing pad on his own phaser and a third beam streaked into the advancing force.

An attacker that walked on three legs and had multiple arms extending from a barrel-shaped body dropped to the floor. Sisko could not determine whether to categorize it as a living being or as a machine. A network of electrical arcs flashed across a many-legged creature that immediately stopped crawling.

The away team continued to fire their phasers, and as more of the peculiar assemblage toppled, Sisko made out more details. Every entity differed considerably from those beside it. The captain noted significant variations in shape, color, composition, and size, and widely diverse numbers and types of appendages and other body parts. Appearances ranged from robotic to animalistic, from the surreal to the sublime. No two individuals hailed from the same species—if any of them evolved as a natural life-form in the first place, rather than being artificially constructed.

More of the entities faltered and collapsed. A large dark-green being that resembled an upright squid fell forward, and another that looked more or less like a red quantum torpedo casing perched atop spider legs crumpled to the floor. But the others kept coming. They'd cut the distance to the away team to twenty meters.

Sisko faced a difficult decision, but he made it at once. "Set phasers to kill," he called out to Rogers and Grandal.

The beams ceased for a moment as the three men adjusted their weapons. When they fired again, intermittent bolts of blue infused the red-yellow streaks. More of the attackers fell, but two continued on. A large humpbacked beast galloped forward on six powerful legs, while a gray wingèd creature took to the air. The lethal phaser beams sliced through the corridor and into the approaching pair, to no effect.

Sisko had no choice, and no time to issue his order. He removed his finger from the trigger pad and reset his weapon, then fired twice in rapid succession. The first brilliant blue-white beam seared out and caught the massive charging animal between its front legs. The luminous glow spread across the creature, consuming it in a haze of vaporization. When the radiance dissipated, it left nothing behind, the molecular integrity of the beast catastrophically destroyed.

The flying entity soared across the remaining distance to the away team. The captain heard it scream as it bore down on its prey. Sisko's second shot struck it at point-blank range. It disappeared in a miasma of deadly phased energy.

The shrill cries of the away team's phasers ended, echoing down the corridor before leaving Sisko and the security officers in an unnatural silence. For a moment, nobody moved. Sisko listened and looked, straining to hear any sound that would signal approaching reinforcements, to see any movement off in the distance.

Rogers consulted his tricorder. "Scans show no other forces headed in this direction," the lieutenant said. "Our path to the children is clear."

"Let's move," Sisko said without hesitation.

As the three *Robinson* officers picked their way through the scene of their downed attackers, Grandal blurted, "What *are* these?"

Sisko had the same question. Some of the entities looked like organic beings, some like machines, while still others evoked a combination of the two. *But not like the Borg,* the captain thought. Before the Collective had been vanquished, they had seized various life-forms, augmented them with technology, and forcibly connected them to their hive consciousness. In the case of the individuals massed on the corridor floor, they did not appear enhanced, but whole—whether born or constructed. *But there's no commonality,* Sisko thought. He considered the Xindi and the Breen and the multiple species that formed their civilizations. The Federation itself comprised numerous races. *Still,* the captain thought, *what's going on here is more than some sort of societal affiliation.*

"I don't know," Sisko told Grandal, but then he remembered an unusual detail about the aliens. "All of their ships were different from one another too. Maybe . . ." *Maybe what?* he asked himself. He didn't know, and at the moment, he didn't care.

Sisko and the two security officers reached the far end of the fallen entities and rushed toward the second intersection. The captain made it there first and quickly peeked around the corner. As Rogers had indicated, the corridor stood empty. Several sets of large doors, all of them different colors, lined the walls at wide intervals.

"It's the first one on the right," Rogers said.

Sisko didn't wait. He ran over to the doors, which came to a peak where they met at the top, reaching almost to the ceiling six or so meters overhead. A dark green, they appeared metal, lined along their edges with large rivets. Rogers scanned them with his tricorder.

"The children are definitely in there, spread out," the lieutenant said. "The doors are composed of a steel alloy that should be susceptible to phasers."

Sisko took a step back and raised his weapon, but then he noticed a hand-size surface protruding from the wall. Shaped like back-to-back crescents, it matched the color of the doors. The captain stepped forward and pushed it. The doors silently swung inward.

Sisko rushed forward with Rogers and Grandal, all brandishing their phasers. They entered a large chamber, perhaps twice the size of *Robinson*'s main engineering compartment. Massive amounts of technological equipment jammed the space, none of which Sisko recognized. Consoles and panels proliferated, featuring incomprehensible readouts, along with oddly shaped dials and what must have been other controls. The air felt heavy and smelled of ozone, the atmosphere laden with a pulsating thrum and the feel of electrical potential.

As the doors swung shut behind the away team, five beings positioned amid the various apparatus turned toward them, obviously startled. None of the entities looked like any they had so far seen, nor did they resemble one another—not in form or hue, not in basic biology or mechanics. Sisko aimed his phaser, as did Rogers and Grandal, but then he saw a pair of legs at the far end of the chamber, atop a flat surface set inside a large, complex piece of machinery. The shins were smaller than those of an adult, their flesh colored blue. The captain moved to his right so that he could see more. He recognized Beschelcorea th'Vrent, the teenage *thei* of Veraldorash ch'Vrent, one of *Robinson*'s nursing staff. The boy appeared strapped down and unconscious.

"There," Sisko said, pointing. "I see one of the children."

"They're all around, Captain," Rogers said, and he gestured to several other points about the chamber. Like th'Vrent, four other children lay insensible and tethered inside various equipment, as did an equal number of the alien beings. The other children were caged in a handful of transparent compartments. When they saw Sisko and the security officers, a few of the older children began waving and shouting, though the captain could not hear them. He wondered how they could breathe in the enclosed space, but saw tubes and conduits attached to their containment cells.

Sisko did not see his daughter.

The captain moved toward the nearest being, who looked more humanoid than any other entity the away team had so far encountered. *More humanoid,* Sisko thought, *but not fully humanoid.* The being had two pair of arms—one set larger, one smaller—and what looked like a ring of eyes around a squarish head. It stood on a wide single leg that ended not in a foot, but in a horizontal cylinder.

Sisko pointed his phaser at the being. It lifted all of its arms in an obvious gesture of supplication. "Free the children," Sisko ordered Rogers and Grandal. The security officers started forward, but the other beings—one of which looked as though it had been carved out of stone—moved to block their path.

Sisko stepped closer to the first being and shoved the emitter of his phaser against its body. "I am Captain Benjamin Sisko of the United Federation of Planets," he said, unsure if his words would be understood. "We were on a mission of peaceful exploration, but your people attacked our ship and abducted our children."

The being appeared confused. Sisko assumed it lacked the technology to translate his words, but then it exhaled through two wavering tabs on either side of its head. Its voice sounded like somebody moaning. Sisko could not discern individual words or even distinguishable phonemes, but the special comm units he wore in his ears contained a universal translator.

"I am Zonir of the Glant," the being said. "You cannot explore here. This is not [untranslatable]." The translator emitted a low tone for the parts of speech it could not adequately interpret. It bestowed a neutral tone upon the voice, casting it as neither female nor male.

"We are not exploring *here*," Sisko said. "We have come to take back our children."

"You *are* exploring here," Zonir said. "I can see you."

Sisko looked to Rogers and Grandal, and then to the other beings. There seemed to be a disconnect in communication. The captain tried again. "We are here to bring our children back to our ship."

"What do you want for your ship?" Zonir asked. "We do not have what you seek."

"We *want* our children," Sisko said again, raising his voice and pointing with his empty hand toward Corea th'Vrent.

Zonir gestured with two of its arms toward the Andorian child. "That is not what you think it is," it said. "It is an [untranslatable]. It is not for you."

Sisko shook his head. He and Zonir had spoken only a few sentences to each other, but both seemed confused. Some of Zonir's words—and probably some of his own, the captain thought—didn't translate, but Sisko suspected a deeper dissonance, down on a conceptual level.

"Captain," Rogers said, "sensors are showing movement and sporadic life signs heading in this direction."

Sisko had no time to negotiate. He pushed his phaser harder into Zonir's body. "Free the children now."

"What are you talking about?" Zonir said. "We don't have what you want."

Sisko swung his arm to one side and fired past Zonir.

The blue phaser beam engulfed a table and reduced it to atoms. The captain returned his weapon to Zonir's chest. "Move," Sisko ordered. "You and the others, move to the corner of the chamber." He motioned to the point farthest from the doors.

Zonir didn't say anything and didn't move, and the captain thought he might have to use force. But then Zonir spoke to his colleagues, telling them to do as Sisko demanded. They complied. Sisko kept his phaser trained on the motley group—one of them looked to the captain like a gray-striped monkey with five tails. "Do not speak another word," Sisko told them when they reached the corner.

Then he turned to Rogers and Grandal. "Get the children out of the cages." As the security officers acknowledged their orders, the captain went to Corea th'Vrent. The boy lay supine on a slab inside the bay of a large machine. He had been strapped down, and three thick conduits led to dish-shaped appliances that had been attached to his head, though his antennae remained free. A dim glow bathed his entire body.

Sisko reached into the machine, intending to free Corea from his restraints, but as the captain's hand entered the bay, it began to feel numb. He jerked his arm back, realizing that the boy had been placed in a stasis field. Sisko searched instead for a way to release the slab and pull it from the machine. As he did so, he heard the security officers speaking to the children, telling them to back away. A phaser blast rang out, and the captain glanced over to see Grandal helping pull one group of children through the broken door of their cage.

Sisko felt all around the front base of the slab, without success. He was about to demand that Zonir help him when his fingers found a latch. He pressed it, then pulled the slab toward him. It glided easily from within the machine. He quickly unshackled Corea, then tried to puzzle out the three appliances on his head. Sisko didn't know if he could safely remove them, but he also knew they had little time to complete their rescue.

The boy's eyes fluttered open. He peered directly at the captain, his expression mixing confusion and hope. "What . . . what's going on?" he asked in his native Andorian tongue. He rose to his elbows, and the dish-shaped appliances fell from his head. "Where's my *charan*?" He referred to one of his two fathers, the one who served aboard *Robinson*.

"He's aboard the ship," Sisko told Corea. "You've been taken to an alien world, and we've come to bring you home." He helped the boy to a sitting position. "Are you strong enough to walk?"

Corea blinked his eyes, once, twice, a third time, as though trying to clear the confusion from his thoughts. His antennae twisted slowly on his head, then tensed. He looked over to where the five Glant stood in the corner. "They . . . they brought us here," he said, pointing. He spoke in Federation Standard.

"We know," Sisko said. "But we're getting you out of here. Can you walk?"

Corea hopped off the slab. "I'm ready to run, Captain."

Sisko couldn't help but offer an encouraging smile. "Good," he said. "Then go assist Lieutenant Rogers and Ensign Grandal. Help the younger children."

"Yes, sir," Corea said. Fear seemed to drop away from the boy as he headed with a purpose across the chamber.

Sisko moved past a slab on which a vaguely crablike entity lay, seemingly unconscious, and over to the next machine and the next slab. By the time he'd freed the fifth child, Rogers and Grandal had released the other twenty-four. The two security officers each carried one of the younger children, as did Corea and several of the other teenagers. The captain raced over to the group. "How close are the approaching forces?" he asked, but he saw that, with a child in one arm and a phaser in his other hand, Rogers had holstered his tricorder. Sisko grabbed it from the lieutenant's hip and scanned their surroundings. "We have a window, but we have to go now." He bent down and addressed the children. He saw that they all wore the special comm units in their ears, which Rogers and Grandal had brought with them. "We have to walk out of here. I want all of you to stay together, and to stay close to Lieutenant Rogers and Ensign Grandal and me. Okay?"

Most of the children responded, though some—particularly the younger ones—just stared. Sisko could see fear in their eyes. His mind drifted to Rebecca, but he shut that thought down right away. "Phasers on max," he told the security officers quietly. They would have no time to determine if the stun setting would stop all of the forces they encountered—especially with the children in tow. "Come on."

As the captain led the way back to the doors and out into the corridor, he tapped at his combadge. "Sisko to *Styx*."

"*Styx here,*" Weil replied at once. "*Go ahead, Captain.*"

"What's your status?"

"*We're still on the bottom of the lake,*" Weil said. "*Either we've avoided detection or they have no way of getting to us—at least not yet.*"

"Good," Sisko said. "We've got the children and we're on our way back to the transport point. Scan for us and beam us back as soon as you can establish a lock."

"*Aye, sir.*"

"Sisko out."

The captain retraced the away team's steps back toward the main corridor. At the junction, he held up a hand to stop everybody and then peeked around the corner. He saw nobody in either direction, but then a piercing sound erupted behind them, and then another—not the auditory weapon that had been used to render the crew unconscious aboard *Robinson*, but something different. In front of Sisko, on the wall of the main corridor opposite the junction, two capsules of light struck the many-colored surface. Chunks of the wall crashed to the floor. The shots—some sort of hybrid energy and projectile ammunition—had come from behind them, down the secondary corridor.

"Go, go," Sisko said, waving his arm. He looked to Rogers and Grandal. "Take the children. Now." The two security officers didn't question their orders, or what their captain intended to do, even as he stepped past them. Rogers and Grandal rushed the group forward and into the main corridor, out of the line of fire and on the way to the transport point.

Sisko dropped to a knee as he saw multiple muzzle flashes ahead of him. The wall next to him exploded in a hail of destroyed stone. He heard another projectile sizzle past his ear and strike out in the main corridor. He couldn't tell how many entities approached him, but it seemed like a smaller group than earlier. Sisko squeezed the firing pad of his phaser. The blue beam missed his intended target, the being leading the charge, but it caught the one to the leader's right. As the entity vaporized, the captain aimed his phaser again, adjusting for his initial miss. He fired—

Something hot blazed through Sisko's left biceps. He was thrown backward and to the floor, sending his phaser blast tracing a line across the wall and ceiling. Hunks of stone rained down, striking the floor like thunderclaps. A cloud of dust filled the corridor.

More shots rang out, but the veil of stone particles served Sisko well. He heard the energy projectiles slam into the wall behind him, high, and he actually saw one as it streaked over him. The beings hadn't altered their aim toward the floor.

When Sisko glanced to his side, he saw Rogers and Grandal guiding the children away. They had navigated past the beings the away team had earlier stunned or killed. Sisko saw that some of the children had turned around at the sound of the blasts, but the two security guards hurried them back into motion.

The captain realized that he'd been thrown back into the main corridor. He rolled to that side, then scrabbled back to his feet. Pain screamed in his wounded arm, which hung limply by his side, but his adrenaline allowed him to ignore it. He heard more shots striking the wall behind him, as well as the chaotic sound of footfalls nearing.

Sisko sprinted after Rogers and Grandal and their charges. As the captain skipped his way through the fallen beings, he heard a familiar hum from up ahead. When he looked up, he saw the thin white bands of the transporter fading, taking the security guards and the children with them.

The sharp report of an alien weapon sounded behind Sisko. As he darted to one side, a bright projectile sailed past him. He heard another shot, and another, and then a volley. He juked left and right, but expected to feel the hot agony of a weapon strike in his back.

More shots flew past Sisko, and more rang out behind him. He darted to one side in an evasive movement and lost his footing. He stumbled forward, regaining his balance by reaching out and steadying himself against the wall. As he pushed away, he glanced back and saw a flurry of glowing projectiles heading for him. In the instant before they would strike, he thought of his daughter and hoped that one of the other away teams had rescued her.

But then a whine grew in the corridor and Sisko's vision

began to fade. He recognized and welcomed the effects of a Federation transporter. He just hoped that his crew would not end up beaming back their captain's corpse.

Sisko dropped to his knees on the transporter platform and looked down at his chest. He expected to see holes singed into his tunic, as well as his own blood. Instead, he saw only his intact uniform. He reflexively clutched a hand to his torso, relieved to find his body whole.

"Captain," said a voice, and Sisko looked up to see *Robinson*'s chief medical officer approaching him from the rear of the runabout. Beyond him, Rogers and Grandal tended to the children that they had just rescued. "You're hurt," Kosciuszko said. He set down an open medkit as he squatted before Sisko. The doctor already had a medical tricorder in his hand. He activated the device as he waved it over the captain's left arm.

"It's nothing," Sisko said, although the wound had begun to throb angrily. But the captain had more important matters on his mind. He and his away team had recovered a third of the missing children, but that left the others still at risk.

"It's not nothing," Kosciuszko said. He set down the tricorder, then dug into his medkit and pulled out a hypospray. "Your biceps muscle has been damaged. It'll require a surgical procedure to repair it." He fished an ampoule from the medkit and inserted it into the hypo, which he then pressed against the side of Sisko's shoulder. Over its reassuring hiss, Kosciuszko said, "This will protect against infection and also mask your pain."

"Thank you, Doctor," Sisko said. He tried to climb to his feet, but had difficulty with only one functioning arm. Kosciuszko helped him up.

"You really should rest, Captain."

Sisko ignored the doctor and made his way forward from the transporter platform to the runabout's cockpit. Ensign Weil sat at the main console, while Crewwoman Spingeld remained at her position at the transporter controls. The captain did not see Ensign Bevelaqua, who had joined two officers from *Acheron* to form one of the away teams. "Status report," Sisko said.

"The second away team transported back to the *Acheron* just before you beamed up," Weil said. She replied to the captain without taking her eyes from her console. A silver comm receiver jutted from her ear, doubtless so that she could monitor the situation on the second runabout. "They reported that they couldn't get near the chamber holding the children. They faced multiple security forces and sustained two casualties: Lieutenant Stannis and Ensign Bevelaqua both took weapons fire. The ensign is expected to recover, but the lieutenant's condition is critical; Doctor Mensara has him in stasis."

The account of injuries to members of his crew troubled Sisko, but his primary attention remained on the recovery of *Robinson*'s missing children. "What about the third away team?"

"There's no word yet." The main console emitted a series of chirps. Weil studied a readout, then worked her controls. "Sensors show alien ships have entered the lake and are heading in this direction."

"Estimated time to intercept?" Sisko asked.

"Calculating," Weil said, working the console. "At their current speed, the first ships will reach us in twenty-three minutes." The ensign's hand moved up to the receiver in her ear. "Captain, the third away team is transporting to the *Acheron* now." She listened for a few seconds, then said, "I'll put you on with Lieutenant Scalin." She reached forward and toggled a switch on the main console.

Sisko walked forward and sat down heavily beside Weil. "Lieutenant Scalin," he said. "Report."

"The last away team just beamed up, sir," Scalin said. He spoke with the slightly barbed intonations of individuals native to Terah'la, one of Bajor's smaller continents. *"They brought back all thirty-one children from their location. Doctor Mensara is checking them now, but her preliminary report is that they all appear uninjured and in good health."*

"Acknowledged," Sisko said, fighting the urge to ask if his daughter had been among those recovered. He had to focus on the remaining missing children, regardless of their identities. "Stand by." Weil closed the channel.

Sisko rose from his chair and moved to stand beside Spingeld. "Scan the area around the location where the children are being held," he said. "Search for an alternate place to beam us down, and a different route to reach the children."

Spingeld shook her head. "It's difficult to know with certainty because of the inconsistent life signs," she said, "but the aliens appear to have fortified the area with additional forces. There is no obvious way to reach the children without encountering considerable resistance."

"Then determine the best of the bad choices," Sisko said. "I'm going back out there."

"Yes, sir," Spingeld said.

"Captain." Ensign Weil spoke quietly, from directly behind Sisko. He turned to face her where she stood. "Sir, I can't allow you to transport back to the surface."

"You can't—?" Sisko began, but then he stopped, dumbstruck. In the two years she had served aboard *Robinson*, Anissa Weil had performed her duties well, collecting solid, if not flashy, reviews from her superiors. Nothing in her record suggested a capacity for willful insubordination. "I must not have heard you correctly, Ensign."

"I'm sorry, sir," she said, her tone low and contained, "but after you, I am the senior command officer aboard the *Styx*. That makes me your *de jure* first officer. That means that your safety is my responsibility."

"*Ensign*," Sisko said, emphasizing Weil's rank in preparation to dress her down, but then he stopped. She was right, he realized, at least in terms of her responsibilities. "Ensign, we don't have a choice," he told her. "There are children in danger. We need to bring them home."

"With all due respect, sir," Weil said, "you are injured and in no condition to go into battle." She gestured to his left arm, which hung down flaccidly. "And it will be a battle, Captain. We have lost the element of surprise, and the aliens have strengthened security around the last set of children. We've already suffered three casualties among the nine members of the away teams. Sending more of our people into harm's way right now is unlikely to result in the recovery of the children, but it could easily result in more injuries—or worse—to our crew."

Sisko wanted to argue, or even simply to order the ensign to stand down, but he knew she was right. Additionally, the Glant had apparently located *Acheron* and *Styx*, so remaining on the Dyson section would put not only the crews of the two runabouts at risk, but also the children they had already recovered. Reluctantly, the captain moved back to the main console and took his chair again. "Sisko to *Acheron*."

"*Acheron here*," Scalin said.

"Lieutenant, set a return course back the way we came," Sisko said. "Best possible speed. The *Styx* will follow."

"*Yes, sir.*"

"Sisko out." He looked up at Weil. "With my injury, I can't pilot the ship."

"Aye, sir," Weil said. She took her position beside Sisko at the main console.

"Take us home, Ensign."

As the runabout's engines came to life, Sisko leaned back in his chair. He felt drained, both physically and emotionally. In short order, *Acheron* and *Styx* reached the tube that ran between the inner and outer surfaces of the Glant world. The runabouts had traversed half its length when Lieutenant Scalin transmitted a list of the recovered children aboard *Acheron*.

Rebecca was not among them.

Bajor, 2380

Jasmine Tey walked with purpose through the spring night. B'hava'el had set an hour earlier, taking with it the lengthening daylight on the march toward summer. Tey appreciated the warm evening breeze wafting through the city streets, especially since the summer had departed early on the other side of Bajor, at least in Ashalla.

Tey had followed one of the city's main pedestrian thoroughfares after transporting from the capital, but she'd quickly left its bright illumination for narrower, darker avenues. She clung to the shadows as best she could, a departure from her tenure protecting Asarem Wadeen. During her time as part of the minister's security detail, her duties required her constant visibility, a reminder to all of the unceasing guard around the Bajoran leader.

Tey had spent most of the day in Ashalla. She began by visiting Militia headquarters. Seeking an understanding of the debacle on Endalla the previous month, she consulted detailed reports of the incident. Benjamin Sisko and Captain Vaughn had provided their own accounts, and the Militia had taken eyewitness statements from all of the surviving Ohalavaru. Tey read through the official narrative that collated all of the information. Afterward, she worked her way through various analyses, most of which focused on the central player in the confrontation, Rejias Norvan.

Once she'd completed her education about the events on Endalla, Tey skimmed through the material provided by the Ohalavaru participants. More than a few of the testimonies revealed a bitterness for different aspects of Bajoran life: Kai Pralon and the mainstream faithful, First Minister Asarem and the government, the Federation and Starfleet. Tey sorted out those that troubled her the most, the individuals who exhibited enough anger and aggression in their statements to bear further investigation. More than a third of the 173 made it to her list.

Hoping to narrow down her pool of suspects, Tey had then crossed Ashalla to the Ministry of Transportation. There, she requested a roster of all transporter operators and technicians stationed across Bajor over the prior five years, reasoning that the method of Rebecca Sisko's abduction required a degree of expertise not common in the general population. Despite her security clearance, it required the authorization of both Minister Asarem and Overgeneral Manos, as well as a judicial warrant, to acquire the data she wanted.

When Tey eventually received the list, it had contained several thousand names. She cross-referenced it with the sixty-plus Ohalavaru she'd singled out for additional follow-up. Eight names appeared on both lists. Tey found among them two single, middle-aged males, one of whom lived in Johcat, and the other who operated a public transporter there.

Tey had visited the town of Laksie first, and the home of a man named Derwell Kant. She introduced herself as a Militia investigator, telling him that she wanted to ask him just a few supplemental questions about what had taken place on Endalla. He balked, accusing Tey of religious intolerance and governmental intimidation. She agreed wholeheartedly, not about her own motives—after all, she just followed orders—but about those of her superior, who'd ordered her to speak with Derwell.

After Tey had successfully cultivated a sympathetic response, Derwell had agreed to answer her questions. He invited her into his home. She spied nothing out of the ordinary inside. They spoke in the living area, but when she asked to use the refresher, she took a moment to glance into the lone bedroom. In the entire flat, she spotted only two items related to the Ohalavaru: a hardbound volume of *The Book of Ohalu* and a framed print of the famous icon painting, *City of B'hala*.

Tey had spoken with Derwell for three-quarters of an hour. Although he criticized Bajor's government and mainstream religion, he did not seem overly angry. Neither did he acquit himself as particularly bright, though Tey allowed that his behavior could have been an act. Eventually, she maneuvered the conversation to a discussion of his whereabouts three days earlier. He claimed to have attended a daylong training seminar; currently a transporter operator, he hoped to become a technician. Once she left Derwell's flat, she confirmed his presence for the entire seminar, which provided him an alibi at the time of the abduction.

After that, Tey beamed to Johcat. There, she visited a small, two-bedroom house in the outer reaches of the city. To her surprise, she discovered that Endred Koth lived there with his romantic partner. Though Endred and the woman, Fanna Elis, had never married, they told her that they'd been involved for three years, and living together for two. Tey had a pleasant enough conversation with the pair. Because Endred no longer fit her profile, she moved quickly to establish his movements three days prior. The couple spoke easily and imprecisely about what they'd done—a natural occurrence for people with nothing to hide—but they managed to supply enough detail for Tey to verify, which she had done immediately after leaving their home.

With no more suspects, Tey had returned to Ashalla. She visited Militia headquarters again, asking herself if she'd erred in the profile she'd produced for the kidnapper. Others involved in the investigation—most notably, Major Orisin—believed that the abduction of Rebecca Sisko had been accomplished by more than one person. Many also felt that the motivation for the crime had less to do with the girl and more to do with her father, and that a ransom demand of a religious nature—based upon Benjamin Sisko's role as the Emissary rather than upon Rebecca's as the Avatar—would materialize. Tey understood the reasoning. She even granted that it made sense. It just didn't scan with her intuition, a sense constructed not of supposition and guesswork, but of her training and experience. Tey did not believe herself infallible, but she felt strongly about her analysis of the situation.

Back at Militia headquarters, Tey revisited the list of the Ohalavaru who'd been on Endalla with Rejias Norvan. She expanded her efforts to cross-check against the directory of transporter operators and technicians by including all of the individuals who'd survived the incident on the Bajoran moon, rather than just those she considered suspicious based on their recorded statements. By doing so, she found a third name, an unattached man in his forties who crewed a public transporter in the city of Elanda, but who resided in Johcat. Tey immediately beamed back to the city.

As she strode along the narrow pedestrian avenue, Tey moved not from one pool of light to another beneath the streetlamps, but from one stretch of darkness to another. She had no particular reason to move furtively—it seemed unlikely that anybody would recognize her—but she did so out of instinct. She had chosen to wear soft-soled shoes, allowing her to move quietly.

Tey reached her destination and found the outdoor staircase at the end of the building. She climbed to the top story and made her way to the far end of the floor, to what turned out to be the end unit. She looked for a welcome panel but didn't see one, so she raised her hand and rapped with her knuckles on the door. Thirty seconds passed, and then Tey knocked again. She waited for five full minutes, then banged on the door a third time.

Still no answer.

Tey understood that the man could simply be out, that his apparent absence could mean nothing. People left their homes to go to restaurants, to visit friends, or for uncounted other reasons. Despite that night had just fallen, the man might even be inside his flat but asleep, oblivious to her knocking.

Or he could be holed up inside with his kidnapped victim.

Tey had to be certain. She looked around to be sure she was unobserved, then leaned in and pressed her ear to the door. She held her breath and listened. When she heard nothing, she moved to the front windows so that she could attempt to look inside, but she saw that they had been set to reflective—not unusual, especially at night, but that failed to put her mind at ease.

Unwilling to leave, Tey took the stairs back down to the ground level, where she walked back to the far end of the building. There, she peered up at the other windows of the flat in question. She saw that they too had been rendered reflective. But then, so had most of the windows she saw.

Still, Tey believed in being thorough. She circled the building, looking for anything out of the ordinary. She saw nothing unusual, but when she reached the outdoor stairs, she noted that they also descended one flight to a basement. Doubting that the building contained belowground flats, she took the steps down.

The door there had been propped open, a triangular piece of wood wedged below its bottom rail. Tey walked inside to find herself in a hallway that ran the length of the building. Numerous doors ran along one side. She paced over to the first one and saw a number on it, which she surmised corresponded to a flat number.

Storage spaces, Tey thought.

She headed down the hallway. She had no expectations and no plan. Tey knew that she could not legally force her way into the storage space that went with the flat of the man she had come to interview, but she also understood that most successful investigations required an attention to detail.

Tey found the man's storage space, like his flat, at the far end of the building. To Tey's surprise, the door stood slightly ajar. "Hello?" she called out.

No response.

Tey used the toe of her shoe to push the door slowly inward. As it opened, lighting panels overhead switched on. The storage space measured about three meters wide and twice as deep. It contained nothing but two stacks of crates. Tey walked over and examined them. Constructed of a translucent material, they revealed their contents, which looked like personal items: framed photographs, books, articles of clothing.

When Tey saw a thin layer of dust coating the top crates, she looked down at the floor. Grime covered the gray concrete, but for several footprints and a large rectangular area. *He moved something from here,* Tey thought. *Recently.*

It could have been nothing, but in Tey's mind, the pieces added up. It started with the crime itself, which led to her profile of the perpetrator. Juxtaposing all of that with the Ohalavaru individuals extreme enough to support an effort to bomb Endalla in an attempt to prove their beliefs, it all led to one man.

Well, it had led to three, Tey thought, but she'd been able to cross the other two off her list.

Mindful of the passage of time, including the three days that had passed since Rebecca's abduction, Tey had to find her latest suspect. That meant she needed to get into his flat—either to confront him if he was there, or to find clues to his current location. She briefly considered putting her shoulder into the man's door and forcing her way inside, claiming exigent circumstances, but she knew that wouldn't hold up in a court of law—particularly since she had already interviewed and exonerated two other suspects that day. She would have to obtain a judicial warrant.

Tey tapped at the secure comm unit she wore around her wrist, then raised it to her lips. "Jasmine Tey to Minister Menvel," she said.

"This is the minister's office," replied a man's voice *"I'm his aide, Tol Danur. Go ahead, Investigator."* Although she had never before spoken with Tol, Tey knew that the justice minister's entire staff had been informed of her identity and instructed to handle her requests with the highest priority.

"I have a time-sensitive need for a warrant to search the residential premises of a criminal suspect," Tey said. "I will send an encrypted file of the details to Minister Menvel within the next five minutes. I am on-site and require the warrant as soon as possible." Tey would go back outside and find a shadow from which she could observe the flat, just in case anybody entered or left. "The suspect's name," she concluded, "is Radovan Tavus."

* * *

On the outskirts of the city, he saw the ad hoc security checkpoint too late to avoid it. Radovan should have expected it, but even if he had, he couldn't have done anything about it. If he turned the travel pod around, the Militia personnel stationed there would see and pursue him. He would lie, tell them that he'd simply forgotten to bring something—another blanket, perhaps, or extra rations—and that he needed to return home to get it, but that would only focus more attention on him. He knew that security officers believed innocent people didn't try to avoid them, and so doing so would likely lead to increased scrutiny—of him, of the travel pod, of everything he'd brought with him.

As Radovan entered the checkpoint, he told himself to remain calm, but also not to overdo it, not to behave too casually. He saw a number of Militia officers working at a portable kiosk. Another stood in the center of the lane, her hands up in a halting gesture. Radovan slowed the travel pod, bringing it to a halt over the sensor mat that had been laid across the avenue. A second officer stepped up to the side of the vehicle and indicated that he wanted to speak to him. Radovan tapped a control that retracted the window.

"Please shut off the vehicle, sir," the officer said.

Radovan did as instructed. The gentle whirr of the travel pod's power cell faded to silence, and the vehicle settled down onto the ground. The officer—a sergeant by his rank insignia—peered inside the cabin.

"Are you traveling alone, sir?" he asked.

"Yes, I am, Sergeant."

"Can I see your identification, please?"

"Certainly."

Radovan reached to the top of the control panel and tapped a control surface. The isolinear chip with his digital ID popped out of its receptacle. He handed it to the sergeant, who raised a handheld device and inserted the chip into it. He studied the readout for a moment.

"I see you live in Johcat, Mister Radovan," the sergeant said. "Can I ask why you're leaving the city tonight?"

"I'm going camping for a few days out in the Deserak Wilderness," Radovan said. He hiked a thumb up over his shoulder, pointing to the back of the travel pod. "I've got all my gear in the rear compartment."

"Kind of late to be heading out camping, don't you think?" The sun had gone down an hour before.

"Too many things to do, not enough time to do them," Radovan said. "I wanted to get out earlier, but it's all right. I'm going to my uncle's cabin for tonight, then I'll head out to the campsite in the morning."

The officer nodded noncommittally, then handed Radovan's ID chip back to him. "Would you please open the rear compartment and step out of the vehicle, sir?"

"Sure, Sergeant." Radovan reinserted his ID chip in the control panel, then activated the latch release for the rear compartment. Once he heard it open, he slid the door back and exited the travel pod.

"Stay there, sir."

As the officer walked to the back of the vehicle, Radovan asked, "What's this all about, Sergeant?" He didn't expect the officer to answer.

"An important work of art has gone missing from Ophiucus Three," he said. "It was supposedly stolen and brought to Bajor to sell."

"Huh," Radovan said, a reaction he hoped would sound genuine to the sergeant. In actuality, the explanation did interest Radovan. He assumed that the cover story had been created so that the authorities could avoid making public the abduction of the Avatar.

A purr emanated from beneath the travel pod, and

Radovan realized that the sensor mat had been activated. He fought the urge to hold his breath. As time passed, he stood there, suddenly unsure what to do with his hands. He crossed his arms over his chest, which felt both unnatural and conspicuous. He saw the officer who had motioned him to a stop gazing over at him, and he forced a smile onto his face. When she looked away, he dropped his arms and shoved his hands into his pockets.

"Sir," called the sergeant from behind the travel pod, "would you please come here?" Radovan pulled his hands out of his pockets and joined the officer at the back of the vehicle. The hatch of the rear compartment hung open, revealing the items he'd brought with him from home: a large antigrav trunk and a couple duffels of clothing.

"Is all of this yours, sir?" the sergeant asked.

"Yes," Radovan said. "The trunk used to belong to my mother, but . . . her path ended at the Celestial Temple about a year ago." He did not have to feign the pain he still felt over his mother's death—only his belief in an afterlife presided over by the Prophets.

"I'm sorry," the sergeant said, but he quickly moved on. "This is a public travel pod, so we have the right to search it and anything inside. We've scanned it, but would you mind opening the trunk?"

Radovan's heart immediately began to race. He tried to cover his distress with movement, stepping close to the travel pod and reaching for the top of the trunk. "Of course," he said. He unfastened the clasps and pushed open the top. The sergeant looked over the contents of the trunk—concentrated foodstuffs, water, a tent, and other camping equipment—then started to paw through it. Radovan took a pace backward to stay out of the officer's way, and also to hide his anxiety. He wished that he'd chosen to carry the hypospray in his pocket, though he realized that would have made no difference to his situation. Even if he could incapacitate the sergeant, he would still have to face the other Militia officers at the checkpoint; he counted at least four. But escaping their clutches would only demonstrate his guilt and set the authorities on his tail.

The sergeant finished looking through the trunk and turned his attention to the two duffels of clothing. He felt along their lengths, squeezing them as he did so. Radovan waited, trying not to look eager for the search to end.

Finally, the sergeant backed away from the travel pod. "Thank you, Mister Radovan," he said. "You can close it up." Radovan did so, and moments later, he piloted the travel pod away from the security checkpoint and out of Johcat.

Several kilometers outside the city, he guided the vehicle off the thoroughfare that ran through the countryside all the way to the town of Revent. Radovan brought the travel pod to a stop and opened the rear compartment. He quickly emptied his mother's trunk, then pulled up the false bottom he'd constructed inside it. He reached into the shallow hidden recess, which he'd lined with the gray, sensor-resistant material he'd replicated, and collected the tools he'd stored there. He also checked on the girl, who lay unconscious, a breathing mask strapped to her face. She seemed fine.

Returning to the cabin, Radovan utilized the tools he'd retrieved to access the travel pod's transponder, which he then disabled, rendering the vehicle invisible to Bajor's satellite-based tracking system. He then piloted the pod almost halfway back around Johcat and set off in a different direction, out into the wilderness. He spared one last glance back at the city as it faded into the distance behind him.

Radovan still didn't know exactly what he was going to do, although the general form of a plan had begun to take shape in his mind. He wondered how he would be remembered, and what history would say about his role in ending the tyranny that the Avatar brought with her. Many had interpreted *The Book of Ohalu*, but none had read the prophecies with the clarity and understanding that he finally had.

Radovan couldn't predict just what would happen next, but he knew, deep down, that when he eventually returned to the city, he would not be bringing the girl back with him.

Gamma Quadrant, 2386

Kasidy's knees threatened to give out. Her thoughts swirled and she felt faint. Before she could lose consciousness, she lurched over to the desk and sat down in one of the chairs before it.

"How can this be happening?" she heard herself say. It seemed inconceivable that Ben and the *Robinson* crew could mount a rescue operation, bring back more than two-thirds of the stolen children, and Rebecca not be among those recovered. Ben had even led one of the away teams, which had freed twenty-nine of the children, but that had not included his own daughter.

Did he know which of the three groups of children Rebecca was in? Kasidy asked herself. *Couldn't sensors have identified her? Did he even try to explicitly locate our daughter?*

Ben got up from the sofa, where they'd both been sitting when he'd delivered the news. Her disappointment—her *horror*—had driven her to her feet, but she'd become almost instantly light-headed. Ben followed her across his ready room and sat down beside her.

"Kas," he said softly. He reached forward and placed his hand atop both of hers, which she twisted together in her lap. "We're going to get her back."

Kasidy looked up at him and felt a sense of *déjà vu*. Hadn't he said essentially the same thing to her six years prior, when their daughter had first been taken, and then again, when she had been taken from *Robinson* three days earlier? *The first time, on Bajor, he was right,* Kasidy reminded herself. *But at what cost?* Rebecca had seemed fine after her ordeal with the Ohalavaru kidnapper, but Kasidy had never been fully convinced that their daughter hadn't suffered emotional damage that would eventually take a toll on her life.

"Didn't you know which group Rebecca was in?" Kasidy asked her husband. "Didn't you want to lead the away team to rescue her?"

"What?" Ben said, pulling back from her as though she'd slapped him across the face. "Kasidy, how could I? We probably could've isolated Rebecca's DNA on sensors, but that would've taken time away from our actual rescue attempts. But even if that wasn't the case, how could I have done that? How could I have demonstrated to members of the crew that our child was more important than any of theirs? My responsibility—"

"Your responsibility is to your family," Kasidy snapped.

Ben regarded her with hurt in his eyes. He could've gotten angry—probably *should* have—but instead, he reached for her, put his hands on her upper arms. "My responsibility *is* to my family," he said quietly. "But as long as I command this ship, I'm also responsible for the other thirteen hundred lives aboard. I can't elevate one above the other." He squeezed her arms. "You know that. We talked about this."

Kasidy just stared at her husband. He was right, of course, and she knew it. She had channeled her anger and frustration at Ben because she could, because it gave her an outlet for her to vent her voluble emotions. "I'm sorry," she said. "It's just . . ." She didn't finish. She didn't have to; her husband would know what she felt because he felt it too.

"We're not giving up," Ben said. "The Glant—"

"The Glant?"

"That's what they call themselves," Ben said. "We've seen that they have some powerful weapons, but while they're different from ours, they're not formidable. They have the energy bolts that destroy the fabric of space-time, but they're not going to use that on their own world. We've already found a way to defend against their auditory weapon. When we're able to use them, phasers have proven effective. On top of that, the Glant apparently do not have transporter technology, which gives us a tremendous advantage."

"Does that mean you're going back to their world?"

"We're not leaving without the rest of the children," Ben said, his voice filled with a determination Kasidy had heard many times before. "Right now, the crew is keeping the *Robinson* away from their ships while we scan their world. We need to learn how they're reacting to our incursion, how they're changing their defenses, if they're moving the children. Then we'll formulate a new plan of attack. Once we—"

A comm signal interrupted Ben. *"Sickbay to Captain Sisko."* Kasidy recognized the voice of the ship's chief medical officer.

"Sisko here. Go ahead, Doctor."

"We've completed our examination of all the rescued children," Kosciuszko said. *"Physically, they're all fine. A few bumps and bruises here and there, but no significant injuries. Most are showing signs of post-traumatic stress, but we've released many of them to their families so that they can return to a familiar setting and receive emotional support. Doctor Althouse and her staff are speaking to the parents about the best ways to handle the situation. The counselor has also cleared several of the older children for debriefing, knowing you'd want to learn as much as you could about the aliens. She wants you to observe those sessions."*

"Understood," Ben said. "Tell the counselor I'll meet her in her office shortly. Is there anything else?"

"Yes," Kosciuszko said. *"How's your arm?"*

Ben glanced down to where the left sleeve of his uniform had been cut away. His eyebrows rose, as though he'd forgotten about whatever had happened to him down on the strange alien world. A nasty purplish scar arced across the muscle there. Kasidy had noticed it when she'd first entered Ben's ready room.

"It's not the prettiest surgical procedure I've ever had, but it seems to be holding up," Ben said. He flexed his arm and rotated his shoulder, apparently putting his words to the test.

"Best I could do on a runabout while also starting examinations on almost thirty children," Kosciuszko said. *"We can mend the scar tissue later."*

"Thank you, Doctor," Ben said. "Sisko out." As the comm channel closed, Ben stood up and yanked his uniform tunic over his head, then headed into the alcove leading to his refresher.

"What happened down there?" Kasidy asked. "Are you all right?"

"One of the beings shot me with a projectile weapon," Ben called back to her from around the corner. He spoke as though getting wounded in battle didn't matter at all, as though such dangers had become second nature to him.

And why wouldn't they? she thought. *After everything that Ben's been through in his career, in his life.*

Ben reappeared with a fresh uniform tunic. He pulled it on and walked back over to her. He started to say something, but then the comm system signaled again.

"Bridge to Captain Sisko," said the ship's first officer.

"Sisko here. What is it, Commander?"

"Captain, we're being hailed," Rogeiro said.

"Hailed?" Ben said. "By who?"

"*The Glant.*"

Ben turned on his heel and headed for the door. "I'm on my way," he said. He looked back at Kasidy, and she expected him to tell her to go back to their quarters, and that he would contact her as soon as he could. Instead, he said, "Come with me."

Kasidy jumped out of her seat and followed him onto the bridge.

Sisko strode to the center of the bridge. In his peripheral vision, he saw his wife take a position off to one side, along the port ramp. Sisko nodded to Uteln at the tactical station, and the commander operated his console. A voice issued from the comm system.

"*I am Voranesk of the Glant,*" it said, its character distinctly unisex. "*Contacting Captain Benjamin Sisko of the United Federation of Planets.*" It uttered Sisko's title, name, and the government he represented essentially as one word, as though the speaker did not understand the distinct parts of speech, treating the entire grouping of words as a single identifier.

"On-screen," Sisko said, and he faced the main viewer.

The distant view of the Dyson section hanging in front of the stars disappeared, replaced by a strange image, though not one inconsistent with what the captain had so far witnessed of the Glant. He saw a backdrop composed of small stones and wooden dowels. In front of it stood something Sisko might not have distinguished as a living being, or even as a functioning robot, had he not already seen so many members of the Glant—no two of them even remotely alike. It resembled a cluster of balloons attached by flexible metallic necks to a bulky, squarish body, from which emerged half a dozen tentacles, arranged with curious asymmetry. Each of the three balloon-like projections had shaded areas that suggested to the captain some kind of sensory organs.

"This is Captain Sisko. Are you prepared to release the rest of our children?" He saw no reason not to come directly to the point.

"You cannot be here," Voranesk said. When it spoke, a cavity formed at the top of its boxy body, growing and vanishing with a fluid motion. *"Your explorations are [untranslatable]. You must go."*

"We will not leave here without our children," Sisko insisted. "If you return them to us, we will leave your system at once."

Voranesk's balloon-like heads fanned out, shifting away from one another. *"We cannot return what we do not have!"* it said, its words loud and rushed. *"You must go. Your explorations harm us. They are [untranslatable]."*

In her chair at the operations station, Plante spun around to face Sisko. "Captain," she said, her tone urgent.

"Voranesk, stand by," Sisko said. A tone indicated that Uteln had muted the signal with the Glant representative. "What is it?"

"They don't understand the concept of children," Plante said.

"What?" Sivadeki said from the conn. "How could that be? In order for a species to survive, it has to reproduce."

"And if a species reproduces, how could its members not understand the idea of children?" Sisko said, following Sivadeki's logic. The captain glanced back over his shoulder and nodded. Uteln restored the communications link. "Voranesk, we do not wish to explore your world. We—"

"You did *explore,"* Voranesk said, still agitated. *"Many singles saw you. You ended the existence of eight of our number."*

Its balloon-shaped heads came together and dipped forward. When it spoke again, its words came more softly and more slowly. *"It is a terrible tragedy. Our loss is irreplaceable."*

Sisko pondered the universal translator's use of the phrase *ended the existence of*, rather than *killed* or *murdered*. "We visited your world and fought against your people only because we had no other choice," the captain tried to explain. "We wanted our—" Sisko stopped, not wanting to use the word *children* again. "Your people attacked our ship and stole from us," he continued. "We wanted to get back what you stole."

The balloon projections bobbed downward and then back up. They twisted on their metallic necks, first to the left, then to the right, as though Voranesk looked somewhere off-screen for guidance. It took more than a few seconds before it responded. *"Do you speak of Gist?"* it finally asked. *"In taking our Gist, you undermined our efforts to actualize the next Issuance."* Again, its heads huddled together and dipped forward, a movement from which Sisko inferred a sense of sadness. *"Your explorations ended the existence of eight of our number, an unspeakable crime, but then you interfered with an Issuance . . . a monstrous act of which it is almost impossible to conceive."*

Voranesk appeared even more distraught over the *Robinson* crew interfering with an "Issuance"—whatever that meant—than with the deaths they had suffered. Sisko didn't understand, though he could only conclude that the Glant referred to whatever the captain's away team had put a halt to in the chamber where they'd found the children. "Voranesk, I do not comprehend what you are telling me," Sisko said. "And I don't think that you understand all that I am saying."

"Your communication is . . . perplexing," Voranesk agreed. *"So are your explorations."*

Sisko wondered how they could move forward. At that

moment, more than anything, it seemed clear that both sides would benefit from an improvement in their ability to communicate. "Voranesk, I want to understand your people, and I want you to understand my people," Sisko said. "I want a peaceful resolution to this situation. I'm sure you must want that too."

"Peaceful, yes," Voranesk said, though the captain could not tell whether it agreed with his sentiment or simply indicated its grasp of the word. *"No more ending our existence. No more interfering with an Issuance."*

"To that end, can we meet?" Sisko asked. In the corner of his eye, he saw Kasidy whip her head around, taking her gaze from the main viewscreen and placing it squarely on him.

"Meet," Voranesk repeated.

"Face-to-face," Sisko said, hoping that the phrase translated adequately into the Glant language.

"I . . . do not know," Voranesk said. *"I must consult with my people."*

"I understand," Sisko said. "Will you contact us again once you have done so?"

"You will not explore more while I speak with my people?" Voranesk said. Although the tone provided by the universal translator remained effectively impartial, the words conveyed an imploring posture.

"We will take no actions while we wait," Sisko said, "as the long as the Glant also take no actions."

"That is satisfactory."

"Then I look forward to hearing from you," the captain said. "Sisko out."

From where he sat in the first officer's position, Rogeiro spoke first, as Sisko expected he would. "If you're going to meet with representatives of the Glant, you should do so aboard the *Robinson*," the exec said. "That will give us the best chance of guaranteeing your safety."

"My safety is immaterial," Sisko said, still standing in the center of the bridge. He felt the burden of his wife's presence—she would not want to hear everything he had to say, beginning with his assessment of the relative unimportance of his own well-being—but he had asked her to come to the bridge for a reason. "Our only goal right now is to retrieve the rest of the children and then to get away from the Glant."

"Bringing members of the Glant here could provide us with leverage," Uteln said. "If necessary, we could detain them. We could then negotiate for an exchange of prisoners."

Sisko considered the idea. "That is a possibility," he said. "At least, it is if the Glant submit to coming aboard the ship. Right now, they haven't even agreed to meet."

"I'm not particularly sanguine about any meeting that would take place on their world," Rogeiro said. "They've already attacked our ship and taken the children. There's nothing to suggest they wouldn't imprison you if you went down there."

"Which is exactly what you were just talking about doing to them if they agree to come aboard the *Robinson*," Plante said from the ops console.

"With all due respect, Commander, we are speaking about responses to two different situations," Uteln said. "We are merely attempting to recover our children and restore the status quo. The Glant have been aggressors, and remain so by not releasing those they've abducted."

"None of that really matters now," Sisko said. "What matters is recovering the children, and it seems to me that the best way of accomplishing that is to get as close as possible to them. Finding a diplomatic solution with the Glant would be the optimal solution, but we've seen little to suggest that will happen. In that case, we will once more have to use force. The Glant now know about our capabilities in terms of weapons and the transporter, so it makes sense that they will adjust their defenses accordingly. A meeting on their world will get us closer to the children, but it will also allow us to learn about the Glant and, if necessary, how best to mount another rescue operation."

"Does that mean the meeting will be only a ruse?" Sivadeki asked.

"No," Sisko said. "We'll seek a diplomatic solution. Maybe all that will require is to find genuine understanding between our people and the Glant."

"That means discovering why they did what they did," Rogeiro said. "They obviously didn't attack the *Robinson* and abduct the children for no reason."

"And based on our discovery of that old stranded starship, it appears that they've been attacking vessels in the region for a long time," Uteln said. "That might make it particularly difficult to change their minds."

"But maybe we won't have to do that," Sisko said. "If we can determine why they attacked us and what they hoped to get out of it, perhaps we can find an alternative— provide the Glant with something that will satisfy them in exchange for returning the children."

"Do you think that's possible?" Plante asked.

"I don't know," Sisko said. "But it's important to try, and that's why I'm going to bring a first-contact team down with me." The captain glanced over at Kasidy, intending the look itself to signal his plan to include her on such a diplomatic mission—not because she was Rebecca's mother or his wife, but because of her training, because of her expertise.

Rogeiro raised an eyebrow, which told the captain that his first officer had concerns about the inclusion of Kasidy on the mission. Sisko assumed that the exec would have reservations about the presence of any parent with a missing child. The captain understood that concern. Given the tremendous emotional stakes, bringing the mother of a kidnapped child to meet with the Glant could be a mistake. But Sisko believed in Kasidy and her abilities. He also thought that her emotions could prove an asset, expressively demonstrating to the Glant the terrible toll their actions had exacted. Sisko just hoped that, after everything they'd been through—on Deep Space 9, on Bajor, aboard *Robinson*—that she still trusted him, and would accept whatever decisions he had to make.

Bajor, 2380

Tey led Orisin Dever and two of his Militia officers along the third-floor walkway. The major had arrived moments earlier, carrying with him a search warrant that the justice minister had secured from a judge. It had taken three hours, during which time Tey had kept watch on Radovan's flat. Nobody had entered or exited the residence.

At the door, Tey stepped to the side, allowing Orisin to stand directly in front of it. Just as she had done earlier, he lifted his hand and knocked. "This is the Militia," the major said loudly. "We have a warrant to search these premises. Open this door immediately."

Tey did not expect a response. She'd concluded that Radovan had packed up and left—presumably with Rebecca Sisko. While Orisin waited, Tey walked the few steps to the end of the building and glanced around the corner, to where two more Militia officers stood guard. The major had stationed people on every side of the building, on the roof, and in the basement to forestall Radovan's escape through the windows or any unforeseen exit routes.

After a minute had passed, Tey expected Orisin to knock again. He didn't. Instead, he moved aside, drew his phaser, and motioned to the woman and man, whom the major had introduced as Lieutenant Tapren and Sergeant Elvem. The sergeant raised a thick, meter-long metal cylinder with a flanged front end. He held it by a set of straps along one side, while the lieutenant grabbed a second set of straps on the other. The two officers looked at each other, and when Tapren nodded, they swayed backward with the ram, then thrust it forward into the door. When the cylinder struck the hard surface, a piston inside fired, adding to the force of the impact. Pieces of wood flew as both the door and the jamb splintered.

Tapren and Elvem moved away from the doorway, setting down the ram and drawing their own phasers. Orisin darted inside, his weapon raised before him. Tey went in after him.

Inside, the major and the other officers fanned out to search the place for Radovan. Tey's gaze immediately fell on a replicator set into the wall across from her. Panels had been removed and clusters of fiber-optic cables ran from one revealed set of circuitry to another. Along with a pile of hard-copy documents, a number of isolinear chips lay scattered on the table in front of the replicator. Tey saw that one of the chips had fallen to the floor beside a chair.

Orisin and his officers called out to one another as they verified the emptiness of a room or closet, while Tey moved to the table. She examined the top document in the stack and saw that it was Radovan's birth record. Tey riffled through the papers, reading several at random: certification for Radovan as a transporter operator; a transfer deed for a property in Lonar Province; medical reports for Radovan Lena, Tavus's mother; and a death certificate for Radovan Jendo, his brother.

Looking up, Tey eyed the suspiciously modified replicator. She raised her wrist comm and activated it with a touch, then instructed it to download a record of all objects generated in the flat over the past month. The most recent items concerned her, though she could not claim to be surprised: drugs, a medkit, quantities of various chemicals, and several pieces of technological equipment, including a sensor mask and a transporter inhibitor. Tey did not doubt that they had found Rebecca Sisko's kidnapper.

"Freeze!" Sergeant Elvem suddenly yelled. Tey turned to see him with his back against the wall in a short passage. He held his weapon with two hands, raised in front of him and pointed toward an open door. Orisin appeared in the bedroom beyond.

For a few seconds, nobody moved. Tey waited either for Elvem to fire or for somebody to emerge from the closet. Neither of those things happened, and finally the sergeant slowly stepped forward into the open doorway, his phaser still aimed before him. As he crouched down, Tey moved to the closet and looked inside. Beyond Elven, she saw the form of a portly woman on the floor, folded into the corner. Her chin rested against her chest and her eyes were closed.

The sergeant reached forward and placed two fingers against the side of the woman's neck. When Elvem looked back over his shoulder, Tey knew what he would say even before he opened his mouth. "She's dead."

Radovan deactivated the portable gamma-ray generator and stowed its emitter back in the device. He had just finished irradiating both the interior and exterior of the travel pod, destroying any biological traces of himself and the girl. He stood back and waited for the vehicle to activate itself. He had set it for automated operation, programming a haphazard course into the navigational system that would take it far from his current location and any settlements. He'd also wiped the record of the journey he'd made from Johcat, and disabled the automatic logging of the travel pod's speed, direction, and location.

At the edge of the wood, the reflected light of Derna,

Penraddo, and Jeraddo provided the only illumination, casting the world beneath the three moons with a silvern glow. As Radovan waited for the travel pod to power up and move away, he gazed skyward at the trio of orbs that circled Bajor. Endalla had not risen, nor would it until the deepest hours of the night. It didn't matter. Radovan considered himself the embodiment of Bajor's largest natural satellite. Rejias Norvan had been convinced that the Ohalu texts pointed to subterranean evidence on Endalla of the veracity of the Ohalavaru beliefs. Starfleet and the Emissary had interfered with the quest to find that proof, but Radovan had been moving forward ever since then to deliver on that promise. The Ohalavaru hadn't found the confirmation of their beliefs, but he would. He had listened to Rejias, he had read and reread *The Book of Ohalu*, and he had allowed the many dreams he'd experienced since the incident to coalesce in his waking mind. It had come together slowly at first, the pieces not quite fitting together, but he'd followed them, sometimes performing tasks without fully understanding where they would lead.

They led here, Radovan thought. He stood at the edge of the Talveran Forest, staring up at a triad of Bajor's moons, knowing that his path would soon end. He still didn't quite know how, but he could sense his ultimate destination not far ahead. And in truth, he had an inkling of the way forward, in part because of those many tasks his dreams had impelled him to complete: kidnapping the girl, modifying his replicator, stockpiling drugs and chemicals, equipment and technology.

He wondered if he should build something for the Avatar. A platform from which he could broadcast her delivering a message to the Ohalavaru? Or perhaps to *all* of Bajor? Or should he construct some sort of extreme transporter that would deliver her to the heart of Endalla so that she could point the way to the proof Rejias had sought? Could he concoct an elixir that would unleash her consciousness in a way that would embody the teachings of Ohalu?

Or should it be something else? Radovan thought. Should he mix a poison for the girl to take? Cobble together a machine to deliver electric shocks to her tiny body? Should he—

The travel pod droned to life. It slowly lifted from the ground, hovered briefly, redirected itself by spinning on its axis, then sped into the distance. Radovan stood there watching it, the radiance of the visible moons glinting off its metallic surface. It seemed emblematic of his connection with society, growing smaller with each passing moment.

When finally the travel pod faded from view, Radovan switched on the wrist-mounted beacon he wore. Its bright white beam cut through the shadowy night and picked out the nearest trees, tall, leafy sentinels that stood guard at the brink of the Talveran Forest. He followed the light of his beacon into the dark wood, to where the moonglow could not penetrate. He padded along layers of fallen leaves, soft and sodden, his footsteps mere rustles in the night.

Radovan pulled a small padd from his pocket and switched it on. He followed the digital map he'd loaded into it for half a kilometer until he reached a small clearing. He spotted his active sensor mask first, a narrow column mounted on a tripod base and topped by a bowl-shaped emitter. Beside it stood a transporter inhibitor, also switched on. A few paces farther on, his antigrav trunk and two duffels sat on the ground.

Radovan set down the portable gamma-ray generator and placed his padd back in his pocket. He opened the trunk, unloaded its main compartment, then removed the false bottom. The girl still lay there unconscious, the breathing mask still over her face. Radovan noted that her respiration had grown shallow, and he wondered if he'd injected her with too much sedative. He took her wrist—such a small thing, so delicate in his hand—and felt for her pulse. It was still strong.

After grabbing up a couple of items he'd brought with him, Radovan threw the beam of his wrist-mounted beacon out ahead of him and searched the surrounding ground. He had chosen the clearing for his encampment in part because it featured several patches of exposed stone. He located one such area and got down on his knees before it. He found a seam in the rock, centered a metal piton atop it, then used a sledge to drive its barbed end into the rocky earth.

Over the next half hour, Radovan set up his camp. He placed a tarp and sleeping mat beside the exposed stone, then carried the unconscious girl over to it, covering her with a thermal blanket. He fixed a restraint just above her right wrist, then attached it via a chain to the piton he'd sunk into the rock. He erected a tent around her, then set up one for his own use. He brought the sensor mask and the transporter inhibitor closer, though he needn't have, given the considerable ranges over which they functioned.

Radovan drank some water and thought about having something to eat, but he feared that the excitement he felt would disturb his digestion. He climbed inside his tent, lay down on his sleeping mat, and pulled a blanket over him. He waited for sleep to take him in the hope that his dreams would point him to what came next.

But Radovan lay awake in the darkness, his exhilaration for what he'd so far accomplished too great to overcome. He craved sleep, and the images that his slumbering mind would summon, but an hour passed with agonizing slowness. He worried over what he'd left behind in his flat. Radovan had utilized the replicator to recycle the child's toilet seat and step stool he'd gotten, along with the entertainment padd on which the girl had drawn pictures. He'd tried to remove any traces of her from his flat, going so far as to use the gamma-ray generator to destroy any DNA she'd left behind. But none of that addressed the one item that, because of its size and nature, he had been unable to make vanish: Winser Ellevet's corpse.

Finally, unable to sleep, Radovan rose, gathered up his beacon, and decided to check on the girl. Leaving his tent, he saw that Derna and Jeraddo had set, while Penraddo had ascended high overhead. Endalla had just begun to peek over the tops of the trees at the rim of the clearing, and he dared to think that might be a sign of things to come. He made his way over to the other tent and squatted down before it. He turned the beacon on to its dimmest setting and pointed it at the ground. The residual light left him in a murky glow. He quietly pulled back the tent's flap.

The girl stared back at him from within, unmoving.

Startled, Radovan barked out a guttural cry. He lost his balance and fell backward off his haunches, landing on the ground on his backside. His heart pounded in his chest.

She just surprised you, Radovan told himself. *That's all.* But it was more than that and he knew it. The girl's eyes, reflecting the light of the beacon, had appeared otherworldly.

Stop it! he told himself. *Be a man.*

Radovan pushed himself up onto his knees and swept back the flap of the tent again. The girl still sat there looking at him. He flashed the beacon onto her arm to ensure that she remained tethered.

"I have to go," the girl said. She spoke in a normal voice, which seemed too loud for their nighttime surroundings. The girl did not seem scared or even shaken by her current circumstances.

"All right," Radovan said. He pulled a key from his pocket and moved out of the tent, aiming the light on the manacle attached to the piton. He unlocked it, then fastened it about his wrist. He would take no chances of the girl getting away.

After helping her on with her shoes, Radovan moved to pick the girl up. She refused, and so he led her over to his supplies, where he picked up some refresher tissue and another beacon. He led the girl to the edge of the clearing, shining his light ahead of them on the ground. Radovan took her just inside the trees. He offered to help, but she told him no, so he gave her the 'fresher tissue and the second beacon, then stepped back into the clearing. Radovan waited, wondering if the girl might try to escape, even though her wrist remained attached to his via a chain. She didn't, and when she finished, he brought her back to her tent.

"I'm hungry," the girl said as he unfastened the manacle from his wrist and reattached it to the piton.

Radovan got up and walked over to his supplies. He rooted around the foodstuffs. Considering the lateness of the hour, he looked for something bland. He settled on a package of kavameal, emptied it into a bowl, and added water. He found a spoon and mixed the traditional breakfast staple, then carried it back to the second tent. Dropping to his knees once more, he leaned inside and handed it to the girl.

She took the bowl and peered into it. She picked up the spoon and dug around in its contents. Then she lifted the bowl to her face and sniffed at it.

"It's kavameal," Radovan said. "It's good for you."

The girl made a face, clearly not enthralled with what he'd elected to feed her. "It looks yucky," she said. She plopped the bowl down in front of her. Some of the kavameal slopped over the side.

Anger flared in Radovan. He heaved the top of his body into the tent, landing on his hands. He snatched the bowl and flung it backward, out onto the ground, some of the wet, pulpy kavameal spilling onto his arm. He raised his hand and felt it curl into a fist.

From where she sat atop her sleeping mat, the girl didn't flinch away, but simply looked up at Radovan. Her peaceful, unfazed countenance disarmed him. He suddenly felt foolish for threatening to strike a young child. He lowered his hand and sat back on his thighs.

She's not just a child, Radovan reminded himself. *She's the Avatar.* The girl impressed him. He could see in her what the Ohalu texts described: a special individual, whose life would be the price for an age of peace for the people of Bajor.

"You have to take me home," the girl said. She spoke with more confidence, with more of a commanding tone, than should have been possible for a human yet to reach her fourth birthday.

"Even if I wanted to take you home, I can't," Radovan told the girl. "I sent the travel pod away, and I have no comm equipment to contact anybody." He realized that he had essentially just told the girl not only that she would never leave the Talveran Forest alive, but that neither would he. Though he supposed he had known that for some time, it was the first time he'd admitted it to himself. He thought that perhaps the idea should have scared him; instead, he felt relieved.

"They know who you are," the girl said. "They're looking for you . . . for *us*." The pronouncements spoke again to the strangeness of the Avatar. Her words sounded convincingly certain, whether she intended them as a bluff—a tactic that seemed far too adult for such a young girl—or she truly believed what she said.

Radovan gazed down at the bright circle generated by his wrist beacon. He lifted his hand and turned it around, shining the light on his own face from below. He glared back at the girl, though he could no longer see her. "Let them search," he told her.

Radovan backed out of the tent and returned to his supplies. He located the medkit and the ampoules he'd brought with him. He hadn't replicated all of the drugs for Rebecca—and, as it had turned out, for Winser Ellevet. He also produced some to administer to himself, if necessary— to help him sleep and, more important, to spur an active dream state. At that moment, he felt exhausted, not just from everything that had taken place in the past twenty-six hours, but because he craved to know what to do next—or if not precisely *what* to do, then *how* to do it.

When he found the right ampoule, Radovan inserted it into the hypospray, then returned to his own tent. He switched off the beacon and removed it from his wrist. He then lay down on his back, held the hypo to his shoulder, and injected himself.

Radovan felt himself immediately grow calmer, knowing that sleep would soon take him, and that the dreams he needed would not be far behind. He closed his eyes, but before he drifted off, he called out to the girl. "Let them search," he said again. "By the time they find us, it will be too late."

Soon after, he fell asleep. And dreamed. Of Endalla, of the Avatar, and of the explosive fire that would soon consume him and the girl.

Inside the small operators' lounge, Tey brushed her hand across her mouth and chin, affecting a gesture of deep contemplation, but in reality covering her effort to stifle a yawn. The young man seated on the other side of the table did not bore her, but the day had grown long and she would need to sleep soon. She didn't want to—she would have preferred to continue her efforts to find Rebecca Sisko and her kidnapper—but she knew her mind and body well, and she had no illusions about her limitations. She had been awake for more than twenty hours, and if she conducted her investigation much longer without rest, she would risk missing a relevant detail here or an important clue there. She relied first and foremost on her own abilities, but she also understood that nobody could work effectively around the clock, and that solving crimes typically required the efforts of more than a single person. Major Orisin and his team of Militia officers had so far ably demonstrated their professionalism and skills.

When the man across the table finished describing his role at the Elanda District Three Transporter Terminal, Tey dropped her hand from in front of her mouth and asked him about his relationship with Radovan Tavus. Not yet thirty, Derish Koln exuded a naïveté that suggested he would be of little value to the investigation. Still, Tey believed in being thorough, not for its own sake, but because she knew that critical information could come from even the unlikeliest of sources.

At that point, Tey felt certain that she had successfully identified Rebecca Sisko's abductor in Radovan Tavus. A sensor expert would soon arrive at the man's flat to search for Rebecca's DNA, but the evidence that Tey, Orisin, and the other Militia officers had already found there only strengthened her belief. The unlawful modifications to Radovan's home replicator, as well as the items produced with the enhanced device, supported her view, as did the discovery of a dead body stuffed into a closet, which indicated something far worse: a kidnapper willing to kill.

Orisin's staff had identified the lifeless woman as Winser Ellevet, a middle-aged records officer at the main city administration building in Johcat. They had yet to uncover her relationship with Radovan, and it remained unclear what role she had played in the abduction of Rebecca Sisko, or why she had been murdered. Although a full autopsy and toxicological assessment still had to be performed, the medical examiner, in part owing to the lack of any significant external damage to Winser's body, had reached a preliminary conclusion of death either by overdose or by toxin. Radovan had replicated enough drugs in his home to have readily caused either outcome.

While Orisin and his staff had started compiling a register of Radovan's family members and friends, as well as a similar list for Winser, Tey had beamed to Elanda. There, she began questioning Radovan's colleagues at the public transporter in the city's third district. Since the hour had passed midnight, Tey found only a handful of operators on duty at the terminal; interviews of the other personnel assigned there would have to take place at their homes. Derish marked Tey's final conversation before she reported her findings to Orisin and headed home to sleep, while members of the major's staff questioned the absent operators.

"I wouldn't say that I know Tavus particularly well," Derish told her. "I mean, we often see each other coming or going, and we sometimes share a shift. We occasionally talk, mostly when we're both on overnight, when traffic is at its lowest ebb."

"What do you talk about?"

"I don't know," Derish said, offering a halfhearted shrug. "Nothing particularly important. Honestly, Tavus mostly keeps to himself. He doesn't say much, even when you do speak to him."

"Does he ever talk about serious issues?" Tey asked. "Things like politics or religion?" She tried to be circumspect in her questioning. She hadn't categorized Radovan as a suspect, but simply as a person of interest, meaning that he could have been the victim of a crime, or a witness. Neither had she divulged the reason for her investigation.

"Um, no, not that I can recall," Derish said. "I might've

heard him talking to somebody once about the Ohalavaru."
The young man spoke haltingly and with little confidence.

"Do you remember what he said?" Tey asked. "Does he
support them? Or oppose them?"

Derish looked down at the table, where he nervously
twirled a ring around a finger on his right hand. "Um, I can't
recall," he eventually said, shaking his head. "I'm sorry."

"It's all right," Tey said with a smile, attempting to put
Derish at ease. "I'm only asking about what you can remember. This isn't a test."

One side of Derish's lips curled upward, but the expression did nothing to convince Tey that she had in the slightest reduced his anxiety about being questioned. "Well, like
I said, we really don't speak much. And when we do, it's
mostly about what's going on in the transporter terminal."

"I understand," Tey said. "How would you describe—"
Her wrist comm emitted an urgent chirp. She glanced down
and saw Major Orisin attempting to contact her. Looking
up at Derish, Tey said, "I'm afraid I need to respond to this."

"Of course," Derish said, but he made no move to leave
the room.

"Would you mind giving me some privacy?" Tey asked,
again smiling so as to avoid intimidating the young man.

"Oh, right, sorry," Derish said. He quickly stood up and
scampered out of the operators' lounge. Tey followed him
to the door, ensuring that it closed securely behind him.
Then she tapped at her wrist comm.

"This is Tey," she said. "What is it, Major?"

"*I wanted you to know that we distributed Radovan's name
and likeness to the checkpoints in Johcat,*" Orisin said. "*We got
an immediate hit. He left the city in a public travel pod not
long after sunset, under his own name.*"

"He gave his own name? Then he doesn't think we've
identified him yet," Tey said. "Was the girl with him?" She

did not say *Rebecca* in case somebody overheard the conversation.

"*She wasn't visible in the pod, and sensors didn't detect her presence,*" Orisin said. "*But the sergeant who dealt with Radovan said he had camping gear in the pod, including a large antigrav trunk. Considering that he replicated sensor-resistant materials, it's conceivable that he masked her life signs and smuggled her out.*" The major didn't need to mention that, carried from the city in such a manner, Rebecca could have been alive or dead.

"Have you tracked the travel pod's transponder?" Tey asked.

"*Yes, but Radovan disabled it not far from where he left the city. We're utilizing satellite-based sensors now to scan for the pod.*"

"Do we have any idea where he might be headed?" Tey asked.

"*The sergeant at the checkpoint said that he spoke about visiting his uncle's cabin, but a survey of public records shows that Radovan has no uncle—no living family of any kind, actually.*"

"Is he anywhere near the Deserak Wilderness?" Tey asked on a hunch.

"*He did leave the city on a route that took him past there, yes,*" Orisin said. "*We've got eyes on the location of the kidnapping. We're trying to watch the entire region, but Deserak is a massive preserve.*" The major paused, then added, "*We did think it was possible that he might be bringing her back to where he abducted her—maybe so that he could return her, if he's thought better of what he's done.*"

"He's not bringing her back," Tey said decisively. "With the dead body we found at his flat, he's in too deep, but . . ." She thought through her profile of Radovan, then added in what she'd just been told. "He used his own name at the checkpoint, then headed toward the Deserak Wilderness before disabling the travel pod's transponder. It's a ruse. He didn't hide his identity because he didn't think we were onto him; he *wants* us to believe that he's going to Deserak. He's not."

"Does that mean you think we should call off the search there?" Orisin asked. It sounded as though he found the idea troubling.

"No, by all means, maintain surveillance there," Tey told the major. "But I would also spread your efforts out all around the city."

"I agree," Orisin said. *"Have you learned anything in Elanda?"*

"No, not yet, and I don't expect to," Tey said. "It turns out that Radovan was something of a loner." Orisin made a yapping sound that might have been labeled a laugh in less serious circumstances. "I've got one last interview to finish up here, then I'm headed home to get some sleep."

"So am I," said the major. *"I'll leave orders with Captain Fisel to contact both of us if there are any developments overnight. Orisin out."*

Tey deactivated her comm, then sat silently for a moment, trying to put herself inside the mind of Radovan Tavus. Where would he go? Why would he take Rebecca Sisko there?

And once he gets there, what does he intend to do with her?

With no answers apparent to her, Tey went back over to the door, opened it, and looked out into the terminal. She thought she might have to search for Derish in one of the eight chambers housing transporter platforms in the large facility, but the operator hadn't left the concourse. He stood just ten meters away, with his back against a support column. He straightened when he saw Tey, and she motioned him back into the lounge.

Inside, Derish sat back down at the table. Tey once more took a seat across from him. She asked if the young man had ever heard Radovan talk about an uncle—or about any of his family, for that matter.

"Um, no, ma'am," Derish said.

"What about hobbies?" Tey asked. "Does he ever talk about what sorts of activities he enjoys?"

"No, I don't think so."

"Really?" Tey persisted. "He never talks about hiking? Skiing? Camping?"

"No, not any of those. Like I said, he mostly keeps to himself and doesn't say much."

Tey spoke with Derish for another ten minutes, but the character of their conversation didn't change. He provided no information of value about Radovan—other than to further confirm the profile she had developed of the kidnapper. Finally, she thanked the young man for his time.

Back out in the terminal, Derish resumed his post, and Tey had him beam her to the Ashalla District Five Transporter Terminal. She walked home from there, quickly ran through her nightly ablutions, and climbed into bed. As she lay in the darkness, staring up at the shadows on her ceiling, it occurred to her that, as they'd burst into his home that night, Radovan had already slipped away.

Tey concentrated on that frustrating thought for a few seconds, allowing it to motivate her. Then she set it aside and closed her eyes. She fell asleep almost immediately—a habit born out of a career spent in security, where, on occasion, sleep came at irregular and unpredictable intervals.

Vivid dreams visited Tey through the night and into the early morning, but when she woke, they slipped away like a spring mist beneath the rising sun.

Gamma Quadrant, 2386

As Kasidy marched into *Robinson*'s shuttlebay with the rest of the away team, she experienced a mixture of anxiety and eagerness, of fear and anticipation, but she also had confidence that she could handle all of it. For the first time since *Robinson* had been attacked four days earlier, she actually felt rested. While the crew had waited for word from the Glant about the meeting Ben had proposed, he'd insisted that she get some sleep—that they *both* get some sleep. Doctor Kosciuszko prescribed a soporific for them, which helped them get through the night.

Although Kasidy had definitely needed the rest, she believed it even more important that her husband had actually gotten a good night's sleep—or at least six hours' worth. Ben suffered through the same anxieties and fears about their daughter that Kasidy did, but the responsibility of the more than thirteen hundred lives aboard *Robinson* also fell on his shoulders. On top of all that, one of the crew, Lieutenant Stannis, had been shot in the chest during the attempt to rescue the children. The Orion arrived back on the ship in critical condition, but Doctor Mensara, who'd done her residency on his homeworld, successfully operated on him. Although expected to fully recover, he remained in serious condition, and Kasidy knew that the lieutenant's health would weigh on Ben until the medical staff released Stannis.

Inside the shuttlebay, it surprised Kasidy to see a veritable squadron of vessels spread out in a rectangular formation on the landing deck. Three rows of four shuttlecraft, their bows all pointed toward space, stretched from near the outer hatch to the interior bulkhead. Ben led the way past all of those ships toward the front of the bay, where a runabout sat open and waiting.

Kasidy boarded *Styx* amid the group of people Ben had chosen for the mission. They included Doctor Kosciuszko, Counselor Althouse, Ensign Weil, and Crewwoman Spingeld, as well as five of the six security guards who'd already visited the Glant world. Crewwoman Stephanie DeSantis replaced Ensign Bevelaqua, who'd suffered a minor injury when she'd been grazed by weapons fire. The ensign would be fine, but Ben wanted a fresh officer for the mission.

As Kasidy understood it, the plan called for Ensign Weil, the pilot, and Crewwoman Spingeld, the transporter operator, to remain aboard the runabout, along with all but one of the security officers. Kasidy had expected Ben to bring along additional diplomatic and first-contact personnel, but he'd explained that the Glant would allow only five individuals from *Robinson* to meet with five of their representatives. As the captain making command decisions, Ben obviously needed to be there. He also wanted the ship's counselor to attend the meeting in order to help make sense of the Glant—something even the universal translator had difficulty achieving. Further, he wanted to bring medical and security personnel in the event that the away team ended up conducting another operation to recover the children. That left only one opening for somebody with Kasidy's expertise.

As Ben and Ensign Weil took their positions at the main console in the runabout's cockpit, the rest of the away team moved past the high-capacity transporters to the rear compartment. As Kasidy sat down with the others, she wondered why Ben had selected her for the meeting with the Glant. She certainly had the training for such an encounter, along with a modicum of experience, but others among the ship's civilian staff had both more training and more experience than Kasidy.

Ben wants me there because of Rebecca, she thought. The conclusion seemed obvious, but it also didn't quite stand to reason. She knew that Ben trusted in her skills, but did he think that her desperation to get their daughter back would somehow motivate her to do a better job? That didn't track; her personal involvement might just as easily—and perhaps more likely—inhibit her performance and cause her to make mistakes.

Kasidy heard the runabout's hatch close with a reassuringly thick sound. The vessel's engines swelled to life, and then she felt the faintest sensation of movement, which surely meant that *Styx* had launched. Kasidy glanced around the compartment, looking for a port so she could confirm that the runabout had departed *Robinson*, but the vessel had clearly been reconfigured since the last time she'd been aboard. Lieutenant Rogers must have noticed her searching for a nonexistent port, because he rose from his chair and activated a viewscreen on the forward bulkhead. It blinked to life focused on the clearly artificial concave square of the Glant world. Numerous ships buzzed about in the space above it, while distant movement suggested that still other vessels served as sentries closer to the surface.

When he returned to his seat, Lieutenant Rogers leaned over to the chair next to his, to where he had placed a carrying case he'd brought aboard with him. He unfastened the lid and flipped it open. From inside the case, he removed a pair of small devices.

"These are special comm units designed to withstand

the sound weapons of the Glant," Rogers said. "Wear one in each ear the entire time we're on their world. They also function as universal translators."

He placed the comm units back in the case, then drew out a black metal circle. It looked to Kasidy like a bracelet. The lieutenant held it up in front of him.

"This is a transport enhancer," Rogers said. "Commander Relkdahz developed it. Wear one around your dominant wrist at all times." He put both his hands on it and pulled, revealing and spreading a break in the circle. Rogers slid the device onto his right wrist and allowed it to snap closed again. Then he passed the carrying case around so that everybody could take their equipment.

"What does this do?" Kasidy asked as she slipped her transport enhancer on.

"In a way, it's like a combadge," Rogers said. Though Kasidy did not wear a Starfleet uniform—she'd chosen a sleek red-and-black jumpsuit, much like those she'd donned aboard *Xhosa*—she nevertheless sported a combadge on the left side of her chest. "It continuously transmits real-time transporter data, but in a much more granular way."

"But to what end?" Doctor Kosciuszko asked.

Rogers explained a bit of theory about the transport enhancers, and then revealed their practical application. He answered a couple more questions. When everybody had taken one of the devices and a pair of the specialized comm units, the carrying case made its way back to Rogers. The lieutenant secured a second enhancer around his other wrist without explanation. He then selected two more of the devices, as well as two pair of the comm units, and took them up to the cockpit, presumably for Ben and Ensign Weil. He came back shortly, empty-handed.

As *Styx* drew closer to its destination, the viewscreen showed a quartet of alien ships break off from the others and navigate toward the runabout. For a few intense seconds, Kasidy thought that the Glant might be attacking, but she noted that Ben and Ensign Weil took no evasive action. Two of the alien ships—one that looked like a white pretzel, and another that resembled a dappled feather duster—took up positions just forward of *Styx*, to port and starboard. Kasidy assumed that the other pair followed the runabout aft.

After a while, the comm system chimed, and Ben's voice emerged. *"We're about to enter the zone of null space above the Glant world, so we're shutting down the impulse drive."* Even knowing that, Kasidy found the fading sound of the engines ominous.

The runabout coasted for a short distance before it shuddered, as though it had struck something. Kasidy glanced up toward the comm system, expecting Ben to make another announcement. He didn't, but Lieutenant Rogers said, "It's the threshold between the regular continuum and null space." Kasidy nodded her understanding and thanked the security officer with a smile.

When the surface of the Glant world had grown to fill the display, it looked to Kasidy like a view of any normal, naturally formed planet. She saw the browns of soil, the greens of vegetation, the dark blues of water, the whites of clouds. *And somewhere down there,* she could not help thinking, *Rebecca is being held captive.*

The runabout jolted a second time as it obviously left null space, but then it catapulted forward—not forward, but *down*. *Styx* fell, unpowered, toward the surface, the gravity of the Glant world taking hold. Kasidy involuntarily grabbed at the sides of her chair. Her stomach quavered, but then she heard the runabout's drive resume.

Kasidy peered again at the screen, but she didn't see it. *Why am I here?* she asked herself. She *wanted* to be there, it pleased her that Ben had assigned her to the away team, but she still didn't understand her husband's reasoning.

And then, all at once, she did.

Kasidy gazed at the screen. She saw that, down on the surface, a complex of buildings had come into view. As she eyed the away team's apparent destination, she understood that Ben intended for the two of them to bring Rebecca home together—or for both of them to die in the attempt.

Kasidy closed her eyes, nodded ever so slightly to herself, and thought, *I'm on board with that plan.*

Sisko studied the large room to which he, Doctors Kosciuszko and Althouse, Lieutenant Rogers, and Kasidy had been escorted. Roughly rectangular, it featured two sets of wide doors, one pair on each end, and no windows. The walls, which wavered from side to side and from top to bottom, appeared to be composed of buffed shards of glass, piled atop one another with their flat sides oriented horizontally. The room had a light-green cast, and though the floors and ceiling had been constructed of a material different from that of the walls, they had been colored to match. Other than lighting panels overhead and a glass table in a far corner, it featured no other built-in details and no other furnishings. The room contained no chairs—no places to sit other than on the floor.

The captain had piloted *Styx* to the surface coordinates provided by the Glant, with the runabout accompanied for most of its journey by a quartet of their ships. The landing zone—a paved area beside a sprawling complex of buildings—lay thousands of kilometers from the location where the remaining *Robinson* children were being held. Spingeld confirmed via sensors that they hadn't been moved. An attempt to transport them to the runabout failed, just as it had during the first away mission, owing to the local interference of Glant technology.

When Sisko and the other four members of his team had disembarked *Styx*, they'd been met by a score of Glant. As had been the case with every one of their individuals the captain had so far seen, none of them looked like any other. They differed in form and hue, in the type and number of body parts and appendages, and in the amount of flesh, metal, and other materials that covered their bodies.

No member of the Glant had stepped forward to greet the *Robinson* delegation. The individual nearest Sisko—a gaunt, four-legged being with an oversize head, three massive eyes, and a body covered in pink down—said simply, "You are to come with us." Without waiting for a response, half of the group marched away. Sisko and the others followed, with the other half of the Glant contingent behind them.

The *Robinson* delegation had been led into a building, down a corridor Sisko found conspicuously empty, and into the large room. None of their escorts said anything more. They simply left and the doors slid closed behind them.

"Not terribly talkative, are they?" Althouse noted.

"When we did speak, the conversation wasn't easy," Sisko said. "That's one of the reasons you're here." Then, speaking to everybody, the captain said, "That's why we're all here. We have to try to understand the Glant. We need to—"

The doors at the far end of the room glided open to reveal five more of the aliens. As they entered, Sisko recognized one of the individuals—or at least its species. Its stocky, boxy body sprouted six tentacles in no discernible pattern, with a trio of balloon-shaped heads perched on malleable metal necks. Such an entity, which called itself Voranesk, had contacted *Robinson* in an attempt to warn the crew away. Either it was the same individual, or it marked the first time the captain had spotted a duplication—presumably meaning a second member of that particular species. To that point, every member of the Glant he'd seen had been different from every other—including the four others that entered the room. One comprised a series of spherical body parts that connected tangentially to each other and, but for the topmost such structure, continually changed places as the being, or robot, moved. Another walked on four stubby legs, low to the ground, but had a quartet of massive, elegant wings extending from its back. The fourth member of the group slid along like a large snake, though it possessed heads at both ends, and below each, a pair of arms. The final Glant resembled a Minotaur, except that while its lower half looked like that of a bull—albeit an eight-legged bull—its upper half appeared more Gorn than human.

No wonder there are no chairs, Sisko thought. None of them could fit into a humanoid-style seat. Moreover, it wouldn't be possible to craft a standardized piece of furniture to accommodate all of their many forms.

Sisko took a step forward and identified himself by rank and full name, then pointed to each member of his team and similarly introduced them. The squat entity with wings likewise moved up to the captain and said, "I am Pavartic of the Glant." It then gave the names of the others. It identified the balloon-headed creature as Voranesk, the one that had contacted Sisko aboard *Robinson.*

"Are you the leader of the Glant?" the captain asked.

"Am I the what?" Pavartic asked, its confusion plain.

"Do you speak on behalf of the Glant?" Sisko said.

Pavartic turned its lumbering body to one side and then the other, regarding its colleagues. "All Glant speak on behalf of the Glant. How could we do otherwise?"

Sisko felt a light touch on the back of his left shoulder,

and he glanced over to see Kasidy just behind him. "They don't understand the concept of a leader any more than they understand what children are," she said quietly. "It's possible that they have a genuine democracy, with every individual within it contributing equally."

Sisko wondered if that could mean that the Glant also possessed a collective consciousness—a hive mind, not unlike the Borg—but he didn't get that sense from them. They didn't appear to act with any more than an expected degree of coordination among them. To Pavartic, he said, "We seek a peaceful resolution to our encounter with the Glant."

"We seek that as well," Pavartic said. "We mourn the end of the existence of eight of our number by your hand, but there is nothing we do, and nothing you can do, to change what has happened. We can only guide what next will happen."

For a moment, the statement struck Sisko as a threat. The Glant could not undo the killing of the eight that had perished, but they could take consequent action. The captain braced for something to happen, but then nothing did. "We understand that one of the things you want to happen next is for us to end our explorations of your world and your space. We are willing to do that, to depart from here and never return."

"That is what we want," Voranesk said, speaking up for the first time. "But in the wake of the end of the existence of eight Glant, we wish for more."

"Yes," agreed the snake-like entity, which had been introduced as Kerchen. "We want you to return what you stole. We want you to return our Gist."

"Your . . . Gist," Sisko repeated. He understood the Glant meaning of the word no more at that moment than when Voranesk had mentioned it during its contact with *Robinson*. "We admit to 'ending the existence' of eight

Glant. We did not want that to happen, but we were forced to take such actions in order to recover our—" Sisko almost said *children*, but stopped himself, knowing that it meant nothing to the Glant. "In order to recover what you stole from us," the captain said. "We did not steal from you. We only took back what the Glant took from us."

"But you are not [untranslatable]," Kerchen said, Sisko's universal translator filling in the uninterpreted word with a flat tone. "You are not Glant. You have no need for Gist."

"Captain," Althouse said, moving up beside Sisko. "If I may." She motioned toward the Glant, and the captain nodded his authorization for her to speak to them. "Do you understand the notion of individuality, of distinctiveness?"

"The Unique is everything," Pavartic said. "Every Glant is imbued with It. Every Glant lives with It and brings more of It into the world." Pavartic spoke with what Sisko perceived as reverence, as though uniqueness held a primary position among the Glant's spiritual or religious tenets. That made sense to the captain. So much of what he had seen of the Glant underscored their desire for differentiation—in their ships, in their rooms and corridors, in their individual bodies.

Althouse took another step forward and turned to face Sisko and the others. She raised her arm and motioned to include all of them before looking back at the Glant. "Are we unique?" she asked.

None of the Glant replied at first. As the silence extended, Pavartic looked to the other Glant. They seemed uncertain. Finally, Pavartic said, "We do not wish to offend you."

"We're not imbued with the Unique, are we?" Althouse asked.

"You . . . are all the same," Pavartic admitted. "Surely, you can see that."

Sisko pondered the nature of the Glant's idea of humanity's lack of uniqueness. Two arms, two legs, a head, a torso—did those basic commonalities make all human be-ings like all other human beings? That felt wrong to Sisko, flying in the face of individuality, but at the same time, it had been humanity's collective acceptance of itself as a single race that had allowed it to evolve as a society, to rid itself of its internal fears and prejudices.

"All Glant are imbued with the Unique," the counselor went on. "But did the Glant evolve?"

For several seconds, nobody said anything, and then Voranesk replied, "We do not understand this word, this concept. Much of what you convey to us is meaningless."

Althouse nodded, as though she had expected such a response. "How far back in time does your history reach?"

"The Glant have existed for thousands of generations," Pavartic said.

"How do you reproduce?" Althouse asked. The question could have been considered rude, but given that the Glant did not understand the concept of children, Sisko wanted to hear their answer.

Voranesk's balloon-shaped heads spread out above its angular body. "Your words do not translate," it said.

"How does one generation . . . *create* . . . the next genera-tion?" Althouse said.

"By contributing to an Issuance," Voranesk said, as though that explained everything. But Althouse did not seem deterred.

"'By contributing to an Issuance,'" she repeated. "So you conceptualize a new generation, and then you design it, and finally you *build* it."

Pavartic lifted its front two feet and thumped them down on the floor in a gesture that could have indicated frustration or anger, levity or surprise. "One cannot con-ceptualize an *entire* generation," it said. "One present Glant contributes one future Glant."

"There are tales from ancient times that tell of one Glant creating *many* Glant," Voranesk said. "But those are mere myths."

Sisko had numerous questions, but he wanted to allow Althouse to complete her line of reasoning. "One present Glant conceives of one new Glant, drafts a blueprint for it, and then lastly builds it."

"Not 'lastly,'" Kerchen said. "Idea, design, creation, and then, lastly, actualization."

"And you interfered with an attempt to actualize the next Issuance," Voranesk said, its heads coming together and sinking forward.

Sisko saw the pattern forming out of the information Althouse drew from the Glant. He thought he understood the conclusion she had arrived at, the conclusion for which she sought confirmation, but he didn't want to accept it. It was too horrible.

"After the creation of a new Glant," Althouse asked, "that is when you require Gist?"

"Of course," Pavartic said. "Gist actualizes a new Glant."

Beside Sisko, Kasidy gasped. She knew. She had puzzled it out. He had too. The Glant didn't understand the concept of children because they didn't have any. They were wholly artificial life-forms. They might have incorporated organic materials into their creations, they might have grown flesh and organs to be used as building materials, but they created every new individual in a laboratory.

But without minds, Sisko thought. And so they had to harvest existing minds—what they called *Gist*—to transfer into the bodies that they built. Which is why they had taken the *Robinson* children. Perhaps they required brains of a certain form, ones that had not completely grown, or consciousnesses that had not become too rigid, but whatever the case, the Glant had selected those minds aboard *Robinson* that they could transfer into their newest creations.

Sisko reached out and set a hand on Althouse's arm, and she moved back behind him. "You claim that we stole Gist from you," he said. "But you took that Gist from us. It is ours." He knew that he could not argue about the importance of children to the Glant. He needed to speak to them in their own terms.

"We do not steal Gist," Voranesk said.

"How could we steal Gist from you?" Pavartic asked. It lifted one of its forward wings and pointed it at Althouse. "You admitted that you are all the same. Therefore it is not Gist to you, and so we could not steal it from you."

"It may not be Gist to us, but that doesn't mean it is unimportant," Sisko said. "In our society, the small beings you have taken from us are the most important part of our society. They are our next Issuance."

"The Glant have heard such arguments before," Voranesk said. "But our collection of Gist is a liberation, freeing it from the rigors of existence in a homogenous society and the ultimate end of lives all too brief."

"You have taken my daughter from me," Kasidy suddenly said.

"We do not know—" Pavartic said, doubtless objecting to the word *daughter*, but Kasidy interrupted.

"You have taken my creation for the next generation," she said. "I offer my life for hers. Release her and I will stay." While Sisko knew that Kasidy would, if necessary, make such a bargain—because he would too—he understood that she did not intend to forfeit her life. She knew that if they could not negotiate with the Glant for the release of the children, Sisko intended to make another rescue attempt. Kasidy would count on that to free her, but she clearly wanted to take that risk herself rather than have Rebecca remain in danger.

"You . . . do not have Gist," Pavartic said, lowering its head, giving it an apologetic air.

"I have a mind," Kasidy protested. "That's what you're talking about."

"Gist is more than just mind," Voranesk said. "It is a quality of malleability. It is the ability to accept change and a new reality. It is the highest capacity for learning."

Sisko thought for a moment, tried to find the right words, the right ideas, to convince the Glant to release the children. "The Glant see us as all the same," he said. "We don't. We believe that we have our own version of the Unique within each of us." Two of the Glant looked at each other, and Sisko could feel their skepticism. "We are different from you," he went on. "Maybe we are not as advanced as you. But we have created individuals for our next generation, and you have taken them from us. You felt horror when we took back sixty of our children. We felt that same horror when you took them from us. We still feel it for those that remain on your world. They are ours. They belong with us."

"We are sorry for your horror," Pavartic said. "But your claim to the Unique, while moving, is irrational and obviously untrue. The needs of the Glant are real."

"We are willing to negotiate with you," Sisko said. "There must be other things you need, other things that we can provide to you, or services we can perform." He preferred not to threaten the Glant if he could avoid it, but he stood on the cusp of doing just that.

"We appreciate your point of view, as well as your willingness to negotiate," Kerchen said. "But the only thing the Glant want from you is the return of the Gist you stole from us in your attack."

It was unbelievable. Sisko had offered whatever he could for the return of the rest of the *Robinson* children, but all the Glant wanted was for him to give back the children he had already rescued. He could think of nothing more to say.

"It is clear that you will not return the Gist you stole, nor will we give up the Gist we have," Kerchen said.

"The negotiations are ended," Pavartic declared.

"It doesn't matter anyway," Voranesk said. "Very soon, there will be a new Issuance. Once done, it is irreversible."

"What do you mean, 'very soon'?" Sisko demanded.

"The actualization," Voranesk said, "has begun."

Bajor, 2380

Among all of the dead bodies littering the barren crater that had been blasted out of Endalla, one did not belong. Radovan had followed the Emissary's gaze to locate it, then weaved his way toward it across the bottom of the basin, through the multitude of burned and unrecognizable corpses. He arrived at the center of the bowl-shaped depression to discover the lifeless form of a small child. It lay facedown on the polished glass of the ruined terrain. Radovan squatted down beside the diminutive body, reached out, and turned it over, revealing the unblemished face of the Avatar.

The little girl's eyes stared upward without seeing. She did not look at peace. Death had immobilized her face in a rictus of fear and surprise. Radovan did not know what to make of the Avatar's loss at so early an age.

And then the girl blinked.

Radovan almost lost his balance as he quickly stood up. He looked down and saw the Avatar peering up at him. Then her mouth moved and she spoke: "What are you going to do?"

That was the question he had been asking himself for so long. He had no place that he belonged, he had no family. His father had fled shortly after Radovan's birth, his older brother had lost his life in an accident, and his mother had left him in the most painful way of all: bit by bit, her health slipping away like a boulder rolling downhill, building momentum as it became an unstoppable force. *Now what?* he wanted to know, but no answers came.

Radovan expected to feel a hand on his shoulder, so when the touch came, he did not feel shock, but relief. He turned to see Benjamin Sisko, who had somehow escaped the devastation on Endalla. The Emissary looked upon him with an expression of benevolence.

"What am I going to do?" Radovan asked him.

In response, the Emissary reached forward. He held a device in his hands. As Radovan took it, the Emissary nodded his approval.

Radovan smiled. He rounded on his heel and crouched down to where the Avatar still lay. He tried to hand her the device, but her little arms could not hold it aloft, so he settled it atop her midsection.

The device started to tick. Radovan felt joy deep down in his gut, a sensation of pure elation like nothing he had ever known. For the first time in his life, he had purpose.

Radovan opened his mouth to laugh—

—and bolted upright on his sleeping mat. His heart beat in his chest with a rhythm of rapture. He still felt the smile on his face, the laugh in his mouth, that had decorated his dreams like the colorful trappings people hung for the Gratitude Festival.

Radovan threw off the blanket covering him. He stripped off the clothes he'd slept in, then dug through the duffel he'd brought into his tent. He found some of the clothes he sometimes wore to the Elanda District Three Transporter Terminal—dark slacks and a green, long-sleeved sweater—and threw them on.

Outside, the day had dawned brightly. The early-morning

sun threw long shadows across the clearing. Insects buzzed about in the still air, circling in seemingly random orbits above wild *esani* and *kidu* plants before alighting to feast on their colorful blossoms. The trees stood like mute sentinels on the periphery of the field. Above the leaves, on the distant horizon, Radovan saw murky, gray clouds gathering.

Perfect, he thought with satisfaction. *Because there's more than one storm coming.*

Radovan crossed to the girl's tent. He pulled the flap open and looked in to see her sleeping in a knot of covers. The blanket had somehow twisted about the chain that bound her manacled wrist to the piton he'd pounded into stone.

"Wake up," he told her. She stirred briefly, then settled back down, her eyes still closed. "Wake up," Radovan said again, louder, taking hold of the foot of her sleeping mat and shaking it. The girl opened her eyes, looked around as though trying to figure out her location, then seemed to remember and peered over at him. "I'm going to unlock you so you can go," he told her. He repeated his procedure from the night before, getting refresher tissue for the girl, then taking her just past the edge of the wood.

After he brought her back to her tent, as he locked her back up, he told the girl that he would get her some clean clothes for the day, along with something to eat for breakfast. She nodded her little head, but she said nothing. Radovan grabbed the second duffel, which he'd left just outside his own tent, and pulled out beige pants and a patterned blue-and-red sweater, along with socks and underwear. He brought them over to the girl's tent and set them down at the foot of her sleeping mat. He unlocked the manacle and waited as she pulled on the sweater. When she finished, he clapped on her restraint again, then exited the tent.

Back outside, Radovan checked over his supplies. He'd brought enough provisions for a few days, perhaps even a week if he rationed the food and water, but his dreams of the previous night told him that he would need virtually none of it. He cut up a piece of *kurna* fruit and put the slices on a small plate, along with a handful of milaberries. Then he found a container of kava flakes, filled a bowl with them, added kava milk, and poured jumja syrup atop it. After sticking a spoon into the cereal and picking up a small bottle of *pooncheenee*, he put the meal on a tray and carried it over to the girl's tent. He set it down before her and opened the bottle of fruit juice. Unlike the night before, the girl offered no complaints about the food. She'd already begun eating by the time he left her tent.

After having the same breakfast—except the jumja syrup—Radovan examined the items he'd replicated and brought with him. He hadn't settled on a course of action until that morning, until his dreams had showed him the way forward, but he saw at that moment confirmation that he had been guided on his path—by prophecies in *The Book of Ohalu*, by Rejias Norvan, by the events on Endalla, by the nightmares that had haunted his sleep. He knew what he had to do, and he saw that he had brought everything he would need, from the chemicals to the technology, from the parts to the tools.

Knowing he would never see another sunrise, Radovan Tavus set to work.

Tey hovered over the transportation coordinator, watching one of his displays as it tracked the target of his scans across the landscape. She had arrived at the Bajoran Planetary Operations Center in Jalanda only a few minutes prior, after receiving a message early that morning from Lieutenant Tapren. Major Orisin wanted Tey to know that sensor scans outside the perimeter of Johcat had just detected an empty travel pod meandering across the surface. The major wanted her to meet him at the BPOC as soon as she could get there.

It had taken Tey less than thirty minutes after speaking with Tapren to reach her destination. Most of that time had been taken up with walking from her home to a local transporter terminal, and then from a Jalanda terminal to the Planetary Operations Center. She managed to arrive before Orisin.

"Can you superimpose the course that the travel pod has taken?" Tey asked Torken Noth, who crewed the panel. His console stood at the end of a row of similar stations, just one of many such rows in a warehouse-sized room called the Surface Transportation Hub. Civilians oversaw the movement and coordination of travel pods, underground slidewalks, intercity maglevs, and the like. They even monitored the status of major pedestrian thoroughfares.

"I can show you from the point where sensors picked it up, but that wasn't even an hour ago," Torken said. "Before that, we had no record of it because its transponder was disabled. We've been scanning for it half the night."

"I know," Tey said. "Show me anyway."

Torken manipulated his controls. Tey studied the display, which showed an overhead satellite view of the region northeast of Johcat. A sliver of the outermost section of the city cut across the bottom left of the screen, the only blemish on a chart of vast, undeveloped lands. At the top left, a verdant swath showed a small section of the Talveran Forest, while the Deserak Wilderness filled the rest of the display. The travel pod moved inside the enormous nature preserve, and as Tey watched, a glowing red line appeared behind it—a line that zigzagged in a seemingly random fashion, traveling north and south, east and west, sometimes crisscrossing, sometimes doubling back.

Tey heard footsteps behind her and recognized the gait of Major Orisin. She turned to face him. He greeted her as he arrived.

"Good morning, Agent Tey," he said. "Thank you for getting here so quickly. What have we got?" They stood on either side of Torken and examined his display. Tey pointed to the end of the red line.

"This is the point at which orbital sensors finally located the travel pod, and this is the path it's taken since then," she said. "They found it less than an hour ago. Its transponder is disabled and there's nobody aboard. It has to be the travel pod we're looking for." Tey mentioned no details that would identify the case upon which they worked or any of the principals involved, as the abduction of Rebecca Sisko had yet to be made public.

"We need to get a team out there to stop and examine the pod," Orisin said.

"I'll beam aboard and shut it down," Tey said. "I can do a preliminary check on its navigational system, but I'm sure it's been wiped. We won't find any physical evidence aboard either."

"Probably not, but we need to be sure," Orisin said. "Even masterminds can make mistakes." The major looked to the transportation coordinator. "Mister . . . ?"

"Torken, sir. Torken Noth."

"Mister Torken, transfer data on the travel pod to Transporter Room Three," Orisin said. Tey hadn't had authorization to beam directly into the Planetary Operations Center—an oversight in her hasty return to service for the Bajoran government—but it would be no problem for her to beam out.

"Yes, sir."

Orisin headed out of the Surface Transportation Hub, and Tey fell in beside him. Once they'd exited into the corridor, the major said, "After I learned about the travel pod, I heard from the forensics team. They found almost no DNA anywhere in the flat—except under the bed. Samples matched both Rebecca's DNA and Radovan's." The news did not surprise Tey. "Before I came here, I stopped in Adarak to notify the parents."

Orisin led Tey to a large transporter room. The major checked with the operator on duty, who confirmed that they'd received the sensor data from Torken. While Tey beamed aboard the travel pod, Orisin would make arrangements at the provincial Militia headquarters in Renassa for the vehicle to be relocated there using a large-scale cargo transporter. There, computer analysts could fully inspect the travel pod's navigational system and a forensics team could search it for physical evidence.

Tey mounted the transporter platform. The operator worked his console. White streaks clouded Tey's vision as a familiar whine rose and then diminished. Her view of the transporter room faded, replaced by the shifting sight of rolling hills ripe with vegetation. She found beaming from a stationary position to a moving perspective a bit disconcerting, so she closed her eyes for a moment to maintain her equilibrium.

When Tey opened her eyes, the sensation of being off-balance had passed. She sat down and reviewed the travel pod's console. She located its piloting controls and stopped it, then shut the drive down. After accessing the navigational system, she searched through its program and logs. As she'd expected, it had been coded to continuously erase its positioning data, so its course could not be traced backward. Similarly, its logs erased themselves every five minutes.

Tey had one other idea. She called up the travel pod's life-of-service gauges. To her surprise, they hadn't been modified or erased. She could compare the values against the numbers prior to when Radovan had taken out the vehicle. After the pod's previous use, its lifetime hours in service and distance traveled would have been automatically downloaded to the Surface Transportation Hub. Tey could thereby determine how long the vehicle had been in use and how far it had journeyed from the moment Radovan had used it to move Rebecca Sisko. It wouldn't be much to go on, but it would allow her to calculate the limits of where the travel pod could have gone. There would still be a tremendous amount of ground to cover, but it would at least narrow the search area.

After recording the travel pod's amassed time and distance in her wrist comm, she tapped the device to open a channel. "Tey to Major Orisin."

After working for the entire morning and into the afternoon, Radovan finished his creation. He regarded it with satisfaction, with awe, and with a sense of poetry. With satisfaction, because he had labored earnestly and meticulously to complete it. With awe, because even without knowing the role he would play in the life of the Avatar, and thus in the future of Bajor, he had still somehow moved forward unerringly along the path to his destination. And finally with a sense of poetry, because of how the end would mirror the beginning. The Ohalavaru had read and contemplated, talked and debated, until Rejias Norvan had made a choice and taken action. In Radovan's case, spurred by the events on Endalla, he had made his own choices, he had taken—and would take—action, and then the Ohalavaru would talk and debate, read and contemplate.

But not just the Ohalavaru, Radovan thought. All of Bajor would see what he had done, would come to understand the door that he had opened for all their people. They would bless his name for the age of Awareness and Understanding he delivered through his sacrifice.

Now all that I need is a stage, Radovan thought. He could do it there, in the clearing, but he wanted something more . . . memorable. He crossed the open ground and headed deeper into the wood, using a large blade to clear the underbrush. He felt confident that he would find what he needed.

Before too long, he did.

Radovan stopped at a point where the ground fell away. He peered down into a rocky gully, split by a running stream. Moss-covered boulders sat at the center of the hollow, and several trees had toppled down at points around the edge. Roughly round in shape, the depression looked almost like a naturally formed amphitheater.

Radovan smiled as a feeling of bliss washed over him. He plainly saw in the setting before him a parallel with the environment of his latest dream. In the images that had infused his sleeping mind, he had stalked toward the Avatar among the charred, dead bodies inside the crater that Rejias's bombs had carved out of the surface of Endalla.

Back at the clearing, Radovan gathered up the device he had made. It lay on the ground, a silver cylinder not quite a meter in length, which he'd sealed at both ends. He had fashioned the housing from the metal container carrying his transporter inhibitor. He'd utilized the chemicals and fiber-optic cables and other components he'd brought with him to rig the mechanism, and he'd attached a padd to control it all. Finally, he'd cut the metal from his mother's trunk into little pieces to use as shrapnel.

Radovan separated the antigrav from the remnants of the trunk and attached it to the bomb. He also packed some pitons and lengths of chain into a carryall, which he slung across his shoulder. Then he went to the girl's tent.

Inside, she watched him as he unlocked the manacle at the end of her chain and attached it to his wrist. "It's time," he told her. "Get up." When she stood, Radovan saw that she had taken her shoes off. He crawled farther into the tent and put them back on her feet. "Come on," he told her, and he led her outside.

"Where are we going?" the girl asked.

Radovan looked down at her. "Don't you know?" he said. "Both of us . . . we're finally going home."

Gamma Quadrant, 2386

The time had come.

Sisko and his away team had discovered the hybrid nature of the Glant, had learned about how they kindled their artificially crafted physical bodies with organic minds culled from naturally evolved species. The captain had been unable to convince the aliens to return the children stolen from *Robinson*, had failed to negotiate any sort of settlement or exchange that would have brought the children back home. The Glant had just announced that the "actualization"—the irrevocable process by which they transferred existing consciousnesses into their newly constructed creations—had begun.

Sisko stabbed at his combadge, which chirped in response. "Captain to *Styx*," he said. "Alpha one go." Before departing *Robinson*, Sisko had chosen the simple code as a shorthand means of ordering the commencement of the crew's secondary plan for dealing with the Glant. If the away team could not reclaim the children by peaceful means, the captain had decided, they would take them back by force.

Sisko received no reply over his combadge from Ensign Weil, but he immediately heard the high-pitched sound of the transporter. White motes appeared before the captain's eyes, and the five Glant in front of him began to fade from view. As he dematerialized, the captain hoped he had not waited too long to act.

The transporter deposited Sisko in a long corridor, its walls, ceiling, and floor comprising alternating wavy strips of orange and blue. He glanced around to verify that Kasidy, Doctor Kosciuszko, Counselor Althouse, and Lieutenant Rogers had been beamed with him to their new location. They had.

An instant later, the high-pitched hum of the transporter rose again. Sisko saw bright specks and streaks appear at his hand, courtesy of the transport enhancer he wore around his wrist. A phaser appeared, and he wrapped his fingers about the pistol's grip. He quickly checked to ensure that every member of the away team had one. In the case of Lieutenant Rogers, a phaser had materialized in one hand and a tricorder in the other.

"Report," Sisko said.

"Like before, Captain," Rogers said, working the tricorder. "Indeterminate life signs inside and outside the chamber where the children are being held, but a great deal of movement, coming toward us from around the next corner. The other away team has beamed in on the other side of them." Per the plan, the security officers remaining aboard *Styx* had been transported as near as they could be to the location of the children, but in a corridor different from where Sisko and the others had been beamed.

"Time until the Glant arrive?" Sisko asked.

"Just seconds," Rogers said.

"Positions," Sisko called out, sidestepping to take cover against one wall. Kasidy crouched behind him, her phaser already raised. Sisko knew that his wife hadn't had much experience using weapons in the field, but as a member of *Robinson*'s civilian support staff, she had received training, and Starfleet required her to maintain her proficiency.

On the other side of the corridor, Kosciuszko, Althouse, and Rogers likewise took up positions against the opposite wall. Sisko could hear the chaotic sounds of the Glant's approach up ahead. "Here they come," Rogers said.

From around the next corner, a horde of Glant appeared. Sisko didn't wait. "Fire," he said, and the shriek of phasers filled the air.

Rogeiro sat in the command chair on the *Robinson* bridge, eager for word from the captain. When Uteln announced an incoming transmission, Plante glanced back at the first officer from the operations console, her concern evident. A veil of anxiety shrouded the bridge—the entire ship, really. While the crew had breathed a collective sigh of relief when sixty of the missing children had been rescued from the Glant, tensions remained high because of the twenty-seven still held captive.

"Put it through," Rogeiro said.

"Weil to Robinson,*"* came the voice of the officer piloting *Styx.* *"Alpha one go."*

Rogeiro had hoped never to hear the coded message. It meant that diplomacy had failed. It meant that the *Robinson* crew would have to go into battle. It meant that more lives would be put at risk.

"Acknowledged. *Robinson* out," the first officer said, and then, "Rogeiro to all shuttlecraft." He repeated the coded phrase that initiated the next stage of the mission. Powered up in standby mode and fully crewed, a dozen of the small vessels sat in the ship's shuttlebay, poised to launch.

Rogeiro waited. "Shuttles away," Uteln said a few moments later. The first officer rose to his feet and moved to the center of the bridge, his gaze fixed on the main viewscreen. The strange world of the Glant floated in space dead ahead. Almost at once, the first trio of shuttlecraft appeared on-screen, sweeping into view as they raced to provide cover for Captain Sisko and the away team.

As they neared the region of inert space surrounding the Dyson section, Uteln said, "Glant vessels are moving to intercept." The image on the main screen shifted to a magnified view. The Glant world filled the screen, and from it, a score or more of ships grew larger as they sped toward space and the approaching *Robinson* shuttles.

"Shields up full," Rogeiro said. "Phasers and quantum torpedoes at the ready."

Uteln translated the first officer's orders into action as he worked the tactical console. "Shields up, weapons online."

"Commander Sivadeki, take us in," Rogeiro said. At the conn, Sivadeki acknowledged her order as she operated her controls. The impulse engines steeped the bridge in their low pulse. "Battle stations."

As alert lighting bathed the bridge in its blood-red glow and emergency tones blared, *Robinson* surged forward, on its way to engage the Glant.

Weil hauled the runabout sharply to starboard. *Styx* banked hard, the view through the forward ports rolling through nearly ninety degrees. The blue laser fired by the pursuing Glant vessel pierced the air just below the runabout.

"Hold on," Weil said as she pitched *Styx* upward on its lateral axis—at the moment, perpendicular to the surface below. Already strained by the runabout's abrupt movements, the inertial dampers struggled to adjust. For an instant, Weil felt a strong accelerative force pushing her toward the deck as the ship wheeled up and over. "We'll be coming up behind them."

"I see them," Grandal said from a console on the port

side of the cockpit, where he had configured a weapons panel. The captain had ordered the security officer to stay aboard *Styx* with Weil and Spingeld, just in case negotiations with the Glant failed.

When Sisko had contacted the runabout and issued his coded message, Weil had relayed it at once to *Robinson*. Crewwoman Spingeld immediately beamed the captain and his away team as close as she could to where the children were being held. The transporter operator had then sent phasers and a tricorder to them, before beaming the other security officers to a second location near the children.

After setting the captain's plan in motion, Weil had watched and waited for the Glant to respond, expecting them either to attempt to commandeer *Styx* and its crew, or to attack the runabout outright. Before long, sensors showed a pair of their vessels approaching the position of the runabout. Weil lifted off and fled, but soon found *Styx* pursued by ten ships closing in from all directions.

Weil had commenced evasive maneuvers, and Grandal had unleashed *Styx*'s weapons. The runabout's superior firepower destroyed two of the attackers, but the ongoing barrage of Glant lasers took its toll. *Styx*'s defensive shields dropped to less than twenty percent.

As the runabout completed its loop, the Glant vessel that had just fired came into view. The howl of the phasers blared in the cockpit. Weil saw two reddish-yellow rays burst from the bow. They caught the Glant ship astern. The vessel veered away, but Weil followed, expertly adjusting the runabout's course in her pursuit. Grandal continued to fire.

"More Glant approaching from above," Weil called out.

"I see them," Grandal said, but he kept up the assault on the ship ahead of the runabout. Five seconds later, the Glant vessel exploded in a ball of flame. Fragments of its charred hull fell in smoking streamers toward the surface.

Weil navigated directly for the shrinking fireball. She took *Styx* into the destruction, then abruptly changed course when the smoke and debris obscured the ship. She sent the runabout into a steep dive. Only at the last second did she see two more Glant vessels approaching from below. She tried to bring the runabout around, but too late. A volley of lasers pummeled the ship.

"Shields down to eleven percent," Grandal called out. "We can't take many more hits."

Weil pulled *Styx* up, racing away from the vessels nearing from the surface. In the sky above, from all angles, seven Glant ships bore down on the runabout. Grandal opened fire at once, sending serial phaser blasts into one vessel after another. But the Glant ships struck back, doing so en masse. Weil threw *Styx* into desperate evasive action, whisking left and right, climbing, diving, but too many lasers pierced the air. She eluded one, then another, and still another, but finally a bolt landed, and then a second.

"Shields down to three percent," Grandal called out.

Weil gambled. She dropped the runabout's velocity to zero and let *Styx* tumble. "Hold your fire," she told Grandal. "Let them think we're powerless." Sensors would show otherwise, but as the Glant watched *Styx* fall through the sky, the feint might secure the runabout crew a few crucial seconds.

"Acknowledged," Grandal said.

Weil checked her own sensor panel and saw the surface rushing up fast. She also saw the route she wanted to take, and she modified the runabout's descent accordingly, shifting its flight path from straight down to a steep angle.

"The Glant ships are moving away," Grandal suddenly said. "It's the shuttlecraft squadron and the *Robinson* heading for the Dyson section. The Glant are moving to intercept."

Weil glanced at her sensors and saw the ships above peeling off and climbing toward space, but the two below *Styx* remained in place. "We've still got two tracking us. Prepare to fire at both, at close range." Weil accelerated *Styx* and decreased the slope of its trajectory. Visible through the forward ports, the ground grew closer, flashing past in a blur.

And then a field of deep blue appeared. The runabout had made it to one of the large bodies of water on the surface of the Glant world. "Shunt all shield power to the bow," she ordered. Weil waited for Grandal to acknowledge the order, for what seemed like too long.

But then he said, "All shield power has been shunted to the bow."

Weil drove *Styx* downward. The runabout juddered violently as it crashed through the surface of the water. The cockpit grew darker for a moment as the Glant sun vanished, but the overhead lighting panels automatically adapted.

Weil calculated the time it would take the vessels in pursuit to reach the ocean, then brought *Styx* once more to a rapid stop. She quickly spun the runabout around on its perpendicular axis, yawing one hundred eighty degrees about. "Prepare to fire," she said again, just as the two Glant vessels dove into the water. "Now!"

Phasers shot from the bow of *Styx*. The beams looked green so far beneath the ocean surface, the reds, oranges, and yellows absorbed by the water. Each of the twin beams flashed into the Glant vessels head-on, less than a hundred meters away.

The ships exploded.

Weil dipped the bow of the runabout and sped downward. "Shields at normal distribution," she said.

"Normal shields, aye," Grandal said.

The shockwaves of the blasts and a mass of vaporized water still caught *Styx*, shaking it forcefully and filling the ship with a tremendous roar. Pieces of broken hull clanked against the runabout. But then *Styx* outpaced the turbulence and the destruction from the explosions, and the cockpit quieted.

"Any other vessels in pursuit?" Weil asked.

"Negative," Grandal reported. "They may all be dealing with the shuttlecraft squadron and the *Robinson*. Or maybe they think we've been destroyed—which we nearly were. Shields are down to two percent."

"Initiate repairs and start recharging the shields," Weil said. "We still have a mission to complete." The ensign studied the navigational sensors as she took the runabout deeper. The view through the ports looked black, with only a hint of illumination from the runabout itself.

Eventually, *Styx* settled onto the ocean floor.

Bajor, 2380

At the Militia headquarters in Kendra Province, Tey stood in the middle of the room, her arms folded across her chest. Her gaze roamed over the numerous displays that lined three of the walls above the consoles that Major Orisin's staff crewed. Orisin had initially commandeered the Mission Operations Center in Renassa hours after Rebecca Sisko had been kidnapped, activating it for the express purpose of coordinating the search for the missing girl. Various Militia provincial headquarters around the planet housed such emergency facilities. Normally dormant, the MOCs provided centralized assets that could be reconfigured and staffed to support a broad range of mission profiles.

At the moment, much of the operation concentrated on scans of the area to the northeast of Johcat. After finding and studying the travel pod Radovan had used to flee the city, Tey had computed its potential reach and delineated an area in which to search. Orisin immediately requisitioned the use of a satellite in geosynchronous orbit over the region, targeting its sensors to scan for anything that could lead to Radovan and the girl. The major had also ordered Militia personnel to take shuttles into the area to conduct visual surveillance from the sky.

As she looked at the different displays, Tey battled a feel-

ing of helplessness. Since being conscripted by the first minister into joining the operation to recover Rebecca Sisko,
she had stopped only to sleep—and not for very long. She
wanted to do more than merely observe as others continued
the mission.

After shutting down Radovan's travel pod, Tey had read
through the reports of the interviews Orisin's staff had conducted of the other support personnel at the Elanda District Three Transporter Terminal. Nobody had anything
particularly negative to say about Radovan, but neither had
anybody had anything particularly positive to say. Denveer
Cotes, the manager of the transporter terminal, used words
like "prompt" and "technically capable," but he offered no
superlatives. None of his colleagues could recollect ever so-
cializing with him, and a few chose descriptors like "aloof"
and "loner."

All of that had served to reinforce Tey's profile of Radovan, but it had done nothing to narrow the search for
him. Next, she had randomly selected a number of the
Ohalavaru who'd accompanied Rejias Norvan to Endalla
and survived the ordeal. She transported out to their locations and questioned them, but only a few could remember
Radovan at all, and none could recall ever speaking with
him. Tey had better fortunes asking about Winser Ellevet.
It turned out that she had also been an Ohalavaru, which
suggested how she and Radovan had met. Different people
described her in paradoxical terms, some calling her mousy
and shy, while others labeled her sassy and opinionated.
None of what Tey learned bore on the problem of where
Radovan might have taken Rebecca—though the murder
of Winser certainly made finding him as soon as possible
that much more imperative.

"Some deka tea, Agent?" Orisin asked, sidling up beside
Tey with a cup in each hand. He held one out to her, which

she accepted with thanks. The slightly sweet aroma of the tea drifted to her, and she sipped from her cup. "Actually, you look like you can use something stronger than that."

"I'm sure I could," Tey agreed, though as a rule, she did not drink alcohol. In her role as a protector of the first minister, she'd been required to be ready for duty at all times. She generally eschewed anything that impacted her abilities or perceptions. "It's frustrating not to be able to do more."

"That's the duty of an investigator," Orisin said. "Ask questions, seek answers, look for clues, and follow the chain of evidence. It's not glamorous. It takes time and effort, and more often than not, patience." He shrugged, a nonchalant gesture that could not hide the major's own anxieties about the situation.

"I know," Tey said. She regarded the large viewscreen mounted on the wall directly in front of her. It showed a pulsating white circle methodically sliding across a view from above the Deserak Wilderness. "He's got sensor-defeating tech with him," she said, motioning toward the screen with the hand holding the cup of tea. "He has to, otherwise he wouldn't have been able to get past the checkpoint out of Johcat."

"That's assuming he still has the girl with him," Orisin said. "If he has accomplices—"

"He doesn't," Tey said, more sharply than she intended. She took a moment to calm herself, sipping her tea before explaining her point of view. "Radovan's reclusive, an introvert. He doesn't relate to other people."

"So he doesn't have accessories, but maybe somebody engaged him for his transporter expertise," Orisin suggested. "He could have abducted the girl and then handed her off to whoever planned the operation."

"Then why did we find a dead woman in his flat?" Tey asked.

"It could be unrelated," the major said, although his tone betrayed that he didn't believe his own suggestion.

"It could be unrelated, but it isn't," Tey said. "Maybe she helped him with the kidnapping and then had second thoughts about it, although I doubt that's what happened. More likely, Radovan abducted Rebecca on his own, and Winser found out and objected to it."

"That's speculation."

"It's reasoning to fit the facts we have," Tey said. She unwrapped a finger from around her cup and pointed to the viewscreen ahead of them. "And one of the facts we have is that the security officers at the checkpoint didn't find the girl in his travel pod. That means either he left her somewhere in Johcat, or he hid her in the travel pod and masked her life signs." She studied the display, following the painstakingly slow process of pinpointing a Bajoran and a human in a vast expanse filled with wildlife. "Maybe if we searched for an energy source," Tey said. "His sensor mask must require power."

"We are doing that," Orisin said, waving toward a screen off to their left. It showed a pair of concentric green circles sliding across the Deserak landscape. "But if Radovan is using a sensor mask, the device will conceal its own readings."

"What about looking for sensor holes?" Tey asked.

"That's not the way those devices work," Orisin said. "Sensor masks don't eliminate readings in an area, leaving an obvious hole. That would effectively render them useless. They disguise the readings where they're in use, making the masked area blend in with its surroundings."

"Of course," Tey said. She didn't have a lot of experience with such devices, but she should have figured out that they would function the way the major had described.

"It wouldn't matter anyway," Orisin said. "Even if we

were to scan for 'sensor holes,' it wouldn't cut down on the search time. The undeveloped areas northeast of Johcat are substantial. It will take time to locate anything out of the ordinary, whether it be Bajoran or human life signs, a power source, a sensor hole, or anything else."

Tey shook her head. "I'm ready to beam out there myself and search on foot."

"I know; I feel the same way," Orisin said. "I spoke earlier today about that kind of plan with the commandant."

The statement confused Tey. "What kind of plan?"

"A line search," Orisin said. "I spoke with Overgeneral Manos about the possibility of transporting Militia troops to the area to walk it."

"You'd need thousands of troops."

"Thousands of troops and a lot of time," Orisin said. "For right now, sensors and shuttles make more sense."

"Because you don't think we have a lot of time?" Tey asked.

The major looked at her squarely. She thought he would say something, perhaps suggest that they still had plenty of time to find Rebecca Sisko before it was too late. Instead, he cast his gaze downward.

"I know," Tey said to him quietly. "I think we're running out of time too."

Radovan waited as the Avatar trudged across the spongy bed of dead leaves beneath the forest canopy. He had cleared a path through the undergrowth with his large blade on his way to and from the gully, but the footing was proving a hazard for the girl. Her little, unsteady legs made it difficult for her to walk quickly without losing her balance. For the prior ten minutes, Radovan had moved ahead the length of the chain that bound the girl to him, then paused so that she could catch up. It made their journey not only slow, but frustrating. The energy coursing through Radovan made him want to bolt, to race through the wood to the gully so that he could finally realize his fate.

When the girl reached him, she looked up. A wayward beam of sunlight penetrated through the thick crown of the wood and shined on her forehead. Radovan stared at the small dot of light, which looked as though it marked her in some meaningful way.

"We're not going home," the girl said. She did not sound scared or angry, or even petulant. She simply spoke as though relaying her awareness of a fact.

"We're not going anywhere very quickly with you taking so long," Radovan said. He took his carryall from his shoulder and set it down, then opened his arms to the girl. "Why don't I carry you?" he said. "We'll get there much quicker." Radovan expected her to refuse, but instead, she padded over and allowed him to pick her up. He propped her in the crook of his elbow, then carefully bent to retrieve his carryall, which he draped once more over his shoulder. Then he put his free hand on his homemade device, held aloft by the antigrav.

They continued on like that, making their way through the wood, until they finally reached the gully. At the edge of the circular depression, Radovan pushed the floating cylinder off to one side, then pulled the carryall from his shoulder. He tried to measure the distance and the right amount of force to use, then tossed the bag underhand into the air. It landed just a few meters from the center of the gully, striking a smaller stone and sending up a quick metallic rattle.

Radovan peered around the perimeter, trying to determine the best way to make his way down. The girl would not be able to do so on her own. The sides of the depression sloped for ten or so meters and appeared fairly steep, though not quite precipitous.

About a third of the way around, a downed tree reached from the upper edge of the gully almost all the way to the bottom. Deciding that he could place his free hand against the trunk in order to keep his balance, Radovan made his way over to it, still pushing the levitating cylinder ahead of him. "We're going down there," he told the girl, "so put your arms around my neck and hold on tightly."

She looked at where he pointed. "I don't wanna go down there."

Moving the cylinder out of the way, Radovan said, "Well, we're going, so you better grab on to me." Without waiting for a response, he steadied himself against the dead tree and dropped over the edge. His hiking boots came down sideways atop the layer of growth covering the sides of the gully, crashing through it to the dirt beneath. He descended the first few steps without incident, but then his front foot caught on a vine and he started to fall forward. He pulled his hand from the tree trunk—scraping it along the hard, dead bark—instinctively wrapped his arms around the girl, and purposely dropped onto his back. He skidded down the embankment, using his feet as pistons to restrain his descent as best he could. His shirt rode up, allowing earth and stones, vines and leaves, to attack his uncovered flesh.

Radovan came to a stop near the bottom of the gully. His back felt as though it had been whipped raw. He started to ask the girl if she was all right, but immediately realized the absurdity of the question. He pushed himself up with his free hand, which burned from the abrasions caused by the tree. He stutter-stepped his way to level ground and set the girl down.

After setting down the girl and reclaiming his carryall, Radovan went over to the boulders. He dug out the items he'd brought with him. Using the sledge, he plunged a pair of pitons into seams on opposite sides of the boulder. He then unlocked the manacle from around his wrist and attached it to one of them. He took another length of chain and connected the girl's other wrist to the second piton.

"I'll be right back," he told her. He climbed back up the embankment to where he'd left the floating cylinder. Taking more care and moving more slowly, he descended backward into the gully, pulling his device after him. When he reached the bottom, he turned toward the Avatar.

The girl stood as he'd left her, with her back to the boulder, her arms raised to either side, held up by the chains that bound her to the pitons. She should have been complaining, whining to him about her discomfort, about how she didn't want to be there, about how she wanted her mother. But she didn't. She only watched him mutely.

Radovan maneuvered his device into place above another large rock, a meter or so in front of the girl. He powered down the antigrav and the cylinder settled onto the relatively flat surface of the stone. He activated the padd attached to the device by a couple of fiber-optic leads.

"Everything's going to be all right," he told the girl. "We're almost done here, and then all this will be finished. You won't have to spend any more time with me."

The girl looked at him without saying anything, and then down at the device. When she peered back up at him, she seemed to take his measure. "I want to go home."

"You're going home right after this," Radovan told her. "We both are."

Excitement welled within Radovan. All of his designs, all of his careful machinations—all of his *life*—had led to that moment. He had suffered through loss after loss—his father, his brother, his mother. He had endured hardships, never fitting in with anybody, never belonging anywhere. And yet, for all of that, he had come out the other side, searching for something—*any*thing!—and finding the Ohalavaru. He'd listened to Rejias Norvan, followed him, and witnessed his failed plan on Endalla. Radovan had used that disastrous event to reinterpret *The Book of Ohalu*. He would do what Rejias could not: empower the Ohalavaru and reveal the truth to all.

"This will all be over soon," he told the girl. He tapped the surface of the padd, bringing up a timing control that he set for one minute. His finger hovered over the START button. He had coded it so that, once initiated, the countdown could not be stopped.

Radovan hesitated. He wanted to complete his work, wanted to achieve what he had set out to achieve, but the irrevocable nature of what lay ahead gave him pause. *This is the beginning of a new age for Bajor,* he thought, *but do I want it also to be an ending?*

Radovan considered the question, but he didn't have to consider long. His childhood had been torment, his adulthood a slow but relentless descent into an abyss of loneliness, depression, and sorrow. He'd had enough.

Radovan touched his fingertip to the padd, and the timer began to count down.

Rebecca Jae Sisko was tired and hurt. She couldn't put her arms down and they felt weird. The big rock behind her was hard and pointy in her back. She missed Mommy and Daddy. She missed her house and her room and her bed. She just wanted to see her parents. She just wanted to sleep.

I just want to go home.

The man said that they both would be going home soon,

but she knew better. He took her from Mommy and he wasn't going to give her back. He was a bad man.

Rebecca watched him hunch over the big silver tube—over the *bomb*. She was only three and a half, but she knew what she saw. Something like it blew up the month before on one of Bajor's moons. It hurt a lot of people and almost hurt Daddy. She wasn't supposed to know that. Her parents didn't think she knew. But she heard things. She heard things, and sometimes she somehow *knew* things.

The man pushed a button on the padd attached to the silver tube. When he stood up, Rebecca saw Bajoran numbers on the screen. They were changing quickly.

The man watched the screen—and then suddenly he didn't. He ran away from the tube, from Rebecca. He ran up the hill, moving alongside the knocked-over tree. He was running away.

"Mommy," Rebecca said, even though she knew her mother wasn't there and couldn't hear her. She never felt more lost in her life. She watched the man run away and knew that he was even more lost than she was. She didn't hate him, even though she thought Mommy and Daddy probably would if they were there. But Rebecca felt sorry for him. He was sad and she wasn't, but in a lot of other ways, she was a lot like him. She was uncomfortable around most people, feeling different from them—even from Mommy and Daddy—and carrying around a loneliness—a *hollowness*.

The tube in front of her made a buzzing noise—or maybe it was the padd on it. Rebecca looked and saw the number *10* written in Bajoran on the screen. She could count to ten in Bajoran and Federation Standard.

The numbers counted backward. The tube—the bomb—clicked and hummed. Rebecca figured it was preparing to explode.

Maybe it won't, she thought. *Maybe I'm just being a scaredy-cat.*

Rebecca thought that maybe she didn't understand what was going on. Maybe everything with the bad man would turn out to be something else. Maybe it would be nothing at all.

But then the hum coming from the tube got louder. Then it issued a loud whine. Rebecca looked at the screen and watched as the numbers changed from *3* to *2* to *1*, and finally to *0*.

Then the bomb exploded.

Gamma Quadrant, 2386

The doors opened and Sisko leaped through them, his phaser raised. A wall of noise met the captain inside the Glant actualization chamber. To his surprise, the broad space looked just like the one he had entered during the first rescue mission. It marked the first time he had observed two creations of the Glant that even remotely resembled each other.

But unlike in the other actualization chamber Sisko had stormed, all of the equipment before him appeared powered up and operating. Indicator lights flashed on control panels, and information spelled out in alien glyphs marched from right to left across displays. Sisko wanted desperately to find his daughter, but five Glant stationed at various consoles looked over at him. Five *Robinson* security officers took up a position on either side of the captain, all of them with their weapons aimed at the Glant. He knew that Kasidy and the others stood behind them.

"Shut off the equipment and move away," Sisko ordered, raising his voice to be heard over the cacophony of the Glant equipment. He could only hope that he had not arrived too late. It had taken precious time for his away team to battle their way through a legion of Glant defenders. The second away team, composed solely of *Robinson* security officers, helped to shorten the confrontation by attacking from another direction. But according to Voranesk, the process of transferring the minds of the children into newly created Glant had already begun.

"You cannot explore here," one of the alien scientists said, speaking loudly. It had an oblong head and a pyramidal body that looked like a cross section of sedimentary layers mounted atop a wide, rolling track. Extending from each triangular side of its body, a pair of articulated metal arms ended in a hand with at least ten digits. "You cannot stop actualization."

"Watch me," Sisko said, and he pointed his phaser at a shelving unit on the wall to the left of the Glant. The captain squeezed the trigger pad, and a beam of bright blue energy shot out and diffused across the piece of furniture, vaporizing it into nothingness. "You four move into the far corner," Sisko said, pointing in that direction, and they quickly heeded his words. To the first Glant he'd addressed, he said, "Now shut down the equipment."

The Glant's wide track spun beneath it, turning it toward the nearest control panel. As it started toward the console, Sisko peered around. Just as in the other actualization chamber, he saw a number of transparent compartments holding the *Robinson* children. When he didn't see Rebecca, he risked a look at the far wall, to the horizontal slabs housed inside the large, intricate machines.

Suddenly, the chamber quieted. Lights stopped flashing, instead burning constantly or staying dark. The characters scrolling across screens settled down to become static displays. Sisko thought that the Glant had done as he'd instructed, deactivating the equipment, but when he looked back over at him, he saw that the scientist had not even reached a control panel.

"Oh, no," Sisko said. Kasidy called after him as he ran forward. His eyes moved from side to side as he searched for his daughter. He saw her in the second of the five machines that lined the back wall. She lay on her back, motionless, secured to the slab by straps around her arms and legs. A trio of thick tubes ended in dish-shaped instruments that had been affixed to the sides and top of her head. Her eyes were closed, as if she were sleeping or unconscious.

Sleeping, Sisko repeated to himself. *Or unconscious.* His mind would not allow for any other possibilities.

He holstered his phaser as he reached his daughter. "Rebecca," he said, his mouth dry, his voice barely above a whisper. "Rebecca." He reached out and put his hand on her arm, which felt warm beneath his touch. He felt a cautious relief, but as he examined her body, he did not see her chest rising and falling.

But then movement caught his attention. He looked right, to the second bay inside the machine, where the slab there was gliding out. Atop it lay an entity Sisko had trouble comprehending. Its main body seemed a tangle of metal coils interspersed with solid objects—cubes and spheres, cylinders and cones. When it rose up, Sisko could see that it had appendages of some sort, though he could not quite distinguish what kind or how many. The entity had a long neck—another helix of metal. Three discs covered parts of its flat, rectangular head, all of them attached to the surrounding machine by bulky conduits. It opened a quartet of eyes.

Sisko's blood ran cold. He recognized the look in the alien eyes of the entity.

"Daddy," it said.

Bajor, 2380

In less time than the blink of an eye, Rebecca felt many things. A heavy weight pushed her body back into the hardness of the boulder. Fire burned her skin. A tangy ammonia smell reached her nose, and the stink of cooking meat. Tiny, jagged pieces of hot metal punctured her arms and legs, her belly, her chest, her face.

More than anything, Rebecca felt physical pain, like nothing else she had ever experienced. Even as young as she was, she knew she could not live. She was scared. For an instant, she thought of Mommy and Daddy, at how upset they would be when they learned what had happened to her, and at how sad they would be to miss her.

And then Rebecca's pain and fear and sadness changed. Even as the blast began to destroy her body, she got angry—angrier than she had ever been in her short life. Angry at the man who took her from Mommy, angry at spending so much time away from her home, angry at the bomb that exploded, angry that she would never be able to return to her life with her parents, who she loved more than anything.

The world almost stopped as Rebecca's intense anger sparked a hidden part of her. The explosion slowed to a crawl. The burst of flames expanded toward her in tiny steps. Fragments of the bomb's shell floated toward her as though suspended in midair.

Rebecca opened her mouth and screamed: "NOOOOO!"

A pale yellow flash of light surged from her in every direction, like the shockwave of an explosion centered within her.

"Major, there's been an explosion!"

Tey looked over to the left side of the room, to where Lieutenant Tapren crewed one of the consoles in the Mission Operations Center. From where she stood with Orisin in the center of the room, Tey could see a dot flashing red on the lieutenant's display. She and the major rushed over.

Standing on either side of Tapren, Tey and Orisin peered down at the console. The screen showed a tactical display of the northeastern outskirts of Johcat. Tey saw markings defining such topographical features as the border of the city, the edge of the Deserak Wilderness, and the thoroughfare that ran all the way to the town of Revent. In the region marked Talveran Forest, the red dot flared, and concentric circles emanated from it.

"It's . . ." Tapren began, but her voice trailed off.

"What?" Orisin asked. "What is it?"

Tapren tapped at her controls. Labeled columns of digits scrolled up in a dialogue window on the side of the display. "I'm not sure, sir," the lieutenant said. "It reads like the energy of a high-yield quantum torpedo, but . . . the shockwave isn't consistent with that. It resembles something else—like the leading edge of a nuclear detonation, or of a temporal wave, or a warp-field rupture. The power of the explosion is sizable for such a contained area, but the force it's generating—"

Tapren stopped speaking as the blinking red dot vanished from her screen. All of the numerical values on her display dropped either to zero or to some negligible amount. Tey had no idea how to interpret what she'd just seen.

"What happened?" Orisin asked.

The lieutenant worked her controls. She refreshed the display, but it still showed normal readings. "This . . . this shouldn't be possible," Tapren said. "There's no discernible trace of an explosion or its effects." She paused, then ventured that it must have been a fault in the sensor system.

"A fault registering within our search area? That's suspect," Tey said. "Can you pinpoint the location?"

"I've got it," the lieutenant said.

Tey began running for the door as she heard the major tell Tapren to transfer the coordinates to the nearest transporter room.

Tey materialized in the middle of the Talveran Forest alongside Major Orisin and four Militia officers—Lieutenant Strine, Sergeants Elvem and Garvish, and Corporal Tenev. They had beamed to a location a hundred meters from the source of the possible explosion. They had all come armed with phasers, though Tey kept hers mounted on her hip for the moment. She opened a tricorder and scanned their surroundings.

"We're inside the spread of a sensor mask," Tey said. "I'm getting indeterminate readings, but there appears to be a life sign ahead." She pointed the direction.

Orisin moved quickly, and Tey trailed immediately behind him. She heard the others following. As they moved, Tey counted off the distance to their target. At fifty meters, Orisin slowed, as did Tey and the others.

"I don't see anything," the major said as he tried to look past the trees and through the underbrush.

Tey checked her tricorder. "There's a roughly circular depression ahead, like a crater," she told Orisin. She wondered if there had been an explosion after all, though her scans showed no indications of increased radiation or any other type of fallout or damage. "The edge is twenty meters away. The life sign is twenty meters beyond that, below the surrounding ground level."

Orisin turned to Tey and the others. "We're going to advance on the rim of the depression. Try to minimize noise, but we need to get there. Agent Tey, you're with me. Strine and Tenev, take a position ten meters that way." Orisin pointed to his left, and the two women started at once in that direction. "Elvem and Garvish, ten meters that way." The major pointed right, and the man and woman set off through the trees and undergrowth.

Orisin made eye contact with Tey. She drew her phaser and nodded once. Together, they moved toward the location of the explosion.

"I'll be right back," Radovan told the girl. He climbed back up the embankment to where he'd left the floating cylinder. Taking more care and moving slowly, he descended backward into the gully, pulling his device after him. When he reached the bottom, he turned toward the Avatar.

The girl stood as he'd left her, with her back to the boulder, her arms raised to either side, held up by the chains that bound her to the pitons. She should have been complaining, whining to him about her discomfort, about how she didn't want to be there, about how she wanted her mother. But she didn't. She only watched him mutely.

Radovan maneuvered his device into place above another large rock, a meter or so in front of the girl. He powered down the antigrav and the cylinder settled down onto the relatively flat surface of the stone. He activated the padd attached to the device by a couple of fiber-optic leads.

"Everything's going to be all right," he told the girl.

"We're almost done here, and then all this will be finished. You won't have to spend any more time with me."

The girl looked at him without saying anything, and then down at the device. When she peered back up at him, she seemed to take his measure. "I want to go home," she said.

"You're going home right after this," Radovan told her. "We both are."

Excitement welled within Radovan. All of his designs, all of his careful machinations—all of his *life*—had led to that moment. He had suffered through loss after loss—his father, his brother, his mother. He had endured hardships, never fitting in with anybody, never belonging anywhere. And yet, for all of that, he had come out the other side, searching for something—*any*thing!—and finding the Ohalavaru. He'd listened to Rejias Norvan, followed him, and witnessed his failed plan on Endalla. Radovan had used that disastrous event to reinterpret *The Book of Ohalu.* He would do what Rejias could not: empower the Ohalavaru and reveal the truth to all.

"This will all be over soon," he told the girl.

"Bajoran Militia!" a man's voice called out from somewhere above, near the rim of the gully. "Freeze!"

No! They'd found him. Just seconds away from fulfilling his destiny.

Radovan shifted to one side, attempting to interpose his body between where the voice had originated and the bomb. He stopped moving then, trying to appear as though he had complied with the shouted orders. But he tapped at the controls on the padd, bringing up a timing control that he set for ten seconds.

Radovan reached for the START button.

* * *

When Tey arrived at the edge of the depression with Orisin, she peered down into it. At its bottom, near the center, a man stood with his back to them. He appeared to be doing something on the flat surface of a large rock.

"Bajoran Militia!" Orisin called to the man. "Freeze!"

The man took a quick step to one side, then stopped moving. He kept his back to her and the major. Tey could see, just past him, a small, outstretched arm bound to a boulder.

Rebecca!

Tey aimed her phaser and fired.

Gamma Quadrant, 2386

Rebecca felt many things. Gravity pulled at her in a way that it hadn't before, making the hardness of the metal surface on which she sat feel even more solid. Suddenly more sensitive than usual, her body registered the gentle passage of air in the room. Likewise, an abundance of scents—including the sour tang of human perspiration—filled her nose.

More than anything, Rebecca felt joy, born out of a mixture of love and profound relief. Her father, impressive and strong in his captain's uniform, stood in front of her, clearly come to rescue her and the others from their captivity of the strange robots who had seized them from *Robinson*. Because she'd been unconscious much of the time, she couldn't tell how long she and the others had been away, but she was filled with fear and confusion and despair.

"Daddy," Rebecca said.

But her father did not reach for her, did not come to her and wrap her in a paternal embrace promising that, however bad circumstances had been, everything would be all right. Instead, he stood there staring at her, his features rigid. *Did I do something wrong?*

"Rebecca!"

She heard her name and turned her head to see her mother rushing past *Robinson* crew members. She sprinted across the chamber. Rebecca could have wept at the sight of her.

But her mother didn't run over to her. Instead, she raced to Rebecca's father, who tried to catch her, grasping her by the upper arms and attempting to keep her in place. She struggled to push past him, reaching for—

Rebecca looked beyond her father, to the place her mother fought to reach, and saw her own small body lying on a metal shelf. She felt as though she'd been dropped from a great height. Terror filled her. She tried to think.

If that's me—

Rebecca hopped from the surface on which she sat. Her feet landed on the floor with a hard, metallic thump. She raised her arms and looked at them—

What?!

Rebecca saw three appendages, formed of coiled bits of metal connecting solid structures. Her sense of herself, of her location in space, of the parts of her body in relation to one another, told her that she was seeing her own limbs, but her conscious mind rejected the notion. Rebecca tested the idea by willing her arms to move.

Before Rebecca, the three metal projections rose, flexed at multiple joints, shifted according to her directions. She brought them into her body and heard them chink against other pieces of metal. She gazed down and saw a figure she did not recognize, an artificial alien physique that could not possibly have belonged to her. Except that her senses told her something different.

This is me!

Days earlier, Rebecca had awoken in a transparent cage with other children. They had all obviously been kidnapped from *Robinson*. Their strange, robotic captors had said little to them, but the peculiar aliens clearly abducted them for a reason.

This is why, Rebecca thought, staring down at her new self. The aliens had taken her away from *Robinson,* away from her parents. They had stolen not just her life from her, but her very existence as a human. The reality horrified her.

And then Rebecca's horror and shock and dread changed. As she recognized the hopelessness of the situation, she got angry—angrier than she had been in a long time, angrier than she had almost ever been. Angry at the entities who had taken her from Mommy and Daddy, angry at spending so much time away from her home, angry at the machines that had pulled her from her own body, angry that she would never be able to return to a normal life with her parents, who she loved more than anything.

Rebecca opened whatever orifice passed for her mouth and screamed: "NOOOOO!"

A pale yellow flash of light surged from her in every direction, like the shockwave of an explosion centered within her.

An alert sounded on the tactical console, and Uteln worked quickly to identify it. Sensors registered it as a significant and abrupt increase in energy on the inner surface of the Dyson section. "I'm detecting what looks like an explosion on the surface of the Glant world," he said.

"Where?" Rogeiro asked from the command chair. "Is it near the away team? Or did they cause it?"

Uteln sent his hands darting across his panel. "I'm working to isolate the readings, but it was nowhere near the runabout or the captain's away team." After *Styx* had landed, Ensign Weil had reported that Sisko and four others had disembarked to meet with a contingent of Glant. Aboard *Robinson,* Uteln had tracked their progress across the surface to a large building complex. "Commander . . . it's centered on the location of the children."

"How bad is it?" Rogeiro asked. "Are there survivors?"

Uteln continued attempting to glean information from the readings appearing on his displays, but— "These scans don't make sense," he said. "The yield resembles that of a quantum torpedo, but the pattern of energy waves doesn't match. It reads more like the containment breach of a warp field."

"Did the runabout crash?" Rogeiro asked. "Did one of their ships?"

"Negative," Uteln said. "The *Styx* is intact . . . and there was no sign of a warp field in that area." Suddenly, all indications of the explosion disappeared from the tactical console. "It's gone," Uteln said, operating his controls as he studied the scans. "All readings of an explosion are gone."

Rogeiro asked, "How is that possible?"

"I don't know," Uteln said. "Except that what the sensors detected couldn't have been an explosion."

"Then what was it?" Rogeiro wanted to know.

"Something that generated a massive amount of energy in a confined space," Uteln said.

"What about the children?"

"I don't know," Uteln said again. "If it was an explosion, I don't know if they could have survived it. If it wasn't an explosion . . . then maybe whatever the Glant intended to do to the children . . . maybe it's begun."

Rogeiro jumped up from the command chair. "*Robinson* to Captain Sisko."

Sisko reached out and set a hand on Althouse's arm, and she moved back behind him. "You claim that we stole Gist from you," he said. Before he could continue, his combadge emitted a tone indicating an incoming message. To the Glant, he said, "My crew is contacting me." He did not ask for permission to receive the message; for him to be interrupted during the summit, it had to be important. He pressed his combadge.

"Robinson *to Captain Sisko,*" came the voice of the ship's first officer.

"This is Sisko. Go ahead, Commander."

"Sir, sensors detected a power surge at the children's location," Rogeiro said. *"It initially read like an explosion. But it doesn't now. We think that whatever purpose the Glant have taken the children for, they've begun that process."*

Sisko looked over at the Glant. Voranesk said, "Yes. The actualization has begun."

The captain did not scruple to act. "Alpha one go," he said.

He received no reply over his combadge from Commander Rogeiro. A beat passed, and Sisko knew that his first officer was relaying his coded order to Ensign Weil aboard *Styx.* Then he heard the high-pitched sound of the transporter.

The doors opened and Sisko leaped through them, his phaser raised. A wall of noise met the captain inside the Glant actualization chamber. To his surprise, the broad space looked just like the one he had entered during the first rescue mission. It marked the first time he had observed two creations of the Glant that even remotely resembled each other.

But unlike in the other actualization chamber Sisko had stormed, all of the equipment before him appeared powered up and operating. Indicator lights flashed on control panels, and information spelled out in alien glyphs marched from right to left across displays. Sisko wanted desperately to find his daughter, but five Glant stationed at various consoles looked over at him. Five *Robinson* security officers took up a position on either side of the captain, all of them with their weapons aimed at the Glant. He knew that Kasidy and the others stood behind them.

"Shut off the equipment and move away," Sisko ordered, raising his voice to be heard over the cacophony of the Glant equipment. He could only hope that he had not arrived too late. It had taken precious time for his away team to battle their way through a legion of Glant defenders. The second away team, composed solely of *Robinson* security officers, helped to shorten the confrontation by attacking from another direction. But according to Voranesk, the process of transferring the minds of the children into newly created Glant had already begun.

"You cannot explore here," one of the alien scientists said, speaking loudly. It had an oblong head and a pyramidal body that looked like a cross section of sedimentary layers mounted atop a wide, rolling track. Extending from each triangular side of its body, a pair of articulated metal arms ended in a hand with at least ten digits. "You cannot stop actualization."

"Watch me," Sisko said, and he pointed his phaser at a shelving unit on the wall to the left of the Glant. The captain squeezed the trigger pad, and a beam of bright blue energy shot out and diffused across the piece of furniture, vaporizing it into nothingness. "You four move into the far corner," Sisko said, pointing in that direction, and they quickly heeded his words. To the first Glant he'd addressed, he said, "Now shut down the equipment."

The Glant's wide track spun beneath it, turning it toward the nearest control panel. As it started toward the console, Sisko peered around. Just as in the other actualization chamber, he saw a number of transparent compartments holding the *Robinson* children. When he didn't see Rebecca, he risked a look at the far wall, to the horizontal slabs housed inside the large, intricate machines. He couldn't see her.

Sisko followed the Glant with the pyramid-shaped body over to a console. The entity raised two of its arms over the control panel, but then hesitated. Sisko stepped around to its side so that it could see him. The captain aimed his phaser at its oblong head. "If you don't shut it all down right now, I'm going to shoot you and then I'm going to destroy every piece of equipment in here."

The Glant's many-fingered hands moved across the console. The din diminished, lights and readouts dimmed. Sisko waited to see if the Glant would comply by shutting it all down. Eventually, the chamber quieted completely.

"Now go over there with the others," Sisko said, pointing to the far corner, where the other four Glant huddled. When the entity joined its colleagues, Sisko glanced back over at the security officers. "Free the children," he said, gesturing toward the transparent cages. Then he hurried across the room. Kasidy called after him as he ran forward. His eyes moved from side to side as he searched for his daughter. He saw her in the second of the five machines that lined the back wall. A dim glow illuminated her body. She lay on her back, motionless, secured to the slab by straps around her arms and legs. A trio of thick tubes ended in dish-shaped instruments that had been affixed to the sides and top of her head. Her eyes were closed, as if she were sleeping or unconscious.

Sleeping, Sisko repeated to himself. *Or unconscious.* His mind would not allow for any other possibilities.

He holstered his phaser as he reached his daughter. "Rebecca," he said, his mouth dry, his voice barely above a whisper. "Rebecca." He felt for the latch, pressed it, then eased the slab toward him, pulling his daughter from the stasis field. Sisko reached out and put his hand on her arm, which felt warm beneath his touch. He felt a cautious relief, exhaling loudly when he saw her chest rising and falling. He unfastened the straps holding Rebecca down. With care, he removed the equipment surrounding her head. Rebecca blinked once, twice, then opened her eyes and looked at Sisko.

"Daddy," she said.

Bajor, 2380

Tey charged down into the depression behind Orisin. The two of them picked their way as quickly as they could through the thick growth and fallen trees. The other Militia officers stayed up at the rim of the depression, maintaining a vigil in case Radovan had accomplices in the area.

The major reached Radovan first. Tey's phaser shot had left the kidnapper in a heap on the ground, stunned into unconsciousness. Orisin dropped a knee onto Radovan's back, then exchanged his phaser for a set of restraints, with which he bound the man's wrists.

Tey went to Rebecca. The girl appeared physically unharmed. "It's all right," Tey said, kneeling down to speak with Rebecca at eye level. "My name is Jasmine. We're here to bring you home to your mother and father. Are you okay?"

The girl wriggled against the boulder. "My back hurts," she said in a small voice.

"Okay, let me get you out of these," Tey said, examining the cuffs around Rebecca's wrists. She saw that they required a physical key. She looked over to where Orisin stood by the unconscious form of Radovan. "Would you see if he's got a key on him?"

The major bent to Radovan's inert body and rummaged

through his pants. He checked in one pocket, then another. Orisin's hand came out with a key. He passed it to Tey.

She quickly unlocked one cuff, and Rebecca's arm fell to her side. When Tey undid the second cuff, she expected the girl's other arm to drop as well, but instead, Rebecca threw her arms around Tey's neck and buried her head in Tey's shoulder. The girl squeezed tightly, as though she might never let go.

"It's okay, Rebecca," Tey said softly into her ear. She stroked the girl's hair, trying to soothe her. Rebecca might not have been hurt physically, but who knew what psychological toll the abduction had taken on her—and would continue to take on her. "We're going to take you to your parents now."

With Radovan's sensor mask still in place—and probably a transporter inhibitor, Tey guessed—they couldn't beam out of their location. Along with Orisin, Tey scaled the side of the depression. Then, with the other officers, they tramped back through the trees until they reached a point where they could contact provincial Militia headquarters. It took more than half an hour, but at last they all transported out of the Talveran Forest.

Rebecca didn't let go of Tey the entire time.

Gamma Quadrant, 2386

Sisko started toward the doors of the actualization chamber alongside his wife. Kasidy held their daughter in her arms. Sisko had offered to carry Rebecca, but neither mother nor daughter had any inclination to let go.

While the captain had freed the other children from the Glant machines, the other members of the away team had gotten the rest of the children out of the cages. Doctor Kosciuszko and Crewwoman DeSantis each carried two of the smaller children, while Counselor Althouse held one. The security officers had gathered everybody together by the doors, with the away team encircling the children.

The Glant scientists seemed extremely distraught at the disruption of their actualization process, but the captain offered them no sympathy. Instead, Sisko told them to remain where they were until the away team had exited the chamber with the children. One of the Glant started to protest loudly, and so the captain had little choice but to fire his phaser past it. The entity backed down.

Sisko made his way across the chamber to the doors. He hoped Glant opposition would be minimal so that the away team could bring all of the children safely to the transport point. He looked to Lieutenant Rogers, who consulted his tricorder.

"Captain," Rogers said quietly. The security officer leaned

in and held up his tricorder so that Sisko could see its display. The captain saw two large groups of orange dots on the screen, many of them fluctuating; some of the pinpoint lights blinked on and off in a regular pattern, while others appeared only for an instant before vanishing. "It's difficult to determine exact numbers because of the inconsistent life signs, but I estimate at least thirty Glant approaching down the corridor to the left, and another thirty to the right."

The report alarmed Sisko. The large numbers of Glant and their advance from opposite directions would make it that much more difficult to reach the transport point without incurring casualties—especially traveling with the children. *If only we could transport from here,* Sisko thought.

But then something occurred to him. His crew had been unable to beam an away team into or out of a Glant actualization chamber because of interference with the carrier wave. Spingeld had believed the cause to be the equipment functioning at the location. *But that equipment has been completely shut down here.*

The captain activated his combadge with a touch. "Sisko to *Styx.*"

"*Weil here, Captain.*"

"Ensign, we have the children," Sisko said. "Have Spingeld scan our location for all non-Glant life signs and attempt transport."

"*Aye, sir.*"

Sisko waited anxiously for a report from Weil. He expected to hear that the Glant technology still interfered with Spingeld's ability to beam the away team back to the runabout. Instead, he heard the high-pitched tones of transport rise inside the actualization chamber. The dazzling white light formations of dematerialization appeared throughout the group of *Robinson* personnel and children. Sisko's vision faded.

An imperceptible amount of time later, the large stage of the high-capacity transporter aboard *Styx* appeared. Sisko immediately checked that the children and the entire away team had been beamed back to the runabout. When he verified that everybody had successfully transported aboard, he quickly kissed his wife and daughter on their cheeks, then headed for the cockpit. They had made it to *Styx*, but they all still had to get back to *Robinson*.

The runabout convulsed beneath the onslaught. Through the forward ports, Sisko could see at least six Glant vessels diving toward them from above. Even with the lesser firepower of their ships' laser weapons, the combined attack rocked *Styx*.

"Shields down to thirty-seven percent," Rogers said from the tactical station, where he had taken over for Grandal.

The captain had set course for one of the water conduits connecting the inner and outer surfaces of the Dyson section, intending to return to space without having to run the gauntlet of Glant vessels above the populated surface of their world. But sensors revealed that the Glant had sealed the inner apertures of the tunnels, in addition to stationing ships within them. Sisko might have been able to use the runabout's phasers to blast through one of the sealed entrances, and then to fight past the enemy vessels there, but the composition of the material blocking the tunnels—a diburnium-based alloy—and the close proximity in which a battle would have to take place made neither prospect a certainty. Instead, Sisko piloted *Styx* out of the ocean and pointed it toward space and the *Robinson*.

Sisko heard the tones from the tactical station, signaling the firing of the runabout's phasers. Multiple yellow-red beams lashed out at the Glant vessels, striking three of them, one of which lost drive control and plummeted from the sky. Sisko brought *Styx* about in an attempt to evade the attacking ships, but as he veered away, he saw even more of the enemy vessels descending toward the runabout.

"The Glant ships are breaking off their engagement with our shuttlecraft," said Weil, who sat beside the captain at the main console. "The shuttles are in pursuit. All Glant vessels are converging on the *Styx*." As though to punctuate the ensign's report, two more laser blasts in succession rocked the runabout.

"Shields down to thirty-four percent," Rogers said. The security officer fired the phasers again, but as Sisko pushed *Styx* onto a new course, the beams flew wide of their targets.

Another laser landed on the runabout, and then another. Sisko reeled *Styx* around to starboard, pushed the bow down toward the surface, then pulled back up hard. Two blue beams sliced past the ports, but a third found its mark, shaking the runabout once more.

"Shields at twenty-seven percent," Rogers said.

Glant vessels filled the sky. Sisko saw the yellowish-red streaks of phasers and traced them back to the shuttlecraft that fired them. As he watched, one of the *Robinson* auxiliary ships took two laser strikes on an already blackened warp nacelle. Then another Glant vessel shot past and discharged its weapon at the wounded shuttlecraft, which suddenly exploded in smoke and fire.

No! Sisko thought, even as he diverted *Styx* onto a new evasive route. The captain's goal in tracking down the Glant and traveling to their world had been to save lives, not to end them, not to recover the children at the cost of his crew.

Three more laser blasts pounded into the runabout's hull in rapid succession. The impacts hurled Sisko from his chair. He climbed back to his feet at once, but fell to his knees as a fourth Glant weapon landed on its target.

"Shields down to thirteen percent," Rogers called from the tactical console as Sisko reached his chair.

"Captain, we're being hailed by the *Robinson*," Weil said beside Sisko. "They want us to drop our shields."

"Sir?" Rogers asked.

"Hold on, Lieutenant," Sisko said. "Be ready." The captain pulled the bow of *Styx* up, sending it into a steep climb. He saw Glant vessels approaching from all around, and as he soared past the first group, he glimpsed them adjusting course, moving to follow the runabout upward.

And far above them, but inside the inert space surrounding the Dyson section, *Robinson* soared past.

Sisko hauled the bow back even farther, past vertical, until it looped over itself and charged into a ninety-degree dive angle. *Styx* plunged straight down toward the surface—and a cluster of Glant buildings. Land and sprawling structures filled the view through the forward ports.

"The Glant ships are adjusting course to pursue, but cautiously," Weil said. "They're not rushing to dive after us. We have a window."

"Lower the shields," Sisko ordered.

As *Robinson* flew through the sky above the Dyson section, Rogeiro stood in the center of the bridge, waiting. When he'd witnessed all of the Glant vessels altering their course to pursue *Styx*, he'd made the decision to take the ship into the atmosphere. At the same time, he recalled all of the shuttlecraft. Once *Robinson* successfully crossed the inert region surrounding the Dyson section, seven of the auxiliary vessels made it back to the shuttlebay, while the crew used cargo transporters to bring aboard the other four. The Glant had destroyed the twelfth shuttle, *Transit*, though fortunately not before its three-person crew had been beamed safely to another, *Eclipse*.

Rogeiro studied the main viewscreen. It displayed a magnified image of *Styx* as the runabout circled bow over stern and then headed straight downward, shooting toward the surface. The first officer watched the Glant vessels respond, but slowly, their pilots clearly not wanting to risk taking their ships into dangerous dives, nor wanting to fire for fear of striking the buildings below. Rogeiro hoped the confusion about what to do would provide an opportunity, not just for the away team aboard *Styx*, but for the *Robinson* crew.

"The runabout's shields are down," Uteln said at last.

"Transporter room, energize," Rogeiro ordered across an already open channel.

"*Energizing,*" replied Chief Farid Iravani, the ship's senior transporter officer.

Seconds seemed to elongate as Rogeiro waited again. He looked over his shoulder to Uteln, who raised an eyebrow so slightly as to be almost undetectable. Rogeiro thought it might mark the most concerned expression he'd ever seen on the Deltan's face.

The first officer turned back to the main viewscreen just in time to see *Styx* slam into the surface of the Glant world. The captain had clearly set its course with care, as it crashed in an open area rather than into any buildings. A red fireball rose high into the air. More seconds passed.

"*Transporter room to bridge,*" Iravani finally said. "*We got everybody: all the children and the entire away team.*"

"Good work, Chief," Rogeiro said, but already his mind moved on to his next tasks. "Uteln, shields up. Sivadeki, get us out of here; full impulse to the inert region, warp speed as soon as we're clear." As the two officers acknowledged their orders, Rogeiro said, "Plante, let's see the Glant forces."

The image on the viewscreen changed, pulling back to show more of the Dyson section. Plante worked her controls, highlighting the numerous Glant vessels. "Some of them are modifying their course to chase the *Robinson*, but they're too far back," she said. "They won't catch us."

Rogeiro moved to the command chair and sat down, thinking, *That's what I wanted to hear.*

Bajor, 2380

Benjamin Sisko opened the front door to the natural beauty of Kendra Province and the welcome sounds of laughter. With the autumnal equinox just passed, shades of orange and red had begun to encroach on the leaves, and the green of the grass had begun to seep toward yellow. B'hava'el hung lower in the sky; it sent long shadows crawling across the landscape. Clouds floated above the distant Kendra Mountains, their puffy whiteness reflected in the ribbon of the Yolja River that wound in front of the foothills. Nearby, the creek that ran through the property offered up its bubbly trickle as though the water itself giggled.

Sisko had intended to call his wife and daughter in for dinner—the hearty aroma of jambalaya drifted from the kitchen to fill the house—but instead he leaned against the doorjamb and simply watched them. Kasidy bent low as she capered across the grass, playfully chasing their daughter around a moba tree. Clad in a sky-blue dress, Rebecca ran with abandon, her delighted chortles a testament to the resilience of the young—and perhaps especially to the uncanny constitution of Rebecca herself.

In the five days since their daughter's return, Sisko and Kasidy had showered her with love and attention, alert for any signs of trauma from her ordeal. To their relief, they had seen no indications in Rebecca of emotional distress. *To our* great *relief,* Sisko thought, *and to our surprise.* Although he hadn't spoken directly about it with his wife, he could tell that the lack of any apparent deleterious effects of the kidnapping on Rebecca puzzled her. It did more than that for Sisko: it confused and troubled him. He knew that children could be eminently adaptable, and he also recognized that maybe Rebecca did not understand the gravity of what had happened.

But she's also the Avatar.

Sisko despised that thought. While he knew firsthand the power of Bajoran prophecy, and believed that the Ohalavaru view of the Prophets—that they were not deities, but merely members of an advanced alien species—might be accurate, he chafed at his daughter being accorded a place of prominence in their belief system. *The Book of Ohalu* offered little about her role beyond her birth being a portent of a new and glorious age for the people of Bajor, but Sisko knew that could change. As she got older, Rebecca could encounter new interpretations of her position as the Avatar, and new expectations.

That's already happened, he thought. Her kidnapper had been an Ohalavaru, evidently acting on motives related to his faith, though a full report on Radovan Tavus had yet to be rendered. Still, Sisko wondered if the time had come for his family to leave Bajor—if for no other reason than their own safety.

It's more than that, isn't it? Sisko asked himself. In the three and a half years since his return from the Celestial Temple, his relationship with the Prophets had changed. *Relationship,* he chided himself. *What relationship?* Since sending him back to Bajor, the Prophets had essentially gone silent.

Isn't that what I always wanted?

It had been, at one time. In the beginning, when Kai Opaka had identified him as the Emissary of the Prophets, he had been wildly uncomfortable with the designation, let alone all of the implications and expectations that accompanied it. But that changed over time, until he not only accepted his part in Bajoran spiritual life, but came to embrace it—even when Prophets took him from Kasidy and Jake to reside in the Celestial Temple.

But there could be no question: the Prophets had been hard taskmasters. Cryptic in their communications and demanding in the burdens they placed on Sisko, they enriched his life at the same time that they complicated it. *Where have they gone?*

After returning from the Celestial Temple, Sisko had continued to feel the presence of the Prophets in his life. Or at least, he believed he felt their presence. Lately, he'd begun to have doubts.

At first, all had been well—better than just well; everything had been *good*. Kasidy gave birth to Rebecca, who, though a bit small, arrived in prefect health. Sisko went with his wife and daughter to the home that he had planned, but that Kas and Jake had built in his absence. Together, he and Kasidy and Rebecca lived the life for which he had longed. After years of effort, Bajor finally joined the Federation. Jake met Rena, fell in love, and married her. And in Sisko's dreams and visions, the Prophets still communicated with him.

Or so I thought.

Then other incidents had begun to occur—troubling incidents. The Ascendants arrived through the wormhole, led by Iliana Ghemor. The health of Sisko's father began to fail. Eivos Calan and Audj died in a house fire. Ohalavaru extremists descended on Endalla with explosives, planning to strip-mine the surface of the moon, and when Sisko attempted to defuse the situation, their leader committed suicide and took a number of his followers with him.

And then Rebecca was kidnapped, he thought. She had been rescued and brought home, but Sisko couldn't help feeling that some force was at work—some *bad* force. As time had passed, it seemed to him that terrible events loomed on his horizon. Some had drawn close, some had even struck, but it all reminded him of the warning the Prophets had issued to him back before the end of the Dominion War: if he spent his life with Kasidy, he would know nothing but sorrow. He thought he had escaped such a fate, but with everything that had happened, he could no longer be sure. Sisko wondered if he was beginning to pay the price for having ignored the Prophets' counsel. Worse, he feared that, if so, that price would grow increasingly dear.

Where are the Prophets now? The dreams and visions Sisko had experienced after returning from the Celestial Temple had been few, and they had faded over time, like bright colors in a darkening room. Those experiences felt like pallid facsimiles of his previous contact with the Prophets. As they continued to diminish in number and frequency, until they disappeared entirely, he came to realize that they had been communications not with the Prophets, but simply with his own subconscious.

A sudden movement broke Sisko's inner focus. A shadow fell across his face, and then something struck him—not hard, but it surprised him. He blinked and looked around, his gaze finally coming to rest on an inflatable ball bouncing away from him on the porch.

Rebecca squealed with laughter. She and Kasidy had come over to the foot of the porch and stood looking up at him. "A credit for your thoughts, Mister Sisko," Kas said.

"My thoughts are: it's dinnertime and I'm hungry," he said. He bent to pick up the ball, then sat on the edge of the porch in front of Rebecca. "So do you want to eat this ball—" Sisko playfully held it up in front of his daughter's face. "—or would you rather have jamba-lamba?" Since the first time Rebecca had ever tried to say jambalaya, that had been her word for the Creole dish.

"Jamba-lamba!"

Rebecca opened her arms wide, and Sisko dropped the ball and scooped her up. He perched her on his hip with one arm and reached the other out toward Kasidy. She took his hand, and together, they walked back into the house. Something more than contentment, something more even than happiness, flooded through Sisko. He felt joy.

He could only hope that it would last.

Kasidy cleared the dishes from the dining room into the kitchen as her husband doled out helpings of bread pudding and vanilla ice cream. She brought out a glass of milk for Rebecca, a mug of *raktajino* for Ben, and a cup of apple cinnamon herbal tea for herself. As they sat around the table enjoying their dessert, Kasidy basked in the restoration of their family.

During the days that Rebecca had been gone, Kasidy had experienced fear in an entirely new way. There had been times in the past when she'd been afraid for her own life, and other times—certainly during the Dominion War— when she had worried about Ben. None of it matched the horror of losing of her child. Rebecca had been brought home safely, but the memory of Kasidy's fear remained.

We have to do something, she thought. Since the recovery of their daughter, Kasidy and Ben hadn't let her out of their sight, even to the point of having her sleep with them for the first couple of nights—not for Rebecca's sake, but for their own. Kasidy needed to know at every moment that

their daughter was home, that she hadn't been stolen away
again.

And that's not going to change, she thought. *Not for a long
time.*

Intellectually, Kasidy knew that she hadn't left Rebecca
alone at the time she'd been kidnapped. But that missed the
point. Her sense of safety had been shattered and she would
need to find a way to restore it.

Beside her, Rebecca gleefully shoveled spoonfuls of
bread pudding and ice cream into her mouth. In her days
back at home, her appetite had been good. Likewise, so had
her disposition. Kasidy and Ben had talked about paying
close attention to their daughter, searching for any hints of
emotional damage she might've suffered during her ordeal.

Except that Rebecca seems perfectly fine. That both pleased
Kasidy and concerned her. She wanted Rebecca to be all
right, but she worried that the lack of any perceivable impact on her suggested repressed emotions that could harm
her psychological well-being in the future.

When Major Orisin had contacted them to say that the
Militia had recovered Rebecca and arrested her abductor,
Kasidy and Ben had immediately transported from their
house to Adarak, and from there to Renassa. Kasidy wept
when she finally held their daughter, who had hugged her
right back, but even then, Rebecca appeared unperturbed.
She even tolerated a medical exam, which thankfully revealed that she had suffered no physical trauma.

The next day, they'd all gone back to Renassa so that
Rebecca could be questioned. Kasidy and Ben accompanied their daughter into a playroom that had been set up
for her. While Major Orisin observed from another room, a
counselor—a Bajoran woman named Lennis Delah—came
in to gently probe Rebecca for information. She refused to
answer—not with closed lips and a reluctance to speak with

the counselor, but because she seemed distracted as she entertained herself with various playthings.

Later, Lennis had asked that Kasidy and Ben leave her alone with their daughter, though they could observe the interaction along with the major. The counselor suggested that Rebecca might be reluctant to talk about what had happened because she believed that she had done something wrong. Kasidy and Ben hesitantly agreed.

Eventually, their daughter had answered some of Lennis's questions. Rebecca didn't appear to believe that she'd done anything wrong, but it also seemed that she didn't have any interest in talking about the abduction. She said enough to suggest that Radovan had actually treated her reasonably well, considering the circumstances. Rebecca referred to him as "the sad man," and rather than expressing anger, she said she felt sorry for him.

Afterward, the counselor had been cautiously optimistic that whatever psychological damage Rebecca had suffered would not be debilitating and could be readily addressed. Lennis recommended starting with an hour-long session three times a week, adjusting the schedule as dictated by how the therapy unfolded. She offered to recommend another counselor, but because of Rebecca's ease with her during their initial meeting, Kasidy and Ben asked her to continue seeing their daughter.

Lennis had been to the house twice. According to her, the sessions had gone well—remarkably so, given Rebecca's age and the nature of what she'd just endured. The counselor was due out at the house again in two days.

"Can I have some more, please?" Rebecca asked. Roused from her thoughts, Kasidy looked over and saw that Rebecca had cleaned her plate.

"More?" Ben asked. "Where's all that food going? You must have hollow legs."

Rebecca snickered. "Nooooo," she said, drawing the word out. "It's going in my belly." She pointed demonstratively to her midsection.

"I think maybe you've had enough to eat," Kasidy said. "You don't want to get a stomachache, do you?"

"No," Rebecca said. "I want to get some more ice cream." She made her request sound perfectly reasonable.

"Well—" Kasidy started, but then the front-door signal chimed.

Ben glanced at her with raised eyebrows. "Who could that be?" he asked. "Jake and Rena aren't due back on Bajor for three more days."

Kasidy shrugged, then stood up and walked between the small sitting area before the fireplace to the right, and the larger living area to the left. At the front door, she tapped at the panel beside it, which then displayed their visitor. "Oh," Kasidy said. "It's Jasmine Tey."

Rebecca immediately jumped from her chair and ran toward the door. "Auntie Jasmine, Auntie Jasmine."

The reaction surprised Kasidy, though she supposed it shouldn't have. From the way Rebecca's recovery had been described by Major Orisin, the agent had been the one to reach her first and free her. But Kasidy experienced a knot of concern at Tey's unexpected appearance at their house.

Kasidy opened the door. Tey stood on the porch wearing a light-blue A-line dress beneath a cropped white cardigan, open at the front. "Good evening, Ms. Yates," she said. "I'm sorry for—" She stopped speaking as Rebecca darted past Kasidy and threw her arms around Tey's legs.

"Hello there, Miss Rebecca," Tey said. "It's good to see you."

"Look," Rebecca said, pointing first to Tey's blue dress, and then at her own. "We match."

Tey peered down at herself, as though she'd forgotten

what she'd worn that day. "You're right, we do match," she said. "Are you copying me?"

Rebecca reached her pointing finger forward until it rested on the skirt of Tey's dress. "You're copying me."

"I guess you're right, but who wouldn't want to copy a pretty girl like you?" Tey said with a smile, and she looked up at Kasidy. "I'm sorry for arriving unannounced, but I was hoping that I could speak with you and Mister Sisko. If I'm intruding, I can come back another time."

"Don't," Rebecca protested, grabbing Tey's hand and trying without success to pull her inside. "Come have ice cream with us."

"Rebecca, why don't you go back to the table with your father," Kasidy said. "Let me talk to Ms. Tey for a moment." Rebecca tried once more to pull Tey inside, then gave up and stomped back to the dining room. Kasidy stepped aside so that Tey could enter, then closed the door and quietly asked, "Is everything all right?"

"Yes," Tey said, also speaking softly. "I'm sorry if I alarmed you by just showing up. I only wanted to update you about the investigation." She gazed past Kasidy, then said, "To be completely honest, I also wanted to see how Miss Rebecca was doing."

"She obviously wants to see you too," Kasidy said. "Why don't you come in and have dessert with us? We can talk after Rebecca goes to bed."

"That would be fine, thank you," Tey said. She joined them in the dining room, and while she didn't partake of either the bread pudding or the ice cream, she did have a cup of Kasidy's herbal tea.

Tey's visit lasted longer than Kasidy had expected it to when it began, and perhaps longer than Tey had expected, though if that were the case, she gave no indication. Rather, she engaged in pleasant conversation with Kasidy and Ben when she could. She mostly found herself the center of attention for Rebecca, who took her on a tour of her room, proudly showed her several drawings that she had done, and introduced her to all of her dolls and stuffed animals.

With the last shreds of the day gone and night fully descended, Rebecca's energy flagged. When Ben took their daughter down the hall and into the refresher to get her ready for bed, Kasidy asked about the real purpose of Tey's visit. "I know you said that everything was all right, but . . ."

Tey apologized again for not contacting Kasidy and Ben before coming to their house. "I wanted to tell you that Radovan Tavus confessed to kidnapping Rebecca," she said. "We've confirmed all of the information he's given us, as well as details he hasn't. I thought you'd want to know that we're certain that he acted alone."

"What about the woman you found in his flat?" The discovery of a dead body in the kidnapper's home, where he had evidently kept Rebecca hostage, continued to chill Kasidy.

"Winser Ellevet," Tey said. "She was someone Radovan knew in the Ohalavaru, but we don't believe she played any part in the abduction. It appears that she accidentally learned about it when she visited him and saw Rebecca. He killed her for it, though he claims he only meant to incapacitate her."

Kasidy listened and tried to take it all in without allowing it to overwhelm her. Although the specific danger of Radovan had passed, it felt as though other perils might lay in wait. Kasidy considered asking if they had identified his motive, but wasn't sure she really wanted to know. If the beliefs of the Ohalavaru had pushed one person to threaten Rebecca, that might mean that more could follow. But Kasidy asked anyway.

"Radovan claimed to be doing the work of Ohalu as imparted to him by the teacher Prophets," Tey said, confirming Kasidy's fears. "But his explanation of what drove him doesn't make much sense. He's quoted *The Book of Ohalu*, except that the words he uses are nowhere in its pages. More than that, his interpretation of Ohalavaru tenets is unique; we haven't been able to find even a splinter group that construes their beliefs in the way that he does. All of which supports the results of his psychological evaluation: he's mentally ill."

Kasidy's vision blurred as tears formed in her eyes.

"Ms. Yates, I'm sorry," Tey said. "I didn't come here to upset you."

"You didn't," Kasidy said. She took a napkin and dabbed at her eyes. "What you just told me actually helps. That this man was just sick . . . that there probably aren't more like him out there . . . other Ohalavaru plotting to kidnap Rebecca . . . it's reassuring."

"I'm glad," Tey said. "I was hoping it would help you find a measure of closure."

"Thank you."

"Well, I won't take up any more of your time." Tey pushed back from the table and stood up, plainly intending to leave, but then Ben and Rebecca emerged from the refresher. Rebecca ran down the hall and back into the dining room, dressed in pink pajamas decorated with drawings of Bajoran animals—*batos* and *pylchyk*s, among others.

"Good night, Auntie Jasmine." Rebecca held her arms out wide. Tey crouched down and hugged her.

"Good night, Miss Rebecca."

After Kasidy kissed her daughter and said good night, Ben took Rebecca to her room to put her to bed. As Kasidy accompanied Tey toward the front door, the young woman said, "I have to tell you that I'm touched that you wanted Rebecca to call me 'Auntie.'"

"I'm glad she likes you enough to want to call you that, but we didn't tell her to."

"What?" Tey said. "You mean—?"

"Rebecca just decided to do that on her own," Kasidy said. "She really must like you a lot."

At the door, Tey offered thanks for welcoming her into the house, and then she turned to go. Kasidy stopped her with a touch to her arm. "May I ask what you intend to do now?" she asked. "I know you recently stepped down from the first minister's security detail, but do you have any plans for what you're going to do next?"

"I've been exploring different options," Tey said. "I was considering leaving Bajor, but now I'm not so sure. Major Orisin asked me if I would join his investigative team, or at least consult with them, so I'm thinking about those opportunities."

"You'd obviously be very good at that," Kasidy said, and meant it. The major had lauded Tey for her efforts, which had led directly to the identification of the kidnapper. Kasidy and Ben could not have been happier with the recommendation of the first minister, whom they'd contacted to thank after Rebecca's return. After seeing her daughter with Tey that evening, another idea had occurred to Kasidy. "I was wondering if you might consider another possibility."

Tey stepped from the porch and onto the grass, to the edge of the illumination thrown by the outside lights. She raised her wrist, ostensibly to activate her comm, but then she dropped her arm back to her side and gazed up at the night sky. Endalla had already risen and hung three-quarters of the way up from the horizon. Even after more than two years, Tey had yet to grow accustomed to the shades of gray coloring its surface; until the Ascendants' attack, the moon had been a living world, painted mainly in the greens of vegetation and the browns of soil.

Her visit to Kendra Valley gratified Tey. She had stopped by to inform Yates and Sisko about the investigation, and to check on the welfare of Rebecca. Tey had wanted the parents to know that their probe into Radovan and the details of their daughter's abduction had yielded no surprises, and that they had found no other threats to their daughter—credible or otherwise.

One detail still gnawed at Tey—not because she thought it held any significance, but because it had not yet been definitively explained. They had found Radovan and Rebecca in the Talveran Forest when scans conducted from the Mission Operations Center in Renassa had detected an explosion there, but when she, Orisin, and the Militia team had arrived at the location, there had been no evidence whatsoever of any kind of detonation. Subsequent detailed scans of the site confirmed that.

Orisin's staff had suspected a malfunction in the sensors, but a complete diagnostic had refuted that—and in any event, it had seemed exceedingly unlikely to Tey that a system failure would have coincidentally led them directly to Rebecca and her kidnapper. Other theories included glitches in Radovan's sensor mask or transporter inhibitor, but all of that equipment had likewise checked out as fully functional. Somebody suggested that the bomb had somehow manufactured the erroneous reading, but analysis of the homemade explosive failed to uncover any mechanism for that to happen.

Tey shrugged to herself at the edge of the pool of light, peering out into the darkness. She would pursue the question as far as she could, but she suspected that she would never find a satisfactory answer. Things always happened for a reason, but that didn't mean those reasons always divulged themselves.

Tey glanced back over her shoulder at the house. Though she barely knew them, she genuinely liked both Yates and Sisko, and she had a particular affinity for their daughter. Perhaps because she had no family of her own—none to speak of, anyway—she found herself considering the proposal she'd just been offered. Tey had left her position on First Minister Asarem's security detail because she had tired of the routine, and in some ways, what Yates had suggested would be more of the same: safeguarding a single individual. Still, providing continuous security for a head of state could hardly be deemed on a par with protecting a little girl, even if the Ohalavaru believed Rebecca to hold the prophesied position of the Avatar.

Yates had explained that she and her husband would spend most of their time with their daughter, but that they would appreciate some occasional assistance, so that they could spend some time alone or attend to other matters—perhaps several hours a day, a few times per week. It would provide Rebecca with security, her parents with peace of mind, and Tey with enough downtime to pursue other interests.

"Maybe," she said aloud, the single word swallowed up by the wide-open space before her.

Tey tapped her wrist comm. "Tey to Adarak Transporter Terminal," she said.

"Adarak Terminal," a woman's voice replied. *"This is Coste Sholl."*

"One to transport." Tey took a deep breath of the crisp, fresh night air. Then she dematerialized.

Gamma Quadrant, 2386

Sisko watched as his wife peeked into Rebecca's room. Just inside the doorway, her dark skin disappeared in the shadows, but the light in the main part of their cabin caught her eye, which gleamed like a bedewed jewel. Even in darkness, Kasidy had a presence.

The captain sat in the living area of their quarters aboard *Robinson*, still in his uniform even though alpha shift had ended hours earlier. He intended to visit the bridge before retiring for the night. He just needed to talk with his wife.

Five days had passed since the *Styx* away team had saved the last of the abducted children from the Glant. Since then, Doctor Kosciuszko and his medical staff had conducted full workups on all of them, each one receiving a clean bill of health. Counselors Althouse, al-Jarjani, and Vint had begun therapy for the children, sometimes in individual settings, sometimes with their families. At the urging of Althouse, Kasidy continued to lead a support group for the parents.

Most of the children reported remembering only fragments of their experiences, although they all knew that they had been kidnapped by a strange and uncommunicative alien species. But the Glant's aural weapon had rendered all of them unconscious before they'd been abducted, and they'd mostly been kept that way during their captivity. The notable exceptions were those children who had at some point been connected to the actualization equipment. Not surprisingly, that group exhibited the highest levels of post-traumatic stress.

Kasidy withdrew from the entryway to Rebecca's room, and the door closed silently behind her. As she walked across the wide cabin, she said, "She's out."

"I'm not surprised," Sisko said as Kasidy edged past the low table and slipped onto the sofa beside him. "Today was a big day." For the first time since their ordeal, the children who had been taken had returned to school. In their first days back aboard ship, they'd had to deal with reunions with their families, extensive medical exams, and the start of counseling sessions. As a result, Althouse recommended allowing a few days to pass before making additional demands on them—although she also suggested not waiting too long before renewing their routines. "Rebecca seemed like she was happy to get back to school. That's all she talked about at dinner."

"I think, more than anything, she just wanted to see Elent again." An animated girl, Elent Dorson had become Rebecca's best friend aboard ship. An unjoined Trill a year older than Rebecca, she too had been abducted by the Glant, though the two had not been held in the same group.

Sisko pointed toward the dining area in the inner corner of their cabin. "I was going to get something to drink," he said. "Can I pour you a glass of wine?"

"Are you having some?"

"No, I've got to head up to the bridge in a few minutes," Sisko said.

"Then no, I'll just have water," Kasidy said. "So why the late duty on the bridge?"

As Sisko rose and walked over to the replicator, he said, "We're supposed to finally set sail out of Glant space, and

I want to make sure we're on schedule." He ordered two glasses of chilled water.

"I'll be glad when the Glant are well behind us," Kasidy said.

"I think the entire crew feels the same way." Since fleeing from the Dyson section, the crew had kept their distance from Glant vessels, but Sisko had ordered *Robinson* to remain in the region. He and his senior staff had debated about their responsibilities with respect to the Glant. They considered returning to the Dyson section to mount an offensive to pinpoint and destroy all of the actualization equipment, but even if they could do that without any risk to the ship—which they assuredly couldn't—Sisko argued that it wouldn't prevent the Glant from constructing new machines to accomplish their nefarious goals.

But nobody had wanted to leave the region without trying to prevent what had happened to the *Robinson* crew—and doubtless to the personnel aboard the other ship they'd found floating dead in null space—from happening to anybody else who entered the area. The senior staff suggested several schemes to accomplish that goal, and Sisko eventually chose to employ a variation on the self-replicating minefield that Miles O'Brien, Jadzia Dax, and Rom had constructed during the Dominion War. Relkdahz and his engineers modified a number of warning buoys, incorporating small industrial replicators into them. The *Robinson* crew then seeded them at wide intervals all around Glant space. If one of the buoys failed or was destroyed, its nearest neighbor would create a replacement and deploy it to a slightly different location.

Sisko took a sip of water, then set the two glasses down on the table in front of the sofa. When he sat back down beside Kasidy, he asked, "Do you know if Rebecca and Elent talked about what they went through?" So far, Rebecca had said almost nothing about her experiences on the Glant world, even though other children who had been placed into the actualization equipment had spoken vividly about what that had felt like.

"I don't know, but I hope so," Kasidy said. "I'd rather she talk about it with us, but if she won't do that, then she should still talk about it with somebody."

"Has Counselor Althouse told you anything?"

"Only that Rebecca was reticent during their first session," Kasidy said. She held her hands in front of her, palms up. "You know our little girl, Ben. She's almost always reserved."

"So Rebecca didn't say anything at all?"

"The counselor told me that they mostly spoke about Rebecca's return to the *Robinson*, since she didn't remember much of her time off the ship," Kasidy said. "The counselor did say that she tried to probe Rebecca about how she felt about what the Glant had intended to do to the children . . . to do to *her* . . . and her reaction was that she would never allow that to happen."

"She would never allow *what* to happen?" Sisko asked. "She'd never let the Glant transplant her conscious mind into one of their creations?"

"That's apparently what she told Counselor Althouse."

Sisko shook his head. "I wonder how she thinks she would've been able to stop them."

Kasidy dropped a hand onto Sisko's knee. "She's your daughter, Ben," she said. "Sometimes she thinks she can do anything."

Sisko started to think about that, about the quiet confidence with which their daughter typically conducted herself, but then the boatswain's whistle sounded. *"Bridge to Captain Sisko,"* said the voice of Scalin Resk, the officer of the deck during beta shift.

"This is the captain," Sisko said. "Go ahead, Lieutenant."

"We've just finished placing the last of the warning buoys," Scalin said.

"Understood," the captain said. "I'll be up to the bridge shortly. Sisko out." He leaned in and kissed Kasidy slowly on the lips. After everything that had happened with Rebecca and the other children, it felt good to be on the cusp of leaving Glant space for good. Even with all of his responsibilities as *Robinson*'s commanding officer, Sisko finally felt like he could breathe again. "I shouldn't be long," he told his wife, holding his face just inches from hers and peering deeply into her beautiful eyes. "Maybe then we can open that bottle of wine."

Kasidy smiled. "I'd like that."

Sisko left the cabin with a spring in his step. But as he headed for the turbolift, he thought again about Rebecca. Sisko loved his daughter dearly, and she was special to him for countless reasons, but he also wondered about her—not for the first time. Over the nine-plus years of her life, he had on rare occasions whispered about her—to Kasidy, to Jake, to Jasmine Tey. They all believed her special, and perhaps not just in the way family members and friends felt about any child. Sisko had seldom allowed himself to think about it in any depth.

I don't want to think about it now, he told himself. But he couldn't suppress the relevant details about his daughter that he knew to be true—starting with the fact that a Prophet had inhabited Rebecca's grandmother in order to ensure Sisko's conception and birth. He didn't know if that made him part Prophet—he'd never believed that it had. But he could not deny that he'd had innumerable experiences that few, if any, had ever had.

Regardless of his own status, what did that mean about his daughter? *Could she be part Prophet?* The idea terrified him—because of the implications it held for Rebecca, but also because of how it might affect Kasidy.

Ahead of Sisko, the doors of a turbolift parted. He stepped inside and specified his destination as the bridge. As the lift ascended, the captain shook his head, as though he could physically clear his thoughts. By the time he reached the bridge, he had refocused all his attention on ordering *Robinson* to continue on its mission of exploration.

Epilogue

Agent

Already bored, Rebecca kicked her legs forward and back as they dangled from the chair in Counselor Althouse's office. It was the second time her mother had brought her there, and she guessed that it wouldn't be the last. She actually liked the counselor—she was kind and funny, and Rebecca loved her short, choppy blond hairstyle—but she didn't like having to talk and talk about things.

Especially bad things.

Rebecca remembered when, a long time ago, back on Bajor, her parents had made her talk with somebody else, again and again, for what seemed like *forever*. That was after the sad man had taken her—the sad man who wanted to hurt her, and maybe to hurt himself too. Though she really didn't understand it at the time, she stopped him, and when it was all over, the last thing she wanted to do was talk about it.

"Can you tell me how you're feeling, Rebecca?" the counselor asked her. "Just in general, when you're in school, when you're in your cabin with your parents, when you're with friends?"

"Um," Rebecca said. She raised her shoulders once, then a second time. "Okay." She knew she would have to say something, if only to avoid being rude. But she really didn't want to talk about what had happened down on that planet, with those strange robots. They hadn't wanted to hurt her, not exactly, but they tried to steal her thoughts . . . her mind.

They didn't just try, Rebecca told herself. Just like the sad man on Bajor didn't just try to hurt her; he *did* hurt her. He set off a bomb right in front of her. She saw it and felt it and knew that bad things were going to happen to her.

So she stopped it. She stopped it by relocating herself, by moving to a fork in the path of her life, and putting down a marker for others to follow. She didn't exactly know how she did it, and she didn't even really remember it very well, until the other day, when the strange robots tried to hurt her. She stopped them, too, by shifting her position within her life so that she could take a different path.

Rebecca still didn't know how she'd done it, but she'd undone something that had happened, made time go another way. She didn't know if she was allowed to do that, but she didn't want to talk about it. She thought it would upset Mommy and Daddy.

Even so, Rebecca kind of liked that she could do that. She liked that she had used that ability. Twice, it kept her from being hurt—or worse.

"Rebecca," the counselor asked, "can you tell me how you're feeling right now?"

Rebecca thought about that for a moment. She knew that she should answer, and she wanted to find the right word. Rebecca considered what she had done—considered what she could do under the right circumstances. It felt like a gift, and it made her smile.

"Rebecca," the counselor asked again, "how do you feel?"

"Powerful," she said.

Acknowledgments

It has been said with eloquence and humility that it takes a village to raise a child. A similar statement could be made about publishing a novel. Yes, there's the writer, of course, but the process requires the participation of so many more people. It starts with an acquisitions editor and continues with a content editor, a copyeditor, and a proofreader. In the case of media tie-in works such as *Star Trek* novels, an individual representing the licensing department of the copyright owner must approve the manuscript and give notes. An artist must create a cover. Salespeople must market and sell the book. A slew of people in Production must format and typeset the novel; produce first-pass, second-pass, and final-pass pages for the author to review; and print and bind the book. Folks in Distribution are tasked with packing and shipping copies of the novel to bookstores and other retailers.

In other words, publishing is typically not a one-person operation. To all of the people involved in the creation of *Original Sin*, I offer my thanks. In particular, I want to single out Margaret Clark, who acquired the book in the first place, and then helped me take it from an idea to a narrative outline, from an outline to a first draft, and then on to its final form. She is a fine editor, with a wealth of experience and armed with excellent skills, who just also happens to possess a keen understanding and appreciation of *Star Trek*. Not only are *Trek* writers well served by Margaret, so are *Trek* readers.

I also want to thank Ed Schlesinger, another editor at Simon & Schuster. Ed is my point of contact at S&S and has been involved for the long haul. Without the stationmaster, the trains don't run.

On the personal side of life, I am a very lucky man. I have longtime, stalwart friends who not only support me in all I do but also help keep at bay the ruminations of the seventeenth-century English philosopher Thomas Hobbes, who noted that ". . . without other security . . . the life of man [is] solitary, poore, nasty, brutish, and short." But I have the security of people in my life who bring joy and strength to my days.

There are, for example, the many friends I have made through our shared days on and around the baseball diamond. From my time playing with the Giants and the Silicon Valley Seals, there are Larry and Mary Ann Candelaria, Bill and Mary Dunlap, Mark and Bev Gemello, Ellen Gordon, Richie Hertz and Kathy Rogers, Scott Lueders, Bill Pederson, Doug "J.C." Penney, Phil Rogers and Angela Narvasa, Jackie Roman and her children Becky and Ryan, Steve "Sman" and Gail Schiffman, Carl and Gayle Shanks, Angie and Michael Simon and their sons Alex and Ben, Dan and Lori Steinberg, Jeanette and Rich Thomas, Rob Weber, and Sandi and Mike Weir. From my Dodgers days, there are Art Aaronson and Cynthia Roman, Terry Calhoun, Tom and Judie Ebert, Chris and Kathy Fabos, Harold and Lori Gainey, Carl Hartman, Barb Sennet Hauser, Dan and Debbie Hofstedt, Harry Horowitz, Anne Lewis, Frank Nevarez, Howard Rubin, Steve Samuelson, Alan Shapiro, Jeff Sherman, Gary Stern, Mark and Meri Sullivan and their daughter Katie, Teddy Tannenbaum,

Gary Turner, and Gordie and Joanna Woo. And from my time on the Creoles and the California Condors, there are Don Agronsky, Jerry Carville, Rick Gari, Bud Golditch, and Art Lacher.

I've also made many friends in Los Angeles. From the world of the arts—film and television, music, and theater— there are Patricia Albrecht and Bruce Wallenstein, Michael Andreas and Julie Fleischer, Tony and Kelly Battelle, Skylar Boorman, Van Boudreaux and Pascale Gigon, Adam Conger, Roger Kent Cruz, Yancey Dunham, Kat' Ferson, Dan Frischman, Roger Garcia and Sean Stack, Michelle Gigon, Merritt Graves, Louis Herthum, Therese Lentz and Chris Albright, Arden Lewis and Charlie Mount, Ernie Mc Daniel, Kathleen McEntee, Phil McKeown, David Mingrino, Don and Alexa Moss, Clark Prestridge, Bruce Ravid, Tim and Kelly Reischauer, Kent Rogers and Andy Coakley, Colette Rosario, Gil Roscoe, Chloé Rosenthal, Alan Schack, Ben Scuglia, Julia Silverman, Amy Simon, Galadriel Stineman and Kevin Joy, Trevor Tamboline and Katrina Merrem, Ashley Taylor and Stephen Monroe Taylor and their son Killian, Darryl and Laura Vinyard and their daughters Julia and Grace, Sandy Weinstein, Adlee and Frank Williams, and Pat and Paul Willson. From my wife's time dancing hula, there are Lynn Angeles, Marissa Berg, Laurie McVey, John Luckman and Roberto San Luis, Leslie De Luco, Yoko Foster, Daisy and Quan Huynh, Cindy Scott, Chase Keoki Wang, and Ligaya Ybarra. Also in L.A., there are Phil Althouse and Diana Shaw, Matt Harris and Adam Rogers and their sons Javier and Marcel, Mary Ann Plumley, Vahe Shahinian, and Chandler Smith.

As you might imagine, I also have friends among the community of writers and editors working in the *Star Trek* universe: Kirsten Beyer (to whom this book is dedicated) and David Permenter and their daughter Anorah, Keith

R.A. DeCandido and Wrenn Simms, Kevin Dilmore, Jack Doner and Margaret Wander Bonanno, Michael Jan Friedman, Dave and Simantha Galanter, Allyn Gibson, Bob and Deb Greenberger, Glenn and Brandy Hauman, Bill Leisner, David Mack and Kara Bain, Marco Palmieri, Scott Pearson and Sandra Immerman and their daughter Ella, Aaron Rosenberg, Paul Simpson and Barbara Holroyd, Amy Sisson, and Dayton and Michi Ward.

There are also family members, notably Charlene and John Costello, and Audrey and Bob Nemes. And then there are those who fit into no particular category, but who still occupy important places in my life: John Collins, John H. Collins III, Rich DePascal, Glenn Elder, Gary Friedrich, Ted and Joan Frost, Bud and Tulay Furrow, Kathy Golec, Barbara and Matty Hahn and their daughter Faith, Marilyn Hyler, Rik Palieri, Steve and Cheryl Pilchik and their sons Brian and Josh, John Ratnaswamy and Victoria Zimmerman and their children Alec, Julia, and Lily, Dana and Marie Robitaille, Ryan and Jen Van Riper and their daughters Claire and Audrey, Brenda and Phil Sencer, Michael and Peggy Sperber, Rick Stratos, and Steve Subject and Sally Morrison.

Unfortunately, I have also lost a number of people whose absence I will always feel. Barry Berman enthusiastically shared his love of baseball, and he was the first person to truly welcome me to Los Angeles. I enjoyed many adventures at various tournaments with Dennis McCroskey and Harry Wade, both of whom were singular personalities. Terry Weinstein always made it fun to step onto a diamond, whether playing with him or against him. Tim Hauser played baseball too, but he had a wealth of other interests and abilities, including helping found The Manhattan Transfer and performing with them for forty-five years (for which he won ten Grammy Awards). Herb Lewis provided inspiration to me at every turn, playing baseball well into his nineties, staying joyously married for seventy-four years, and passing away at the ripe old age of one hundred after a long and happy life. My grandfather John Walenista left me with a lifetime of memories that will never leave me, from riding horses with him around Pocono Downs to when he met my future wife for the first time and told us that we were "a peach of a pair." I miss the three grandes dames of my wife's family that are no longer with us: Elizabeth Knezo Ragan, Lillian Ragan, and Audrey Collins Ragan, all of whom always treated me with great love and kindness. Marty Nedboy, also known as America's Guest, was one of the funniest people I've ever met, and I and so many others will tell stories about him until we ourselves are gone. And Paul Roman, with whom I shared a special relationship that started as pitcher-catcher and became one of the most meaningful friendships in my life, stood up with me as a best man at my wedding and left us far too soon.

Last year, we also lost a fine person in Joan Roman. A loving wife and mother, a devoted sister, and a good friend, Joan lived a positive and optimistic life that buoyed the people around her. I met her through her husband, Dan, a good man with whom I have played many baseball games. My heart aches for his loss.

Among all the many people who contribute so much to my life, there are those who stand out. Walter Ragan welcomed me into his family on the first day I met him, and he has done nothing but stand by me ever since. I value the examples he sets, and I feel fortunate to have such a wonderful relationship with him.

Colleen Ragan, the Qveen of All She Surveys, is one of my favorite people. By turns strong and sweet, earnest and funny, she makes every visit memorable. I love her like a sister.

I also love Anita Smith like a sister. A successful woman, she lives a balanced life of hard work and happiness—and more than a little bit of golf. Our family could not have benefited more when Anita chose to join it.

I also have an actual sister. I am proud to be Jennifer George's brother. Sharp, kind, adventurous, accomplished, and funny, she makes the most out of life. Her love and support mean the world to me.

I am also grateful for Patricia Walenista. I cannot count all the intangible gifts has given me—and continues to give me. I marvel and delight at her happy and active life.

Finally, inevitably, gloriously, there is the unparalleled Karen Ragan-George. I am continuously impressed by my wife's spirit—artistic, bold, compassionate, curious, intelligent, kind, loving, principled and informed, strong, supportive, and virtuous. Karen is like no one else I have ever met. Fortune smiled on me when she came into my life, and it has offered a constant grin ever since. I love Karen more than words can say.

About the Author

You can learn all you want to know—and then some—about David R. George III on his website, DRGIII.com. From there, you can access his Facebook, Instagram, Pinterest, Tumblr, and Twitter accounts.